Micah
Clarke

Micah Clarke

SIR ARTHUR CONAN DOYLE

Edited by Virginia Kirkus

With Illustrations by Henry Pitz

DOVER PUBLICATIONS, INC.
Mineola, New York

Bibliographical Note

This Dover edition, first published in 2018, is an unabridged republication of the text of the work originally published by Harper & Brothers Publishers, New York and London, in 1894 [first publication: 1889]. The original full-color frontispiece has been reproduced in black and white for this edition.

Library of Congress Cataloging-in-Publication Data

Names: Doyle, Arthur Conan, 1859–1930, author. | Kirkus, Virginia, 1893– editor. | Pitz, Henry C. (Henry Clarence), 1895–1976, illustrator.
Title: Micah Clarke / Sir Arthur Conan Doyle ; edited by Virginia Kirkus, with illustrations by Henry C. Pitz.
Description: Mineola, New York : Dover Publications, 2018.
Identifiers: LCCN 2017036972| ISBN 9780486813455 (paperback) | ISBN 0486813452 (paperback)
Subjects: | BISAC: FICTION / Historical.
Classification: LCC PR4622 .M5 2018 | DDC 823/.8—dc23
LC record available at https://lccn.loc.gov/2017036972

Manufactured in the United States by LSC Communications
81345201   2017
www.doverpublications.com

TO

MY MOTHER

CONTENTS

CONTENTS

ILLUSTRATIONS

Micah Clarke

CHAPTER ONE

OF CORNET JOSEPH CLARKE OF THE IRONSIDES

I WAS born, then, in the year 1664, at Havant, which is a flourishing village a few miles from Portsmouth off the main London road, and there it was that I spent the greater part of my youth. It is now, as it was then, a pleasant, healthy spot, with a hundred or more brick cottages scattered along in a single irregular street. In the middle of the village stood the old church with the square tower, and the great sundial like a wrinkle upon its gray, weather-blotched face. On the outskirts the Presbyterians had their chapel, but when the Act of Uniformity was passed, their good minister, Master Breckenridge, whose discourses had often crowded his rude benches while the comfortable pews of the church were empty, was cast into jail, and his flock dispersed. As to the Independents, of whom my father was one, they also were under the ban of the law, but they attended conventicle at Emsworth, whither we would trudge, rain or shine, on every Sabbath morning. There were Papists, too, among us, who were compelled to go as far as Portsmouth for their mass.

My father, Joseph Clarke, was better known over the countryside by the name of Ironside Joe, for he had served in his youth in the Yaxley troop of Oliver Cromwell's famous regiment of horse, and had preached so lustily and fought so stoutly that old Noll himself called him out of the ranks after the fight at Dunbar, and raised him to a cornetcy. It chanced, however, that having some little time later fallen into an argument with one of his troopers, the man, who was a half-crazy zealot, smote my father across the face, a favor which he returned by a thrust from his broadsword, which sent his adversary to test in person the truth of his beliefs. A court-martial sat upon my father, and it is likely that he would have been offered up as a sacrifice to appease the angry soldiery had not the Lord Protector interfered, and limited the punishment to dismissal from the army. Cornet Clarke was accordingly stripped of his buff coat and steel cap, and wandered down to Havant, where he settled into business as a leather merchant and tanner, thereby depriving Parliament of as trusty a soldier as ever drew blade in its service. Finding that he prospered in trade, he took as wife Mary Shepstone, a young Churchwoman, and I, Micah Clarke, was the first pledge of their union.

My father, as I remember him first, was tall and straight, with a great spread of shoulder and a mighty chest. His gray eyes were piercing and soldier-like, yet I have seen them lighten

up into a kindly and merry twinkle. His voice was the most tremendous and awe-inspiring that I have ever listened to. Though
he possessed every quality which was needed to raise him to distinction as an officer, he had thrown off his military habits when
he returned to civil life. As he prospered and grew rich he might
well have worn a sword, but instead he would ever bear a small
copy of the Scriptures bound to his girdle, where other men hung
their weapons. He was sober and measured in his speech, and
it was seldom, even in the bosom of his own family, that he would
speak of the scenes in which he had taken part. He was frugal
in his eating, backward in drinking, and allowed himself no pleasures save three pipes a day of Oronooko tobacco, which he kept
ever in a brown jar by the great wooden chair.

Yet, for all his self-restraint, the old leaven would at times
begin to work in him, and bring on fits of what his enemies
would call fanaticism and his friends piety, though it must be
confessed that this piety was prone to take a fierce and fiery
shape.

For the rest, he was an excellent man of business, fair and
even generous in his dealings, respected by all and loved by few,
for his nature was too self-contained to admit of much affection.
To us he was a stern and rigid father, punishing us heavily for
whatever he regarded as amiss in our conduct. He could not
bear that we should play trick-track upon the green, or dance
with the other children upon the Saturday night.

As to my mother, dear soul, it was her calm, peaceful influence
which kept my father within bounds, and softened his austere
rule. Seldom indeed, even in his darkest moods, did the touch
of her gentle hand and the sound of her voice fail to soothe his
fiery spirit. She came of a Church stock, and held to her
religion with a quiet grip which was proof against every attempt
to turn her from it.

Women were good house-keepers fifty years ago, but she was
conspicuous among the best. To see her spotless cuffs and snowy
kirtle one would scarce credit how hard she labored. It was

only the well-ordered house and the dustless rooms which proclaimed her constant industry. She made salves and eye-waters, powders and confects, cordials and persico, orange-flower water and cherry-brandy, each in its due season and all of the best. She was wise, too, in herbs and simples. The villagers and the farm laborers would rather any day have her advice upon their ailments than that of Dr. Jackson of Purbrook, who never mixed a draught under a silver crown. Over the whole countryside there was no woman more deservedly respected and more esteemed both by those above her and by those beneath.

Such were my parents as I remember them in my childhood. As to myself, I shall let my story explain the growth of my own nature. My brothers and my sisters were all brown-faced, sturdy little country children, with no very marked traits save a love of mischief controlled by the fear of their father. These, with Martha, the serving-maid, formed our whole household during those boyish years when the pliant soul of the child is hardening into the settled character of the man.

CHAPTER TWO

OF MY GOING TO SCHOOL AND OF MY COMING THENCE

WITH the home influences which I have described, it may be readily imagined that my young mind turned very much upon the subject of religion, the more so as my father and mother took different views upon it. The old Puritan soldier held that the Bible alone contained all things essential to salvation, and that it was by no means necessary, but rather hurtful and degrading, that any organized body of ministers or of bishops should claim special prerogatives or take the place of mediators between the creature and the Creator.

My mother, on the other hand, held that the very essence of a church was that it should have a hierarchy and a graduated government within itself, with the king at the apex, the archbishops beneath him, the bishops under their control, and so down through the ministry to the common folk. She agreed that religion was based upon the Bible, but the Bible was a book which contained much that was obscure, and unless that obscurity were cleared away by a duly elected and consecrated servant of God, a lineal descendant of the disciples, all human wisdom might not serve to interpret it aright. That was my mother's position, and neither argument nor entreaty could move her from it. The only question of belief on which my two parents were equally ardent was their mutual dislike and distrust of the Roman Catholic forms of worship, and in this the Churchwoman was every whit as decided as the fanatical Independent.

In the days when I was young special causes had inflamed this dislike, and made it all the more bitter because there was a spice of fear mingled with it. Charles was a very lukewarm Protestant, and indeed showed upon his deathbed that he was no Protestant at all. There was no longer any chance of his having legitimate offspring. The Duke of York, his younger brother, was therefore heir to the throne, and he was known to be an austere and narrow Papist, while his spouse, Mary of Modena, was as bigoted as himself. Should they have children there could be no question but that they would be brought up in the faith of their parents, and that a line of Catholic monarchs would occupy the throne of England. To the Church, as represented by my mother, and to Nonconformity, in the person of my father, this was an equally intolerable prospect.

When King James II. ascended the throne he did so amid a sullen silence on the part of a large class of his subjects, and both my father and my mother were among those who were zealous for a Protestant succession.

My childhood was, as I have already said, a gloomy one. Now and again, when there chanced to be a fair at Portsdown Hill, or when a passing raree showman set up his booth in the village, my dear mother would slip a penny or two from her house-keeping money into my hand, and with a warning finger upon her lip would send me off to see the sights. These treats were, however, rare events, and made such a mark upon my mind that when I was sixteen years of age I could have checked off upon my fingers all that I had ever seen.

There were other shows, however, which I might see for nothing, and yet were more real and every whit as interesting as any for which I paid. Now and again upon a holiday I was permitted to walk down to Portsmouth—once I was even taken in front of my father upon his pad nag, and there I wandered with him through the streets with wondering eyes, marvelling over the strange sights around me. The walls and the moats, the gates and the sentinels, the long high street with the great government buildings, and the constant rattle of drums and blare of trumpets, they made my little heart beat quicker beneath my sagathy stuff jacket.

From the day that I first learned my letters from the horn-book at my mother's knee I was always hungry to increase my knowledge, and never a piece of print came in my way that I did not eagerly master. My father pushed the sectarian hatred of learning to such a length that he was averse to having any worldly books within his doors. I was dependent, therefore, for my supply upon one or two of my friends in the village, who lent me a volume at a time from their small libraries. These I would carry inside my shirt, and would only dare to produce when I could slip away into the fields, and lie hid among the long grass, or at night when the rushlight was still burning, and my father's snoring assured me that there was no danger of his detecting me.

When I was fourteen years of age, a yellow-haired, brown-faced lad, I was packed off to a small private school at Peters-field, and there I remained for a year, returning home for the last Saturday in each month. I took with me only a scanty outfit of school-books, with Lilly's "Latin Grammar," and Rosse's "View of all the Religions in the World from the Creation down to our Own Times," which was shoved into my hands by my good mother as a parting present. With this small stock of letters I might have fared badly, had it not happened that my master, Mr. Thomas Chillingfoot, had himself a good library, and took a pleasure in lending his books to any of his scholars who showed a desire to improve themselves. Under this good old man's care I not only picked up some smattering of Latin and Greek, but I found means to read good English translations of many of the classics, and to acquire a knowledge of the history of my own and other countries. I was rapidly growing in mind as well as in body, when my school career was cut short by no less an event than my summary and ignominious expulsion.

Petersfield had always been a great stronghold of the Church, having hardly a non-conformist within its bounds. The reason of this was that most of the house property was owned by zealous Churchmen, who refused to allow any one who differed from the Established Church to settle there. The vicar, whose name was Pinfold, possessed in this manner great power in the town, and, as he was a man with a highly inflamed counte-nance and a pompous manner, he inspired no little awe among the quiet inhabitants. This proud priest made a point of know-ing the history of every one within his parish, and having learned that I was the son of an Independent, he spoke severely to Mr. Chillingfoot upon the indiscretion which he had shown in admit-ting me to his school. Indeed, nothing but my mother's good name for orthodoxy prevented him from insisting upon my dismissal.

At the other end of the village there was a large day-school. A constant feud prevailed between the scholars who attended it and the lads who studied under our master. No one could tell how the war broke out, but for many years there had been a standing quarrel between the two, which resulted in skirmishes, sallies, and ambuscades, with now and then a pitched battle. No great harm was done in these encounters, for the weapons were usually snowballs in winter and pine-cones or clods of earth in the summer. Even when the contest got closer, and we came to fisticuffs, a few bruises and a little blood was the worst that could come of it. Our opponents were more numerous than we, but we had the advantage of being always together, and of having a secure asylum upon which to retreat, while they, living in scattered houses all over the parish, had no common rallying-point. A stream, crossed by two bridges, ran through the centre of the town, and this was the boundary which separated our territories from those of our enemies. The boy who crossed the bridge found himself in hostile country.

It chanced that in the first conflict which occurred after my arrival at the school I distinguished myself by singling out the most redoubtable of our foemen, and smiting him such a blow that he was knocked helpless and was carried off by our party as a prisoner. This feat of arms established my good name as a warrior, so I came at last to be regarded as the leader of our forces, and to be looked up to by bigger boys than myself. This promotion tickled my fancy so much that I set to work to prove that I deserved it by devising fresh and ingenious schemes for the defeat of our enemies.

One winter's evening news reached us that our rivals were about to make a raid upon us under cover of night, and that they proposed coming by the little-used plank bridge, so as to escape our notice. This bridge lay almost out of the town, and consisted of a single broad piece of wood without a rail, erected for the good of the town-clerk, who lived just opposite to it. We proposed to hide ourselves among the bushes on our side of the stream, and make an unexpected attack upon the invaders as they crossed. As we started, however, I bethought me of an ingenious stratagem which I had read of as being practised in the German wars, and having expounded it, to the great delight of my companions, we took Mr. Chillingfoot's saw and set off for the seat of action.

On reaching the bridge all was quiet and still. It was quite dark and very cold, for Christmas was approaching. There were no signs of our opponents. We exchanged a few whispers as to who should do the daring deed, but as the others shrank from it, and as I was too proud to propose what I dare not execute, I griped the saw, and, sitting astraddle upon the plank, set to work upon the very centre of it.

My purpose was to weaken it in such a way that, though it would bear the weight of one, it would collapse when the main body of our foremen was upon it, and so precipitate them into the ice-cold stream. The water was but a couple of feet deep at the place, so that there was nothing for them but a fright and a ducking. I had no compunction about the destruction of the bridge, for I knew enough of carpentry to see that a skilful joiner could in an hour's work make it stronger than ever by putting a prop beneath the point where I had divided it. When at last I felt by the yielding of the plank that I had done enough, and that the least strain would snap it, I crawled quietly off, and, taking up my position with my school-fellows, awaited the coming of the enemy.

I had scarce concealed myself when we heard the steps of some one approaching down the foot-path which led to the bridge. We crouched behind the cover, convinced that the sound must come from some scout whom our foemen had sent on in front—a big boy, evidently, for his step was heavy and slow, with a clinking noise mingling with it, of which we could make nothing. It was only as he was setting foot upon the plank and beginning gingerly to pick his way across it, that we discerned the outlines of the familiar form, and realized the dreadful truth that the stranger whom we had taken for the advance guard of our enemy was in truth none other than Vicar Pinfold, and that it was the rhythmic pat of his stick which we heard mingling with his footfalls. Fascinated by the sight, we lay bereft of all power to warn him—a line of staring eyeballs. One step, two steps, three steps did the haughty Churchman take, when there was a rending crack, and he vanished with a mighty splash into the swift-flowing stream. He must have fallen upon his back, for we could see the curved outline of his portly figure standing out above the surface, as he struggled desperately to regain his feet. At last he managed to get erect, and came sputtering for the bank with such a mixture of godly ejaculations and of profane oaths that, even in our terror, we could not keep from laughter. Rising from under his feet like a covey of wild-fowl, we scurried off across the fields and so back to the school, where, as you may imagine, we said nothing to our good master of what had occurred.

The matter was too serious, however, to be hushed up. The sudden chill set up some manner of disturbance in the bottle of sack which the vicar had just been drinking with the town-clerk, and an attack of gout set in which laid him on his back for a fortnight. Meanwhile, an examination of the bridge had shown that it had been sawn across, and an inquiry traced the matter to Mr. Chillingfoot's boarders. To save a wholesale expulsion of the school from the town, I was forced to acknowledge myself as both the inventor and perpetrator of the deed. Chillingfoot was entirely in the power of the vicar, so he was forced to read me a long homily in public—which he balanced by an affectionate leave-taking in private—and to expel me solemnly from the school.

This adventure shocked my dear mother, but it found great favor in the eyes of my father, who laughed until the whole village resounded with his stentorian merriment. Even of the Church folk many were secretly glad at the misfortune which had overtaken the vicar, for his pretensions and his pride had made him hated throughout the district.

By this time I had grown into a sturdy, broad-shouldered

lad, and every month added to my strength and my stature. When I was sixteen I could carry a bag of wheat or a cask of beer against any man in the village, and I could throw the fifteen-pound putting-stone to a distance of thirty-six feet, which was four feet farther than could Ted Dawson, the blacksmith. Once when my father was unable to carry a bale of skins out of the yard, I whipped it up and bare it away upon my shoulders. The old man would often look gravely at me from under his heavy, thatched eyebrows, and shake his grizzled head, as he sat in his arm-chair puffing his pipe. "You grow too big for the nest, lad," he would say. "I doubt some of these days you'll find your wings and away!" In my heart I longed that the time would come, for I was weary of the quiet life of the village, and was anxious to see the great world of which I had heard and read so much.

CHAPTER THREE

OF TWO FRIENDS OF MY YOUTH

I FEAR that you will think that the prologue is over-long for the play; but be patient while I speak of the old friends of my youth, some of whom you may hear more of hereafter, while others remained behind in the country hamlet, and yet left traces of our early intercourse upon my character.

Foremost for good among all whom I knew was Zachary Palmer, the village carpenter, a man whose aged and labor-warped body contained the simplest and purest of spirits. Yet his simplicity was by no means the result of ignorance, for from the teachings of Plato to those of Hobbes, there were few systems ever thought out by man which he had not studied and weighed. Books were far dearer in my boyhood than they are now, and carpenters were less well paid, but old Palmer had neither wife nor child, and spent little on food or raiment. Thus it came about that, on the shelf over his bed, he had a more choice collection of books—few as they were in number—than the squire or the parson, and these books he had read until he not only understood them himself, but could impart them to others.

This white-bearded and venerable village philosopher would sit by his cabin door upon a summer evening, and was never so pleased as when some of the young fellows would slip away from their bowls and their quoit-playing, in order to lie in the grass at his feet and ask him questions about the great men of old, their words and their deeds. But of all the youths I and Reüben Lockarby, the innkeeper's son, were his two favorites, for we would come the earliest and stop the latest to hear the old man talk.

A very different teacher was the sea-dog Solomon Sprent, who lived in the second last cottage on the left-hand side of the main street of the village. He was one of the old tarpaulin breed, who had fought under the red-cross ensign against Frenchman, Don, Dutchman, and Moor, until a round shot carried off his foot and put an end to his battles forever. In person he was thin and hard and brown, as lithe and active as a cat, with a

short body and very long arms, each ending in a great hand, which was ever half-closed, as though shutting upon a rope.

Old Solomon was a never-failing source of amusement and of interest to my friend Lockarby and myself. On gala-days he would have us in to dine with him, for he had a famous trick of cooking, and could produce the delicacies of all nations. And all the time that we were with him he would tell us the most marvellous stories. Stirring as were Solomon Sprent's accounts of his old commanders, their effect upon us was not so great as when, about his second or third glass, the floodgates of his memory would be opened, and he would pour out long tales of the lands which he had visited and the peoples which he had seen. Leaning forward in our seats, with our chins resting upon our hands, we two youngsters would sit for hours, with our eyes fixed upon the old adventurer, drinking in his words, while he, pleased at the interest which he excited, would puff slowly at his pipe and reel off story after story of what he had seen or done. After such a flight as that, we would feel, as we came back to the Hampshire village and the dull realities of country life, like wild birds who had been snared by the fowler and clapped into narrow cages. Then it was that the words of my father, "You will find your wings some day and fly away," would come back to me and set up such a restlessness as all the wise words of Zachary Palmer could not allay.

CHAPTER FOUR

OF THE STRANGE FISH THAT WE CAUGHT AT SPITHEAD

ONE evening in the month of May, 1685, about the end of the first week of the month, my friend Reuben Lockarby and I borrowed Ned Marley's pleasure-boat, and went a-fishing out of Langston Bay. At that time I was close on one-and-twenty years of age, while my companion was one year younger. A great intimacy had sprung up between us, founded on mutual esteem; for he, being a little, undergrown youth, was proud of my strength and stature, while my melancholy and somewhat heavy spirit took a pleasure in the energy and joviality which never deserted him, and in the wit which gleamed as bright and as innocent as summer lightning through all that he said. In person he was short and broad, round-faced, ruddy-cheeked, and, in truth, a little inclined to be fat. The stern test of common danger and mutual hardship entitle me to say that no man could have desired a stancher or more trusty comrade. As he was destined to be with me in the sequel, it was but fitting that he should have been at my side on that May evening which was the starting-point of our adventures.

We pulled out beyond the Warner Sands to a place half-way between them and the Nab, where we usually found bass in plenty. There we cast the heavy stone which served us as an anchor overboard, and proceeded to set our lines. The sun, sinking slowly behind a fog-bank, had slashed the whole western sky with scarlet streaks, against which the wooded slopes of the Isle of Wight stood out vaporous and purple. A fresh breeze was blowing from the south-east, flecking the long, green waves with crests of foam, and filling our eyes and lips with the smack of the salt spray. Over near St. Helen's Point a king's ship was making her way down the channel, while a single large brig was tacking about a quarter of a mile or less from where we lay. So near were we that we could catch a glimpse of the figures upon her deck as she heeled over to the breeze, and could hear the creaking of her yards and the flapping of her weather-stained canvas as she prepared to go about.

"Look ye, Micah," said my companion, looking up from his fishing-line. "That is a most weak-minded ship—a ship which

will make no way in the world. See how she hangs in the wind, neither keeping on her course nor tacking. She is a trimmer of the seas—the Lord Halifax of the ocean."

"Why, there is something amiss with her," I replied, staring across with hand-shaded eyes. "She yaws about as though there were no one at the helm. Her main-yard goes aback! Now it is forward again! The folk on her deck seem to me to be either fighting or dancing. Up with the anchor, Reuben, and let us pull to her."

"Up with the anchor and let us get out of her way," he answered, still gazing at the stranger. "Why will you ever run that meddlesome head of yours into danger's way? She flies Dutch colors, but who can say whence she really comes? A pretty thing if we were snapped up by a buccaneer and sold in the plantations!"

"A buccaneer in the Solent!" cried I, derisively. "We shall be seeing the black flag in Emsworth Creek next. But, hark! What is that?"

The crack of a musket sounded from aboard the brig. Then came a moment's silence, and another musket shot rang out, followed by a chorus of shouts and cries. Simultaneously the yards swung round into position, the sails caught the breeze once more, and the vessel darted away on a course which would take her past Bembridge Point out to the English Channel. As she flew along her helm was put hard down, a puff of smoke shot out from her quarter, and a cannon-ball came hopping and splashing over the waves, passing within a hundred yards of where we lay. With this farewell greeting she came up into the wind again and continued her course to the southward.

"Heart o' grace!" ejaculated Reuben, in loose-lipped astonishment. "The murdering villains!"

"I would to the Lord that king's ship would snap them up!" cried I, savagely, for the attack was so unprovoked that it stirred my bile. "What could the rogues have meant! They are surely drunk or mad."

"Pull at the anchor, man, pull at the anchor!" my companion shouted, springing up from his seat. "I understand it! Pull at the anchor!"

"What, then?" I asked, helping him to haul the great stone up, hand over hand, until it came dripping over the side.

"They are not firing at us, lad. They were aiming at some one in the water between us and them. Pull, Micah! Put your back into it! Some poor fellow may be drowning."

"Why, I declare!" said I, looking over my shoulder as I rowed, "there is his head upon the crest of a wave. Easy, or we shall be over him! Two more strokes and be ready to seize him! Keep up, friend! There's help at hand!"

"Take help to those who need help," said a voice out of the sea. "Zounds, man, keep a guard on your oar! I fear a pat from it very much more than I do the water."

These words were delivered in so calm and self-possessed a tone that all concern for the swimmer was set at rest. Drawing in our oars we faced round to have a look at him. The drift of the boat had brought us so close that he could have grasped the gunwale had he been so minded.

"Sapperment!" he cried, in a peevish voice, "to think of my brother Nonus serving me such a trick! What would our blessed mother have said could she have seen it? My whole kit gone, to say nothing of my venture in the voyage! And now I have kicked off a pair of new jack-boots that cost sixteen rix-dollars at Vanseddar's at Amsterdam. I can't swim in jack-boots, nor can I walk without them."

"Won't you come in out of the wet, sir?" asked Reuben, who could scarce keep serious at the stranger's appearance and address. A pair of long arms shot out of the water, and in a moment, with a lithe, snake-like motion, the man wound himself into the boat and coiled his great length upon the stern-sheets. Very lanky he was and very thin, with a craggy, hard face, clean-shaven and sunburned, with a thousand little wrinkles intersecting it in every direction. He had lost his hat, and his short, wiry hair, slightly flecked with gray, stood up in a bristle all over his head. It was hard to guess at his age, but he could scarce have been under his fiftieth year, though the ease with which he had boarded our boat proved that his strength and energy were unimpaired. Of all his characteristics, however, nothing attracted my attention so much as his eyes, which were almost covered by their drooping lids, and yet looked out through the thin slits which remained with marvellous bright-ness and keenness. A passing glance might give the idea that he was languid and half asleep, but a closer one would reveal those glittering, shifting lines of light, and warn the prudent man not to trust too much to his first impressions.

"I could swim to Portsmouth," he remarked, rummaging in the pockets of his sodden jacket; "I could swim wellnigh anywhere. Take my advice, young men, and always carry your tobacco in a water-tight metal box."

As he spoke he drew a flat box from his pocket and several wooden tubes which he screwed together to form a long pipe. This he stuffed with tobacco, and having lit it by means of a flint and steel with a piece of touch-paper from the inside of his box, he curled his legs under him in Eastern fashion and settled down to enjoy a smoke. There was something so peculiar about the whole incident, and so preposterous about the man's appearance and actions, that we both broke into a roar of laughter, which lasted until, for very exhaustion, we were compelled to stop. He neither joined in our merriment nor expressed offence at it, but continued to suck away at his long wooden tube with a perfectly stolid and impassive face, save that the half-covered eyes glinted rapidly backward and forward from one to the other of us.

"You will excuse our laughter, sir," I said at last; "my friend and I are unused to such adventures, and are merry at the happy ending of it. May we ask whom it is that we have picked up?"

"Decimus Saxon is my name," the stranger answered; "I am the tenth child of a worthy father, as the Latin implies. There are but nine betwixt me and an inheritance. Who knows? Small-pox might do it, or the plague!"

"We heard a shot aboard the brig," said Reuben.

"That was my brother Nonus shooting at me," the stranger observed, shaking his head sadly.

"But there was a second shot."

"Ah, that was me shooting at my brother Nonus."

"Good lack!" I cried. "I trust that thou hast done him no hurt."

"But a flesh wound, at the most," he answered. "I thought it best to come away, however, lest the affair grow into a quarrel. I am sure that it was he who trained the nine-pounder on me when I was in the water. It came near enough to part my hair. He was always a good shot with a carronade or a mortar-piece. He could not have been hurt, however, to get down from the poop to the main-deck in the time."

There was a pause after this, while the stranger drew a long knife from his belt and cleaned out his pipe with it. Reuben and I took up our oars, and, having pulled up our tangled fishing-lines, which had been streaming behind the boat, we proceeded to pull in towards the land.

"The question now is," said the stranger, "where we are to go to?"

"We are going down Langston Bay," I answered.

"Oh, we are, are we?" he cried, in a mocking voice; "you are sure of it—eh? You are certain we are not going to France? We have a mast and sail there, I see, and water in the beaker. All we want are a few fish, which I hear are plentiful in these waters, and we might make a push for Barfleur."

"We are going down Langston Bay," I repeated, coldly.

"You see, might is right upon the waters," he explained, with a smile which broke his whole face up into crinkles. "I am an old soldier, a tough fighting-man, and you are two raw lads. I have a knife, and you are unarmed. D'ye see the line of argument? The question now is: Where are we to go?"

I faced round upon him with the oar in my hand. "You boasted that you could swim to Portsmouth," said I, "and so you shall. Into the water with you, you sea-viper, or I'll push you in as sure as my name is Micah Clarke."

"Throw your knife down, or I'll drive the boat-hook through you!" cried Reuben, pushing it forward to within a few inches of the man's throat.

"Sink me, but this is most commendable!" he said, sheathing his weapon, and laughing softly to himself. "I love to draw spirit out of the young fellows."

"Give up that knife," said I, sternly.

"Certainly," he replied, handing it over to me with a polite bow. "Is there any other reasonable matter in which I can oblige ye? I will give up anything to do ye pleasure—save only my good name and soldierly repute."

I sat down beside him with the knife in my hand. "You pull both oars," I said to Reuben; "I'll keep guard over the fellow and sees that he plays us no trick. I believe that you are right, and that he is nothing better than a pirate. He shall be given over to the justices when we get to Havant."

I thought that our passenger's coolness deserted him for a moment, and that a look of annoyance passed over his face.

"Wait a bit!" he said; "your name, I gather, is Clarke, and your home is Havant. Are you a kinsman of Joseph Clarke, the old Roundhead of that town?"

"He is my father," I answered.

"Hark to that, now!" he cried, with a throb of laughter; "I have a trick of falling on my feet. Look at this, lad! Look at this!" He drew a packet of letters from his inside pocket, wrapped in a bit of tarred cloth, and, opening it, he picked one out and placed it upon my knee. "Read!" said he, pointing at it with his long, thin finger.

It was inscribed in large, plain characters, "To Joseph Clarke, leather merchant of Havant, by the hand of Master Decimus Saxon, part owner of the ship *Providence,* from Amsterdam to Portsmouth." At each side it was sealed with a massive red seal, and was additionally secured with a broad band of silk.

"I have three-and-twenty of them to deliver in the neighborhood," he remarked. "That shows what folk think of Decimus Saxon. Three-and-twenty lives and liberties are in my hands. I risk my life in carrying this letter to your father; and you, his son, threaten to hand me over to the justices! For shame! For shame! I blush for you!"

"I don't know what you are hinting at," I answered. "You must speak plainer if I am to understand you."

"Can we trust him?" he asked, jerking his head in the direction of Reuben.

"As myself."

"How very charming!" said he, with something between a smile and a sneer. "David and Jonathan—or, to be more classical and less scriptural, Damon and Pythias—eh? These papers, then, are from the faithful abroad, the exiles in Holland, ye understand, who are thinking of making a move and of coming over to see King James in his own country with their swords strapped on their thighs. The letters are to those from whom they expect sympathy, and notify when and where they will make a landing. Now, my dear lad, you will perceive that instead of my being in your power, you are so completely in mine that it needs but a word from me to destroy your whole family. Decimus Saxon is stanch, though, and that word shall never be spoken."

"If all this be true," said I, "and if your mission is indeed as you have said, why did you, even now, propose to make for France?"

"Aptly asked, and yet the answer is clear enough," he replied; "sweet and ingenuous as are your faces, I could not read upon them that ye would prove to be Whigs and friends of the good old cause. Ye might have taken me to where excisemen or others would have wanted to pry and peep, and so endangered my commission. Better a voyage to France in an open boat than that."

"I will take you to my father," said I, after a few moments' thought. "You can deliver your letter and make good your story to him. If you are indeed a true man, you will meet with a warm welcome; but should you prove, as I shrewdly suspect, to be a rogue, you need expect no mercy."

"Bless the youngster! He speaks like the Lord High Chancellor of England!"

All this time Reuben had been swinging away at his oars, and we had made our way into Langston Bay, down the sheltered waters of which we were rapidly shooting. Sitting in the sheets, I turned over in my mind all that this waif had said. I had glanced over his shoulder at the addresses of some of the letters —Steadman of Bassingstoke, Wintle of Alresford, Fortescue of Bognor, all well-known leaders of the Dissenters. If they were what he represented them to be, it was no exaggeration to say that he held the fortunes and fates of these men entirely in his hands. Government would be only too glad to have a valid reason for striking hard at the men whom they feared. On the whole, it was well to tread carefully in the matter, so I restored our prisoner's knife to him, and treated him with increased consideration. It was wellnigh dark when we beached the boat, and entirely so before we reached Havant, which was fortunate, as the bootless and hatless state of our dripping companion could not have failed to set tongues wagging, and perhaps to excite the inquiries of the authorities. As it was, we scarce met a soul before reaching my father's door.

CHAPTER FIVE

OF THE MAN WITH THE DROOPING LIDS

M Y MOTHER and my father were sitting in their high-backed chairs on either side of the empty fireplace when we arrived, he smoking his evening pipe of Oronooko, and she working at her embroidery. The moment that I opened the door the man whom I had brought stepped briskly in, and, bowing to the old people, began to make glib excuses for the lateness of his visit, and to explain the manner in which we had picked him up. I could not help smiling at the utter amazement expressed upon my mother's face as she gazed at him, for the loss of his jack-boots exposed a pair of interminable spindle shanks which were in ludicrous contrast to the baggy, Low Country knee-breeches which surmounted them. His tunic was made of coarse, sad-colored kersey stuff with flat, new-gilded brass buttons, beneath which was a whitish callamanca vest edged with silver. Round the neck of his coat was a broad white collar after the Dutch fashion, out of which his long, scraggy throat shot upward, with his round head and bristle of hair balanced upon the top of it, like the turnip on a stick at which we used to throw at the fairs. In this guise he stood blinking and winking in the glare of light, and pattering out his excuses with as many bows and scrapes as Sir Peter Witling in the play. I was in the act of following him into the room, when Reuben plucked at my sleeve to detain me.

"Nay, I won't come in with you, Micah," said he; "there's mischief likely to come of all this. My father may grumble over his beer jugs, but he's a Churchman and a Tantivy for all that. I'd best keep out of it."

25

"You are right," I answered. "There is no need for you to meddle in the business. Be mum as to all that you have heard."

"Mum as a mouse," said he, and, pressing my hand, turned away into the darkness. When I returned to the sitting-room I found that my mother had hurried into the kitchen, where the crackling of sticks showed that she was busy building a fire. Decimus Saxon was seated at the edge of the iron-bound oak chest at the side of my father, and was watching him keenly

with his little twinkling eyes, while the old man was fixing his horn glasses and breaking the seals of the packet which his strange visitor had just handed to him.

I saw that when my father looked at the signature at the end of the long, closely written letter, he gave a whiff of surprise, and sat motionless for a moment or so staring at it. Then he turned to the commencement and read it very carefully through, after which he turned it over and read it again. Clearly it brought no unwelcome news, for his eyes sparkled with joy when he looked up from his reading, and more than once he laughed aloud. Finally he asked the man Saxon how it had come into his possession, and whether he was aware of the contents.

"Why, as to that," said the messenger, "it was handed to me by no less a person than Dicky Rumbold himself, and in the presence of others whom it's not for me to name. As to the contents, your own sense will tell you that I would scarce risk my neck by bearing a message without I knew what the message was. I am no chicken at the trade, sir."

"Indeed!" quoth my father. "You are yourself one of the faithful?"

"I trust that I am one of those who are on the narrow and thorny track," said he, speaking through his nose, as was the habit of the extreme sectaries.

"A track upon which no prelate can guide us," said my father.

"Where man is naught, and the Lord is all," rejoined Saxon.

"Good! good!" cried my father. "Micah, you shall take this worthy man to my room and see that he hath dry linen and my second-best suit of Utrecht velvet. It may serve until his own are dried. My boots, too, may perchance be useful, my riding ones of untanned leather. A hat with silver braiding hangs above them in the cupboard. See that he lacks for nothing which the house can furnish. Supper will be ready when he hath changed his attire. I beg that you will go at once, good Master Saxon, lest you take a chill."

Master Decimus Saxon, in my father's black Utrecht velvet and untanned riding-boots, looked a very different man from the bedraggled castaway who had crawled like a conger eel into our fishing-boat. It seemed as if he had cast off his manner with his raiment, for he behaved to my mother during supper with an air of demure gallantry which sat upon him better than the pert and flippant carriage which he had shown towards us in the boat. Truth to say, if he was now more reserved, there was a very good reason for it, for he had played such havoc among the eatables that there was little time for talk. At last, after passing from the round of cold beef to a capon pasty, and topping up with a two-pound perch, washed down by a great jug of ale, he smiled upon us all and told us that his fleshly necessities were satisfied for the nonce. "It is my rule," he remarked, "to obey the wise precept which advises a man to rise from the table feeling that he could yet eat as much as he has partaken of."

"I gather from your words, sir, that you have yourself seen hard service," my father remarked when the board had been cleared and my mother had retired for the night.

"I am an old fighting man," our visitor answered, screwing his pipe together, "a lean old dog of the holdfast breed. This body of mine bears the mark of many a cut and slash received for the most part in the service of the Protestant faith, though some few were caught for the sake of Christendom in general when warring against the Turk."

"Your weapon on such occasions was, I suppose, the sword?" my father asked, shifting uneasily in his seat, as he would do when his old instincts were waking up.

"Broadsword, rapier, Toledo, spontoon, battle-axe, pike or half-pike, morgenstiern, and halberd. I speak with all due modesty, but with backsword, sword and dagger, sword and buckler, single falchion, case of falchions, or any other such exercise, I will hold mine own against any man that ever wore neat's leather, save only my elder brother Quartus."

"By my faith," said my father, with his eyes shining, "were I twenty years younger I should have at you! My backsword play hath been thought well of by stout men of war. God forgive me that my heart should still turn to such vanities."

"I have heard godly men speak well of it," remarked Saxon. "Master Richard Rumbold himself spake of your deeds of arms to the Duke of Argyle. Was there not a Scotsman, one Storr or Stour?"

"Aye, aye! Storr of Drumlithie. I cut him nigh to the saddle-bow in a skirmish on the eve of Dunbar. So Dicky Rumbold had not forgotten it, eh? He was a hard one both at praying and at fighting. We have ridden knee to knee in the field, and we have sought truth together in the chamber. So, Dick will be in harness once again! He could not be still if a blow were to be struck for the trampled faith. If the tide of war set in this direction, I too—who knows? who knows?"

"And here is a stout man at arms," said Saxon, passing his hand down my arm. "He hath thew and sinew, and can use proud words too upon occasion, as I have good cause to know, even in our short acquaintance. Might it not be that he too should strike in in this quarrel?"

"We shall discuss it," my father answered, looking thoughtfully at me from under his heavy brows. "But I pray you, friend Saxon, to give us some further account upon these matters. My son Micah, as I understand, hath picked you out of the waves. How came you there?"

Decimus Saxon puffed at his pipe for a minute or more in silence, as one who is marshalling facts each in its due order.

"It came about in this wise," he said, at last. "When John of Poland chased the Turk from the gates of Vienna, peace broke out in the Principalities, and many a wandering cavaliero like myself found his occupation gone. At last, however, on reaching the Lowlands, I chanced to hear that the *Providence,* owned and commanded by my two brothers, Nonus and Quartus, was about to start from Amsterdam for an adventure to the Guinea coast. I proposed to them that I should join them, and was accordingly taken into partnership on condition that I paid one-third of the cost of the cargo. While waiting at the port, I chanced to come across some of the exiles, who, having heard of my devotion to the Protestant cause, brought me to the duke and to Master Rumbold, who committed these letters to my charge. This makes it clear how they came into my possession."

"But not how you and they came into the water," my father suggested.

"Why, that was but the veriest chance," the adventurer answered, with some little confusion of manner. "I had asked my brothers to put into Portsmouth that I might get rid of these letters, on which they replied in a boorish and unmannerly fashion that they were still waiting for the thousand guineas which represented my share of the venture. To this I answered with brotherly familiarity that it was a small thing, and should be paid for out of the profits of our enterprise. Their base mercantile souls prompted them, however, to catch up two muskets, one of which Nonus discharged at me, and it is likely that Quartus would have followed suit had I not plucked the gun from his hand and unloaded it to prevent further mischief. In unloading it I fear that one of the slugs blew a hole in brother Nonus. Seeing that there was a chance of further disagreements aboard the vessel, I at once decided to leave her, in doing which I was forced to kick off my beautiful jack-boots, which were said by Vanseddars himself to be the finest pair that ever went out of his shop, square-toed, double-soled—alas! alas!"

"Strange that you should have been picked up by the son of the very man to whom you had a letter."

"The working of Providence," Saxon answered. "I have two-and-twenty other letters which must all be delivered by hand. If you will permit me to use your house for a while, I shall make it my headquarters."

"Use it as though it were your own," said my father.

"Your most grateful servant, sir," he cried, jumping up and bowing, with his hand over his heart. "This is indeed a haven of rest after the ungodly and profane company of my brothers. Shall we, then, put up a hymn, and retire from the business of the day?"

My father willingly agreed, and we sang "Oh, happy land!" after which our visitor followed me to his room, bearing with him the unfinished bottle of usquebaugh which my mother had left on the table. He took it with him, he explained, as a precaution against Persian ague, contracted while battling against the Ottoman, and liable to recur at strange moments. I left him in our best spare bedroom, and returned to my father, who was still seated, heavy with thought, in his old corner.

"What think you of my find, dad?" I asked.

"A man of parts and of piety," he answered; "but in truth he has brought me news so much after my heart that he could not be unwelcome were he the pope of Rome."

"What news, then?"

"This, this!" he cried, joyously, plucking the letter out of his bosom. "I will read it to you, lad. Nay, perhaps I had best sleep the night upon it, and read it to-morrow when our heads are clearer. May the Lord guide my path, and confound the tyrant! Pray for light, boy, for my life and yours may be equally at stake."

CHAPTER SIX

OF THE LETTER THAT CAME FROM THE LOWLANDS

IN THE morning I was up betimes, and went forthwith, after the country fashion, to our guest's room to see if there was aught in which I could serve him. On pushing at his door, I found that it was fastened, which surprised me the more as I knew that there was neither key nor bolt upon the inside. On my pressing against it, however, it began to yield, and I gave a butt with my shoulder which cleared a chest out of the way, and enabled me to enter the room.

The man Saxon was sitting up in bed, staring about him as though he were not very certain for the moment where he was.

"Ah, my young friend!" he said, at last. "Is it, then, the custom of this part of the country to carry your visitor's rooms by storm in the early hours of the morning?"

"Is it the custom," I answered, sternly, "to barricade up your door when you are sleeping under the roof-tree of an honest man? What did you fear, that you should take such a precaution?"

"Nay, you are indeed a spitfire," he replied, sinking back upon the pillow, and drawing the clothes round him.

"Know, then, that the bearer of papers of import, *documenta preciosa sed periculosa,* is bound to leave nought to chance, but to guard in every way the charge which hath been committed to him. True it is that I am in the house of an honest man, but I know not who may come or who may go during the hours of the night. Indeed, for the matter of that—but enough is said. I shall be with you anon."

"Your clothes are dry and are ready for you," I remarked.

"Enough! enough!" he answered. "I have no quarrel with the suit which your father has lent me. It may be that I have been used to better, but they will serve my turn. The camp is not the court."

It was evident to me that my father's suit was infinitely better, both in texture and material, than that which our visitor had brought with him. As he had withdrawn his head, however, entirely beneath the bedclothes, there was nothing more to be said, so I descended to the lower room, where I found my father busily engaged fastening a new buckle to his sword-belt, while my mother and the maid were preparing the morning meal.

"Come into the yard with me, Micah," quoth my father; "I would have a word with you." The workmen had not yet come to their work, so we strolled out into the sweet morning air, and seated ourselves on the low stone bankment on which the skins are dressed.

"I have been out here this morning trying my hand at the broadsword exercise," said he; "I find that I am as quick as ever on a thrust, but my cuts are sadly stiff. Yet, if I am old and worn, there is the fruit of my loins to stand in my place and to wield the same sword in the same cause. You shall go in my place, Micah."

"Go! Go whither?"

"Hush, lad, and listen! Let not your mother know too much, for the hearts of women are soft. When Abraham offered up his eldest born, I trow that he said little to Sarah on the matter. Here is the letter. Know you who this Dicky Rumbold is?"

"Surely I have heard you speak of him as an old companion of yours."

"The same—a stanch man and true. So faithful was he —faithful even to slaying—that when the army of the righteous dispersed, he did not lay aside his zeal with his buff-coat. He took to business as a maltster at Hoddesdon, and in his house was planned the famous Rye-House Plot, in which so many good men were involved. When the plot failed, Rumbold had to fly for his life, but he succeeded in giving his pursuers the slip and in making his way to the Lowlands. There he found that many enemies of the government had gathered together. Repeated messages from England, especially from the western counties and from London, assured them that if they would but attempt an invasion they might rely upon help both in men and in money. They were, however, at fault for some time for want of a leader of sufficient weight to carry through so large a project; but now at last they have one, who is the best that could have been singled out—none other than the well-beloved Protestant chieftain James, Duke of Monmouth, son of Charles II."

"Illegitimate son," I remarked.

"That may or may not be. There are those who say that Lucy Walters was a lawful wife. Bastard or no, he holds the sound principles of the true Church, and he is beloved by the people. Let him appear in the west, and soldiers will rise up like the flowers in the spring-time."

He paused, and led me away to the farther end of the yard, for the workmen had begun to arrive and to cluster round the dipping-trough.

"Monmouth is coming over," he continued, "and he expects every brave Protestant man to rally to his standard. The Duke of Argyle is to command a separate expedition, which will set the Highlands of Scotland in a blaze. Between them they hope to bring the persecutor of the faithful on his knees. But I hear the voice of the man Saxon, and I must not let him say that I have treated him in a churlish fashion. Here is the letter, lad. Read it with care, and remember that when brave men are striving for their rights it is fitting that one of the old rebel house of Clarke should be among them."

I took the letter, and, wandering off into the fields, I settled myself under a convenient tree, and set myself to read it.

"To my friend and companion in the cause of the Lord, Joseph Clarke: Know, friend, that aid and delivery is coming.

"It has chanced from time to time that many of the suffering Church, both from our own land and from among the Scots, have assembled in this good Lutheran town of Amsterdam, until enough are gathered together to take a good work in hand.

"It has now come to pass, however, that Monmouth, who has long lived in dalliance with the Midianitish woman known by the name of Wentworth, has at last turned him to higher things, and has consented to make a bid for the crown. It was found that the Scots preferred to follow a chieftain of their own, and it has therefore been determined that Argyle shall command a separate expedition, landing upon the western coast of Scotland. There he hopes to raise five thousand Campbells, and to be joined by all the Covenanters and western Whigs, men who would make troops of the old breed had they but God-fearing officers with an experience of the chance of fields and the usages of war. With such a following he should be able to hold Glasgow, and to draw away the king's force to the north. Ayloffe and I go with Argyle. It is likely that our feet may be upon Scottish ground before thy eyes read these words.

"The stronger expedition starts with Monmouth, and lands at a fitting place in the west, where we are assured that we have many friends. I cannot name the spot lest this letter miscarry, but thou shalt hear anon. I have written to all good men along the coast, bidding them to be prepared to support the rising. The king is weak, and hated by the greater part of his subjects. It doth but need one good stroke to bring his crown in the dust. Monmouth will start in a few weeks, when his equipment is finished and the weather favorable. If thou canst come, mine old comrade, I know well that thou wilt need no bidding of mine to bring thee to our banner. Should, perchance, a peaceful life and waning strength forbid thy attendance, I trust that thou wilt wrestle for us in prayer, even as

the holy prophet of old; and perchance, since I hear that thou
hast prospered according to the things of this world, thou mayst
be able to fit out a pikeman or two, or to send a gift towards
the military chest, which will be none too plentifully lined.
Should we fall, we fall like men and Christians. Should we
succeed, we shall see how the perjured James, the persecutor of
the saints, we shall see how manfully he can bear adversity when
it falls to his lot. May the hand of the Almighty be over us!"

"I know little of the bearer of this, save that he professes to
be of the elect. Shouldst thou go to Monmouth's camp, see
that thou take him with thee, for I hear that he hath had good
experience in the German, Swedish, and Ottoman wars.

"Yours, in the faith of Christ,
"RICHARD RUMBOLD.

"Present my services to thy spouse. Let her read Timothy,
chapter two, ninth to fifteenth verses."

This long letter I read very carefully, and then, putting it
in my pocket, returned in-doors to my breakfast. My father
looked at me as I entered with questioning eyes, but I had no
answer to return him, for my own mind was clouded and uncertain.

That day Decimus Saxon left us, intending to make a round
of the country and to deliver his letters, but promising to be back
again ere long. As he started off down the village street, his
long, stringy figure and strange gnarled visage, with my father's
silver-braided hat cocked over his eye, attracted rather more
attention than I cared to see, considering the importance of the
missives which he bore, and the certainty of their discovery
should he be arrested as a masterless man. He had left golden
opinions behind him. My father's good wishes had been won
by his piety and by the sacrifices which he claimed to have made
for the faith. My mother he had taught how wimples are worn
among the Serbs, and had also demonstrated to her a new

THAT DAY DECIMUS SAXON LEFT US

method of curing marigolds in use in some parts of Lithuania. For myself, I confess that I retained a vague distrust of the man, and was determined to avoid putting faith in him more than was needful. At present, however, we had no choice but to treat him as an ambassador from friends.

And I? What was I to do? Should I follow my father's wishes, and draw my maiden sword on behalf of the insurgents, or should I stand aside and see how events shaped themselves? It was more fitting that I should go than he. But, on the other hand, I was no keen religious zealot. James might be a perjurer and a villain, but he was, as far as I could see, the rightful king of England, and no tales of secret marriages or black boxes could alter the fact that his rival was apparently an illegitimate son, and as such ineligible to the throne. It was a weighty question for a country-bred lad to have to settle, and yet settled it must be, and that speedily. I took up my hat and wandered away down the village street, turning the matter over in my head.

But it was no easy thing for me to think seriously of anything in the hamlet; for I was in some way, though I say it myself, a favorite with the young and with the old, so that I could not walk ten paces without some greeting or address.

Zachary Palmer was planing a plank as I passed. Looking up, he bade me good-morrow.

"I have a book for you, lad," he said.

"I have but now finished the 'Comus,'" I answered, for he had lent me John Milton's poem. "But what is this new book, daddy?"

"It is by the learned Locke, and treateth of states and statecraft. A good man is Master Locke. Is he not at this moment a wanderer in the Lowlands, rather than bow his knee to what his conscience approved not of?"

"There are many good men among the exiles, are there not?" said I.

"The pick of the country," he answered. "Ill fares the land

that drives the highest and bravest of its citizens away from
it. The day is coming, I fear, when every man will have to
choose betwixt his beliefs and his freedom. I am an old man,
Micah boy, but I may live long enough to see strange things
in this once Protestant kingdom."

"But if these exiles had their way," I objected, "they would
place Monmouth upon the throne, and so unjustly alter the succession."

"Nay, nay," old Zachary answered, laying down his plane.
"If they use Monmouth's name it is but to strengthen their
cause, and to show that they have a leader of repute. Were
James driven from the throne, the Commons of England in
Parliament assembled would be called upon to name his suc-
cessor. There are men at Monmouth's back who would not
stir unless this were so."

"Then, daddy," said I, "since I can trust you, and since you
will tell me what you do really think, would it be well, if Monmouth's standard be raised, that I should join it?"

The carpenter stroked his white beard and pondered for a
while. "It is a pregnant question," he said at last, "and yet
methinks that there is but one answer to it, especially for your
father's son. It is treasonable and dangerous counsel—counsel
which might lead to a short shrift and a bloody death—but, as
the Lord liveth, if you were child of mine I should say the same."

So spoke the old carpenter, with a voice which trembled
with earnestness, and went to work upon his plank once more,
while I, with a few words of gratitude, went on my way, pon-
dering over what he had said to me.

And why should I refuse? Had it not long been the secret
wish of my heart to see something of the great world, and what
fairer chance could present itself? My wishes, my friend's
advice, and my father's hopes all pointed in the one direction.

"Father," said I, when I returned home, "I am ready to go
where you will."

CHAPTER SEVEN

OF THE HORSEMAN WHO RODE FROM THE WEST

M Y FATHER set to work forthwith preparing for our equipment, furnishing Saxon out as well as myself on the most liberal scale, for he was determined that the wealth of his age should be as devoted to the cause as was the strength of his youth. These arrangements had to be carried out with the most extreme caution, for there were many Prelatists in the village, and in the present disturbed state of the public mind any activity on the part of so well known a man would have at once attracted attention. So carefully did the wary old soldier manage matters, however, that we soon found ourselves in a position to start at an hour's notice, without any of our neighbors being a whit the wiser.

It was, then, towards nightfall upon the twelfth day of June, 1685, that the news reached our part of the country that Monmouth had landed the day before at Lyme, a small seaport on the boundary between Dorsetshire and Devonshire. A great beacon blaze upon Portsdown Hill was the first news that we had of it, and then came a rattling and a drumming from Portsmouth, where the troops were assembled under arms. Mounted messengers clattered through the village street with their heads low on their horses' necks, for the great tidings must be carried to London, that the governor of Portsmouth might know how to act. We were standing at our doorway in the gloaming, watching the coming and the going, and the line of beacon fires which were lengthening away to the eastward, when a little man galloped up to the door and pulled up his panting horse.

"Is Joseph Clarke here?" he asked.

"I am he," said my father.

"Are these men true?" he whispered, pointing with his whip at Saxon and myself. "Then the trysting place is Tauton. Pass it on to all whom ye know. Give my horse a bait and a drink, I beg of ye, for I must get on my way."

My young brother Hosea looked to the tired creature, while we brought the rider inside and drew him a stoup of beer. A wiry, sharp-faced man he was, with a birth-mark upon his temple. His face and clothes were caked with dust, and his limbs were so stiff from the saddle that he could scarce put one foot before another.

"One horse hath died under me," he said, "and this can scarce last another twenty miles. I must be in London by

morning, for we hope that Danvers and Wildman may be able to raise the city. Yester evening I left Monmouth's camp. His blue flag floats over Lyme."

"What force hath he?" my father asked, anxiously.

"He hath but brought over leaders. The force must come from you folk at home. He has with him Lord Grey of Wark, with Wade, the German Buyse, and eighty or a hundred more."

The messenger staggered to his feet. "I hope to find a relay at Chichester, and time presses. Work for the cause now, or be slaves forever. Farewell!" He clambered into his saddle, and we heard the clatter of his hoofs dying away down the London road.

"The time hath come for you to go, Micah," said my father, solemnly. "Nay, wife, do not weep, but rather hearten the lad on his way by a blithe word and a merry face. I need not tell you to fight manfully and fearlessly in this quarrel. Should the tide of war set in this direction, you may find your old father riding by your side. Let us now bow down and implore the favor of the Almighty upon this expedition."

The prayer finished, we all rose with the exception of Saxon, who remained with his face buried in his hands for a minute or so before starting to his feet. I shrewdly suspect that he had been fast asleep, though he explained that he had paused to offer up an additional supplication. My father placed his hands upon my head and invoked the blessing of Heaven upon me. He then drew my companion aside, and I heard the jingling of coin, from which I judge that he was giving him something wherewith to start upon his travels. My mother clasped me to her heart, and slipped a small square of paper into my hand, saying that I was to look at it at my leisure, and that I should make her happy if I would but conform to the instructions contained in it. This I promised to do, and, tearing myself away, I set off down the darkened village street, with my long-limbed companion striding by my side.

It was close upon one in the morning, and all the country folk had been long abed. Passing the Wheatsheaf and the house of old Solomon, I could not but wonder what they would think of my martial garb were they afoot. I had scarce time to form the same thought before Zachary Palmer's cottage when his door flew open, and the carpenter came running out, with his white hair streaming in the fresh night breeze.

"I have been awaiting you, Micah," he cried. "I had heard that Monmouth was up, and I knew that you could not lose a night ere starting. God bless you, lad, God bless you! Strong of arm and soft of heart, tender to the weak and stern to the oppressor, you have the prayers and the love of all who know you." I pressed his extended hands, and the last I saw of my native hamlet was the shadowy figure of the carpenter as he waved his good wishes to me through the darkness.

We made our way across the fields to the house of Whittier, the Whig farmer, where Saxon got into his war harness. We found our horses ready saddled and bridled, for my father had at the first alarm sent a message across that we should need them. By two in the morning we were breasting Portsdown Hill, armed, mounted, and fairly started on our journey to the rebel camp.

CHAPTER EIGHT

OF OUR START FOR THE WARS

ALL along the ridge of Portsdown Hill we had the lights of Portsmouth and of the harbor ships twinkling beneath us on the left, while on the right the Forest of Bere was ablaze with the signal fires which proclaimed the landing of the invader. One great beacon throbbed upon the summit of Butser, while beyond that, as far as eye could reach, twinkling sparks of light showed how the tidings were being carried north into Berkshire and eastward into Sussex. Of these fires, some were composed of fagots piled into heaps and others of tar barrels set upon poles. We passed one of these last just opposite to Portchester and the watchers around it, hearing the tramp of our horses and the clank of our arms, set up a loud huzza, thinking doubtless that we were king's officers bound for the west.

Master Decimus Saxon had flung to the winds the precise demeanor which he had assumed in the presence of my father, and rattled away with many a jest and scrap of rhyme or song as we galloped through the darkness.

"Gadzooks!" said he, frankly, "it is good to be able to speak freely without being expected to tag every sentence with a hallelujah or an amen."

"You were ever the leader in those pious exercises," I remarked, dryly.

"Aye, indeed. You have nicked it there! If a thing must be done, then take a lead in it, whatever it may be."

We passed through Fareham and Botley in conversation, and were now making our way down the Bishopstoke road. The soil changes about here from chalk to sand, so that our horses' hoofs did but make a dull, subdued rattle, which was no bar to our talk—or rather to my companion's, for I did little more than listen. In truth, my mind was so full of anticipations of what was before us, and of thoughts of the home behind, that I was in no humor for sprightly chatter. The sky was somewhat clouded, but the moon glinted out between the rifts, showing us the long road which wound away in front of us. On either side were scattered houses with gardens sloping down towards the road. The heavy, sickly scent of strawberries was in the air.

"Hast ever slain a man in anger?" asked Saxon, as we galloped along.

"Never," I answered.

"Ha! You will find that when you hear the clink of steel against steel, and see your foeman's eyes, you will straightway forget all rules, maxims, and precepts of the fence which your father or others may have taught you."

"I have learned little of the sort," said I. "My father did but teach me to strike an honest, downright blow. This sword can shear through a square inch of iron bar."

"Scanderbeg's sword must have Scanderbeg's arm," he remarked. "I have observed that it is a fine piece of steel. One of the real old text-compellers and psalm-expounders which the faithful drew in the days of yore, when they would

> " 'Prove their religion orthodox,
> By Apostolic blows and knocks.'

You have not fenced much, then?"

"Scarce at all," said I.

"It is as well. With an old and tried swordsman like myself, knowledge of the use of his weapon is everything, but with a young Hotspur of your temper, strength and energy go for much. I make no doubt, Master Clarke, that we shall make trusty comrades. What saith old Butler?

> " 'Never did trusty squire with knight,
> Or knight with squire e'er jump more right.'

I have scarce dared to quote Hudibras for these weeks past, lest I should set the Covenant fermenting in the old man's veins."

"If we are indeed to be comrades," said I, sternly, "you must learn to speak with more reverence and less flippancy of my father, who would assuredly never have harbored you had he heard the tale which you have told me even now."

"Belike not," the adventurer answered, chuckling to himself. "But be not so hot-headed, my friend. You lack that repose of character which will come to you, no doubt, in your more mature years. Remember that you go now among men who fight on small occasion of quarrel. A word awry may mean a rapier thrust."

"Do you bear the same in mind," I answered, hotly; "my temper is peaceful, but covert threats and veiled menace I shall not abide."

"Odd's mercy!" he cried. "I see that you will start carving me anon, and take me to Monmouth's camp in sections.

Nay, nay, we shall have fighting enow without falling out among ourselves. What houses are those on the left?"

"The village of Swathling," I replied. "The lights of Bishopstoke lie to the right, in the hollow."

"Then we are fifteen miles on our way, and methinks there is already some faint flush of dawn in the east. This, you say, is Bishopstoke. What are the lights over yonder?"

"They come, I think, from Bishop's Waltham," I answered.

"We must press on, for I would fain be in Salisbury before it is broad day. There we shall put our horses up until evening and have some rest, for there is nothing gained by man or beast coming jaded to the wars. All this day the western roads will be crowded with couriers, and mayhap patrolled by cavalry as well, so that we cannot show our faces upon it without a risk of being stopped and examined. Now, if we lie by all day, and push on at dusk, keeping off the main road and making our way across Salisbury Plain and the Somersetshire downs, we shall be less likely to come to harm."

"But what if Monmouth be engaged before we come up to him?" I asked.

"Then we shall have missed a chance of getting our throats cut. Why, man, supposing that he has been routed and entirely dispersed, would it not be a merry conceit for us to appear upon the scene as two loyal yeomen, who had ridden all the way from Hampshire to strike in against the king's enemies? We might chance to get some reward in money or in land for our zeal. Nay, frown not, for I was but jesting. Breathe our horses by walking them up this hill. My jennet is as fresh as when we started, but those great limbs of thine are telling upon the gray."

"Anent Monmouth," he remarked, coming back suddenly to the realities of our position. "It is unlikely that he can take the field for some days, though much depends upon his striking a blow soon, and so raising the courage of his followers before the king's troops can come down upon him. He has, mark ye, not only his troops to find, but their weapons, which is like to prove a more difficult matter. Suppose he can raise five thousand men—and he cannot stir with less—he will not have one musket in five, so the rest must do as they can with pikes and bills, or such other rude arms as they can find. All this takes time, and, though there may be skirmishes, there can scarce be any engagement of import before we arrive."

"He will have been landed three or four days ere we reach him," said I.

"Hardly time for him, with his small staff of officers, to enroll his men and divide them into regiments. I scarce expect to find him at Taunton, though we were so directed. Hast ever heard whether there are any rich Papists in those parts?"

"I know not," I replied.

"If so, there might be plate-chests and silver chargers, to say nothing of my lady's jewels and other such trifles to reward a faithful soldier. What would war be without plunder? A bottle without the wine—a shell without the oyster. See the house yonder that peeps through the trees. I warrant there is a store of all good things under that roof, which you and I might have for the asking, did we but ask with the swords in our grip. You are my witness that your father did give and not lend me this horse."

"Why say you that, then?"

"Lest he claim a half of whatever booty I may chance to gain."

"I can promise you," I answered, "that no such claim shall ever be made by my father upon you. See yonder, over the brow of the hill, how the sun shines upon the high cathedral tower, which points upward with its great stone finger to the road that every man must travel."

It chanced that Saxon's mare had gained a stride or two upon mine while he spoke, so that I was able to get a good view of him without turning my head. I had scarce had light during our ride to see how his harness sat upon him, but now I was amazed on looking at him to mark the change which it had wrought in the man. In his civil dress his lankiness and length of limb gave him an awkward appearance, but on horseback, with his lean, gaunt face looking out from his steel cap, his breastplate and buff jacket filling out his figure, and his high boots of untanned leather reaching to the centre of his thighs, he looked the veteran man at arms which he purported to be. The ease with which he sat his horse, the high, bold expression upon his face, and the great length of his arms, all marked him as one who could give a good account of himself in a fray. In his words alone I could have placed little trust, but there was that in his bearing which assured even a novice like myself that he was indeed a trained man of war.

"That is the Avon which glitters among the trees," I remarked. "We are about three miles from Salisbury town."

"It is a noble spire," said he, glancing at the great stone spire in front of us. "The men of old would seem to have spent all their days in piling stones upon stones. And yet we read of tough battles and shrewd blows struck, showing that they had some time for soldierly relaxation, and were not always at this mason work."

"The Church was rich in those days," I answered, shaking my bridle, for Covenant was beginning to show signs of laziness. "But here comes one who might perhaps tell us something of the war."

A horseman who bore traces of having ridden long and hard was rapidly approaching us. Both rider and steed were gray with dust and splashed with mire, yet he galloped with loosened rein and bent body, as one to whom every extra stride is of value.

"What ho, friend!" cried Saxon, reining his mare across the road so as to bar the man's passage. "What news from the west?"

"I must not tarry," the messenger gasped, slackening his

speed for an instant. "I bear papers of import from Gregory Alford, Mayor of Lyme, to his majesty's council. The rebels make great head, and gather together like bees in the swarming time. There are some thousands in arms already, and all Devonshire is on the move. The rebel horse under Lord Grey hath been beaten back from Bridport by the red militia of Dorset, but every prick-eared Whig from the Channel to the Severn is making his way to Monmouth." With this brief summary of the news, he pushed his way past us and clattered on in a cloud of dust upon his mission.

"The broth is fairly on the fire, then," quoth Decimus Saxon as we rode onward. "Now that skins have been slit the rebels may draw their swords and fling away their scabbards, for it's either victory for them or their quarters will be dangling in every market-town of the county. Heh! lad! we throw a main for a brave stake."

"Marked ye that Lord Grey had met with a check?" said I.

"Pshaw! it is of no import. A cavalry skirmish at the most, for it is impossible that Monmouth could have brought his main forces to Bridport; nor would he if he could, for it is out of his track. It was one of those three-shots-and-a-gallop affrays, where each side runs away and each claims the victory. But here we are in the streets of Salisbury. Now leave the talking to me, or your wrongheaded truthfulness may lay us by the heels before our time."

Passing down the broad high street, we dismounted in front of the Blue Boar inn, and handed our tired horses over to the hostler, to whom Saxon, in a loud voice and with many rough military oaths, gave strict injunctions as to their treatment. He then clanked into the inn parlor, and, throwing himself into one chair with his feet upon another, he summoned the landlord up before him and explained our needs in a tone and manner which should give him a due sense of our quality.

"Of your best, and at once," quoth he. "Have your largest double-couched chamber ready, with your softest lavender-scented sheets, for we have had a weary ride and must rest. And hark ye, landlord, no palming off your stale, musty goods as fresh, or of your washy French wines for the true Hainault vintage. I would have you to understand that my friend here and I are men who meet with some consideration in the world, though we care not to speak our names to every underling. Deserve well of us, therefore, or it may be the worse for you."

This speech, combined with my companion's haughty manner and fierce face, had such an effect upon the landlord that he straightway sent us in the breakfast which had been prepared for three officers of the Blues, who were waiting for it in the next apartment. This kept them fasting for another half-hour, and we could hear their oaths and complaints through the partition, while we were devouring their capon and venison pie. Having eaten a hearty meal and washed it down with a bottle of Burgundy, we sought our room, and, throwing our tired limbs upon the bed, were soon in a deep slumber.

CHAPTER NINE

OF A PASSAGE OF ARMS AT THE BLUE BOAR

I HAD slept several hours when I was suddenly aroused by a prodigious crash, followed by the clash of arms and shrill cries from the lower floor. Springing to my feet, I found that the bed upon which my comrade had lain was vacant, and that the door of the apartment was opened. As the uproar still continued, and as I seemed to discern his voice in the midst of it, I caught up my sword, and, without waiting to put on either head-piece, steel-breast, or arm-plates, I hurried to the scene of the commotion.

The hall and passage were filled with silly maids and staring drawers, attracted, like myself, by the uproar. Through

these I pushed my way into the apartment where we had break-
fasted in the morning, which was a scene of the wildest disorder.
The round table in the centre had been tilted over upon its
side, and three broken bottles of wine, with apples, pears, nuts,
and the fragments of the dishes containing them, were littered
over the floor. A couple of packs of cards and a dice-box lay
among the scattered feast. Close by the door stood Decimus
Saxon, with his drawn rapier in his hand and a second one beneath his feet, while facing him there was a young officer in a
blue uniform, whose face was reddened with shame and anger,
and who looked wildly about the room as though in search of
some weapon to replace that of which he had been deprived.
He might have served Cibber or Gibbons as a model for a
statue of impotent rage. Two other officers, dressed in the
same blue uniform, stood by their comrade, and, as I observed
that they had laid their hands upon the hilts of their swords,
I took my place by Saxon's side and stood ready to strike in
should the occasion arise.

"What would the maître d'armes say—the maître d'escrime?"
cried my companion. "Methinks he should lose his place for
not teaching you to make a better show. Out on him! Is this
the way that he teaches the officers of his majesty's guard to
use their weapons?"

"This raillery, sir," said the elder of the three, a squat,
brown, heavy-faced man, "is not undeserved, and yet might
perchance be dispensed with. I am free to say that our friend
attacked you somewhat hastily, and that a little more deference
should have been shown by so young a soldier to a cavalier of
your experience."

The other officer, who was a fine-looking, noble-featured
man, expressed himself in much the same manner. "If this
apology will serve," said he, "I am prepared to join in it. If,
however, more is required, I shall be happy to take the quarrel upon myself."

"Nay, nay, take your brad-awl!" Saxon answered, good-humoredly, kicking the sword towards his youthful opponent. The youth sheathed his sword, but was so overcome by his own easy defeat, and the contemptuous way in which his opponent had dismissed him, that he turned and hurried out of the room. Meanwhile, Decimus Saxon and the two officers set to work getting the table upon its legs and restoring the room to some sort of order, in which I did what I could to assist them.

That settled, I was right glad to have the opportunity of making their closer acquaintance over a flask of excellent wine. My father's prejudices had led me to believe that a king's officer was ever a compound of the coxcomb and the bully, but I found on testing it that this idea, like most others which a man takes upon trust, had very little foundation upon truth. As a matter of fact, had they been dressed in less warlike garb and deprived of their swords and jack-boots, they would have passed as particularly mild-mannered men, for their conversation ran in the learned channels, and they discussed Boyle's researches in chemistry and the ponderation of air with much gravity and show of knowledge. At the same time, their brisk bearing and manly carriage showed that in cultivating the scholar they had not sacrificed the soldier.

The officers finally rose from their chairs, for the bottle was empty and the evening beginning to draw in. "We have work to do here," said the one addressed as Ogilvy. "Besides, we must find this foolish boy of ours, and tell him that it is no disgrace to be disarmed by so expert a swordsman. We have to prepare the quarters for the regiment, who will be up to join Churchill's forces not later than to-night. Ye are yourselves bound for the west, I understand?"

"We belong to the Duke of Beauford's household," said Saxon.

"Indeed! I thought ye might belong to Portman's yellow

regiment of militia. I trust that the duke will muster every man he can, and make play until the royalist forces come up."

"How many will Churchill bring?" asked my companion, carelessly.

"Eight hundred horses at the most, but my Lord Feversham will follow after with close on four thousand foot."

"We may meet on the field of battle, if not before," said I, and we bade our friendly enemies a very cordial adieu.

"A skilful equivoque, that last of yours, Master Micah," quoth Decimus Saxon, "though smacking of double dealing in a truth-lover like yourself. If we meet them in battle I trust that it may be with chevaux-de-frise of pikes and morgenstierns before us, and a litter of caltrops in front of them, for Monmouth has no cavalry that could stand for a moment against the Royal Guards."

"How came you to make their acquaintance?" I asked.

"I slept a few hours, but I have learned in camps to do with little rest. Finding you in sound slumber, and hearing the rattle of the dice-box below, I came softly down and found means to join their party—whereby I am a richer man by fifteen guineas."

I proposed that we should order an evening meal, and should employ the remaining hour or two of daylight in looking over the city. It was wellnigh dark before we returned to the hostel, and entirely so by the time that we had eaten our suppers, paid our reckoning, and got ready for the road.

Before we set off I bethought me of the paper which my mother had slipped into my hand on parting, and, drawing it from my pouch, I read it by the rushlight in our chamber. It still bore the splotches of the tears which she had dropped on it, poor soul, and ran in this wise:

"Instructions from Mistress Mary Clarke to her son Micah, on the twelfth day of June, in the year of our Lord sixteen hundred and eighty-five.

"On occasion of his going forth, like David of old, to do battle with the Goliath of Papistry, which hath overshadowed and thrown into disrepute that true and reverent regard for ritual which should exist in the real Church of England, as ordained by law.

"Let these points be observed by him, namely, to wit.

"1. Change your hosen when the occasion serves. You have two pairs in your saddle-bag, and can buy more, for the wool work is good in the west.

"2. A hare's foot suspended round the neck driveth away colic.

"3. Say the Lord's Prayer night and morning. Also read the Scriptures, especially Job, the Psalms, and the Gospel according to St. Matthew.

"4. Daffy's Elixir possesses extraordinary powers in purifying the blood and working off all phlegms, humors, vapors, or rheums. The dose is five drops. A small phial of it will be found in the barrel of your left pistol, with wadding around it lest it come to harm.

"5. Ten golden pieces are sewn into the hem of your under doublet. Touch them not, save as a last resource.

"6. Fight stoutly for the Lord, and yet, I pray you, Micah, be not too forward in battle, but let others do their turn also. Press not into the heart of the fray, and yet flinch not from the standard of the Protestant faith.

"And, oh, Micah, my own bright boy, come back safe to your mother, or my heart will break!

"And the deponent will ever pray."

The sudden gush of tenderness in the last few lines made the tears spring to my eyes, and yet I could scarce forbear from smiling at the whole composition, for my dear mother had little time to cultivate the graces of style, and it was evidently her thought that, in order to make her instructions binding, it was needful to express them in some sort of legal form.

I had little time to think over her advice, however, for I had scarce finished reading it before the voice of Decimus Saxon and the clink of the horses' hoofs upon the cobblestones of the yard informed me that all was ready for our departure.

CHAPTER TEN

OF OUR PERILOUS ADVENTURE ON THE PLAIN

WE WERE not half a mile from the town before the roll of kettle-drums and the blare of bugles swelling up musically through the darkness announced the arrival of the regiment of horse which our friends at the inn had been expecting.

"It is as well, perhaps," said Saxon, "that we gave them the slip, for that young springald might have smelt a rat and played us some ill turn. Have you chanced to see my silken kerchief?"

"Not I," I answered.

"Nay, then it must have fallen from my bosom during our ruffle. I can ill afford to leave it, for I travel light in such matters. Eight hundred men, quoth the major, and three thousand to follow. Should I meet this same Oglethorpe or Ogilvy when the little business is over, I shall read him a lesson on

59

thinking less of chemistry and more of the need of preserving military precautions. It is well always to be courteous to strangers, and to give them information, but it is well, also, that the information should be false."

"As his may have been," I suggested.

"Nay, nay, the words came too glibly from his tongue. So ho, Chloe, so ho! She is full of oats, and would fain gallop, but it is so plaguy dark that we can scarce see where we are going."

We had come to the point where a by-road branches off from the main highway, when we heard the clatter of horses' hoofs behind us.

"Here comes some one who is not afraid to gallop," I remarked.

"Halt here in the shadow!" cried Saxon, in a short, quick whisper. "Have your blade loose in the scabbard. He must have a set errand who rides so fast o' nights."

Looking down the road, we could make out, through the darkness, a shadowy blur, which soon resolved itself into man and horse. The rider was wellnigh abreast of us before he was aware of our presence, when he pulled up his steed in a strange, awkward fashion and faced round in our direction.

"Is Micah Clarke there?" he said, in a voice which was strangely familiar to my ears.

"I am Micah Clarke," said I.

"And I am Reuben Lockarby," cried our pursuer, in a mock-heroic voice. "Ah, Micah, lad, I'd embrace you were it not that I should assuredly fall out of the saddle if I attempted it, and perchance drag you along. That sudden pull up wellnigh landed me on the roadway. I have been sliding off and clambering on ever since I bade good-bye to Havant. Sure, such a horse for slipping from under one was never bestridden by man."

"Good heavens, Reuben!" I cried, in amazement, "what brings you all this way from home?"

"The very same cause which brings you, Micah, and also Don Decima Saxon, late of the Solent, whom methinks I see in the shadow behind you. How fares it, O illustrious one?"

"It is you, then, young cock of the woods!" growled Saxon, in no very overjoyed voice.

"No less a person," said Reuben. "And now, my gay cavalieros, round with your horses and trot on your way, for there is no time to be lost. We ought all to be at Taunton to-morrow."

"But, my dear Reuben," said I, "it cannot be that you are coming with us to join Monmouth. What would your father say?"

"Forward, lads, forward!" cried he, spurring on his horse. "It is all arranged and settled. I am about to offer my august person, together with a sword which I borrowed and a horse which I stole, to his most Protestant highness, James, Duke of Monmouth."

"But how comes it all?" I asked, as we rode on together. "It warms my very heart to see you, but you were never concerned either in religion or in politics. Whence, then, this sudden resolution?"

"Well, truth to tell," he replied, "I am neither a king's man nor a duke's man. I am a Micah Clarke man, though, from the crown of my head to the soles of my feet; and, if he rides to the wars, may the plague strike me if I don't stick to his elbow!" He raised his hand excitedly as he spoke, and, instantly losing his balance, he shot into a dense clump of bushes by the road-side, whence his legs flapped helplessly in the darkness.

"That makes the tenth," said he, scrambling out and clambering into his saddle once more. "My father used to tell me not to sit a horse too closely. 'A gentle rise and fall,' said the old man. Egad! there is more fall than rise, and it is anything but gentle."

"Odd's truth!" exclaimed Saxon. "How, in the name of

all the saints in the calendar, do you expect to keep your seat in the presence of an enemy if you lose it on a peaceful high-road?"

"I can but try, my illustrious," he answered, rearranging his ruffled clothing. "Perchance the sudden and unexpected character of my movements may disconcert the said enemy."

"Well, well, there may be more truth in that than you are aware of," quoth Saxon, riding upon Lockarby's bridle arm, so that there was scarce room for him to fall between us. "I had sooner fight a man like that young fool at the inn, who knew a little of the use of his weapon, than one like Micah here, or yourself, who knows nothing."

"If want of knowledge maketh a dangerous swordsman," quoth Reuben, "then am I deadly indeed. To continue my story, however, which I broke off in order to step down from my horse, I found out early in the morning that ye were gone, and Zachary Palmer was able to tell me whither. I made up my mind, therefore, that I would out into the world also. To this end I borrowed a sword from Solomon Sprent, and, my father having gone to Gosport, I helped myself to the best nag in his stables—for I have too much respect for the old man to allow one of his flesh and blood to go ill-provided to the wars. All day I have ridden, since early morning, being twice stopped on suspicion of being ill-affected, but having the good-luck to get away each time. I knew that I was close at your heels, for I found them searching for you at the Salisbury inn."

Decimus whistled. "Searching for us?" said he.

"Yes. It seems that they had some notion that ye were not what ye professed to be, so the inn was surrounded as I passed, but none knew which road ye had taken."

"Said I not so?" cried Saxon. "That young viper hath stirred up the regiment against us. We must push on, for they may send a party on our track."

"We are off the main road now," I remarked; "even should they pursue us, they would be unlikely to follow this side-track."

"Yet it would be wise to show them a clean pair of heels," said Saxon, spurring his mare into a gallop. Lockarby and I followed his example, and we all three rode swiftly along the rough moorland track.

At last we had slackened our pace, under the impression that all fear of pursuit was at an end, and Reuben was amusing us by an account of the excitement which had been caused in Havant by our disappearance, when, through the stillness of the night, a dull, muffled rat-tat-tat struck upon my ear. At the same moment Saxon sprang from his horse and listened intently, with sidelong head.

"Boot and saddle!" he cried, springing into his seat again. "They are after us, as sure as fate. A dozen troopers, by the sound. We must shake them off, or good-bye to Monmouth."

"Give them their heads," I answered, and, striking spurs into our steeds, we thundered on through the darkness. Covenant and Chloe were as fresh as could be wished, and soon settled down into a long, springy gallop. Our friend's horse, however, had been travelling all day, and its long-drawn, labored breathing showed that it could not hold out for long. Through the clatter of our horses' hoofs I could still, from time to time, hear the ominous murmur from behind us.

"This will never do, Reuben," said I, anxiously, as the weary creature stumbled, and the rider came perilously near to shooting over its head.

"The old horse is nearly foundered," he answered, ruefully. "We are off the road now, and the rough ground is too much for her."

"Yes, we are off the track," cried Saxon, over his shoulder —for he led us by a few paces. "Bear in mind that the Bluecoats have been on the march all day, so that their horses may also be blown. How in Himmel came they to know which road we took?"

As if in answer to his ejaculation, there rose out of the

still night behind us a single clear, bell-like note, swelling and increasing in volume, until it seemed to fill the whole air with its harmony.

"A blood-hound!" cried Saxon.

A second, sharper, keener note, ending in an unmistakable howl, answered the first.

"Another of them," said he. "They have loosed the brutes that we saw near the cathedral. Keep a firm knee and a steady seat, for a slip now would be your last."

"Holy mother!" cried Reuben, "I had steeled myself to die in battle—but to be dog's-meat! It is something outside the contract."

"They hold them in leash," said Saxon, between his teeth; "else they would outstrip the horses and be lost in the darkness. Could we but come on running water, we might put them off our track."

"My horse cannot hold on at this pace for more than a very few minutes," Reuben cried. "If I break down, do ye go on, for ye must remember that they are upon your track and not mine. They have found cause for suspicion of the two strangers of the inn, but none of me."

"Nay, Reuben, we shall stand or fall together," said I, sadly, for at every step his horse grew more and more feeble. "In this darkness they will make little distinction between persons."

"Keep a good heart," shouted the old soldier, who was now leading us by twenty yards or more. "We can hear them because the wind blows from that way, but it's odds whether they have heard us. Methinks they slacken in their pursuit."

"The sound of their horses has indeed grown fainter," said I, joyfully.

"So faint that I can hear it no longer," my companion cried.

We reined up our panting steeds and strained our ears, but not a sound could we hear save the gentle murmur of the breeze among the whin-bushes, and the melancholy cry of the night-jar. Behind us the broad, rolling plain, half light and half shadow, stretched away to the dim horizon without sign of life or movement.

"We have either outstripped them completely, or else they have given up the chase," said I. "What ails the horses that they should tremble and snort?"

"My poor beast is nearly done for," Reuben remarked, leaning forward and passing his hand down the creature's reeking neck.

"For all that we cannot rest," said Saxon. "We may not be out of danger yet. Another mile or two may shake us clear. But I like it not."

"Like not what?"

"These horses and their terrors. The beasts can at times both see and hear more than we, as I could show by divers examples drawn from mine own experience on the Danube and in the Palatinate, were the time and place more fitting. Let us on, then, before we rest."

The weary horses responded bravely to the call, and struggled onward over the broken ground for a considerable time. At last we were thinking of pulling up in good earnest, and of congratulating ourselves upon having tired out our pursuers, when of a sudden the bell-like baying broke upon our ears far louder than it had been before—so loud, indeed, that it was evident that the dogs were close upon our heels.

"The accursed hounds!" cried Saxon, putting spurs to his horse and shooting ahead of us; "I feared as much. They have freed them from the leash. There is no escape from the devils, but we can choose the spot where we shall make our stand."

"Come on, Reuben," I shouted. "We have only to reckon with the dogs now. Their masters have let them loose, and turned back for Salisbury."

"Pray Heaven they break their necks before they get there!" he cried. "They set dogs on us as though we were rats in a cock-pit. Yet they call England a Christian country! It's no use, Micah. Poor Dido can't stir another step."

As he spoke, the sharp, fierce bay of the hounds rose again, clear and stern, on the night air, swelling up from a low, hoarse growl to a high, angry yelp. There seemed to be a ring of exultation in their wild cry, as though they knew that their quarry was almost run to earth.

"Not another step!" said Reuben Lockarby, pulling up and drawing his sword. "If I must fight I shall fight here."

"There could be no better place," I replied. Two great jagged rocks rose before us, jutting abruptly out of the ground, and leaving a space of twelve or fifteen feet between them. Through this gap we rode, and I shouted loudly for Saxon to join us. His horse, however, had been steadily gaining upon ours, and at the renewed alarm had darted off again, so that he was already some hundred yards from us. It was useless to summon him, even could he hear our voices, for the hounds would be upon us before he could return.

"Never heed him," I said, hurriedly. "Do you rein your steed behind that rock, and I behind this. They will serve to break the force of the attack. Dismount not, but strike down and strike hard."

On either side in the shadow of the rock we waited in silence for our terrible pursuers. Nor had we long to wait. Another long, deep, thunderous bay sounded in our ears, followed by a profound silence, broken only by the quick, shivering breathing of the horses. Then, suddenly and noiselessly, a great tawny brute, with its black muzzle to the earth, and its overhung cheeks flapping on either side, sprang into the band of moonlight between the rocks, and on into the shadow beyond. It never paused or swerved for an instant, but pursued its course straight onward without a glance to right or to left. Close behind it came a second, and behind that a third, all of enormous size, and looking even larger and more terrible than they were in the dim, shifting light. Like the first, they took no notice of our presence, but bounded on along the trail left by Decimus Saxon.

The first and second I let pass, for I hardly realized that they so completely overlooked us. When the third, however, sprang out into the moonlight, I drew my right-hand pistol from its holster, and, resting its long barrel across my left forearm, I fired at it as it passed. The bullet struck the mark, for the brute gave a fierce howl of rage and pain, but, true to the scent, it never turned or swerved. Lockarby fired also, as it disappeared among the brushwood, but with no apparent effect. So swiftly and so noiselessly did the great hounds pass that they might have been grim, silent spirits of the night, the phantom dogs of Herne the Hunter, but for that one fierce yelp which followed my shot.

"What brutes!" my companion ejaculated; "what shall we do, Micah?"

"They have clearly been laid on Saxon's trail," said I. "We must follow them up, or they will be too many for him. Can you hear anything of our pursuers?"

"Nothing."

"They have given up the chase, then, and let the dogs loose as a last resource. Doubtless the creatures are trained to return to the town. But we must push on, Reuben, if we are to help our companion."

"One more spurt, then, little Dido," cried Reuben; "can you muster strength for one more? Nay, I have not the heart to put spurs to you. If you can do it, I know you will."

The brave mare snorted, as though she understood her rider's words, and stretched her weary limbs into a gallop. So stoutly did she answer the appeal that, though I pressed Covenant to his topmost speed, she was never more than a few strides behind him.

"He took this direction," said I, peering anxiously out into the darkness. "He can scarce have gone far, for he spoke of making a stand. Or, perhaps, finding that we are not with him, he may trust to the speed of his horse."

"What chance hath a horse of outstripping these brutes?" Reuben answered. "They must run him to earth, and he knows it. Hullo! what have we here?"

A dark, dim form lay stretched in the moonlight in front of us. It was the dead body of a hound—the one, evidently, at which I had fired.

"There is one of them disposed of,"I cried, joyously; "we have but two to settle with now."

As I spoke we heard the crack of two pistol-shots some little distance to the left. Heading our steeds in that direction, we pressed on at the top of our speed. Presently out of the darkness in front of us there arose such a roaring and a yelping as sent the hearts into our mouths. It was not a single cry, such as the hounds had uttered when they were on the scent, but a continuous, deep-mouthed uproar, so fierce and so prolonged that we could not doubt that they had come to the end of their run.

"Pray God that they have not got him down!" cried Reuben, in a faltering voice.

Bursting through a thick belt of scrub and tangled gorse bushes, we came upon a scene so unlike what we expected that we pulled up our horses in astonishment.

A circular clearing lay in front of us, brightly illuminated by the silvery moonshine. In the centre of this rose a giant stone, one of those high, dark columns which are found all over the plain, and especially in the parts round Stonehenge. On the top of this ancient stone, cross-legged and motionless, like some strange, carved idol of former days, sat Decimus Saxon, puffing sedately at the long pipe which was ever his comfort in moments of difficulty. Beneath him, at the base of the mono-lith, as our learned men call them, the two great blood-hounds were rearing and springing, clambering over each other's backs in their frenzied and futile eagerness to reach the impassive

ON THE TOP OF THIS ANCIENT STONE, CROSS-LEGGED AND MOTIONLESS,
SAT DECIMUS SAXON

figure perched above them, while they gave vent to their rage and disappointment in the hideous uproar which had suggested such terrible thoughts to our mind.

We had little time, however, to gaze at this strange scene, for upon our appearance the hounds abandoned their helpless attempts to reach Saxon, and flew with a fierce snarl of satisfaction at Reuben and myself. One great brute, with flaring eyes and yawning mouth, his white fangs glistening in the moonlight, sprang at my horse's neck; but I met him fair with a single sweeping cut, which shore away his muzzle and left him wallowing and writhing in a pool of blood. Reuben, meanwhile, had spurred his horse forward to meet his assailant; but the poor, tired steed flinched at the sight of the fierce hound, and pulled up suddenly, with the result that her rider rolled headlong into the very jaws of the animal. It might have gone ill with Reuben had he been left to his own resources. At the most he could only have kept the cruel teeth from his throat for a very few moments; but, seeing the mischance, I drew my remaining pistol, and, springing from my horse, discharged it full into the creature's flank while it struggled with my friend. With a last yell of rage and pain it brought its fierce jaws together in one wild, impotent snap, and then sank slowly over upon its side, while Reuben crawled from beneath it, scared and bruised, but none the worse otherwise for his perilous adventure.

"I owe you one for that, Micah," he said, gratefully. "I may live to do as much for you."

"And I owe ye both one," said Saxon, who had scrambled down from his place of refuge. "I pay my debts, too, whether for good or evil. I might have stayed up there until I had eaten my jack-boots, for all the chance I had of ever getting down again. Sancta Maria! but that was a shrewd blow of yours, Clarke! The brute's head flew in halves like a rotten pumpkin. No wonder that they stuck to my track, for I have left both my spare girth and my kerchief behind me, which would serve to put them on Chloe's scent as well as mine own."

"And where is Chloe?" I asked, wiping my sword.

"Chloe had to look out for herself. I found the brutes gaining on me, you see, and I let drive at them with my barkers; but with a horse flying at twenty miles an hour, what chance is there for a single slug finding its way home? As luck would have it, just as I was fairly puzzled, what should I come across but this handy stone which the good priests of old did erect, as far as I can see, for no other purpose than to provide worthy cavalieros with an escape from such ignoble and scurvy enemies. I had no time to spare in clambering up it, for I had to tear my heel out of the mouth of the foremost of them, and might have been dragged down by it had he not found my spur too tough a morsel for his chewing. But surely one of my bullets must have reached its mark." Lighting the touch-paper in his tobacco-box, he passed it over the body of the hound which had attacked me, and then of the other.

"Why, this one is riddled like a sieve!" he cried. "What do you load your petronels with, good Master Clarke?"

"With two leaden slugs."

"Yet two leaden slugs have made a score of holes at the least! And, of all things in this world, here is the neck of a bottle stuck in the brute's hide!"

"Good heavens!" I exclaimed. "I remember. My dear mother packed a bottle of Daffy's Elixir in the barrel of my pistol."

"And you have shot it into the blood-hound!" roared Reuben. "Ho! ho! When they hear that tale at the tap of the Wheatsheaf, there will be some throats dry with laughter. Saved my life by shooting a dog with a bottle of Daffy's Elixir!"

"And a bullet as well, Reuben, though I dare warrant the gossips will soon contrive to leave that detail out. It is a mercy the pistol did not burst. But what do you propose to do now, Master Saxon?"

"Why, to recover my mare if it can anywise be done," said the adventurer. "Though, on this vast moor, in the dark, she will be as difficult to find as a Scotsman's breeches or a flavorless line in 'Hudibras.'"

"And Reuben Lockarby's steed can go no farther," I remarked. "But do mine eyes deceive me, or is there a glimmer of light over yonder?"

"Where there is light there is life," cried Reuben. "Let us make for it, and see what chance of shelter we may find there."

"It cannot come from our dragoon friends," remarked Decimus. "A murrain on them! how came they to guess our true character; or was it on the score of some insult to the regiment that that young Fahnführer has set them on our track? If I have him at my sword's point again, he shall not come off so free. Well, do ye lead your horses, and we shall explore this light, since no better course is open to us."

Picking our way across the moor, we directed our course for the bright point which twinkled in the distance.

As we approached we saw that the light did indeed come from a small cottage, which was built in a hollow, so as to be invisible from any quarter save that from which we approached it. In front of this humble dwelling a small patch of ground had been cleared of shrub, and in the centre of this little piece of sward our missing steed stood grazing at her leisure upon the scanty herbage. The same light which had attracted us had doubtless caught her eye, and drawn her towards it by hopes of oats and of water. With a grunt of satisfaction Saxon resumed possession of his lost property, and, leading her by the bridle, approached the door of the solitary cottage.

CHAPTER ELEVEN

OF THE LONELY MAN AND THE GOLD CHEST

THE strong yellow glare which found its way out through a single narrow slit alongside the door changed suddenly to red, and that again to green, throwing a ghastly pallor over our faces. At the same time we became aware of a most subtle and noxious odor which poisoned the air all round the cottage. This worked upon the old man at arms' superstitious feelings to such an extent that he paused and looked back at us inquiringly. Both Reuben and I were determined, however, to carry the adventure through, so walking up to the door, I rapped upon it with the hilt of my sword and announced that we were weary travellers who were seeking a night's shelter.

The first result of my appeal was a sound as of some one bustling rapidly about, with the clinking of metal and noise of the turning of locks. This died away into a hush, and I was about to knock once more when a crackling voice greeted us from the other side of the door.

"There is little shelter here, gentlemen, and less provisions," it said. "It is but six miles to Amesbury, where at the Cecil Arms ye shall find, I doubt not, all that is needful for man and for beast."

"Nay, nay, mine invisible friend," quoth Saxon, who was much reassured by the sound of a human voice. "This is surely but a scurvy reception. One of our horses is completely foundered, and none of them are in very good plight, so that we could no more make for the Cecil Arms at Amesbury than for the Grüner Mann at Lubeck. I prithee, therefore, that you will allow us to pass the remainder of the night under your roof."

At this appeal there was much creaking of locks and rasping of bolts, which ended in the door swinging slowly open, and disclosing the person who had addressed us.

By the strong light which shone out from behind him we could see that he was a man of venerable aspect, with snow-white hair and a countenance which bespoke a thoughtful and yet fiery nature. His lofty bearing and his rich though severe costume of black velvet were at strange variance with the humble nature of the abode which he had chosen for his dwelling-place.

"Ho!" said he, looking keenly at us. "Two of ye unused to war, and the other an old soldier. Ye have been pursued, I see!"

"How did you know that, then?" asked Decimus Saxon.

"Ah, my friend, I too have served in my time. Your story, however, can keep. Every true soldier thinks first of his horse, so I pray that you will tether yours without."

The strange dwelling into which we presently entered had been prolonged into the side of the little hill against which it had been built, so as to form a very long, narrow hall. The ends of this great room, as we entered, were wrapped in shadow, but in the centre was a bright glare from a brazier full of coals, over which a brass pipkin was suspended. The vile smell which had greeted us outside was very much worse within the chamber, and arose apparently from the fumes of the boiling, bubbling contents of the brazen pot.

"Ye behold in me," said our host, bowing courteously to us, "the last of an ancient family. I am Sir Jacob Clancing of Snellaby Hall."

"Smellaby it should be, methinks," whispered Reuben in a voice which fortunately did not reach the ears of the old knight.

"I pray that ye be seated," he continued, "and that ye lay aside your plates and head-pieces, and remove your boots. Consider this to be your inn, and behave as freely. Ye will hold me excused if for a moment I turn my attention from you to this operation on which I am engaged, which will not brook delay."

Saxon began forthwith to undo his buckles and to pull off his harness, while Reuben, throwing himself into a chair, appeared to be too weary to do more than unfasten his sword-belt. For my own part, I was glad to throw off my gear, but I kept my attention all the while upon the movements of our host, whose graceful manners and learned appearance had aroused my curiosity and admiration.

He approached the evil-smelling pot, and stirred it up with a face which indicated so much anxiety that it was clear that he had pushed his courtesy to us so far as to risk the ruin of some important experiment. Taking a handful of a whitish powder from a trencher at his side, he threw it into the pipkin. This treatment had the effect of clearing the fluid, for the chemist was enabled to pour off into a bottle a quantity of perfectly watery transparent liquid, while a brownish sediment remained in the vessel, and was emptied out upon a sheet of paper. This done, Sir Jacob Clancing pushed aside all his bottles, and turned towards us with a smiling face and a lighter air.

"We shall see what my poor larder can furnish forth," said he. "Meanwhile, this odor may be offensive to your untrained nostrils, so we shall away with it." He threw a few grains of some balsamic resin into the brazier, which at once filled the chamber with a most agreeable perfume. He then laid a white cloth upon the table, and, taking from a cupboard a dish of cold trout and a large meat pasty, he placed them upon it, and invited us to draw up our settles and set to work.

"I would that I had more toothsome fare to offer ye," said he. "Were we at Snellaby Hall, ye should not be put off in this scurvy fashion, I promise ye. This may serve, however, for hungry men, and I can still lay my hands upon a brace of bottles of the old Alicant." So saying, he brought a pair of flasks out from a recess, and, having seen us served and our

TAKING A HANDFUL OF A WHITISH POWDER FROM A TRENCHER AT HIS
SIDE, HE THREW IT INTO THE PIPKIN

glasses filled, he seated himself in a high-backed oaken chair and presided with old-fashioned courtesy over our feast. As we supped, I explained to him what our errand was, and narrated the adventures of the night, without making mention of our destination.

"You are bound for Monmouth's camp," he said, quietly, when I had finished, looking me full in the face with his keen dark eyes. "I know it, but ye need not fear lest I betray you, even were it in my power. What chance, think ye, hath the duke against the king's forces?"

"As much chance as a farm-yard fowl against a spurred game-cock, did he rely only on those whom he hath with him," Saxon answered. "He hath reason to think, however, that all England is like a powder magazine, and he hopes to be the spark to set it alight."

The old man shook his head sadly. "The king hath great resources," he remarked. "Where is Monmouth to get his trained soldiers?"

"There is the militia," I suggested.

"And there are many of the old Parliamentary breed, who are not too far gone to strike a blow for their belief," said Saxon.

"I should judge from your speech, sir," our host observed, "that you are not one of the sectaries. How comes it, then, that you are throwing the weight of your sword and your experience into the weaker scale?"

"For the very reason that it is the weaker scale," said the soldier of fortune. "Since I must be doing something, I choose to fight for Protestantism and Monmouth. It is nothing to me whether James Stuart or James Walters sits upon the throne, but the court and army of the king are already made up. Now, since Monmouth hath both courtiers and soldiers to find, it may well happen that he may be glad of my services and reward them with honorable preferment."

"Your logic is sound," said our host, "save only that you

have omitted the very great chance which you will incur of losing your head if the duke's party are borne down by the odds against them."

"A man cannot throw a main without putting a stake on the board," said Saxon.

"And you, young sir," the old man asked, "what has caused you to take a hand in so dangerous a game?"

"I come of a Roundhead stock," I answered, "and my folk have always fought for the liberty of the people and the humbling of tyranny. I come in the place of my father."

"And you, sir?" our questioner continued, looking at Reuben.

"I have come to see something of the world, and to be with my friend and companion here," he replied.

"And I have stronger reasons than any of ye," Sir Jacob cried, "for appearing in arms against any man who bears the name of Stuart. Had I not a mission here which cannot be neglected, I might myself be tempted to hie westward with ye. For where now is the noble castle of Snellaby, and where those glades and woods amid which the Clancings have grown up, and lived and died, ere ever Norman William set his foot on English soil? A man of trade is now the owner of all that fair property."

"And how comes so sudden a reverse of fortune?" I asked.

"Fill up your glasses," cried the old man, suiting the action to the word. "Here's a toast for you. Perdition to all faithless princes! How came it about, ye ask? Why, when the troubles came upon the first Charles, I stood by him as though he had been mine own brother. At Edgehill, at Naseby, in twenty skirmishes and battles, I fought stoutly in his cause, maintaining a troop of horse at my own expense, formed from among my own gardeners, grooms, and attendants. Then the military chest ran low, and money must be had to carry on the contest. My silver chargers and candlesticks were thrown into the melting-pot, as were those of many another cavalier. They went in metal, and they came out as troopers and pikemen. So we tided over a few months until again the purse was empty, and again we filled it among us. This time it was the home farm and the oak-trees that went. Then came Marston Moor, and every penny and man was needed to repair that great disaster. I flinched not, but gave everything. And so I held out until the final ruin of Worcester, when I covered the retreat of the young prince, and may indeed say that save in the Isle of Man I was the last Royalist who upheld the authority of the crown. The Commonwealth had set a price upon my head as a dangerous malignant, so I was forced to take my passage in a Harwich ketch, and arrived in the Lowlands with nothing save my sword and a few broad pieces in my pocket."

"A cavalier might do well even then," remarked Saxon. "There are ever wars in Germany where a man is worth his hire."

"I did indeed take arms for a time in the employ of the United Provinces, by which means I came face to face once more with mine old foes, the Roundheads. However, my soldiering was of no great duration, for peace was soon declared, and I then pursued the study of chemistry, for which I had a strong turn."

"Truly," said Saxon, "there seemeth to be some fatal attraction in this same chemistry, for we met two officers of the Blue Guards in Salisbury, who, though they were stout, soldierly men in other respects, had also a weakness in that direction."

"Ha!" cried Sir Jacob, with interest. "To what school did they belong?"

"Nay, I know nothing of the matter," Saxon answered, "save that they denied that Gervinus of Nürnberg, whom I guarded in prison, or any other man, could transmute metals."

"For Gervinus I cannot answer," said our host, "but for the possibility of it I can pledge my knightly word. However, of that anon. The time came at last when the second

Charles was invited back to his throne, and all of us were in
high feather at the hope of regaining our own once more. I
waited and waited, but no word came, so at last I betook myself to the levée and was duly presented to him. 'Ah,' said he
greeting me with the cordiality which he could assume so well,
'you are, if I mistake not, Sir Jasper Killigrew?' 'Nay, your
majesty,' I answered, 'I am Sir Jacob Clancing, formerly of
Snellaby Hall in Staffordshire'; and with that I reminded him
of Worcester fight and of many passages which had occurred
to us in common. 'Od's fish!' he cried, 'how could I be so
forgetful! And how are all at Snellaby?' I then explained to
him that the Hall had passed out of my hands, and told him,
in a few words, the state to which I had been reduced. His face
clouded over and his manner chilled me at once. 'They are
all on to me for money and for places,' he said, 'and truly the
Commons are so niggardly to me that I can scarce be generous
to others. However, Sir Jacob, we shall see what can be done
for thee,' and with that he dismissed me. That same night
the secretary of my Lord Clarendon came to me, and announced,
with much form and show, that, in consideration of my long
devotion and the losses which I had sustained, the king was
graciously pleased to make me a lottery cavalier."

"And pray, sir, what is a lottery cavalier?"

"It is nothing else than a licensed keeper of a gambling-
house. This was his reward to me. I was to be allowed to
have a den in the piazza of Covent Garden, and there to de-
coy the young sparks of the town and fleece them at ombre.
To restore my own fortunes I was to ruin others. My honor,
my family, my reputation, they were all to weigh for nothing
so long as I had the means of bubbling a few fools out of
their guineas."

"I have heard that some of the lottery cavaliers did well,"
remarked Saxon, reflectively.

"Well or ill, it was no employment for me. I waited upon
the king and implored that his bounty would take another

form. His only reply was that for one so poor I was strangely fastidious. For weeks I hung about the court—I and other poor cavaliers like myself—watching the royal brothers squandering upon their gaming and their harlots sums which would have restored us to our patrimonies. I have seen Charles put upon one turn of a card as much as would have satisfied the most exacting of us. At last I received a second message from him. It was that unless I could dress more in the mode he could dispense with my attendance. That was his message to the old, broken soldier who had sacrificed health, wealth, position, everything, in the service of his father and himself."

"Shameful!" we cried, all three.

"Can you wonder, then, that I cursed the whole Stuart race, false-hearted, lecherous, and cruel? For the Hall, I could buy it back to-morrow if I chose, but why should I do so when I have no heir?"

"Ho, you have prospered, then!" said Decimus Saxon, with one of his shrewd, sidelong looks. "Perhaps you have yourself found out how to convert pots and pans into gold in the way you have spoken of. But that cannot be, for I see iron and brass in this room, which would hardly remain there could you convert it to gold."

"Gold has its uses, and iron has its uses," said Sir Jacob, oracularly. "The one can never supplant the other."

"Yet these officers," I remarked, "did declare to us that it was but a superstition of the vulgar."

"Then these officers did show that their knowledge was less than their prejudice. It can indeed be done, but only slowly and in order, small pieces at a time, and with much expenditure of work and patience. For a man to enrich himself at it he must labor hard and long; yet in the end I will not deny that he may compass it. And now, since the flasks are empty and your young comrade is nodding in his chair, it will perhaps be as well for you to spend as much of the night as is left in repose." He drew several blankets and rugs from a corner and scattered them over the floor. "It is a soldier's couch," he remarked; "but ye may sleep on worse before ye put Monmouth on the English throne. For myself, it is my custom to sleep in an inside chamber, which is hollowed out of the hill." With a few last words and precautions for our comfort he withdrew with the lamp, passing through a door which had escaped our notice at the farther end of the apartment.

Reuben, having had no rest since he left Havant, had already dropped upon the rugs and was fast asleep, with a saddle for a pillow. Saxon and I sat for a few minutes longer by the light of the burning brazier.

"One might do worse than take to this same chemical business," my companion remarked, knocking the ashes out of his pipe. "See you yon iron-bound chest in the corner?"

"What of it?"

"It is two-thirds full of gold, which this worthy gentleman hath manufactured."

"How do you know that?" I asked, incredulously.

"When you did strike the door panel with the hilt of your sword, as though you would drive it in, you may have heard some scuttling about and the turning of a lock. Well, thanks to my inches, I was able to look through yon slit in the wall, and I saw our friend throwing something into the chest with a chink, and then lock it. It was but a glance at the contents, yet I could swear that that dull yellow light could come from no metal but gold. Let us see if it be indeed locked." Rising from his seat he walked over to the box and pulled vigorously at the lid.

"Forbear, Saxon, forbear!" I cried, angrily. "What would our host say should he come upon you?"

"Nay, then, he should not keep such things beneath his roof. With a chisel or a dagger now this might be prized open."

"By Heaven!" I whispered, "if you should attempt it I shall lay you on your back."

"Well, well, young Anak! it was but a passing fancy to

see the treasure again. Now, if he were but well-favored to the king, this would be fair prize of war. Marked ye not that he claimed to have been the last Royalist who drew sword in England? and he confessed that he had been proscribed as a malignant. Your father, godly as he is, would have little compunction in despoiling such an Amalekite. Besides, bethink you, he can make more as easily as your good mother maketh cranberry dumplings."

"Enough said!" I answered, sternly. "It will not bear discussion. Get ye to your couch, lest I summon our host and tell him what manner of man he hath entertained."

With many grumbles Saxon consented at last to curl his long limbs up upon a mat, while I lay by his side and remained awake until the mellow light of morning streamed through the chinks between the ill-covered rafters. Truth to tell, I feared to sleep, lest the freebooting habits of the soldier of fortune should be too strong for him, and he should disgrace us in the eyes of our kindly and generous entertainer. At last, however, his long-drawn breathing assured me that he was asleep, and I was able to settle down to a few hours of welcome rest.

CHAPTER TWELVE

OF CERTAIN PASSAGES UPON THE MOOR

IN THE morning, after a breakfast furnished by the remains of our supper, we looked to our horses and prepared for our departure. Ere we could mount, however, our kindly host came running out to us with a load of armor in his arms.

"Come hither," said he, beckoning to Reuben. "It is not meet, lad, that you should go barebreasted against the enemy when your comrades are girt with steel. I have here mine own old breastplate and head-piece, which should, methinks, fit you, for if you have more flesh than I, I am a larger frame-work of a man. Ah, said I not so! Were't measured for you by Silas Thomson, the court armorer, it could not grip better. Now on with the head-piece. A close fit again. You are now a cavalier whom Monmouth or any other leader might be proud to see ride beneath his banner."

Both helmet and body-plates were of the finest Milan steel, richly inlaid with silver and with gold, and carved all over in rare and curious devices. So stern and soldierly was the effect that the ruddy, kindly visage of our friend staring out of such a panoply had an ill-matched and somewhat ludicrous appearance.

"Nay, nay," cried the old cavalier, seeing a smile upon our features, "it is but right that so precious a jewel as a faithful heart should have a fitting casket to protect it."

"I am truly beholden to you, sir," said Reuben; "I can scarce find words to express my thanks. Holy mother! I have a mind to ride straight back to Havant, to show them how stout a man-at-arms hath been reared among them."

"It is steel of proof," Sir Jacob remarked; "a pistol-bullet might glance from it. And you," he continued, turning to me, "here is a small gift by which you shall remember this meeting. I did observe that you did cast a wistful eye upon my book-shelf. It is Plutarch's lives of the ancient worthies, done into English by the ingenious Mr. Latimer. Carry this volume with you, and shape your life after the example of the giant men whose deeds are here set forth. In your saddle-bag I place a small but weighty packet, which I desire you to hand over to Monmouth upon the day of your arrival in his camp. As to you, sir," addressing Decimus Saxon, "here is a slug of virgin gold for you, which may fashion into a pin or such like ornament. You may wear it with a quiet conscience, for it is fairly given to you, and not filched from your entertainer while he slept."

Saxon and I shot a sharp glance of surprise at each other at this speech, which showed that our words of the night before were not unknown to him. Sir Jacob, however, showed no signs of anger, but proceeded to point out our road, and to advise us as to our journey.

Thanking our venerable host for his great kindness towards us, we gave rein to our horses and left him once more to the strange solitary existence in which we had found him.

The pathway was so narrow that only one of us could ride upon it at a time, but we presently abandoned it altogether, using it simply as a guide, and galloping along side by side over the rolling plain. We were all silent—Reuben meditating upon his new corslet, as I could see from his frequent glances at it, while Saxon, with his eyes half closed, was brooding over some matter of his own. For my own part, my thoughts ran upon the ignominy of the old soldier's designs upon the gold chest, and the additional shame which rose from the knowledge that our host had in some way divined his intention. No good could come of an alliance with a man so devoid of all feelings of honor or of gratitude. So strongly did I feel upon it that I at last broke the silence by pointing to a cross-path, which turned away from the one which we were pursuing, and recommending him to follow it, since he had proved that he was no fit company for honest men.

"By the living road!" he cried, laying his hand upon the hilt of his rapier; "have you taken leave of your senses? These are words such as no honorable cavaliero can abide."

"They are none the less words of truth," I answered.

His blade flashed out in an instant, while his mare bounded twice her length under the sharp dig of his spurs.

"We have here," he cried, reining her round, with his fierce lean face all of a quiver with passion, "an excellent level stretch on which to discuss the matter. Out with your bilbo and maintain your words."

"By all the saints in heaven!" cried Reuben, "whichever of ye strikes first at the other I'll snap this pistol at his head. None of your jokes, Don Decimo, for by the Lord I'll let drive at you if you were my own mother's son. Put up your sword, for the trigger falls easy, and my finger is a-twitching."

"Curse you for a spoil-sport!" growled Saxon, sulkily sheathing his weapon. "Nay, Clarke," he added, after a few moments of reflection, "this is but child's play, that two camarados with a purpose in view should fall out over such a trifle. I, who am old enough to be your father, should have known better than to have drawn upon you, for a boy's tongue wags on impulse and without due thought. Do but say that you have said more than you meant."

"My way of saying it may have been over-plain and rough," I answered, for I saw that he did but want a little salve where my short words had galled him. "At the same time, our ways differ from your ways, and that difference must be mended, or you can be no true comrade of ours."

"All right, Master Morality," quoth he, "I must e'en unlearn some of the tricks of my trade. Touching that same incident last night, of the chest filled, as I surmise, with gold, which I was inclined to take as lawful plunder. I am now ready to admit that I may have shown an undue haste and precipitance, considering that the old man treated us fairly."

"Say no more of it," I answered, "if you will but guard against such impulses for the future."

"They do not properly come from me," he replied, "but from Will Spotterbridge, who was a man of no character at all."

"And how comes he to be mixed up in the matter?" I asked, curiously.

"Why, marry, in this wise. My father married the daughter of this same Will Spotterbridge, and so weakened a good old stock by an unhealthy strain. Will was a rake-hell of Fleet Street in the days of James, a chosen light of Alsatia, the home of bullies and of braw-lers. His blood hath, through his daughter, been transmitted to the ten of us, though I rejoice to say that I, being the tenth, it had by that time lost much of its virulence, and indeed amounts to little more than a proper pride and a laudable desire to prosper."

Reuben and I could not but laugh over this frank family confession, which our companion delivered without a sign of shame or embarrass-ment. "Ye have paid a heavy price for your father's want of discretion," I remarked. "But what in the name of fate is this upon our left?"

"A gibbet, by the look of it," said Saxon, peering across at the gaunt framework of wood which rose up from a little knoll.

As we approached this lonely gibbet we saw that a dried-up wisp of a thing, which could hardly be recognized as having once been a human being, was dangling from the centre of it. We had pulled up our horses, and were gazing in silence at this sign-post of death, when what had seemed to us to be a bundle of rags thrown down at the foot of the gallows began suddenly to move, and turned towards us the wizened face of an aged woman, so marked with evil passions and so malignant in its expression that it inspired us with even more horror than the unclean thing which dangled above her head.

"Gott in Himmel!" cried Saxon. "It is ever thus! A gibbet draws witches as a magnet draws needles. All the hexerei of the countryside will sit round one, like cats round a milk-pail. Beware of her! she hath the evil eye!"

"Poor soul! It is the evil stomach that she hath," said Reuben, walking his horse up to her. "Who ever saw such a bag of bones! I warrant that she is pining away for want of a crust of bread."

The creature whined, and thrust out two skinny claws to grab the piece of silver which our friend had thrown down to her.

"What use is money in the wilderness?" I remarked. "She cannot feed herself upon a silver piece."

She tied the coin hurriedly into the corner of her rags, as though she feared that I might try to wrest it from her. "It will buy bread," she croaked.

"But who is there to sell it, good mistress?" I asked.

"They sell it at Fovant, and they sell it at Hindon," she answered. "I bide here o' days, but I travel at night."

"I warrant she does, and on a broomstick," quoth Saxon; "but tell us, mother, who is it who hangs above your head?"

"It is he who slew my youngest born," cried the old woman, casting a malignant look at the mummy above her, and shaking a clinched hand at it which was hardly more fleshy than its own. "It is he who slew my bonny boy. And here, come rain, come shine, shall I, his mother, sit while two bones hang together of the man who slew my heart's darling." She nestled down in her rags as she spoke, and leaning her chin upon her hands, stared up with an intensity of hatred at the hideous remnant.

"Come away, Reuben," I cried, for the sight was enough to make one loathe one's kind. "She is a ghoul, not a woman."

"Pah! it gives me a foul taste in the mouth," quoth Saxon. "Who is for a fresh gallop over the Downs? Away with care and carrion! Hark away, lads, with a loose rein and a bloody heel!"

We spurred our steeds and galloped from the unholy spot as fast as our brave beasts could carry us. To all of us the air had a purer flavor and the heath a sweeter scent by contrast with the grim couple whom we had left behind us.

When we at last pulled up we had set some three or four miles between the gibbet and ourselves. Right over against us, on the side of a gentle slope, stood a bright little village, with a red-roofed church rising up from amid a clump of trees. To our eyes, after the dull sward of the plain, it was a glad sight to see the green spread of the branches and the pleasant gardens which girt the hamlet round.

"This," said I, "must be the village of Mere, which we were to pass before coming to Bruton. We shall soon be over the Somersetshire border."

"I trust that we shall soon be over a dish of beefsteaks," groaned Reuben. "I am wellnigh famished. So fair a village must needs have a passable inn, though I have not seen one yet upon my travels which would compare with the old Wheat-sheaf."

"Neither inn nor dinner for us just yet," said Saxon. "Look yonder to the north, and tell me what ye see."

On the extreme horizon there was visible a long line of gleaming, glittering points, which shone and sparkled like a string of diamonds. These brilliant specks were all in rapid motion, and yet kept their positions to each other.

"What is it, then?" we both cried.

"Horse upon the march," quoth Saxon. "It may be our friends of Salisbury, who have made a long day's journey; or, as I am inclined to think, it may be some other body of the king's horse. They are far distant, and what we see is but the sun shining on their casques; yet they are bound for this very village, if I mistake not. It would be wisest to avoid entering it, lest the rustics set them upon our track. Let us skirt it and push on for Bruton, where we may spare time for bite and sup."

"Alas, alas, for our dinners!" cried Reuben, ruefully. "I have fallen away until my body rattles about inside this shell of armor like a pea in a pod. However, lads, it is all for the Protestant faith."

"One more good stretch to Bruton, and we may rest in peace," said Saxon. "It is ill dining when a dragoon may be served up as a grace after meat. Our horses are still fresh, and we should be there in little over an hour."

We pushed on our way accordingly, passing at a safe distance from Mere, which is the village where the second Charles did conceal himself after the battle of Worcester. The road beyond was much crowded by peasants. We questioned many as to the news from the war, but though we were now on the outskirts of the disturbed country, we could gain no clear account of how matters stood, save that all agreed that the rising was on the increase. We learned, too, from an old woman of the place, that though a troop of the Wiltshire Yeomanry had passed through the day before, there were no soldiers quartered at present in the neighborhood. Thus assured, we rode boldly into the town, and soon found our way to the principal inn.

CHAPTER THIRTEEN

OF SIR GERVAS JEROME, KNIGHT BANNERET OF THE COUNTY OF SURREY

THE inn was very full of company, being occupied not only by many government agents and couriers on their way to and from the seat of the rising, but also by all the local gossips, who gathered there to exchange news and consume Dame Hobson the landlady's home-brewed. In spite, however, of this stress of custom and the consequent uproar, the hostess conducted us into her own private room, where we could consume her

94

excellent cheer in peace and quietness. This favor was due, I think, to a little sly manœuvring and a few whispered words from Saxon, who, never failed, in spite of his fifty years, to make his way into the good graces of the fair sex by the help of his voluble tongue and assured manner.

"We are your grateful servants, mistress," said he, when the smoking joint and the batter-pudding had been placed upon the table. "We have robbed you of your room. Will you not honor us so far as to sit down with us and share our repast?"

"Nay, kind sir," said the portly dame, much flattered by the proposal. "It is not for me to sit with gentles like yourselves."

"Nay, by my troth, you shall not leave us," cried Saxon, with his little twinkling eyes fixed in admiration upon her buxom countenance. "I shall lock the door first. If you will not eat, you shall at least drink a cup of alicant with me."

"Nay, sir, it is too much honor," cried Dame Hobson, with a simper. "I shall go down into the cellars and bring a flask of the best."

"Nay, by my manhood, you shall not," said Saxon, springing up from his seat. "What are all these infernal lazy drawers here for if you are to descend to menial offices?" Handing the widow to a chair, he clanked away into the tap-room, where we heard him swearing at the men-servants.

"Here is the wine, fair mistress," said he, returning presently with a bottle in either hand. "Let me fill your glass. Ha! it flows clear and yellow like a prime vintage. These rogues can stir their limbs when they find that there is a man to command them."

"Would that there were ever such," said the widow, meaningly, with a languishing look at our companion. "Here is to you, sir—and to ye too, young sirs," she added, sipping at her wine. "May there be a speedy end to the insurrection, for I judge, from your gallant equipment, that ye be serving the king."

"His business takes us to the west," said Reuben, "and we

have every reason to hope that there will be a speedy end to the insurrection."

"Aye, aye, though blood will be shed first," she said, shaking her head. "They tell me that the rebels are as many as seven thousand, and that they swear to give an' take no quarter, the murderous villains! Alas! how any gentleman can fall to such bloody work when he might have a clean, honorable occupation, such as innkeeping or the like, is more than my poor mind can understand." She again looked hard at Saxon as she spoke, while Reuben and I nudged each other beneath the table.

"This business hath doubtless increased your trade, fair mistress," quoth Saxon.

"Aye, and in the way that payeth best," said she. "The few kilderkins of beer which are drunk by the common folk make little difference one way or the other. But now, when we have lieutenants of counties, officers, mayors, and gentry spurring it for very life down the highways, I have sold more of my rare old wines in three days than ever I did before in a calendar month."

"So indeed!" quoth Saxon, thoughtfully. "A snug home and a steady income."

"Would that my poor Peter had lived to share it with me," said Dame Hobson, laying down her glass, and rubbing her eyes with a corner of her kerchief. "He was a good man, poor soul, though in very truth and between friends he did at last become as broad and as thick as one of his own puncheons. Ah, well, the heart is the thing! Marry come up! if a woman were ever to wait until her own fancy came her way, there would be more maids than mothers in the land."

"Prithee, good dame, how runs your own fancy?" asked Reuben, mischievously.

"Not in the direction of fat, young man," she answered, smartly, with a merry glance at our plump companion.

"She has hit you there, Reuben," said I.

"I would have no pert young springald," she continued, "but

one who hath knowledge of the world and ripe experience. Tall he should be, and of sinewy build, free of speech that he might lighten the weary hours, and help entertain the gentles when they crack a flagon of wine. Of business habits he must be too, forsooth, for is there not a busy hostel and two hundred good pounds a year to pass through his fingers? If Jane Hobson is to be led to the altar again it must be by such a man as this."

Saxon had listened with much attention to the widow's words, and had just opened his mouth to make some reply to her when a clattering and bustle outside announced the arrival of some traveller. Our hostess drank off her wine and pricked up her ears, but when a loud authoritative voice was heard in the passage, demanding a private room and a draught of sack, her call to duty overcame her private concerns, and she bustled off with a few words of apology to take the measure of the newcomer.

"Body o' me, lads!" quoth Decimus Saxon the moment that she disappeared, "ye can see how the land lies. I have half a mind to let Monmouth carve his own road, and to pitch my tent in this quiet English township."

"Your tent, indeed!" cried Reuben; "it is a brave tent that is furnished with cellars of such wine as we are drinking. And as to the quiet, my illustrious, if you take up your residence here I'll warrant that the quiet soon comes to an end."

"You have seen the woman," said Saxon, with his brow all in a wrinkle with thought. "She hath much to commend her. A man must look to himself. But what in the name of the devil have we here?"

Our companion's ejaculation was called forth by a noise as of a slight scuffle outside the door, with a smothered "Oh, sir!" and "What will the maids think?" The contest was terminated by the door being opened, and Dame Hobson re-entering the room with her face in a glow, and a slim young man dressed in the height of fashion at her heels.

"I am sure, good gentlemen," said she, "that ye will not

object to this young nobleman drinking his wine in the same room with ye, since all the others are filled with the townsfolk and commonalty."

"Faith! I must needs be mine own usher," said the stranger, sticking his gold-laced cap under his left arm and laying his hand upon his heart, while he bowed until his forehead nearly struck the edge of the table. "Your very humble servant, gentlemen, Sir Gervas Jerome, knight banneret of his Majesty's county of Surrey, and at one time custos rotulorum of the district of Beacham Ford."

"Welcome, sir," quoth Reuben, with a merry twinkle in his eye. "You have before you Don Decimo Saxon of the Spanish nobility, together with Sir Micah Clarke and Sir Reuben Lockarby, both of his Majesty's county of Hampshire."

"Proud and glad to meet ye, gentlemen!" cried the newcomer, with a flourish. "But what is this upon the table? Alicant? Fie, fie, it is a drink for boys. Let us have some good sack with plenty of body in it. Claret for youth, say I, sack for maturity, and strong waters in old age. Fly, my sweetest, move those dainty feet of thine, for, egad, my throat is like leather. Od's 'oons, I drank deep last night, and yet it is clear that I could not have drunk enough, for I was as dry as a concordance when I awoke."

Saxon sat silently at the table, looking so viciously at the stranger out of his half-closed glittering eyes that I feared that we should have another such brawl as occurred at Salisbury, with perhaps a more unpleasant ending. Finally, however, his ill-humor at the gallant's free and easy attention to our hostess spent itself in a few muttered oaths, and he lit his long pipe, the never-failing remedy of a ruffled spirit. As to Reuben and myself, we watched our new companion half in wonder and half in amusement, for his appearance and manners were novel enough to raise the interest of inexperienced youngsters like ourselves.

I have said that he was dressed in the height of fashion,

and such indeed was the impression which a glance would give; but when looked at closely, each and all of his articles of attire bore evidence of having seen better days. Besides the dust and stains of travel, there was a shininess or a fading of color here and there, which scarce accorded with the costliness of their material or the bearing of their wearer. While we were noting these peculiarities he was reclining upon Dame Hobson's best taffeta-covered settee, tranquilly combing his wig with a delicate ivory comb which he had taken from a small satin bag which hung upon the right of his sword-belt.

"Lard preserve us from country inns!" he remarked. "What with the boors that swarm in every chamber, and the want of mirrors and jasmine water and other necessaries, blister me if one has not to do one's toilet in the common room. 'Oons! I'd as soon travel in the land of the Great Mogul!"

"When you shall come to be my age, young sir," Saxon answered, "you may know better than to decry a comfortable country hostel."

"Very like, sir, very like!" the gallant answered, with a careless laugh. "For all that, being mine own age, I feel the wilds of Wiltshire and the inns of Bruton to be a sorry change after the Mall, and the fare of Pontack's or the Coca Tree. Ah, Lud! here comes the sack! Open it, my pretty Hebe, and send a drawer with fresh glasses, for these gentlemen must do me the honor of drinking with me."

Our hostess, having brought fresh glasses, withdrew, and Decimus Saxon soon found an opportunity for following her. Sir Gervas Jerome continued, however, to chatter freely to Reuben and myself over the wine, rattling along as gayly and airily as though we were old acquaintances.

"Sink me, if I have not frighted your comrade away!" he remarked. "Or is it possible that he hath gone on the slot of the plump widow? Methought he looked in no very good temper when I kissed her at the door. Yet it is a civility which I seldom refuse to anything which wears a cap. Your friend's appearance smacked more of Mars than of Venus, though, indeed, those who worship the god are wont to be on good terms with the goddess. A hardy old soldier, I should judge, from his features and attire."

"One who hath seen much service abroad," I answered.

"Ha! ye are lucky to ride to the wars in the company of so accomplished a cavalier. For I presume that it is to the wars that ye are riding, since ye are all so armed and accoutred."

"We are indeed bound for the West," I replied, with some reserve, for in Saxon's absence I did not care to be too loose-tongued.

"And in what capacity?" he persisted. "Will ye risk your crowns in defence of King James's one, or will ye strike in, hit or miss, with these rogues of Devon and Somerset? Stop my vital breath, if I would not as soon side with a clown as with the Crown, with all due respect to your own principles!"

"You are a daring man," said I, "if you air your opinions thus in every inn parlor. Dost not know that a word of what you have said, whispered to the nearest justice of the peace, might mean your liberty, if not your life?"

"Anything for a change," cried Sir Gervas, filling up a bumper. "Here's to the maid that's next our heart, and here's to the heart that loves the maids. War, wine, and women— 'twould be a dull world without them. But you have not answered my question."

"Why, truly, sir," said I, "frank as you have been with us, I can scarce be equally so with you without the permission of the gentleman who has just left the room. He is the leader of our party. Pleasant as our short intercourse has been, these are parlous times, and hasty confidences are apt to lead to repentance."

"A Daniel come to judgment!" cried our new acquaintance. "What ancient, ancient words from so young a head! You are, I'll warrant, five years younger than a scatterbrain like myself, and yet you talk like the seven wise men of Greece. Wilt take me as a valet?"

"A valet!" I exclaimed.

"Aye, a valet, a man-servant. I have been waited upon so long that it is my turn to wait now, and I would not wish a more likely master. By the Lard, I must, in applying for a place, give an account of my character and a list of my accomplishments. So my rascals ever did with me, though in good truth I seldom listened to their recital. Honesty—there I score a trick. Sober—Ananias himself could scarce say that I am that. Trustworthy—indifferently so. Steady—hum! about as much so as Garraway's weathercock. Hang it, man, I am chock-full of good resolutions, but a sparkling glass or a roguish eye will deflect me, as the mariners say of the compass. So much for my weaknesses. Now let me see what qualifications I can produce. A steady nerve, save only when I have my morning qualms, and a cheerful heart; I score two on that. I can dance, fence, ride, and sing. Good Lard! who ever heard a valet urge such accomplishments? I can play the best game of piquet in London. But that won't advance me much, either. What is there, then, to commend me? Why, marry, I can brew a bowl of punch, and I can broil a devilled fowl. It is not much, but I can do it well."

"Truly, good sir," I said, with a smile, "neither of these accomplishments is like to prove of much use to us on our present errand. You do, however, but jest, no doubt, when you talk of descending to such a position."

"Not a whit! not a whit!" he replied, earnestly. " 'To such base uses do we come,' as Will Shakespeare has it. If you would be able to say that you have in your service Sir Gervas Jerome, knight banneret, and sole owner of Beacham Ford Park, with a rent-roll of four thousand good pounds a year, he is now up for sale, and will be knocked down to the bidder who pleases him best. Say but the word, and we'll have another flagon of sack to clinch the bargain."

"But," said I, "if you are indeed owner of this fair property, why should you descend to so menial an occupation?"

"The Jews, the Jews, oh most astute and yet most slow-witted master! Never was Agag, king of Amalek, more completely in the hands of the chosen, and the sole difference is that they have hewed into pieces mine estate instead of myself."

"Have you lost all, then?" Reuben asked, open-eyed.

"Why, no, not all—by no means all," he answered, with a merry laugh; "I have a gold Jacobus and a guinea or two in my purse. 'Twill serve for a flask or so yet. There is my silver-hilted rapier, my rings, my gold snuffbox, and my watch by Tompion at the sign of the Three Crowns. It was never bought under a hundred, I'll warrant. Then there are such relics of grandeur as you see upon my person, though they begin to look as frail and worn as a waiting-woman's virtue. In this bag, too, I retain the means for preserving that niceness and elegance of person which made me, though I say it, as well groomed a man as ever set foot in St. James's Park. Here are French scissors, eyebrow-brush, toothpick-case, patch box, powder-bag, comb, puff, and my pair of red-heeled shoes. What could a man wish for more? These, with a dry throat, a cheerful heart, and a ready hand, are my whole stock in trade."

Reuben and I could not forbear from laughing at the curious inventory of articles which Sir Gervas had saved from the wreck of his fortunes. He, upon seeing our mirth, was so tickled at his own misfortunes that he laughed in a high treble key until the whole house resounded with his merriment. "By the mass," he cried at last, "I have never had so much honest amusement out of my prosperity as hath been caused in me by my downfall. Fill up your glasses!"

"We have still some distance to travel this evening, and must not drink more," I observed, for prudence told me that it was dangerous work for two sober country lads to keep pace with an experienced toper.

"So?" said he, in surprise. "I should have thought that

would be a *'raison de plus,'* as the French say. But I wish your long-legged friend would come back, even if he were intent upon slitting my weasand for my attention to the widow. He is not a man to flinch from his liquor, I'll warrant. Curse this Wiltshire dust that clings to my periwig!"

"Until my comrade returns, Sir Gervas," said I, "you might, since the subject does not appear to be a painful one to you, let us know how these evil times, which you bear with such philosophy, came upon you."

"The old story," he answered, flicking away a few grains of snuff with his deeply-laced cambric handkerchief. "The old, old story. My father, a good, easy country baronet, finding the family purse somewhat full, must needs carry me up to town to make a man of me. There as a young lad I was presented at court, and being a slim, active youngster, with a pert tongue and assured manner, I caught the notice of the queen, who made me one of her pages of honor. This post I held until I grew out of it, when I withdrew from town; but, egad, I found I must get back to it again, for Beacham Ford Park was as dull as a monastery after the life which I had been living. Well, it was rare sport while it lasted, and sink me if I wouldn't do the same again if I had my time once more. It is like sliding down a greased plank, though, for at first a man goes slow enough, and thinks he can pull himself up, but presently he goes faster and faster until he comes with a crash on to the rocks of ruin at the bottom."

"And did you run through four thousand pounds a year?" I exclaimed.

"Od's bodikins, man, you speak as if this paltry sum were all the wealth of the Indies."

"And your noble friends," I asked, "did none of them stand by you in your adversity?"

"Well, well, I have naught to complain of," exclaimed Sir Gervas. "They were brave-hearted boys for the most part.

I' faith, I care not what I turn my hand to among strangers, but I would fain leave my memory sweet in town."

"As to what you proposed, of serving us as a valet," said I, "it is not to be thought of. We are, in spite of my friend's waggishness, but two plain, blunt countrymen, and have no more need of a valet than one of those poets which you have spoken of. On the other hand, if you should care to attach yourself to our party, we shall take you where you will see service which shall be more to your taste than the curling of periwigs or the brushing of eyebrows."

"Goths! Perfect Goths!" cried the exquisite, throwing up his white hands. "But here comes a heavy tread and the clink of armor in the passage. 'Tis our friend the knight of the wrathful countenance, if I mistake not."

It was indeed Saxon, who strode into the room to tell us that our horses were at the door and that all was ready for our departure. Taking him aside, I explained to him in a whisper what had passed between the stranger and ourselves, with the circumstances which had led me to suggest that he should join our party. The old soldier frowned at the news.

"What have we to do with such a coxcomb?" he said. "We have hard fare and harder blows before us. He is not fit for the work."

"You said yourself that Monmouth will be weak in horse," I answered. "Here is a well-appointed cavalier, who is to all appearance a desperate man and ready for anything. Why should we not enroll him?"

"I fear," said Saxon, "that his body may prove to be like the bran of a fine cushion, of value only for what it has around it. However, it is perhaps for the best. The handle to his name may make him welcome in the camp, for from what I hear there is some dissatisfaction at the way in which the gentry stand aloof from the enterprise."

"I had feared," I remarked, still speaking in a whisper, "that we were about to lose one of our party instead of gaining one in this Bruton inn."

"I have thought better of it," he answered, with a smile. "Nay, I'll tell you of it anon. Well, Sir Gervas Jerome," he added, aloud, turning to our new associate, "I hear that you are coming with us. For a day you must be content to follow without question or remark. Is that agreed?"

"With all my heart," cried Sir Gervas.

"Then here's a bumper to our better acquaintance," cried Saxon, raising his glass.

"I pledge ye all," quoth the gallant. "Here's to a fair fight, and may the best men win."

"Dennerblitz, man!" said Saxon. "I believe there's mettle in you for all your gay plumes. I do conceive a liking for you. Give me your hand!"

The soldier of fortune's great brown grip enclosed the delicate hand of our new friend in a pledge of comradeship. Then, having paid our reckoning and bade a cordial adieu to Dame Hobson, who glanced, methought, somewhat reproachfully or expectantly at Saxon, we sprang on our steeds and continued our journey amid a crowd of staring villagers, who huzzaed lustily as we rode out from among them.

CHAPTER FOURTEEN

OF THE STIFF-LEGGED PARSON AND HIS FLOCK

OUR way lay through Castle Carey and Somerton, which are small towns lying in the midst of a most beautiful pastoral country, well wooded and watered by many streams. The road was crowded with peasants who were travelling in two strong currents, the one setting from east to west, and the other from west to east. The latter consisted principally of aged people and of children, who were being sent out of harm's way to reside in the less disturbed counties until the troubles should be over.

The countrymen who were making for the west were upon the other hand men in the prime of life, with little or no baggage. Their brown faces, heavy boots, and smock-frocks proclaimed most of them to be mere hinds, though here and there we overtook men who, by their top-boots and corduroys, may have been small farmers or yeomen.

"We are in Monmouth's country at last," said Saxon to me, for Reuben Lockarby and Sir Gervas Jerome had ridden on ahead. "This is the raw material which we shall have to lick into soldiership."

"And no bad material, either," I replied, taking note of the sturdy figures and bold hearty faces of the men. "Think ye that they are bound for Monmouth's camp, then?"

"Aye, are they. See you yon long-limbed parson on the left—him with the pent-house hat. Markest thou not the stiffness wherewith he moves his left leg?"

"Why, yes; he is travel-worn, doubtless."

"Ho, ho!" laughed my companion. "I have seen such a stiffness before now. The man hath a straight sword within the leg of his breeches. A regular Parliamentary tuck, I'll warrant. When he is on safe ground he will produce it, aye, and use it too, but until he is out of all danger of falling in with the king's horse he is shy of strapping it to his belt. I warrant there is not one of the rascals but hath a pike-head or sickle-blade concealed somewhere about him. I begin to feel the breath of war once more, and to grow younger with it. Hark ye, lad! I am glad that I did not tarry at the inn."

"You seemed to be in two minds about it," said I.

"Aye, aye. She was a fine woman, and the quarters were comfortable. I do not gainsay it. But marriage, d'ye see, is a citadel that it is plaguy easy to find one's way into; but once in, old Tilly himself could not bring one out again with credit. I did succeed in gaining the ear of one of the gossips, and asking him what he could tell me of the good dame and her inn. It seemeth that she is somewhat of a shrew upon occasion, and that her tongue had more to do with her husband's death than the dropsy which the leech put it down to. Again, a new inn hath been started in the village, which is well managed, and is like to draw the custom from her. It is, too, as you have said, a dull, sleepy spot. All these reasons weighed with me, and I decided that it would be best to raise my siege of the widow, and to retreat while I could yet do so with the credit and honors of war."

" 'Tis best so," said I; "you could not have settled down

to a life of toping and ease. But our new comrade, what think you of him?"

"Faith!" Saxon answered, "we shall extend into a troop of horse if we add to our number every gallant who is in want of a job. As to this Sir Gervas, however, I think, as I said at the inn, that he hath more mettle in him than one would judge at first sight. These young sprigs of the gentry will always fight, but I doubt if he is hardened enough or hath constancy enough for such a campaign as this is like to be. His appearance, too, will be against him in the eyes of the saints; and though Monmouth is a man of easy virtue, the saints are like to have the chief voice in his councils. Now do but look at him as he reins up that showy gray stallion and gazes back at us. He will have to change his style if he is to fight by the side of the fanatics. But hark! I am much mistaken if they have not already got themselves into trouble."

Our friends had pulled up their horses to await our coming. They had scarce halted, however, before the stream of peasants who had been moving along abreast of them slackened their pace, and gathered round them with a deep ominous murmur and threatening gestures. Other rustics, seeing that there was something afoot, hurried up to help their companions. Saxon and I put spurs to our horses, and pushing through the throng, which was becoming every instant larger and more menacing, made our way to the aid of our friends, who were hemmed in on every side by the rabble. Reuben had laid his hand upon the hilt of his sword, while Sir Gervas was placidly chewing his toothpick and looking down at the angry mob with an air of amused contempt.

"A flask or two of scent among them would not be amiss," he remarked; "I would I had a casting bottle."

"Stand on your guard, but do not draw," cried Saxon. "What the henker hath come over the chaw-bacons? They mean mischief. How now, friends, why this uproar?"

This question, instead of allaying the tumult, appeared to make it tenfold worse. All around us twenty deep were savage faces and angry eyes, with the glint here and there of a weapon, half drawn from its place of concealment. The uproar, which had been a mere hoarse growl, began to take shape and form. "Down with the Papists!" was the cry. "Down with the Prelatists!" "Smite the Erastian butchers!" "Smite the Philistine horsemen!" "Down with them!"

A stone or two had already whistled past our ears, and we had been forced in self-defence to draw our swords, when the tall minister whom we had already observed shoved his way through the crowd, and by dint of his lofty stature and commanding voice prevailed upon them to be silent.

"How say ye," he asked, turning upon us, "fight ye for Baal or for the Lord? He who is not with us is against us."

"Which is the side of Baal, most reverend sir, and which of the Lord?" asked Sir Gervas Jerome. "Methinks if you were to speak plain English instead of Hebrew we might come to an understanding sooner."

"This is no time for light words," the minister cried, with a flush of anger upon his face. "If ye would keep your skins whole, tell me, are ye for the bloody usurper James Stuart, or are ye for his most Protestant Majesty King Monmouth?"

"What! He hath come to the title already?" exclaimed Saxon. "Know, then, that we are four unworthy vessels upon our way to offer our services to the Protestant cause."

"He lies, good Master Pettigrue, he lies most foully!" shouted a burly fellow from the edge of the crowd. "Who ever saw a good Protestant in such a Punchinello dress as yonder? Is not Amalekite written upon his raiment? Is he not attired as becometh the bridegroom of the harlot of Rome? Why, then, should we not smite him?"

"I thank you, my worthy friend," said Sir Gervas, whose attire had moved this champion's wrath. "If I were nearer I should give you some return for the notice which you have taken of me."

"What proof have we that ye are not in the pay of the

usurper, and on your way to oppress the faithful?" asked the Puritan divine.

"I tell you, man," said Saxon, impatiently, "that we have travelled all the way from Hampshire to fight against James Stuart. We will ride with ye to Monmouth's camp, and what better proof could ye desire than that?"

"It may be that ye do but seek an opportunity of escaping from our bondage," the minister observed, after conferring with one or two of the leading peasants. "It is our opinion, therefore, that before coming with us ye must deliver unto us your swords, pistols, and other carnal weapons."

"Nay, good sir, that cannot be," our leader answered. "A cavalier may not with honor surrender his blade or his liberty in the manner ye demand. Keep close to my bridle-arm, Clarke, and strike home at any rogue who lays hands on you."

A hum of anger rose from the crowd, and a score of sticks and scythe-blades were raised against us, when the minister again interposed and silenced his noisy following.

"Did I hear aright?" he asked. "Is your name Clarke?"

"It is," I answered.

"Your Christian name?"

"Micah."

"Living at?"

"Havant."

The clergyman conferred for a few moments with a grizzly-bearded, harsh-faced man dressed in black buckram who stood at his elbow.

"If you are really Micah Clarke of Havant," quoth he, "you will be able to tell us the name of an old soldier, skilled in the German wars, who was to have come with ye to the camp of the faithful."

"Why, this is he," I answered; "Decimus Saxon is his name."

"Aye, aye, Master Pettigrue," cried the old man. "The very name given by Dicky Rumbold. He said that either the old

Roundhead Clarke or his son would go with him. But who are these?"

"This is Master Reuben Lockarby, also of Havant, and Sir Gervas Jerome of Surrey," I replied. "They are both here as volunteers desiring to serve under the Duke of Monmouth."

"Right glad I am to see ye, then," said the stalwart minister, heartily. "Friends, I can answer for these gentlemen that they favor the honest folk and the old cause."

At these words the rage of the mob turned in an instant into the most extravagant adulation and delight. We walked our horses in the midst of them while the clergyman strode along between Saxon and myself.

"Joshua Pettigrue is my name, gentlemen," said he. "I am an unworthy worker in the Lord's vineyard, testifying with voice and with arm to His holy covenant. These are my faithful flock, whom I am bringing westward that they may be ready for the reaping when it pleases the Almighty to gather them in. I received from Monmouth, or rather from Master Ferguson, instructions to be on the lookout for ye and for several others of the faithful we expect to join us from the east. By what route came ye?"

"Over Salisbury Plain, and so through Bruton."

"And saw ye or met ye any of our people upon the way?"

"None," Saxon answered. "We left the Blue Guards at Salisbury, however, and we saw either them or some other horse regiment near this side of the Plain, at the village of Mere."

"Ah, there is a gathering of the eagles," cried Master Joshua Pettigrue, shaking his head. "They are men of fine raiment, with war-horses and chariots and trappings like the Assyrians of old, yet shall the angel of the Lord breathe upon them in the night. Yea, He shall cut them off utterly in His wrath, and they shall be destroyed."

"Amen! Amen!" cried as many of the peasants as were within ear-shot.

"Shall we not lighten it by a song of praise? Where is Brother Thistlethwaite, whose voice is as the cymbal, the tabor, and the dulcimer."

"Lo, most pious Master Pettigrue," said Saxon, "I have myself at times ventured to lift up my voice before the Lord." Without any further apology he broke out in stentorian tones into the following hymn, the refrain of which was caught up by pastor and congregation:

" 'The Lord He is a morion
     That guards me from all wound:
   The Lord He is a coat of mail
     That circles me all round.
        Who, then, fears to draw the sword,
        And fight the battle of the Lord?

" 'My faith is like a citadel
     Girt round with moat and wall,
   No mine, or sap, or breach, or gap
     Can e'er prevail at all.
        Who, then, fears to draw the sword,
        And fight the battle of the Lord?' "

Saxon ceased, but the Rev. Joshua Pettigrue waved his long arms and repeated the refrain, which was taken up again and again by the long column of marching peasants.

"It is a godly hymn," said our companion, who had, to my disgust and to the evident astonishment of Reuben and Sir Gervas, resumed the snuffling, whining voice which he had used in the presence of my father. "It hath availed much on the field of battle."

"Truly," returned the clergyman, "if your comrades are of as sweet a savor as yourself, ye will be worth a brigade of pikes to the faithful," a sentiment which raised a murmur of assent from the Puritans around. "Since, sir," he continued, "you have had much experience in the wiles of war, I shall be glad to hand over to you the command of this small body of the faithful, until such time as we reach the army."

"It is time, too, in good faith, that ye had a soldier at your head," Decimus Saxon answered, quietly. "My eyes deceive me strangely if I do not see the gleam of sword and cuirass upon the brow of yonder declivity. Methinks our pious exercises have brought the enemy upon us."

CHAPTER FIFTEEN

OF OUR BRUSH WITH THE KING'S DRAGOONS

SOME little distance from us a branch road ran into that along which we and our motley assemblage of companions in arms were travelling. This road curved down the side of a well-wooded hill, and then over the level for a quarter of a mile or so before opening on the other. Just at the brow of the rising ground there stood a thick bristle of trees, amid the trunks of which there came and went a bright shimmer of sparkling steel, which proclaimed the presence of armed men. So peaceful, however, was the long sweep of countryside, that it was hard to think that the thunder-cloud of war was really lowering over that fair valley.

The country-folk, however, appeared to have no difficulty at all in understanding the danger to which they were exposed. The fugitives from the west gave a yell of consternation, and ran wildly down the road or whipped up their beasts of burden in the endeavor to place as safe a distance as possible between themselves and the threatened attack. When, however, the loud brazen shriek from a bugle broke from the wood, and the head of a troop of horse began to descend the slope, the panic became greater still, and it was difficult for us to preserve any order at all amid the wild rush of the terrified fugitives.

"Stop that cart, Clarke," cried Saxon, vehemently, pointing with his sword to an old wagon, piled high with furniture and bedding, which was lumbering along, drawn by two raw-boned colts. At the same moment I saw him drive his horse into the crowd and catch at the reins of another similar one. Giving Covenant's bridle a shake I was soon abreast of the cart which he had indicated, and managed to bring the furious young horses to a stand-still.

"Bring it up!" cried our leader, working with the coolness which only a long apprenticeship to war can give. "Now friends, cut the traces!" A dozen knives were at work in a moment, and the kicking, struggling animals scampered off, leaving their burdens behind them. Saxon sprang off his horse and set the example in dragging the wagon across the roadway, while some of the peasants, under the direction of Reuben Lockarby and of Master Joshua Pettigrue, arranged a couple of other carts to block the way fifty yards farther down. The latter precaution was to guard against the chance of the royal horse riding through the fields and attacking us from behind. So speedily was the scheme conceived and carried out that within a very few minutes of the first alarm we found ourselves protected front and rear by a lofty barricade, while within this improvised fortress was a garrison of a hundred and fifty men.

"What fire-arms have we among us?" asked Saxon, hurriedly.

"A dozen pistols at the most," replied the elderly Puritan, who was addressed by his companions as Hope-above Williams. "John Rodway, the coachman, hath his blunderbuss. There are also two godly men from Hungerford, who are keepers of game, and who have brought their pieces with them."

"Let all who have pistols line the wagon," said Saxon, tying his mare to the hedge—an example which we all followed. "Clarke, do you take charge upon the right with Sir Gervas, while Lockarby assists Master Pettigrue upon the left. Ye others shall stand behind with stones. Should they break through our barricade, slash at the horses with your scythes. Once down, the riders are no match for ye."

A low, sullen murmur of determined resolution rose from the peasants, mingled with pious ejaculations and little scraps of hymn or of prayer. They had all produced from under their smocks rustic weapons of some sort.

"By the mass!" whispered Sir Gervas, "it is magnificent! An hour of this is worth a year in the Mall. The old Puritan bull is fairly at bay. Let us see what sort of sport the bull-pups make in the baiting of him! I'll lay five pieces to four on the chaw-bacons!"

"Nay, it's no matter for idle betting," said I, shortly, for his light-hearted chatter annoyed me at so solemn a moment.

"Five to four on the soldiers, then!" he persisted. "It is too good a match not to have a stake on it one way or the other."

"Our lives are the stake," said I.

"Faith, I had forgot it!" he replied, still mumbling his toothpick. " 'To be or not to be?' as Will of Stratford says. Kynaston was great on the passage. But here is the bell that rings the curtain up."

While we had been making our dispositions the troop of

horse—for there appeared to be but one—had trotted down the cross-roads, and had drawn up across the main highway. They numbered, as far as I could judge, about ninety troopers, and it was evident from their three-cornered hats, steel plates, red sleeves, and bandoliers that they were dragoons of the regular army. The main body halted a quarter of a mile from us, while three officers rode to the front and held a short consultation, which ended in one of them setting spurs to his horse and cantering down in our direction. A bugler followed a few paces behind him, waving a white kerchief and blowing an occasional blast upon his trumpet.

"Here comes an envoy," cried Saxon, who was standing up in the wagon. "Now, my brethren, we have neither kettledrum nor tinkling brass, but we have the instrument wherewith Providence hath endowed us. Let us show the redcoats that we know how to use it.

> " 'Who, then, dreads the violent,
>   Or fears the man of pride?
>   Or shall I flee from two or three
>   If He be by my side?' "

Seven score voices broke in, in a hoarse roar, upon the chorus:
> " 'Who, then, fears to draw the sword,
>   And fight the battle of the Lord?' "

I could well believe at that moment that the Spartans had found the lame singer Tyrtæus the most successful of their generals, for the sound of their own voices increased the confidence of the country-folk, while the martial words of the old hymn roused the dogged spirit in their breasts. In the midst of this clamor and turmoil the young dragoon officer, a handsome, olive-faced lad, rode fearlessly up to the barrier, and, pulling up his beautiful roan steed, held up his hand with an imperious gesture which demanded silence.

"Who is the leader of this conventicle?" he asked.

"Address your message to me, sir," said our leader, from

the top of the wagon, "but understand that your white flag will only protect you while you use such language as may come from one courteous adversary to another. Say your say or retire."

"Courtesy and honor," said the officer, with a sneer, "are not extended to rebels who are in arms against their lawful sovereign. If you are the leader of this rabble, I warn you if they are not dispersed within five minutes by this watch"—he pulled out an elegant gold timepiece—"we shall ride down upon them and cut them to pieces."

"The Lord can protect His own," Saxon answered, amid a fierce hum of approval from the crowd. "Is this all thy message?"

"It is all, and you will find it enough, you Presbyterian traitor," cried the dragoon cornet. "Listen to me, misguided fools," he continued, standing up upon his stirrups and speaking to the peasants at the other side of the wagon. "What chance have ye with your whittles and cheese-scrapers? Ye may yet save your skins if ye will but deliver up your leaders, throw down what ye are pleased to call your arms, and trust to the king's mercy."

"This exceedeth the limitations of your privileges," said Saxon, drawing a pistol from his belt and cocking it. "If you say another word to seduce these people from their allegiance, I fire."

"Hope not to benefit Monmouth," cried the young officer, disregarding the threat and still addressing his words to the peasants. "The whole royal army is drawing round him, and——"

"Have a care!" shouted our leader, in a deep, harsh voice.

"His head within a month shall roll upon the scaffold."

"But you shall never live to see it," said Saxon, and stooping over he fired straight at the cornet's head. At the flash of the pistol the trumpeter wheeled round and galloped for his life, while the roan horse turned and followed, with its master still seated firmly in the saddle.

"Verily you have missed the Midianite!" cried Hope-above Williams.

"He is dead," said our leader, pouring a fresh charge into his pistol. "It is the law of war, Clarke," he added, looking round at me. "He hath chosen to break it and must pay forfeit."

As he spoke I saw the young officer lean gradually over in his saddle, until, when about half-way back to his friends, he lost his balance, and fell heavily in the roadway, turning over two or three times with the force of his fall, and lying at last still and motionless, a dust-colored heap. A loud yell of rage broke from the troopers at the sight, which was answered by a shout of defiance from the Puritan peasantry.

"Down on your faces!" cried Saxon; "they are about to fire."

The crackle of musketry and a storm of bullets, pinging on the hard ground, or cutting twigs from the hedges on either side of us, lent emphasis to our leader's order. Many of the peasants crouched behind the feather-beds and tables which had been pulled out of the cart. Some lay in the wagon itself, and some sheltered themselves behind or underneath it. Others again lined the ditches on either side or lay flat upon the roadway, while a few showed their belief in the workings of Providence by standing upright without flinching from the bullets. Among these latter were Saxon and Sir Gervas, the former to set an example to his raw troops, and the latter out of pure laziness and indifference.

The cornet's death did not remain long unavenged. A little old man with a sickle, who had been standing near Sir Gervas, gave a sudden sharp cry, and springing up into the air with a loud "Glory to God!" fell flat upon his face, dead. A bullet had struck him just over the right eye. Almost at the same moment one of the peasants in the wagon was shot through the chest, and sat up coughing blood all over the wheel. I saw Master Joshua Pettigrue catch him in his long arms, and settle some bedding under his head, so that he lay breathing heavily and pattering forth prayers. The minister showed himself a man that day, for amid the fierce carbine fire he walked boldly up and down, with a drawn rapier in his left hand—for he was a left-handed man—and his Bible in the other. "This is what you are dying for, dear brothers," he cried, continually, holding the brown volume up in the air; "are ye not ready to die for this?" And every time he asked the question a low eager murmur of assent rose from the ditches, the wagon, and the road.

"They aim like yokels at a wappinschaw," said Saxon, seating himself on the side of the wagon. "Like all young soldiers, they fire too high. When I was an adjutant it was my custom to press down the barrels of the muskets until my eye told me that they were level. These rogues think that they have done their part if they do but let the gun off, though they are as like to hit the plovers above us as ourselves."

"Five of the faithful have fallen," said Hope-above Williams. "Shall we not sally forth and do battle with the children of Antichrist? Are we to lie here like so many popinjays at a fair for the troopers to practise upon?"

"There is a stone barn over yonder on the hill-side," I remarked. "If we who have horses, and a few others, were to keep the dragoons in play, the people might be able to reach it, and so be sheltered from the fire."

"At least let my brother and me have a shot or two back at them," cried one of the marksmen beside the wheel.

To all our entreaties and suggestions, however, our leader only replied by a shake of the head, and continued to swing his long legs over the side of the wagon, with his eyes fixed intently upon the horsemen, many of whom had dismounted and were leaning their carbines over the cruppers of their chargers.

"This cannot go on, sir," said the pastor, in a low, earnest voice; "two more men have just been hit."

"If fifty more men are hit we must wait until they charge," Saxon answered. "What would you do, man? If you leave this shelter you will be cut off and utterly destroyed. Ha, my brave boys, they are mounting! We shall not have to wait long now."

The dragoons were indeed climbing into their saddles again, and forming across the road, with the evident intention of charging down upon us. At the same time about thirty men detached themselves from the main body, and trotted away into the fields upon our right. Saxon growled a hearty oath under his breath as he observed them.

"They have some knowledge of warfare, after all," said he. "They mean to charge us flank and front. Master Joshua, see that your scythemen line the quickset hedge upon the right. Stand well up, my brothers, and flinch not from the horses. You men with the sickles, lie in the ditch there, and cut at the legs of the brutes. A line of stone-throwers behind that. A heavy stone is as sure as a bullet at close quarters. If ye would see your wives and children, make that hedge good against the horsemen. Now for the front attack. Let the men who carry petronels come into the wagon. Two of yours, Clarke, and two of yours, Lockarby. I can spare one also. That makes five. Now here are ten other of a sort and three muskets. Twenty shots in all. Have you no pistols, Sir Gervas?"

"No, but I can get a pair," said our companion, and springing upon his horse he forced his way through the ditch, past the barrier, and so down the road in the direction of the dragoons.

The movement was so sudden and so unexpected that there was a dead silence for a few seconds, which was broken by a general howl of hatred and execration from the peasants. "Shoot upon him! Shoot down the false Amalekite!" they shrieked. "He hath gone to join his kind! He hath delivered us up into the hands of the enemy! Judas! Judas!" As to the horsemen, who were still forming up for a charge and waiting for the flanking party to get into position, they sat still and silent, not knowing what to make of the gayly-dressed cavalier who was speeding towards them.

We were not left long in doubt, however. He had no sooner reached the spot where the cornet had fallen than he sprang from his horse and helped himself to the dead man's pistols, and to the belt which contained his powder and ball. Mounting at his leisure, amid a shower of bullets which puffed up the white dust all around him, he rode onward towards the dragoons and discharged one of his pistols at them. Wheeling round, he politely raised his cap, and galloped back to us, none the worse for his adventure, though a ball had grazed his horse's fetlock and another had left a hole in the skirt of his riding-coat. The peasants raised a shout of jubilation as he rode in, and from that day forward our friend was permitted to wear his gay trappings and to bear himself as he would, without being suspected of having mounted the livery of Satan or being wanting in zeal for the cause of the saints.

"They are coming," cried Saxon. "Let no man draw trigger until he sees me shoot. If any does, I shall send a bullet through him, though it was my last shot and the troopers were among us."

As our leader uttered this threat, and looked grimly round upon us with an evident intention of executing it, a shrill blare of a bugle burst from the horsemen in front of us, and was answered by those upon our flank. At the signal both bodies set spurs to their horses and dashed down upon us at the top of their speed. Those in the field were delayed for a few moments, and thrown into some disorder, by finding that the ground immediately in front of them was soft and boggy; but having made their way through it, they reformed upon the other side and rode gallantly at the hedge. Our own opponents, having a clear course before them, never slackened for an instant, but came thundering down with a jingling of harness and a tempest of oaths upon our rude barricade.

To inexperienced soldiers like ourselves, it seemed impossible that our frail defence and our feeble weapons could check for an instant the impetus and weight of the dragoons. To right and left I saw white set faces, open-eyed and rigid, unflinching, with a stubbornness which rose less from hope than from despair. All round rose exclamations and prayers. "Lord, save Thy people!" "Mercy, Lord, mercy!" "Be with us this day!" "Receive our souls, oh merciful Father!" Saxon lay across the wagon with his eyes glinting like diamonds and his petronel presented at the full length of his rigid arm. Following his example, we all took aim as steadily as possible at the first rank of the enemy. Our only hope of safety lay in making that one discharge so deadly that our opponents should be too much shaken to continue their attack.

Would the man never fire? They could not be more than ten paces from us. I could see the buckles on the men's plates and the powder charges in their bandoliers. One more stride yet, and at last our leader's pistol flashed and we poured in a close volley, supported by a shower of heavy stones from the sturdy peasants behind. I could hear them splintering against casque and cuirass like hail upon a casement. The cloud of smoke veiling for an instant the line of galloping steeds and gallant riders drifted slowly aside to show a very different scene. A dozen men and horses were rolling in one wild blood-spurting heap, the unwounded falling over those whom our balls and stones had just brought down. Struggling, snorting chargers, iron-shod feet, staggering figures rising and falling, wild, hatless, bewildered men half stunned by a fall, and not knowing which way to turn. That was the foreground of the picture, while behind them the remainder of the troop were riding furiously back, wounded and hale, all driven by the one desire of getting to a place of safety where they might rally their shattered formation. A great shout of praise and thanksgiving rose from the delighted peasants, and surging over the barricade, they struck down or secured the few uninjured troopers who had been unable or unwilling to join their companions in their flight. The carbines, swords, and bandoliers were eagerly pounced upon by the victors, some of whom had served in the militia, and knew well how to handle the different weapons which they had won.

The victory, however, was by no means completed. The flanking squadron had ridden boldly at the hedge, and a dozen or more had forced their way through, in spite of the showers of stones and the desperate thrusts of the pikemen and scythemen. Once among the peasants, the long swords and the armor of the dragoons gave them a great advantage. A dragoon sergeant, a man of great resolution and of prodigious strength, appeared to be the leader of the party, and encouraged his followers both by word and example. A stab from a half-pike brought his horse to the ground, but he sprang from the saddle as it fell, and avenged its death by a sweeping back-handed cut from his broadsword. Waving his hat in his left hand, he continued to rally his men, and to strike down every Puritan who came against him, until a blow from a hatchet brought him on his knees and a flail stroke broke his sword close by the hilt. At the fall of their leader his comrades turned and fled through the hedge, but the gallant fellow, wounded and bleeding, still showed fight, and would assuredly have been knocked upon the head for his pains had I not picked him up and thrown him into a wagon, where he had the good sense to lie quiet until the skirmish was at an end. Of the dozen who broke through, not more than four escaped, and several others lay dead or wounded upon the other side of the hedge, empaled by scythe-blades or knocked off their horses by stones. The remainder of the troop fired a single, straggling, irregular volley, and then galloped away down the cross-road, disappearing among the trees from which they had emerged.

All this, however, had not been accomplished without severe loss upon our side. Our total losses were eight killed and the same wounded, which could not but be regarded as a very moderate number, when we consider the fierceness of the skirmish and the superiority of our enemy both in discipline and in equipment.

Within an hour of the ending of the skirmish we found ourselves pursuing our way once more, and looking back through the twilight at the scattered black dots upon the white road, where the bodies of the dragoons marked the scene of our victory.

CHAPTER SIXTEEN

OF OUR COMING TO TAUNTON

THE purple shadows of evening had fallen over the country side, and the sun had sunk behind the distant Quantock and Brandon hills, as our rude column of rustic infantry plodded through Curry Rivell, Wrantage, and Henlade. At every way-side cottage and red-tiled farm-house the people swarmed out as we passed, with jugs of milk or beer, shaking hands with our yokels and pressing food and drink upon them.

The skirmish had reduced our numbers, but it had done much to turn our rabble of peasants into a real military force. The leadership of Saxon, and his stern, short words of praise or of censure, had done even more. The men kept some sort of formation, and stepped together briskly in a compact body. The old soldier and I rode at the head of the column, with Master Pettigrue still walking between us.

I observed that Saxon rode with his chin upon his shoulder, casting continual uneasy glances behind him, and halting at every piece of rising ground to make sure that there were no pursuers at our heels. It was not until, after many weary miles of marching, the lights of Taunton could be seen twinkling far off in the valley beneath us, that he at last heaved a deep sigh of relief, and expressed his belief that all danger was over.

"I am not prone to be fearful upon small occasion," he remarked, "but, hampered as we are with wounded men and prisoners, it might have puzzled Petrinus himself to know what we should have done had the cavalry overtaken us. I can now, Master Pettigrue, smoke my pipe in peace, without pricking up my ears at every chance rumble of a wheel or shout of a village roisterer."

"Even had they pursued us," said the minister, stoutly, "as long as the hand of the Lord shall shield us, why should we fear them?"

"Aye, aye!" Saxon answered, impatiently, "but the devil prevaileth at times. Were not the chosen people themselves overthrown and led into captivity? How say you, Clarke?"

"One such skirmish is enough for a day," I remarked. "Faith! if instead of charging us they had continued that carbine fire, we must either have come forth or been shot where we lay."

"For that reason I forbade our friends with the muskets to answer it," said Saxon. "Our silence led them to think that we had but a pistol or two among us, and so brought them to charge us. Thus our volley became the more terrifying since it was unexpected. I'll wager there was not a man among them who did not feel that he had been led into a trap. Mark you how the rogues wheeled and fled with one accord, as though it had been part of their daily drill!"

"The peasants stood to it like men," I remarked.

"There is nothing like a tincture of Calvinism for stiffening a line of battle," said Saxon. So austere and holy was his expression, so solemn his demeanor, and so frequent the upturnings of his eyes, clasping of his hands, and other signs which marked the extreme sectary, that I could not but marvel at the depths and completeness of the hypocrisy which had cast so complete a cloak over his rapacious self. For very mischief's sake I could not refrain from reminding him that there was one at least who valued his professions at their real value.

"Have you told the worthy minister," said I, "of your captivity among the Mussulmans, and of the noble way in which you did uphold the Christian faith at Stamboul?"

"Nay," cried our companion, "I would fain hear the tale. I marvel much that one so faithful and unbending as thyself was ever let loose by the unclean and blood-thirsty followers of Mohammed."

"It does not become me to tell the tale," Saxon answered, with great presence of mind, casting at the same time a most venomous sidelong glance at me. "It is for my comrades in misfortune and not for me to describe what I endured for the faith. I have little doubt, Master Pettigrue, that you would have done as much had you been there. The town of Taunton lies very quiet beneath us, and there are few lights for so early an hour, seeing that it has not yet gone ten. It is clear that Monmouth's forces have not reached it yet, else had there been some show of camp-fires in the valley; for though it is warm enough to lie out in the open, the men must have fires to cook their victual."

"The army could scarce have come so far," said the pastor. "They have, I fear, been much delayed by the want of arms and by the need of discipline. Bethink ye, it was on the eleventh day of the month that Monmouth landed at Lyme, and it is now but the night of the fourteenth. There was much to be done in the time."

"Four whole days!" growled the old soldier. "Yet I expected no better, seeing that they have, so far as I can hear, no tried soldiers among them. By my sword, Tilly or Wallenstein would not have taken four days to come from Lyme to Taunton, though all James Stuart's cavalry barred the way. Great enterprises are not pushed through in this halting fashion. The blow should be sharp and sudden. But tell me, worthy sir, all that you know about the matter, for we have heard little upon the road save rumor and surmise. Was there not some fashion of onfall at Bridport!"

"There was indeed some shedding of blood at that place. The first two days were consumed, as I understand, in the enrolling of the faithful and the search for arms wherewith to equip them. You may well shake your head, for the hours were precious. At last five hundred men were broken into some sort of order, and marched along the coast under the command of Lord Grey, of Wark, and Wade, the lawyer. At Bridport they were opposed by the red Dorset militia and part of Portman's yellow-coats. If all be true that is said, neither side had much to boast of. Grey and his cavalry never tightened bridle until they were back in Lyme once more, though it is said their flight had more to do with the hard mouths of their horses than with the soft hearts of the riders. Wade and his footmen did bravely, and had the best of it against the king's troops. There was much outcry against Grey in the camp, but Monmouth can scarce afford to be severe upon the only nobleman who hath joined his standard."

"Pshaw!" cried Saxon, peevishly. "There was no great stock of noblemen in Cromwell's army, I trow, and yet they held their own against the king, who had as many lords by him as there are haws in a thicket. If ye have the people on your side, why should ye crave for these bewigged fine gentlemen, whose white hands and delicate rapiers are of as much service as so many ladies' bodkins?"

"Faith!" said I, "if all the fops are as careless for their lives as our friend Sir Gervas, I could wish no better comrades in the field."

"In good sooth, yes!" cried Master Pettigrue, heartily. "What though he be clothed in a Joseph's coat of many colors, and hath strange turns of speech, no man could have fought more stoutly or shown a bolder front against the enemies of Israel. Surely the youth hath good in his heart, and will become a seat of grace and a vessel of the Spirit, though at present he be entangled in the net of worldly follies and carnal vanities."

"It is to be hoped so," quoth Saxon, devoutly. "And what else can you tell us of the revolt, worthy sir?"

"Very little, save that the peasants have flocked in in such numbers that many have had to be turned away for want of arms. Every tithing-man in Somersetshire is searching for axes and scythes. There is not a blacksmith but is at his forge from morn to night at work upon pike-heads. There are six thousand men of a sort in the camp, but not one in five carries a musket. They have advanced, I hear, upon Axminster, where they must meet the Duke of Albemarle, who hath set out from Exeter with four thousand of the train-bands."

"Then we shall be too late, after all," I exclaimed.

"You will have enough of battles before Monmouth exchanges his riding-hat for a crown, and his laced roquelaure for the royal purple," quoth Saxon. "Should our worthy friend here be correctly informed, and such an engagement take place, it will but be the prologue to the play. When Feversham and Churchill come up with the king's own troops, it is then that Monmouth takes the last spring that lands him either on the throne or the scaffold."

While this conversation had been proceeding we had been walking our horses down the winding track which leads along the eastern slope of Taunton Deane. For some time past we had been able to see in the valley beneath us the lights of Taunton town and the long silver strip of the river Tone. The moon was shining brightly in a cloudless heaven, throwing a still and peaceful radiance over the fairest and richest of English valleys. Suddenly, in the stillness, a strong fervent voice was heard calling upon the source of all life to guard and preserve that which He had created. It was Joshua Pettigrue, who had flung himself upon his knees, and who, while asking for future guidance, was returning thanks for the safe deliverance which his flock had experienced from the many perils which had beset them upon their journey.

Master Pettigrue had concluded his thanksgiving, and was in the act of rising to his feet, when the musical peal of a bell rose up from the sleeping town before us. For a minute or more it rose and fell in its sweet, clear cadence. Then a second, with a deeper, harsher note, joined in, and then a third, until the air was filled with the merry jangling. At the same time a buzz of shouting or huzzaing could be heard, which increased and spread until it swelled into a mighty uproar. Lights flashed in the windows, drums beat, and the whole place was astir. These sudden signs of rejoicing coming at the heels of the minister's prayer were seized upon as a happy omen by the superstitious peasants, who set up a glad cry, and pushing onward, were soon within the outskirts of the town.

CHAPTER SEVENTEEN

OF THE GATHERING IN THE MARKET-SQUARE

THE fair town in which we now found ourselves was, although Monmouth had not yet reached it, the real centre of the rebellion. It was a prosperous place, with a great woollen and kersey trade, which gave occupation to as many as seven thousand inhabitants. Taunton from time immemorial had been a rallying point for the party of liberty, and for many years it had leaned to the side of Republicanism in politics and of Puritanism in religion. After the Restoration the Privy Council had shown their recollection of the part played by the Somersetshire town, by issuing a special order that the battlements which fenced round the maiden stronghold should be destroyed. Thus, at the time of which I speak, nothing but a line of ruins and a few unsightly mounds represented the massive line of wall which had been so bravely defended by the last generation of townsmen. There were not wanting, however, many other relics of those stormy times. The houses on the outskirts were still scarred and splintered from the effects of the bombs and grenades of the Cavaliers. Indeed, the whole town bore a grimly martial appearance, as though she were a veteran among boroughs who had served in the past, and was not averse to seeing the flash of guns and hearing the screech of shot once more.

A large body of the burghers had already set out to join the rebel army, but a good number had remained behind to guard the city, and these were reinforced by gangs of peasants, like the one to which we had attached ourselves, who had trooped in from the surrounding country, and now divided their time between listening to their favorite preachers and learning to step in line and to handle their weapons. In yard, street, and market-square there was marching and drilling, night, morning, and noon. As we rode out after breakfast the whole town was ringing with the shouting of orders and the clatter of arms. Our own friends of yesterday marched into the market-place at the moment we entered it, and no sooner did they catch sight of us than they plucked off their hats and cheered lustily, nor would they desist until we cantered over to them and took our places at their head.

"They have vowed that none other should lead them," said the minister, standing by Saxon's stirrup.

"I could not wish to lead stouter fellows," said he. "Let them deploy into double line in front of the town-hall. So, so, smartly there, rear rank!" he shouted, facing his horse towards them. "Now swing round into position. Keep your ground, left flank, and let the others pivot upon you. So—did ever an unhappy soldier find himself called upon to make order among so motley a crew!"

"Shoulder scythe, port scythe, present scythe—mow!" whispered Reuben to Sir Gervas, and the pair began to laugh, heedless of the angry frowns of Saxon.

"Let us divide them," he said, "into three companies of eighty men. Or, stay—how many musketeers have we in all? Five-and-fifty. Let them stand forward, and form the first line or company. Sir Gervas Jerome, you have officered the militia of your county, and have doubtless some knowledge of the manual exercise. If I am commandant of this force I hand over the captaincy of this company to you. It shall be the first line in battle—a position which I know you will not be averse to."

"Gad, they'll have to powder their heads," said Sir Gervas, with decision.

"You shall have the entire ordering of them," Saxon answered. "Let the first company take six paces to the front— so! Now let the pikemen stand out. Eighty-seven, a serviceable company. Lockarby, do you take these men in hand, and never forget that the German wars have proved that the best of horse has no more chance against steady pikemen than the waves against a crag. Take the captaincy of the second company, and ride at their head."

"Faith! if they don't fight better than their captain rides," whispered Reuben, "it will be an evil business. I trust they will be firmer in the field than I am in the saddle."

"The third company of scythesmen I commit to your charge, Captain Micah Clarke," continued Saxon. "Good Master Joshua Pettigrue will be our field-chaplain. His voice and his presence be to us as manna in the wilderness, and as springs of water in dry places. The underofficers I see that you have yourselves chosen, and your captains shall have power to add to the number from those who smite boldly and spare not. Now, one thing I have to say to you, and I speak it that all may hear, and that none may hereafter complain that the rules he serves under were not made clear to him. When we are in arms and the good work is to be done, on the march, in the field, or on parade, then let your bearing be strict, soldierly, and scrupulous, quick to hear and alert to obey, for I shall have no sluggards or laggards, and if there be any such my hand shall be heavy upon them, yea, even to the cutting of them off. I say there shall be no mercy for such." Here he paused and surveyed his force with a set face and his eyelids drawn low over his glinting, shifting eyes. "If, then," he continued, "there is any man among you who fears to serve under a hard discipline, let him stand forth now, and let him betake him to some easier leader, for I say to you that while I command this corps, Saxon's regiment of Wiltshire foot shall be worthy to testify in this great and soul-raising cause."

The colonel stopped and sat silent upon his mare. The long lines of rustic faces looked up, some stolidly, some admiringly, some with an expression of fear at his stern, gaunt face and baneful eyes. None moved, however; so he continued:

"Worthy Master Timewell, the mayor of this fair town of

Taunton, who has been a tower of strength to the faithful during these long and spirit-trying times, is about to inspect us when
the others shall have assembled. Captains, to your companies,
then! Close up there on the musketeers, with three paces between each line. Scythesmen, take ground to your left. Let
the underofficers stand on the flanks and rear. So! 'tis smartly
done for a first venture, though a good adjutant with a prugel
after the Imperial fashion might find work to do."

While we were thus rapidly and effectively organizing ourselves into a regiment, other bodies of peasantry more or less
disciplined had marched into the market-square and had taken
up their position there. Those on our right had come from
Frome and Radstock, in the north of Somersetshire, and were
a mere rabble armed with flails, hammers, and other such
weapons, with no common sign of order or cohesion save the
green boughs which waved in their hat-bands. The body upon
our left, who bore a banner among them announcing that they
were men of Dorset, were fewer in number but better equipped,
having a front rank, like our own, entirely armed with muskets.

The good townsmen of Taunton, with their wives and their
daughters, had meanwhile been assembling on the balconies and
at the windows which overlooked the square, whence they might
have a view of the pageant. The sidewalks were crowded with
the commoner folk—old white-bearded wool-workers, stern-
faced matrons, country lasses with their shawls over their heads,
and swarms of children, who cried out with their treble voices
for King Monmouth and the Protestant succession.

"By my faith!" said Sir Gervas, reining back his steed until
he was abreast of me, "our square-toed friend need not be in
such post-haste to get to heaven when they have so many angels
among them on earth. Gad's wounds, are they not beautiful?
Never a patch or a diamond among them, and yet what would
not our faded belles of the Mall or the Piazza give for their
innocence and freshness?"

"Nay, for Heaven's sake, do not smile and bow at them,"

said I. "These courtesies may pass in London, but they may be misunderstood among simple Somerset maidens and their hot-headed, hard-handed kinsfolk."

I had hardly spoken before the folding doors of the town-hall were thrown open, and a procession of the city fathers emerged into the market-place. In rear of these walked a pursy little red-faced man, the town-clerk, bearing a staff of office in his hand, while the line of dignitaries was closed by the tall and stately figure of Stephen Timewell, Mayor of Taunton.

Having passed round the front and rear of the various bodies, and inspected them with a minuteness and attention which showed that his years had not dulled his soldier's faculties, the mayor faced round with the evident intention of addressing us. His clerk instantly darted in front of him, and waving his arms began to shout "Silence, good people!—silence for his most worshipful the Mayor of Taunton!—silence for the worthy Master Stephen Timewell!" until in the midst of his gesticulations and cries he got entangled once more with his overgrown weapon, and went sprawling on his hands and knees in the kennel.

"Silence yourself, Master Tetheridge," said the chief magistrate, severely. "If your sword and your tongue were both clipped, it would be as well for yourself and us. Shall I not speak a few words in season to these good people but you must interrupt with your discordant bellowings?"

The busybody gathered himself together and slunk behind the group of councilmen, while the mayor slowly ascended the steps of the market cross. From this position he addressed us, speaking in a high, piping voice which gathered strength as he proceeded, until it was audible at the remotest corners of the square.

A deep irrepressible hum of approval at the close of his speech burst from the ranks of the insurgent infantry, with a clang of arms as musketoon or pike was grounded upon the stone pavement. Saxon half turned his fierce face, raising an

STEPHEN TIMEWELL—MAYOR OF TAUNTON

impatient hand, and the hoarse murmur died away among our men, though our less-disciplined companions to right and left continued to wave their green boughs and to clatter their arms. The Taunton men opposite stood grim and silent, but their set faces and bent brows showed that their townsman's oratory had stirred the deep fanatic spirit which distinguished them.

"In my hands," continued the mayor, drawing a roll of paper from his bosom, "is the proclamation which our royal leader hath sent in advance of him. Know, therefore, that it is hereby proclaimed that James, Duke of Monmouth, is now and henceforth rightful King of England; that James Stuart, the Papist and fratricide, is a wicked usurper, upon whose head, dead or alive, a price of five thousand guineas is affixed; and that the assembly now sitting at Westminster, and calling itself the Commons of England, is an illegal assembly, and its acts are null and void in the sight of the law. God bless King Monmouth and the Protestant religion!"

The trumpeters struck up a flourish and the people huzzaed, but the mayor raised his thin white hands as a signal for silence. "A messenger hath reached me this morning from the king," he continued. "He sends a greeting to all his faithful Protestant subjects, and having halted at Axminster to rest after his victory, he will advance presently, and be with ye in two days at the latest."

The old Puritan gravely rolled up his papers, and having stood for a few moments with his hands folded across his breast in silent prayer, he descended from the market-cross and moved off, followed by the aldermen and councilmen. The crowd began likewise to disperse in sedate and sober fashion, with grave, earnest faces and downcast eyes. A large number of the country-folk, however, more curious and less devout than the citizens, gathered round our regiment to see the men who had beaten off the dragoons.

CHAPTER EIGHTEEN

OF MASTER STEPHEN TIMEWELL, MAYOR OF TAUNTON

WITHIN the town-hall all was bustle and turmoil. At one side, behind a low table covered with green baize, sat two scriveners with great rolls of paper in front of them. A long line of citizens passed slowly before them, each in turn putting down a roll or bag of coins which was duly noted by the receivers. A square iron-bound chest stood by their side, into which the money was thrown, and we noted as we passed that it was half full of gold-pieces. We could not but mark that many of the givers were men whose threadbare doublets and pinched faces showed that the wealth which they were dashing down so readily must have been hoarded up for such a purpose at the cost of scanty fare and hard living. Most of them accompanied their gift by a few words of prayer, or by some pithy text anent the treasure which rusteth not, or the lending to the Lord. The town-clerk stood by the table giving forth the vouchers for each sum, and the constant clack of his tongue filled the hall, as he read aloud the names and amounts, with his own remarks between.

At the other side of the hall were several long wooden drinking-troughs, which were used for the storing of pikes and scythes. Special messengers and tithing-men had been sent out to scour the country for arms, who, as they returned, placed their prizes here under the care of the armorer-general.

In the midst of the coming and the going stood Master Timewell, the mayor, ordering all things, like a skilful and provident commander. I could understand the trust and love which his townsmen had for him, as I watched him laboring with all the wisdom of an old man and the blithesomeness of a young one. He was hard at work as we approached in trying the lock of a falconet; but perceiving us, he came forward, and saluted us with much kindliness.

"I have heard much of ye," said he; "how ye caused the faithful to gather to a head, and so beat off the horsemen of the usurper. It will not be the last time, I trust, that ye shall see their backs. I hear, Colonel Saxon, that ye have seen much service abroad."

"I have been the humble tool of Providence in much good work," said Saxon, with a bow. "I have fought with the Swedes against the Brandenburgers, and again with the Brandenburgers against the Swedes, my time and conditions with the latter having been duly carried out. I have afterwards, in the Bavarian service, fought against Swedes and Brandenburgers combined, besides having undergone the great wars on the Danube against the Turk, and two compaigns with the Messieurs in the Palatinate, which latter might be better termed holiday-making than fighting."

"A soldierly record in very truth," cried the mayor, stroking his white beard. "I hear that you are also powerfully borne onward in prayer and song. You are, I perceive, one of the old breed of '44, colonel—the men who were in the saddle all day, and on their knees half the night. When shall we see the like of them again? A few such broken wrecks as I are left, with the fire of our youth all burned out, and naught left but the ashes of lethargy and lukewarmness."

"Nay, nay," said Saxon, "your position and present business will scarce jump with the modesty of your words. But here are young men who will find the fire if their elders bring the brains. This is Captain Micah Clarke, and Captain Lockarby, and Captain the Honorable Sir Gervas Jerome, who have all come far to draw their swords for the down-trodden faith."

"Taunton welcomes ye, young sirs," said the mayor, looking a trifle askance, as I thought, at the baronet, who had drawn out his pocket mirror, and was engaged in the brushing of his eyebrows. "I trust that during your stay in this town ye will all four take up your abode with me. 'Tis a homely roof and simple fare, but a soldier's wants are few. And now, colonel, I would fain have your advice as to these three drakes, whether if rehooped they may be deemed fit for service; and also to these demi-cannons, which were used in the old Parliamentary days, and may yet have a word to say in the people's cause."

The old soldier and the Puritan instantly plunged into a deep and learned disquisition upon the merits of wall-pieces, drakes, demi-culverins, sakers, minions, mortar-pieces, falcons, and pattereroes. We slipped away at last, leaving him still discussing the effects produced by the Austrian grenadoes upon a Bavarian brigade of pikes at the battle of Ober-Graustock.

"Curse me if I like accepting this old fellow's offer," said Sir Gervas, in an undertone. "I have heard of these Puritan households. Much grace to little sack, and text flying about as hard and as jagged as flint stones. To bed at sundown, and a sermon ready if ye do but look kindly at the waiting-wench or hum the refrain of a ditty."

"His home may be larger, but it could scare be stricter than that of my own father," I remarked.

"I'll warrant that," cried Reuben. "When we have been a morris-dancing, or having a Saturday night game of 'kiss-in-the-ring,' or 'parson-has-lost-his-coat,' I have seen Ironside Joe stride past us, and cast a glance at us which hath frozen the smile upon our lips. I warrant that he would have aided Colonel Pride to shoot the bears and hack down the maypoles."

"'Twere fratricide for such a man to shoot a bear," quoth Sir Gervas, "with all respect, friend Clarke, for your honored progenitor."

"No more than for you to shoot at a popinjay," I answered, laughing; "but as to the mayor's offer, we can but go to meat with him now; and should it prove irksome, it will be easy for you to plead some excuse, and so get honorably quit of it. But bear in mind, Sir Gervas, that such households are in very truth different from any with which you are acquainted, so curb your tongue or offence may come of it. Should I cry 'hem!' or cough, it will be a sign to you that you had best beware."

"Agreed, young Solomon!" cried he. "It is, indeed, well to have a pilot like yourself who knows these godly waters. For my own part I should never know how near I was to the shoals. But our friends have finished the battle of Ober what's-its-name, and are coming towards us. I trust, worthy Mr. Mayor, that your difficulties have been resolved?"

"They are, sir," replied the Puritan. "I have been much edified by your colonel's discourse, and I have little doubt that by serving under him ye will profit much by his ripe experience."

"Very like, sir, very like," said Sir Gervas, carelessly.

"But it is nigh one o'clock," the mayor continued; "our frail flesh cries aloud for meat and drink. I beg that you will do me the favor to accompany me to my humble dwelling, where we shall find the household board already dressed."

With these words he led the way out of the hall and paced slowly down Fore Street, the people falling back to right and to left as he passed, and raising their caps to do him reverence.

The chief magistrate's house was a squat square-faced stone building within a court which opened on to East Street. The peaked oak door, spangled with broad iron nails, had a gloomy and surly aspect, but the hall within was lightful and airy, with a bright polished cedar planking, and high panelling of some dark-grained wood which gave forth a pleasant smell as of violets. A broad flight of steps rose up from the farther end of the hall, down which as we entered a young sweet-faced maid came tripping, with an old dame behind her, who bore in her hands a pile of fresh napery. At the sight of us the elder one retreated up the stairs again, while the younger came flying down three steps at a time, threw her arms around the old mayor's neck, and kissed him fondly, looking hard into his face the while, as a mother gazes into that of a child with whom she fears that aught may have gone amiss.

"Weary again, daddy, weary again," she said, shaking her head anxiously, with a small white hand upon each of his shoulders. "Indeed and indeed, thy spirit is greater than thy strength."

"Nay, nay, lass," said he, passing his hand fondly over her rich brown hair. "The workman must toil until the hour of rest is rung. This, gentlemen, is my granddaughter Ruth, the sole relic of my family and the light of mine old age. The whole grove hath been cut down, and only the oldest oak and the youngest sapling left. These cavaliers, little one, have come from afar to serve the cause, and they have done us the honor to accept of our poor hospitality."

"Ye are come in good time, gentlemen," she answered, looking us straight in the eyes with a kindly smile, as a sister might greet her brothers. "The household is gathered round the table, and the meal is ready."

"But not more ready than we," cried the stout old burgher. "Do thou conduct our guests to their places, while I seek my room and doff these robes of office, with my chain and tippet, ere I break my fast."

Following our fair guide, we passed into a very large and lofty room, the walls of which were wainscoted with carved oak, and hung at either end with tapestry. Down the centre of this room there ran a long and massive table, which was surrounded by thirty or forty people, the greater part of whom were men of all ages, from graybeards down to lads scarce out of their teens, all with the same solemn and austere expression of countenance, and clad in the same homely and sombre garb.

Our young hostess led us to the end of the table, where a high carved chair with a black cushion upon it marked the position of the master of the house. Mistress Timewell seated herself upon the right of the mayor's place, with Sir Gervas beside her, while the post of honor upon the left was assigned to

Saxon. On my left sat Lockarby, whose eyes, I observed, had been fixed in undisguised and all-absorbing admiration upon the Puritan maiden from the first moment that he had seen her. The table was of no great breadth, so that we could talk across in spite of the clatter of plates and dishes, the bustle of servants, and the deep murmur of voices.

"This is my father's household," said our hostess, addressing herself to Saxon. "There is not one of them who is not in his employ. He hath many apprentices in the wool trade. We sit down forty to meat every day in the year."

"And to right good fare, too," quoth Saxon, glancing down the table. "Salmon, ribs of beef, loin of mutton, veal, pasties —what could man wish for more? Plenty of good home-brewed, too, to wash it down. If worthy Master Timewell can arrange that the army be victualled after the same fashion, I for one shall be beholden to him. A cup of dirty water and a charred morsel cooked on a ramrod over the camp-fire are like to take the place of these toothsome dainties."

"Is it not best to have faith?" said the Puritan maiden. "Shall not the Almighty feed His soldiers even as Elisha was fed in the wilderness and Hagar in the desert?"

"Aye!" exclaimed a lanky-haired and swarthy young man who sat upon the right of Sir Gervas. "He will provide for us, even as the stream of water gushed forth out of dry places, even as the quails and the manna lay thick upon barren soil."

"So I trust, young sir," quoth Saxon; "but we must none the less arrange a victual-train, with a staff of wains, duly numbered, and an intendant over each, after the German fashion. Such things should not be left to chance."

Pretty Mistress Timewell glanced up with a half-startled look at this remark, as though shocked at the want of faith implied in it. Her thoughts might have taken the form of words had not her father entered the room at that moment, the whole company rising and bowing to him as he advanced to his seat.

"Be seated, friends," said he, with a wave of his hand. "We

are a homely folk, Colonel Saxon, and the old-time virtue of respect for our elders has not entirely forsaken us. I trust, Ruth," he continued, "that thou hast seen to the wants of our guests."

We all protested that we had never received such attention and hospitality.

" 'Tis well, 'tis well," said the good wool-worker. "But your plates are clear and your glasses empty. William, look to it. A good workman is ever a good trencherman. If a prentice of mine cannot clean his platter I know that I shall get little from him with carder and teazel. Thew and sinew need building up. A slice from that round of beef, William. Touching that same battle of Ober-Graustock, colonel, what part was played in the fray by that regiment of Pandour horse in which, as I understand, thou didst hold a commission?"

This was a question on which, as may be imagined, Saxon had much to say, and the pair were soon involved in a heated discussion. While this friendly strife was proceeding between the elders, Sir Gervas Jerome and Mistress Ruth had fallen into conversation at the other side of the table. I have seldom seen so beautiful a face as that of this Puritan damsel; the perfectly moulded body appeared to be but the outer expression of the perfect spirit within. Her dark brown hair swept back from a broad and white forehead, which surmounted a pair of well-marked eyebrows and large, blue, thoughtful eyes. The whole cast of her features was gentle and dove-like, yet there was a firmness in the mouth and delicate prominence of the chin which might indicate that in times of trouble and danger the little maid would prove to be no unworthy descendant of the Roundhead soldier and Puritan magistrate. It amused me much to listen to the efforts which Sir Gervas made to converse with her, for the damsel and he lived so entirely in two different worlds that it took all his gallantry and ready wit to keep on ground which would be intelligible to her.

"No doubt you spend much of your time in reading, Mistress

Ruth," he remarked. "It puzzles me to think what else you can do so far from town."

"Town!" said she, in surprise. "What is Taunton but a town?"

"Heaven forbid that I should deny it," replied Sir Gervas, "more especially in the presence of so many worthy burghers, who have the name of being somewhat jealous of the honor of their native city. Yet the fact remains, fair mistress, that the town of London so far transcends all other towns that it is called, even as I called it just now, *the* town."

"Is it so very large, then?" she cried, with pretty wonder. "But new houses are building in Taunton, outside the old walls, and beyond Shuttern, and some even at the other side of the river. Perhaps in time it may be as large."

"If all the folks in Taunton were to be added to London," said Sir Gervas, "no one there would observe that there had been any increase."

"Nay, there you are laughing at me. That is against all reason," cried the country maiden.

"Your grandfather will bear out my words," said Sir Gervas. "But to return to your reading, I'll warrant that there is not a page of Scudéry and her 'Grand Cyrus' which you have not read. You are familiar, doubtless, with every sentiment in Cowley, or Waller, or Dryden?"

"Who are these?" she asked. "At what church do they preach?"

"Faith!" cried the baronet, with a laugh, "honest John preaches at the church of Will Unwin, commonly known as Will's, where many a time it is two in the morning before he comes to the end of his sermon. But why this question? Do you think that no one may put pen to paper unless they have also a right to wear a gown and climb up to a pulpit? I had thought that all of your sex had read Dryden. Pray what are your own favorite books?"

"There is Alleine's 'Alarm to the Unconverted,'" said she.

"It is a stirring work, and one which hath wrought much good. Hast thou not found it to fructify within thee?"

"I have not read the book you name," Sir Gervas confessed.

"Not read it?" she cried, with raised eyebrows. "Truly I had thought that every one had read the 'Alarm.' What dost thou think, then, of 'Faithful Contendings'?"

"I have not read it."

"Or of Baxter's sermons?" she asked.

"I have not read them."

"Of Bull's 'Spirit Cordial,' then?"

"I have not read it."

Mistress Ruth Timewell stared at him in undisguised wonder. "You may think me ill-bred to say it, sir," she remarked, "but I cannot but marvel where you have been, or what you have done all your life. Why, the very children in the street have read these books."

"In truth, such works come little in our way in London," Sir Gervas answered. "A play of George Etherege's, or a jingle of Sir John Suckling's is lighter, though mayhap less wholesome food for the mind. A man in London may keep pace with the world of letters without much reading, for what with the gossip of the coffee-houses and the news-letters that fall in his way, and the babble of poets or wits at the assemblies, with mayhap an evening or two in the week at the playhouse, with Vanbrugh or Farquhar, one can never part company for long with the muses. Then, after the play, if a man is in no humor for a turn of luck at the green table at the Groom Parter's, he may stroll down to the Coca Tree if he be a Tory, or to St. James's if he be a Whig, and it is ten to one if the talk turn not upon the turning of alcaics, or the contest between blank verse or rhyme. Then one may, after an arrière supper, drop into Will's or Slaughter's, and find Old John, with Tickell and Congreve and the rest of them, hard at work on the dramatic unities, or poetical justice, or some such matter. I confess that my own tastes lay little in that line, for about that hour I was likely to be worse employed with wine-flask, dice-box, or ——"

"Hem! hem!" cried I, warningly, for several of the Puritans were listening with faces which expressed anything but approval.

"What you say of London is of much interest to me," said the Puritan maiden, "though these names and places have little meaning to my ignorant ears. You did speak, however, of the playhouse. Surely no worthy man goes near those sinks of iniquity, the baited traps of the Evil One!"

"Well and truly spoken, Mistress Timewell," cried the lean young Puritan upon the right, who had been an attentive listener to the whole conversation. "There is more evil in such houses than even in the cities of the plain. I doubt not that the wrath of the Lord will descend upon them, and destroy them, and wreck them utterly, together with the dissolute men and abandoned women who frequent them."

"Your strong opinions, friend," said Sir Gervas, quietly, "are borne out doubtless by your full knowledge of the subject. How often, prithee, have you been in these playhouses which you are so ready to decry?"

"I thank the Lord that I have never been so far tempted from the straight path as to set foot within one," the Puritan answered, "nor have I ever been in that great sewer which is called London. I trust, however, that I with others of the faithful may find our way thither and leave not one stone upon another, and sow the spot with salt, that it may be a hissing and a by-word among the people."

"You are right, John Derrick," said the mayor, who had overheard the latter part of his remarks. "Yet methinks that a lower tone and a more backward manner would become you better when you are speaking with your master's guests. Have you ever been in London, Captain Clarke?"

"Nay, sir; I am country born and bred."

"The better man you," said our host. "I have been there

twice. The first time was in the days of the Rump, when
Lambert brought in his division to overawe the Commons. All
was quiet and sober then, I promise you, and you might have
walked from Westminster to the Tower in the dead of the
night without hearing aught save the murmur of prayer and
the chanting of hymns. Not a ruffler or a wench was in the
streets after dark, nor any one save staid citizens upon their
business, or the halberdiers of the watch. The second visit which
I made was over this business of the levelling of the ramparts,
when I and neighbor Foster, the glover, were sent at the head
of a deputation from this town to the Privy Council of Charles.
Who could have credited that a few years would have made
such a change? Every evil thing that had been stamped under-
ground had spawned and festered until its vermin brood flooded
the streets, and the godly were themselves driven to shun the
light of day. A quiet man could not walk the highways without
being elbowed into the kennel by swaggering swashbucklers, or
accosted by painted hussies. Even in the solitude of one's coach
one was not free from the robber."

"How that, sir?" asked Reuben.

"Why, marry, in this wise. As I was the sufferer, I have
the best right to tell the tale. Ye must know that after our
reception—which was cold enough, for we were about as welcome to the Privy Council as the hearth-tax man is to the village
housewife—we were asked, more as I guess from derision than
from courtesy, to the evening levee at Buckingham Palace. We
would both fain have been excused from going, but we feared
that our refusal might give undue offence, and so hinder the success of our mission. My homespun garments were somewhat
rough for such an occasion, yet I determined to appear in them,
with the addition of a new black baize waistcoat faced with silk,
and a good periwig, for which I gave three pounds ten shillings
in the Haymarket."

The young Puritan opposite turned up his eyes and murmured something about "sacrificing to Dagon," which, fortunately for him, was inaudible to the high-spirited old man.

"It was but a worldly vanity," quoth the mayor; "for, with all deference, Sir Gervas Jerome, a man's own hair arranged with some taste, and with perhaps a sprinkling of powder, is to my mind the fittest ornament to his head. It is the contents, and not the case, which availeth. Having donned this frippery, good Master Foster and I hired a calash and drove to the palace. We were deep in grave, and, I trust, profitable converse, speeding through the endless streets, when of a sudden I felt a sharp tug at my head, and my hat fluttered down on to my knees. I raised my hands, and lo! they came upon my bare pate. The wig had vanished. We were rolling down Fleet Street at the moment, and there was no one in the calash save neighbor Foster, who sat as astounded as I. We looked high and low, on the seats and beneath them, but not a sign of the periwig was there. It was gone utterly and without a trace."

"Whither, then?" we asked, with one voice.

"That was the question which we set ourselves to solve. We hallooed to the coachman, and told him what had occurred to us. The fellow came down from his perch, and having heard our story, he burst straightway into much foul language, and walking round to the back of his calash, showed us that a slit had been made in the leather wherewith it was fashioned. Through this the thief had thrust his hand, and had drawn my wig through the hole, resting the while on the crossbar of the coach. It was no uncommon thing, he said, and the wig-snatchers were a numerous body who waited beside the peruke-makers' shops, and when they saw a customer come forth with a purchase which was worth their pains, they would follow, and, should he chance to drive, deprive him of it in this fashion. Be that as it may, I never saw my wig again, and had to purchase another before I could venture into the royal presence."

"A strange adventure, truly!" exclaimed Saxon. "How fared it with you for the remainder of the evening?"

"But scurvily, for Charles's face, which was black enough at all times, was blackest of all to us; nor was his brother the Papist more complaisant. They had but brought us there that they might dazzle us with their glitter and gewgaws, in order that we might bear a fine report of them back to the west with us. So we stood throughout the evening, until, finding that they could get little sport from us, my Lord Clarendon, the Chancellor, gave us the word to retire, which we did at our leisure, after saluting the king and the company."

"Nay, that I should never have done!" cried the young Puritan, who had listened intently to his elder's narrative. "Would it not have been more fitting to have raised up your hands and called down vengeance upon them, as the holy man of old did upon the wicked cities?"

"More fitting, quotha!" said the mayor, impatiently. "It is most fitting that youth should be silent until its opinion is asked on such matters."

The young apprentice, for such he was, bowed his head sullenly to the rebuke, while the mayor, after a short pause, resumed his story.

When he ended his tale, a general shuffling and rising announced the conclusion of the meal. The company filed slowly out in order of seniority, all wearing the same gloomy and earnest expression, with grave gait and downcast eyes. These Puritan ways were, it is true, familiar to me from childhood, yet I have never before seen a large household conforming to them, or marked their effect upon so many young men.

"You shall bide behind for a while," said the mayor, as we were about to follow the others. "William, do you bring a flask of the old green-sealed sack. These creature comforts I do not produce before my lads, for beef and honest malt is the fittest food for such. On occasion, however, I am of Paul's opinion, that a flagon of wine among friends is no bad thing for mind or for body. You can away now, sweetheart, if you have aught to engage you."

"Do you go out again?" asked Mistress Ruth.

"Presently, to the town-hall. The survey of arms is not yet complete."

"I shall have your robes ready, and also the rooms of our guests," she answered; and so, with a bright smile to us, tripped away upon her duty.

"I would that I could order our town as that maiden orders this house," said the mayor. "There is not a want that is not supplied before it is felt. She reads my thoughts and acts upon them, ere my lips have time to form them. If I have still strength to spend in the public service, it is because my private life is full of restful peace. Do not fear the sack, sirs. It cometh from Brooke & Hellier's, of Abchurch Lane, and may be relied upon."

"Which showeth that one good thing cometh out of London," remarked Sir Gervas.

"Aye, truly," said the old man, smiling. "But what think ye of my young men, sir? They must needs be of a very different class to any with whom you are acquainted, if, as I understand, you have frequented court circles."

"Why, marry, they are good enough young men, no doubt." Sir Gervas answered, lightly. "Methinks, however, that there is a want of sap about them. It is not blood, but sour butter-milk that flows in their veins."

"Nay, nay," the mayor responded, warmly. "There you do them an injustice. Their passions and feelings are under control, as the skilful rider keeps his horse in hand; but they are as surely there as are the speed and endurance of the animal. Did you observe the godly youth who sat upon your right, whom I had occasion to reprove more than once for overzeal? He is a fit example of how a man may take the upperhand of his feelings, and keep them in control."

"And how has he done so?" I asked.

"Why, between friends," quoth the mayor, "it was but last Lady-day that he asked the hand of my granddaughter Ruth in marriage. His time is nearly served, and his father, Sam Derrick, is an honorable craftsman, so that the match would have been no unfitting one. The maiden turned against him, however—young girls will have their fancies—and the matter came to an end. Yet here he dwells under the same roof-tree, at her elbow from morn to night, with never a sign of that passion which can scarce have died out so soon. Twice my wool warehouse hath been nigh burned to the ground since then, and twice he hath headed those who fought the flames. There are not many whose suit hath been rejected who would bear themselves in so resigned and patient a fashion."

"I am prepared to find that your judgment is the correct one," said Sir Gervas Jerome. "I have learned to distrust too hasty dislikes, and bear in mind that couplet of John Dryden:

" 'Errors, like straws, upon the surface flow.
He who would search for pearls must dive below.' "

"Or worthy Dr. Samuel Butler," said Saxon, "who, in his immortal poem of 'Hudibras,' says:

" 'The fool can only see the skin:
The wise man tries to peep within.' "

"I wonder, Colonel Saxon," said our host, severely, "that you should speak favorably of that licentious poem, which is composed, as I have heard, for the sole purpose of casting ridicule upon the godly."

"It is true that I contemn and despise the use which Butler hath made of his satire," said Saxon, adroitly. "Yet I may admire the satire itself, just as one may admire a damascened blade without approving of the quarrel in which it is drawn."

"These distinctions are, I fear, too subtle for my old brain," said the stout old Puritan. "This England of ours is divided into two camps, that of God and that of Antichrist. He who is not with us is against us, nor shall any who serve under the devil's banner have anything from me save my scorn and the sharp edge of my sword."

"Well, well," said Saxon, filling up his glass, "I am no Laodicean or time-server. The cause shall not find me wanting with tongue or with sword."

"Of that I am well convinced, my worthy friend," the mayor answered, "and if I have spoken over-sharply you will hold me excused. But I regret to have evil tidings to announce to you. Argyle's rising has failed, and he and his companions are prisoners in the hands of the man who never knew what pity was."

We all started in our chairs at this, and looked at one another aghast, save only Sir Gervas Jerome, whose natural serenity was, I am well convinced, proof against any disturbance. For you may remember that the hopes of Monmouth's party rested very much upon the raid which Argyle and the Scottish exiles had made upon Ayrshire, where it was hoped that they would create such a disturbance as would divert a good share of King James's forces, and so make our march to London less difficult. This sudden news of his total defeat and downfall was therefore a heavy blow, since it turned the whole forces of the Government upon ourselves.

"Have you the news from a trusty source?" asked Decimus Saxon, after a long silence.

"It is beyond all doubt or question," Master Stephen Timewell answered. "Yet I can well understand your surprise, for the duke had trusty counsellors with him. There was Sir Patrick Hume of Polwarth——"

"All talk and no fight," said Saxon.

"And Richard Rumbold."

"All fight and no talk," quoth our companion. "He should, methinks, have rendered a better account of himself."

"Then there was Major Elphinstone."

"A bragging fool!" cried Saxon.

"And Sir John Cochrane."

"A captious, long-tongued, short-witted sluggard," said the soldier of fortune. "The expedition was doomed from the first with such men at its head. Yet I had thought that could they have done naught else, they might at least have flung themselves into the mountain country, where these barelegged caterans could have held their own amid their native clouds and mists. All taken, you say! It is a lesson and a warning to us. I tell you, that unless Monmouth infuses more energy into his councils, and thrusts straight for the heart instead of fencing and foining at the extremities, we shall find ourselves as Argyle and Rumbold. What mean these two days wasted at Axminster at a time when every hour is of import?"

"You are very right, Colonel Saxon," the mayor answered. "And I trust that when the king comes here we may stir him up to more prompt action. He has much need of more soldierly advisers, for since Fletcher hath gone there is hardly a man about him who hath been trained to arms."

"Well," said Saxon, moodily, "now that Argyle hath gone under we are face to face with James, with nothing but our own good swords to trust to."

"To them and to the justice of our cause. How like ye the news, young sirs? Has the wine lost its smack on account of it? Are ye disposed to flinch from the standard of the Lord?"

"For my own part I shall see the matter through," said I.

"And I shall bide where Micah Clarke bides," quoth Reuben Lockarby.

"And to me," said Sir Gervas, "it is a matter of indifference so long as I am in good company and there is something stirring."

"In that case," said the mayor, "we had best each turn to his own work, and have all ready for the king's arrival. Until then I trust that ye will honor my humble roof."

"I fear that I cannot accept your kindness," Saxon answered. "When I am in harness I come and go early and late. I shall therefore take up my quarters in the inn, which is not very well furnished with victual, and yet can supply me with the simple fare which, with a black Jack of October and a pipe of Trinidado, is all I require."

As Saxon was firm in this resolution, the mayor forbore to press it upon him, but my two friends gladly joined with me in accepting the worthy wool-worker's offer, and took up our quarters for the time under his hospitable roof.

CHAPTER NINETEEN

OF A BRAWL IN THE NIGHT

DECIMUS SAXON refused to avail himself of Master
Timewell's house and table for the reason, as I afterwards
learned, that, the mayor being a firm Presbyterian, he thought
it might stand him in ill stead with the Independents and other
zealots were he to allow too great an intimacy to spring up
between them. For he had a firm belief that in all such out-
breaks as that in which we were engaged, the most extreme
party is sure in the end to gain the upperhand. "Fanatics,"
he said to me one day, "mean fervor, and fervor means hard
work, and hard work means power." That was the centre
point of all his plotting and scheming.

And first of all he set himself to show how excellent a soldier he was, and he spared neither time nor work to make this
apparent. From morn till mid-day, and from afternoon till
night, we drilled and drilled until in very truth the shouting
of the orders and the clatter of the arms became wearisome
to our ears.

As we became more soldierly we increased in numbers, for
our smart appearance drew the pick of the new-comers into
our ranks. My own company swelled until it had to be divided, and the others enlarged in proportion. The baronet's
musketeers mustered a full hundred, skilled for the most part

in the use of the gun. Altogether, we sprang from three hundred to four hundred and fifty, and our drill improved until we received praise from all sides on the state of our men.

Late in the evening I was riding slowly back to the house of Master Timewell when Reuben clattered after me, and besought me to turn back with him to see a noteworthy sight. Though feeling little in the mood for such things, I turned Covenant and rode with him down the length of High Street, and into the suburb which is known as Shuttern, where my companion pulled up at a bare barn-like building, and bade me look in through the window.

The interior, which consisted of a single great hall, the empty warehouse in which wool had used to be stored, was all alight with lamps and candles. A great throng of men, whom I recognized as belonging to my own company, or that of my companion, lay about on either side, some smoking, some praying, and some burnishing their arms. Down the middle a line of benches had been drawn up, on which there were seated astraddle the whole hundred of the baronet's musketeers, each engaged in plaiting into a queue the hair of the man who sat in front of him. A boy walked up and down with a pot of grease, by the aid of which, with some whipcord, the work was going forward merrily. Sir Gervas himself, with a great flour-dredger, sat perched upon a bale of wool at the head of the line, and as quickly as any queue was finished he examined it through his quizzing-glass, and, if it found favor in his eyes, daintily powdered it from his dredger, with as much care and reverence as though it were some service of the Church. No cook seasoning a dish could have added his spices with more nicety of judgment than our friend displayed in whitening the pates of his company. Glancing up from his labors, he saw our two smiling faces looking in at him through the window, but his work was too engrossing to allow him to leave it, and we rode off at last without having speech with him.

By this time the town was very quiet and still, for the folk in those parts were early bed-goers, save when some special occasion kept them afoot. We rode slowly together through the silent streets, our horses' hoofs ringing out sharply against the cobble-stones, talking about such light matters as engage the mind of youth. The moon was shining very brightly above us, silvering the broad streets, and casting a fretwork of shadows from the peaks and pinnacles of the churches. At Master Timewell's court-yard I sprang from my saddle, but Reuben, attracted by the peace and beauty of the scene, rode onward, with the intention of going as far as the town-gate.

I was still at work upon my girth-buckles, undoing my harness, when of a sudden there came from the street a shouting and a rushing, with the clinking of blades, and my comrade's voice calling upon me for help. Drawing my sword, I ran out. Some little way down there was a clear space, white with the moonshine, in the centre of which I caught a glimpse of the sturdy figure of my friend, springing about with an activity for which I had never given him credit, and exchanging sword-thrusts with three or four men who were pressing him closely. On the ground there lay a dark figure, and behind the struggling group Reuben's mare reared and plunged in sympathy with her master's peril. As I rushed down, shouting and waving my sword, the assailants took flight down a side street, save one, a tall, sinewy swordsman, who rushed in upon Reuben, stabbing furiously at him, and cursing him the while for a spoil-sport. To my horror I saw, as I ran, the fellow's blade slip inside my friend's guard, who threw up his arms and fell prostrate, while the other, with a final thrust, dashed off down one of the narrow winding lanes which lead from East Street to the banks of the Tone.

"For Heaven's sake, where are you hurt?" I cried, throwing myself upon my knees beside his prostrate body. "Where is your injury, Reuben?"

"In the wind, mostly," quoth he, blowing like a smithy

SOME LITTLE WAY DOWN WAS A CLEAR SPACE, WHITE WITH MOONSHINE

bellows. "Likewise on the back of my pate. Give me your hand, I pray."

"And are you indeed scathless?" I cried, with a great lightening of the heart as I helped him to his feet. "I thought that the villain had stabbed you."

"As well stab a Warsash crab with a bodkin," said he. "Thanks to good Sir Jacob Clancing, once of Snellaby Hall, and now of Salisbury Plain, their rapiers did no more than scratch my plate of proof. But how is it with the maid?"

"The maid?" said I.

"Aye, it was to save her that I drew. She was beset by these night-walkers. See, she rises! They threw her down when I set upon them."

"How is it with you, mistress?" I asked; for the prostrate figure had arisen and taken the form of a woman, young and graceful to all appearance, with her face muffled in a mantle. "I trust that you have met with no hurt."

"None, sir," she answered, in a low sweet voice; "but that I have escaped is due to the ready valor of your friend and the guiding wisdom of Him who confutes the plots of the wicked. Doubtless a true man would have rendered this help to any damsel in distress, and yet it may add to your satisfaction to know that she whom you have served is no stranger to you." With these words she dropped her mantle and turned her face towards us in the moonlight.

"Good lack, it is Mistress Timewell!" I cried in amazement.

"Let us homeward," she said, in firm, quick tones. "The neighbors are alarmed, and there will be a rabble collected anon. Let us escape from the babblement."

Windows had indeed begun to clatter up in every direction, and loud voices to demand what was amiss. Far away down the street we could see the glint of lanterns swinging to and fro as the watch hurried thitherward. We slipped along in the shadow, however, and found ourselves safe within the mayor's court-yard without let or hinderance.

"I trust, sir, that you have really met with no hurt," said the maiden to my companion.

Reuben had said not a word since she had uncovered her face, and bore the face of a man who finds himself in some pleasant dream, and is vexed only by the fear lest he wake up from it. "Nay, I am not hurt," he answered; "but I would that you could tell us who these roving blades may be, and where they may be found."

"Nay, nay," said she, with uplifted finger, "you shall not follow the matter further. As to the men, I cannot say with certainty who they may have been. I had gone forth to visit Dame Clatworthy, who hath the tertian ague, and they did beset me on my return. Perchance they are some who are not of my grandfather's way of thinking in affairs of state, and who struck at him through me. But ye have both been so kind that ye will not refuse me one other favor which I shall ask ye?"

We protested that we could not, with our hands upon our sword-hilts.

"Nay, keep them for the Lord's quarrel," said she, smiling at the action. "All that I ask is that ye will say nothing of this matter to my grandsire. He is choleric, and a little matter doth set him in a flame, so old as he is. I would not have his mind turned from the public needs to a private trifle of this sort. Have I your promises?"

"Mine," said I, bowing.

"And mine," said Lockarby.

"Thanks, good friends. Alack! I have dropped my gauntlet in the street. But it is of no import. I thank God that no harm has come to any one. My thanks once more, and may pleasant dreams await ye." She sprang up the steps and was gone in an instant.

Reuben and I unharnessed our horses and saw them cared

for in silence. We then entered the house and ascended to our chambers, still without a word. Outside his room door my friend paused.

"I have heard that long man's voice before, Micah," said he.

"And so have I," I answered. "The old man must beware of his 'prentices. I have half a mind to go back for the little maiden's gauntlet."

A merry twinkle shot through the cloud which had gathered on Reuben's brow. He opened his left hand, and showed me the doeskin glove crumpled up in his palm.

"I would not barter it for all the gold in her grandsire's coffers," said he, with a sudden outflame; and then half laughing, half blushing at his own heat, he whisked in and left me to my thoughts.

And so I learned for the first time that my good comrade had been struck by the little god's arrows. Heaven only knows what match it was that had set the tow alight. I can but say that from that day on my comrade was sad and cloudy one hour, gay and blithesome the next. His even flow of good spirits had deserted him, and he became as dismal as a moulting chicken, which has ever seemed to me to be one of the strangest outcomes of what poets have called the joyous state of love.

On the night of Wednesday, June 17th, we learned that the king, as Monmouth was called throughout the west, was lying less than ten miles off with his forces, and that he would make his entry into the loyal town of Taunton the next morning. Every effort was made, as ye may well guess, to give him a welcome which should be worthy of the most Whiggish and Protestant town in England. Late into the night there was planing and hammering, working and devising, until when the sun rose upon Thursday, June 18th, it shone on as brave a show of bunting and evergreen as ever graced a town. Taunton had changed as by magic from a city into a flower-garden. Master Stephen Timewell had busied himself in these preparations, but he had borne in mind at the same time that the most welcome sight which he could present to Monmouth's eyes was the large body of armed men who were prepared to follow his fortunes. There were sixteen hundred in the town, two hundred of which were horse, mostly well armed and equipped. These were disposed in such a way that the king should pass them in his progress. The townsmen lined the market-place three deep from the Castle gate to the entrance to the High Street. When all were in their places, and the burghers and their wives had arrayed themselves in their holiday gear, with gladsome faces and baskets of new-cut flowers, all was ready for the royal visitor's reception.

"My orders are," said Saxon, riding up to us as we sat our horses beside our companions, "that I and my captains should fall in with the king's escort as he passes, and so accompany him to the market-place. Your men shall present arms, and shall then stand their ground until we return."

We all three drew our swords and saluted.

"If ye will come with me, gentlemen, and take position to the right of the gate here," said he, "I may be able to tell ye something of these folks as they pass. Thirty years of war in many climes should give me the master craftsman's right to expound to his apprentices."

We all very gladly followed his advice, and passed out through the gate, which was now nothing more than a broad gap among the mounds which marked the lines of the old walls. "There is no sign of them yet," I remarked, as we pulled up upon a convenient hillock. "I suppose that they must come by this road which winds through the valley before us."

"There are two sorts of bad general," quoth Saxon, "the man who is too fast and the man who is too slow. His majesty's advisers will never be accused of the former failing, whatever other mistakes they may fall into. But mark ye the folk upon yonder tower! They are waving their kerchiefs as though something were visible to them."

"I can see nothing," I answered, shading my eyes and gazing down the tree-sprinkled valley which rose slowly in green uplands to the grassy Blackdown hills.

"Those on the house-tops are waving and pointing," said Reuben. "Methinks I can myself see the flash of steel among yonder woods."

"There it is," cried Saxon, extending his gauntleted hand, "on the western bank of the Tone, hard by the wooden bridge. Follow my finger, Clarke, and see if you cannot distinguish it."

"Yes, truly," I exclaimed, "I see a bright shimmer coming and going. And there to the left, where the road curves over the hill, mark you that dense mass of men? Ha! the head of the column begins to emerge from the trees."

As we gazed, the van of the army began to roll out from the cover of the trees and to darken the white, dusty roads. The long line slowly extended itself, writhing out of the forest-land like a dark snake with sparkling scales, until the whole rebel army—horse, foot, and ordnance—were visible beneath us. The gleam of the weapons, the waving of numerous banners, the plumes of the leaders, and the deep columns of marching men, made up a picture which stirred the very hearts of the citizens, who, from the house-tops and from the ruinous summit of the dismantled walls, were enabled to gaze down upon the champions of their faith. Of all the ties that unite men in this world, that of a common danger is the strongest.

It all appeared to be most warlike and most imposing to my inexperienced eyes, and I thought as I looked at the long array that our cause was as good as won. To my surprise, however, Saxon pished and pshawed under his breath, until at last, unable to contain his impatience, he broke out in hot discontent.

"Do but look at that vanguard as they breast the slope," he cried. "Where is the advance party, or Vorreiter, as the Germans call them? Where, too, is the space which should be left between the fore-guard and the main battle? By the sword of Scanderbeg, they remind me more of a drove of pilgrims, as I have seen them approaching the shrine of St. Arnold of Neuerstadt with their banners and streamers. There in the centre, amid that cavalcade of cavaliers, rides our new monarch, doubtless. Pity he hath not a man by him who can put this swarm of peasants into something like campaign order."

"Good sport, colonel," said the baronet, with a touch of color in his white cheeks. "I warrant that you did keep your Pandours on the trot."

"Aye, the rogues had to work or hang—one or t'other. But methinks our friends here are scarce as numerous as reported. I reckon them to be a thousand horse, and mayhap five thousand two hundred foot. I have been thought a good tallyman on such occasions. With fifteen hundred in the town that would bring us to close on eight thousand men, which is no great force to invade a kingdom and dispute a crown."

"If the west can give eight thousand, how many can all the counties of England afford?" I asked. "Is not that the fairer way to look at it?"

"Monmouth's popularity lies mostly in the west," Saxon answered. "It was the memory of that which prompted him to raise his standard in these counties."

"His standards, rather," quoth Reuben. "Why, it looks as though they had hung their linen up to dry all down the line."

"True! They have more ensigns than ever I saw with so small a force," Saxon answered, rising in his stirrups. "One or two are blue, and the rest, as far as I can see for the sun shining upon them, are white, with some motto or device."

While we had been conversing the body of horse which formed the vanguard of the Protestant army had approached within a quarter of a mile or less of the town, when a loud, clear bugle-call brought them to a halt. In each successive regiment or squadron the signal was repeated, so that the sound passed swiftly down the long army array until it died away in the distance. As the coil of men formed up upon the white road,

with just a tremulous shifting motion along the curved and
undulating line, its likeness to a giant serpent occurred again
to my mind.

"I could fancy it a great boa," I remarked, "which was drawing its coils round the town."

"A rattlesnake, rather," said Reuben, pointing to the guns
in the rear. "It keeps all its noise in its tail."

"Here comes its head, if I mistake not," quoth Saxon. "It
were best, perhaps, that we stand at the side of the gate."

As he spoke a group of gayly-dressed cavaliers broke away
from the main body and rode straight for the town. Their
leader was a tall, slim, elegant young man, who sat his horse
with the grace of a skilled rider, and who was remarkable among
those around him for the gallantry of his bearing and the richness of his trappings. As he galloped towards the gate a roar
of welcome burst from the assembled multitude, which was taken
up and prolonged by the crowds behind, who, though unable
to see what was going forward, gathered from the shouting
that the king was approaching.

CHAPTER TWENTY

OF THE MUSTER OF THE MEN OF THE WEST

MONMOUTH was at that time in his thirty-sixth year, and was remarkable for those superficial graces which please the multitude and fit a man to lead in a popular cause. He was young, well spoken, witty, and skilled in all martial and manly exercises. As he reined up his beautiful black horse at the gate of the city, and raised his plumed montero cap to the shouting crowd, the grace and dignity of his bearing were such as might befit the knight-errant in a romance who is fighting at long odds for a crown which a tyrant has filched from him.

He was reckoned well-favored, but I cannot say that I found him so. His face was, I thought, too long and white for comeliness, yet his features were high and noble, with well-marked nose and clear, searching eyes. In his mouth might perchance be noticed some trace of that weakness which marred his character, though the expression was sweet and amiable. He wore a dark-purple roquelaure riding-jacket, a velvet suit of a lighter shade than the jacket, a pair of high yellow Cordovan boots. Again and again he raised his cap and bent to the saddle-bow in response to the storm of cheering. "A Monmouth! A Monmouth!" cried the people; "Hail to the Protestant chief!" "Long live the noble King Monmouth!" while from every window and roof and balcony fluttering kerchief or waving hat brightened the joyous scene. The rebel van caught fire at the sight and raised a great deep-chested shout, which was taken up again and again by the rest of the army, until the whole countryside was sonorous.

In the meanwhile the city elders, headed by our friend the mayor, advanced from the gate in all the dignity of silk and fur to pay homage to the king. Sinking upon one knee by Monmouth's stirrup, he kissed the hand which was graciously extended to him.

"Nay, good Master Mayor," said the king, in a clear, strong voice, "it is for my enemies to sink before me, and not for my friends. Your name, good Master Mayor, is Stephen Timewell, as I understand?"

"The same, your majesty."

"Too curt a name for so trusty a man," said the king, drawing his sword and touching him upon the shoulder with it. "I shall make it longer by three letters. Rise up, Sir Stephen, and may I find that there are many other knights in my dominions as loyal and as stout."

Amid the huzzas which broke out afresh at this honor done to the town, the mayor withdrew with the councilmen to the left side of the gate, while Monmouth with his staff gathered upon the right. At a signal a trumpeter blew a fanfare, the drums struck up a point of war, and the insurgent army, with serried ranks and waving banners, resumed its advance upon the town. As it approached, Saxon pointed out to us the various leaders and men of note who surrounded the king, giving us their names and some few words as to their characters.

While our companion was talking, the whole Protestant army had been streaming towards the town, and the head of the fore-guard was abreast with the gateway. Four troops of horse led the way, badly equipped and mounted, with ropes instead of bridles, and in some cases squares of sacking in place of saddles. These horse-soldiers were made up of yeomen's and farmers' sons, unused to discipline, and having a high regard for themselves as volunteers, which caused them to cavil and argue over every order. For this cause, though not wanting in natural courage, they did little service during the war, and were a hinderance rather than a help to the army.

Behind the horse came the foot, walking six abreast, divided into companies of varying size, each company bearing a banner which gave the name of the town or village from which it had been raised. This manner of arranging the troops had been chosen because it had been found to be impossible to separate men who were akin and neighbors to each other. They would fight, they said, side by side, or they would not fight at all.

When the last soldier had passed through the Shutterngate, Monmouth and his leaders rode slowly in, the mayor walking by the king's charger. As we saluted, they all faced round to us, and I saw a quick flush of surprise and pleasure come over Monmouth's pale face as he noted our close lines and soldierly bearing.

"By my faith! gentlemen," he said, glancing round at his staff, "our worthy friend, the mayor, must have inherited Cadmus's dragon teeth. Where raised ye this pretty crop, Sir Stephen? How came ye to bring them to such perfection too, even, I declare, to the hair-powder of the grenadiers?"

"I have fifteen hundred in the town," the old wool-worker answered, proudly—"though some are scarce as disciplined. These men come from Wiltshire, and the officers from Hampshire. As to their order, the credit is due not to me, but to the old soldier, Colonel Decimus Saxon, whom they have chosen as their commander, as well as to the captains who served under him."

"My thanks are due to you, colonel," said the king, turning to Saxon, who bowed, and sank the point of his sword to the earth, "and to you also, gentlemen. I shall not forget the warm loyalty which brought you from Hampshire in so short a time. Would that I could find the same virtue in higher places! But, Colonel Saxon, you have, I gather, seen much service abroad. What think you of the army which hath just passed before you?"

"If it please your majesty," Saxon answered, "it is like so much uncarded wool, which is rough enough in itself, and yet may in time come to be woven into a noble garment."

"Hem! There is not much leisure for the weaving," said Monmouth. "But they fight well. You should have seen them fall on at Axminster! We hope to see you, and to hear your views at the council-table. But how is this? Have I not seen this gentleman's face before?"

"It is the Honorable Sir Gervas Jerome, of the county of Surrey," quoth Saxon.

"Your majesty may have seen me at St. James's," said the baronet, raising his hat, "or in the balcony at Whitehall. I was much at court during the latter years of the late king."

"Yes, yes; I remember the name as well as the face," cried Monmouth. "You see, gentlemen," he continued, turning to his staff, "the courtiers begin to come in at last. Were you not the man who did fight Sir Thomas Killigrew behind Dunkirk House? I thought as much. Will you not attach yourself to my personal attendants?"

"If it please your majesty," Sir Gervas answered, "I am of opinion that I could do your royal cause better service at the head of my musketeers."

"So be it! so be it!" said King Monmouth. Setting spurs to his horse, he raised his hat in response to the cheers of the troops, and cantered down the High Street under a rain of flowers, which showered from roof and window upon him, his staff, and his escort. We had joined in his train, as commanded, so that we came in for our share of this merry cross-fire. One rose, as it fluttered down, was caught by Reuben, who, I observed, pressed it to his lips, and then pushed it inside his breast-plate. Glancing up, I caught sight of the smiling face of our host's daughter, peeping down at us from a casement.

"Well caught, Reuben," I whispered. "At trick-track or trap and ball you were ever our best player."

"Ah, Micah," said he, "I bless the day that ever I followed you to the wars. I would not change places with Monmouth this day."

"Has it gone so far, then?" I exclaimed. "Why, lad, I thought that you were but opening your trenches, and you speak as though you had carried the city."

"Perhaps I am over-hopeful," he cried, turning from hot to cold, as a man doth when he is in love. "God knows that I am little worthy of her, and yet ——"

"Set not your heart too firmly upon that which may prove to be beyond your reach," said I. "The old man is rich, and will look higher."

"I would he were poor!" sighed Reuben, with all the self-ishness of a lover. "If this war last, I may win myself some honor or title—who knows? Others have done it, and why not I?"

"Of our three from Havant," I remarked, "one is spurred onward by ambition and one by love. Now what am I to do, who care neither for high office nor for the face of a maid? What is to carry me into the fight?"

"Our motives come and go, but yours is ever with you," said Reuben. "Honor and duty are the two stars, Micah, by which you have ever steered your course."

"Faith, Mistress Ruth has taught you to make pretty

speeches," said I, "but methinks she ought to be here amid the beauty of Taunton."

As I spoke we were riding into the market-place, which was now crowded with our troops. Round the cross were grouped a score of maidens, clad in white muslin dresses with blue scarfs around their waists. As the king approached, these little maids, with much pretty nervousness, advanced to meet him and handed him a banner which they had worked for him, and also a dainty gold-clasped Bible. Monmouth handed the flag to one of his captains, but he raised the book above his head, exclaiming that he had come there to defend the truths contained within it; at which the cheering and acclamations broke forth with redoubled vigor. It had been expected that he might address the people from the cross, but he contented himself with waiting while the heralds proclaimed his titles to the crown, when he gave the word to disperse, and the troops marched off to the different centres where food had been provided for them.

CHAPTER TWENTY-ONE

OF MY HAND-GRIPES WITH THE
BRANDENBURGER

KING MONMOUTH had called a council meeting for the evening, and summoned Colonel Decimus Saxon to attend it, with whom I went, bearing with me the small package which Sir Jacob Clancing had given over to my keeping. On arriving at the castle, we found that the king had not yet come out from his chamber, but we were shown into the great hall to await him, a fine room with lofty windows and a noble ceiling of carved wood-work. Here were assembled the principal chiefs of the army, with many of the inferior commanders, town-officers, and others who had petitions to offer. Lord Grey, of Wark, stood silently by the window, looking out over the countryside with a gloomy face. A few of the more gayly dressed gathered round the empty fireplace, and listened to a tale from one of their number which appeared to be shrouded in many oaths, and which was greeted with shouts of laughter. In another corner was a numerous group of zealots, and a few plain, homely soldiers, who were neither sectaries nor courtiers, wandered up and down. To one of these, remarkable for his great size and breadth of shoulder, Saxon led me, and, touching him on the sleeve, he held out his hand as to an old friend.

"Mein Gott!" cried the German soldier of fortune, for it was the same man whom my companion had pointed out in the morning, "I thought it was you, Saxon, when I saw you by the gate, though you are even thinner than of old. How a man could suck up so much good Bavarian beer as you have done, and yet make so little flesh upon it, is more than I can verstehen. How have all things gone with you?"

"As of old," said Saxon. "More blows than thalers, and greater need of a surgeon than of a strong-box. When did I see you last, friend? Was it not at the onfall at Nürnberg, when I led the right and you the left wing of the heavy horse? But you remember the old hand-gripe which no man in the Palatinate could exchange with you? Here is my captain, Micah Clarke. Let him see how warm a North German welcome may be."

The Brandenburger showed his white teeth in a grin as he held out his broad brown hand to me. The instant that mine was enclosed in it, he suddenly bent his whole strength upon it, and squeezed my fingers together until the blood tingled in the nails, and the whole hand was limp and powerless.

"Donnerwetter!" he cried, laughing heartily at my start of pain and surprise. "It is a rough Prussian game, and the English lads have not much stomach for it."

"Truly, sir," said I, "it is the first time that I have seen the pastime, and I would fain practice it under so able a master."

"What, another!" he cried. "Why, you must be still pringling from the first. Nay, if you will, I shall not refuse you, though I fear it may weaken your hold upon your swordhilt."

He held out his hand as he spoke, and I grasped it firmly, thumb to thumb, keeping my elbow high, so as to bear all my force upon it. His own trick was, as I observed, to gain command of the other hand by a great output of strength at the onset. This I prevented by myself putting out all my power. For a minute or more we stood motionless, gazing into each other's faces. Then I saw a bead of sweat trickle down his forehead, and I knew that he was beaten. Slowly his gripe relaxed, and his hand grew limp and slack while my own tightened ever upon it, until he was forced, in a surly, muttering voice, to request that I should unhand him.

"Teufel und hexerei!" he cried, wiping away the blood which oozed from under his nails. "I might as well put my fingers in a rat-trap. You are the first man that ever yet exchanged fair hand-gripes with Anthony Buyse."

"We breed brawn in England as well as in Brandenburg," said Saxon, who was shaking with laughter over the German soldier's discomfiture. "Why, I have seen that lad pick up a full-size sergeant of dragoons and throw him into a cart as though he had been a clod of earth."

"Strong he is," grumbled Buyse, still wringing his injured hand, "strong as old Götz mit de iron gripe. But what good is strength alone in the handling of a weapon? It is not the force of a blow, but the way in which it is geschlagen that makes the effect. Your sword now is heavier than mine by the look of it and yet my blade would bite deeper. Eh? Is not that a more soldierly sport than kinderspiel, such as hand-grasping and the like?"

"He is a modest youth," said Saxon. "Yet I would match his stroke against yours."

"For what?" snarled the German.

"For as much wine as we can take at a sitting."

"No small amount, either," said Buyse; "a brace of gallons at the least. Well, be it so. Do you accept the contest?"

"I shall do what I may," I answered, "though I can scarce hope to strike as heavy a blow as so old and tried a soldier."

"Henker take your compliments," he cried, gruffly. "It was with sweet words that you did coax my fingers into that fool-catcher of yours. Now, here is my old head-piece of Spanish steel. It has, as you can see, one or two dints of blows, and a fresh one will not hurt it. I place it here upon this oaken stool, high enough to be within fair sword-sweep. Have at it, Junker, and let us see if you can leave your mark upon it!"

"Do you strike first, sir," said I, "since the challenge is yours."

"I must bruise my own head-piece to regain my soldierly credit," he grumbled. "Well, well, it has stood a cut or two in its day." Drawing his broadsword, he waved back the crowd who had gathered around us, while he swung the great weapon with tremendous force round his head, and brought it down with a full, clean sweep on to the smooth cap of steel. The head-piece sprang high into the air, and then clattered down upon the oaken floor with a long, deep line bitten into the solid metal.

"Well struck!" "A brave stroke!" cried the spectators. "It is proof steel thrice welded, and warranted to turn a sword-blade," one remarked, raising up the helmet to examine it, and then replacing it upon the stool.

"I have seen my father cut through proof steel with this very sword," said I, drawing the fifty-year-old weapon. "He put rather more of his weight into it than you have done. I have heard him say that a good stroke should come from the back and loins rather than from the mere muscles of the arm."

"It is not a lecture we want, but a beispiel or example," sneered the German. "It is with your stroke that we have to do, and not with the teaching of your father."

"My stroke," said I, "is in accordance with his teaching;" and, whistling round the sword, I brought it down with all my might and strength upon the German's helmet. The good old Commonwealth blade shore through the plate of steel, cut the stool asunder, and buried its point two inches deep in the oaken floor. "It is but a trick," I explained. "I have practised it in the winter evenings at home."

"It is not a trick that I should care to have played upon me," said Lord Grey, amid a general murmur of applause and surprise. "Od's bud, man, you have lived two centuries too late. What would not your thews have been worth before gunpowder put all men upon a level!"

"Wunderbar!" growled Buyse, "wunderbar! I am past my prime, young sir, and may well resign the palm of strength to you. It was a right noble stroke. It hath cost me a runlet or two of canary, and a good old hemlet; but I grudge it not, for it was fairly done. I am thankful that my head was not darin. Saxon, here, used to show us some brave schwertspielerei, but he hath not the weight for such smashing blows as this."

"My eye is still true and my hand firm, though both are perhaps a trifle the worse for want of use," said Saxon, only too glad at the chance of drawing the eyes of the chiefs upon him. "At backsword, sword and dagger, sword and buckler, single falchion, and case of falchions mine old challenge still holds good against any comer, save only my brother Quartus, who plays as well as I do, but hath an extra half inch in reach which gives him the vantage."

"I studied sword-play under Signor Contarini of Paris," then said Lord Grey. "Who was your master?"

"I have studied, my lord, under Signor Stern Necessity of Europe," quoth Saxon. "For five-and-thirty years my life has depended from day to day upon being able to cover myself with this slip of steel. Here is a small trick which showeth some nicety of eye: to throw this ring to the ceiling and catch it upon the rapier point. It seems simple, perchance, and yet is only to be attained by some practice."

"Simple!" cried Wade the lawyer, a square-faced, bold-eyed man. "Why, the ring is but the girth of your little finger. A man might do it once by good-luck, but none could insure it."

"I will lay a guinea a thrust on it," said Saxon; and, tossing the little gold circlet up into the air, he flashed out his rapier and made a pass at it. The ring rasped down the steel blade and tinkled against the hilt, fairly empaled. By a sharp motion of the wrist he shot it up to the ceiling again, where it struck a carved rafter and altered its course; but again, with a quick step forward, he got beneath it and received it on his sword-point. "Surely there is some cavalier present who is as apt at the trick as I am," he said, replacing the ring upon his finger.

"I think, colonel, that I could venture upon it," said a voice; and, looking round, we found that Monmouth had entered the room and was standing quietly on the outskirts of the throng, unperceived in the general interest which our contention had excited. "Nay, nay, gentlemen," he continued, pleasantly, as we uncovered and bowed with some little embarrassment; "how could my faithful followers be better employed than by breathing themselves in a little sword-play? I prithee lend me your rapier, colonel." He drew a diamond ring from his finger, and, spinning it up into the air, he transfixed it as deftly as Saxon had done. "I practised the trick at the Hague, where, by my faith, I had only too many hours to devote to such trifles. But how come these steel links and splinters of wood to be littered over the floor?"

"A son of Anak hath appaired amang us," said Ferguson, turning his face, all scarred and reddened with the king's evil, in my direction. "A Goliath o' Gath wha hath a stroke like untae a weaver's beam. Hath he no the smooth face o' a bairn and the thews o' Behemoth?"

"A shrewd blow indeed," King Monmouth remarked, picking up half the stool. "How is our champion named?"

"He is my captain, your majesty," Saxon answered, resheathing the sword which the king had handed to him; "Micah Clarke, a man of Hampshire birth."

"They breed a good old English stock in those parts," said Monmouth; "but how comes it that you are here, sir? I summoned this meeting for my own immediate household, and for the colonels of the regiments. If every captain is to be admitted into our councils, we must hold our meetings on the Castle Green, for no apartment could contain us."

"I ventured to come here, your majesty," I replied, "because on my way hither I received a commission which was that I should deliver this small but weighty package into your hands. I therefore thought it my duty to lose no time in fulfilling my errand."

"What is in it?" he asked.

"I know not," I answered.

Dr. Ferguson whispered a few words into the king's ear, who laughed and held out his hand for the packet.

"Tut! tut!" said he. "The days of the Borgias and the Medicis are over, doctor. Besides, the lad is no Italian conspirator, but hath honest blue eyes and flaxen hair as nature's certificate to his character. This is passing heavy—an ingot of lead, by the feel. Lend me your dagger, Colonel Holmes. It is stitched round with packthread. Ha! It is a bar of gold —solid virgin gold, by all that is wonderful. Take charge of it, Wade, and see that it is added to the common fund. This little piece of metal may furnish ten pikemen. What have we here? A letter and an enclosure. 'To James, Duke of Monmouth'—hum! It was written before we assumed our royal state. 'Sir Jacob Clancing, late of Snellaby Hall, sends greeting and a pledge of affection. Carry out the good work. A hundred more such ingots await you when you have crossed Salisbury Plain.' Bravely promised, Sir Jacob! I would that you had sent them. Well, gentlemen, ye see how support and tokens of goodwill come pouring in upon us. Is not the tide upon the turn? Can the usurper hope to hold his own? Will his men stand by him? Within a month or less I shall see ye all gathered round me at Westminster, and no duty will then be so pleasing to me as to see that ye are all, from the highest to the lowest, rewarded for your loyalty to your monarch in this the hour of his darkness and his danger."

A murmur of thanks rose up from the courtiers at this gracious speech, but the German plucked at Saxon's sleeve and whispered, "He hath his warm fit upon him. You shall see him cold anon."

"Fifteen hundred men have joined me here where I did but expect a thousand at the most," the king continued. "If we had high hopes when we landed at Lyme Cobb with eighty at our back, what should we think now when we find ourselves in the chief city of Somerset with eight thousand brave men around us? 'Tis but one other affair like that at Axminster, and my uncle's power will go down like a house of cards. But gather round the table, gentlemen, and we shall discuss matters in due form."

"There is yet a scrap of paper which you have not read, sire," said Wade, picking up a little slip which had been enclosed in the note.

"It is a rhyming catch or the posy of a ring," said Monmouth, glancing at it. "What are we to make of this?

> " 'When thy star is in trine,
> Between darkness and shine,
> Duke of Monmouth, Duke of Monmouth,
> Beware of the Rhine!'

Thy star in trine! What tomfoolery is this?"

"If it please your majesty," said I, "I have reason to believe that the man who sent you this message is one of those who are deeply skilled in the arts of divination, and who pretend from the motions of the celestial bodies to foretell the fates of men."

"This gentleman is right, sir," remarked Lord Grey. " 'Thy star in trine' is an astrological term, which signifieth when your natal planet shall be in a certain quarter of the heavens."

"Gentlemen, if this be indeed a prophecy," said the king, "it should, methinks, bode well for our enterprise. It is true that I am warned against the Rhine, but there is little prospect of our fighting this quarrel upon its banks."

"Worse luck!" murmured the German, under his breath.

"We may, therefore, thank this Sir Jacob and his giant messenger for his forecast as well as for his gold. But here comes the worthy Mayor of Taunton, the oldest of our councillors and the youngest of our knights. Captain Clarke, I desire you to stand at the inside of the door and to prevent intrusion. What passes among us will, I am well convinced, be safe in your keeping."

I bowed and took up my post as ordered, while the councilmen and commanders gathered round the great oaken table which ran down the centre of the hall. Monmouth paced with quick, uneasy steps up and down the farther end of the room until all were seated, when he turned towards them and addressed them.

"You will have surmised, gentlemen," he said, "that I have called you together to-day that I might have the benefit of your collective wisdom in determining what our next steps should be. We have now marched some forty miles into our kingdom, and we have met wherever we have gone with the warm welcome which we expected. Close upon eight thousand men follow our standards, and as many more have been turned away for want of arms. We have twice met the enemy, with the effect that we have armed ourselves with their muskets and field-pieces. From first to last there hath been nothing which has not prospered with us. We must look to it that the future be as successful as the past. To insure this I have called ye together, and I now ask ye to give me your opinions of our situation, leaving me after I have listened to your views to form our plan of action. There are statesmen among ye, and there are soldiers among ye, and there are godly men among ye who may chance to get a flash of light when statesman and soldier are in the dark. Speak fearlessly, then, and let me know what you have in your minds."

From my central post by the door I could see the lines of faces on either side of the board—the solemn, close-shaven Puritans, sunburnt soldiers, and white-wigged, mustachioed courtiers. My eyes rested particularly upon Ferguson's scorbutic features, Saxon's hard, aquiline profile, the German's burly face, and the peaky, thoughtful countenance of the Lord of Wark.

"If naebody else will gie an opeenion," cried the fanatical doctor, "I'll een speak mysel' as led by the inward voice. Have we no heard that Argyle is cutten off? And why was he cutten off? Because he hadna due faith in the workings o' the Almighty, and must needs reject the help o' the children o' light in favor o' the barelegged spawn o' Prelacy, wha are half pagan, half Popish. Why did he no gird up his loins and march straight onward wi' the banner o' light, instead o' dallying here and biding there like a half-hairted Didymus? And the same or waur will fa' upon us if we dinna march on intae the land, and plant our ensigns afore the wicked toun o' London—the toun where the Lord's wark is tae be done, and the tares tae be separated frae the wheat and piled up for the burning."

"Your advice, in short, is that we march on?" said Monmouth.

A hum of assent and approval rose up from the more Puritan members of the council at this expression of opinion, while the courtiers glanced at each other and curled their lips in derision. Monmouth took two or three turns, and then called for another opinion.

"You, Lord Grey," he said, "are a soldier and a man of experience. What is your advice? Should we halt here or push forward towards London?"

"To advance to the east would, in my humble judgment, be fatal to us," Grey answered, speaking slowly, with the manner of a man who has thought long and deeply before delivering an opinion. "James Stuart is strong in horse, and we have none. We can hold our own among hedge-rows or in broken country, but what chance could we have in the middle of Salisbury Plain? Unless, therefore, we hear of some great outbreak elsewhere, or of some general movement in London in our favor, we would do best to hold our ground and wait an attack."

"You argue shrewdly and well, my Lord Grey," said the king. "But how long are we to wait for this outbreak which never comes, and for this support which is ever promised and never provided? We have now been seven long days in England, and during that time of all the House of Commons no single man hath come over to us, and of the lords none save my Lord Grey, who was himself an exile. Not a man hath moved save only these good peasants. I have been deluded, ensnared, trapped—trapped by vile agents who have led me into the shambles." He paced up and down, wringing his hands and biting his lips, with despair stamped upon his face. I observed that Buyse smiled, and whispered something to Saxon —a hint, I suppose, that this was the cold fit of which he spoke.

"Tell me, Colonel Buyse," said the king, mastering his emotion by a strong effort, "do you, as a soldier, agree with my Lord Grey?"

"Ask Saxon, your majesty," the German answered. "My opinion in a Raths-Versammlung is, I have observed, ever the same as his."

"Then we turn to you, Colonel Saxon," said Monmouth. "We have in this council a party who are in favor of an advance and a party who wish to stand their ground. Their weight and numbers are, methinks, nearly equal. If you had the casting vote, how would you decide?" All eyes were bent upon our leader, for his martial bearing and the respect shown to him by the veteran Buyse made it likely that his opinion might really turn the scale. He sat for a few moments in silence, with his hands before his face.

"I will give my opinion, your majesty," he said at last. "Feversham and Churchill are making for Salisbury with three thousand foot, and they have pushed on eight hundred of the Blue Guards and two or three dragoon regiments. We should, therefore, as Lord Grey says, have to fight on Salisbury Plain, and our foot, armed with a medley of weapons, could scarce make head against their horse. On the other hand, sire, it appears to me that to remain here is equally impossible. Your majesty's friends throughout England would lose all heart if the army lay motionless and struck no blow. We cannot hope to end this business until we get to London. London, then, must be our goal. But there are many ways of reaching it. You have, sire, as I have heard, many friends at Bristol and in the Midlands. If I might advise, I should say let us march round in that direction. Every day that passes will serve to swell your forces and improve your troops, while all will feel something is a-stirring. If all goes well with us, we could make our way to

London through Gloucestershire and Worcestershire. In the meantime I might suggest that a day of fast and humiliation be called, to bring down a blessing on the cause."

This address, skilfully compounded of worldly wisdom and of spiritual zeal, won the applause of the whole council, and especially that of King Monmouth, whose melancholy vanished as if by magic.

"By my faith, colonel," said he, "you make it all as clear as day. Of course, if we make ourselves strong in the west, and my uncle is threatened with disaffection elsewhere, he will have no chance to hold out against us. Should he wish to fight us upon our own ground, he must needs drain his troops from north, south, and east, which is not to be thought of. We may very well march to London by way of Bristol."

"I think that the advice is good," Lord Grey observed, "but I should like to ask Colonel Saxon what warrant he hath for saying that Churchill and Feversham are on their way, with three thousand regular foot and several regiments of horse."

"The word of an officer of the Blues with whom I conversed at Salisbury," Saxon answered. "He confided in me, believing me to be one of the Duke of Beaufort's household. As to the horse, one party pursued us on Salisbury Plain with blood-hounds, and another attacked us not twenty miles from here and lost a score of troopers and a cornet."

"We heard something of the brush," said the king. "It was bravely done. But if these men are so close, we have no great time for preparation."

"Their foot cannot be here before a week," said the mayor. "By that time we might be behind the walls of Bristol."

"There is one point which might be urged," observed Wade, the lawyer. "We have, as your majesty most truly says, met with heavy discouragement in the fact that no noblemen and few commoners of repute have declared for us. The reason is, I opine, that each doth wait for his neighbor to make a move.

Should one or two come over, the others would soon follow. How, then, are we to bring a duke or two to our standards?"

"There's the question, Master Wade," said Monmouth, shaking his head despondently.

"I think that it might be done," continued the Whig lawyer. "Mere proclamations addressed to the commonalty will not catch these goldfish. They are not to be angled for with a naked hook. I should recommend that some form of summons or writ be served upon each of them, calling upon them to appear in our camp within a certain date under pain of high-treason."

"There spake the legal mind," quoth King Monmouth, with a laugh. "But you have omitted to tell us how the said writ or summons is to be conveyed to these same delinquents."

"There is the Duke of Beaufort," continued Wade, disregarding the king's objection. "He is President of Wales, and he is, as your majesty knows, lieutenant of four English counties. His influence overshadows the whole west. He hath two hundred horses in his stables at Badminton, and a thousand men, as I have heard, sit down at his tables every day. Why should not a special effort be made to gain over such a one, the more so as we intend to march in his direction?"

"Henry, Duke of Beaufort, is unfortunately already in arms against his sovereign," said Monmouth, gloomily.

"He is, sire, but he may be induced to turn in your favor the weapon which he hath raised against you. He is a Protestant. He is said to be a Whig. Why should we not send a message to him? Flatter his pride. Appeal to his religion. Coax and threaten him. Who knows? He may have private grievances of which we know nothing, and may be ripe for such a move."

"Your counsel is good, Wade," said Lord Grey, "but methinks his majesty hath asked a pertinent question. Your messenger would, I fear, find himself swinging upon one of the Badminton oaks if the duke desired to show his loyalty to James

Stuart. Where are we to find a man who is wary enough and bold enough for such a mission, without risking one of our leaders, who could be ill spared at such a time?"

"It is true," said the king. "It were better not to venture it at all than to do it in a clumsy and halting fashion. Beaufort would think that it was a plot not to gain him over, but to throw discredit upon him. But what means our giant at the door by signing to us?"

"If it please your majesty," I asked, "have I permission to speak?"

"We would fain hear you, captain," he answered, graciously. "If your understanding is in any degree corresponding to your strength, your opinion should be of weight."

"Then, your majesty," said I, "I would offer myself as a fitting messenger in this matter. My father bid me spare neither life nor limb in this quarrel, and if this honorable council thinks that the duke may be gained over, I am ready to guarantee that the message shall be conveyed to him if man and horse can do it."

"I'll warrant that no better herald could be found," cried Saxon. "The lad hath a cool head and a stanch heart."

"Then, young sir, we shall accept your royal and gallant offer," said Monmouth. "Are ye all agreed, gentlemen, upon the point?"

A murmur of assent rose from the company.

"You shall draw up the paper, Wade. Offer him money, a seniority among the dukes, the perpetual Presidentship of Wales —what you will, if you can but shake him. If not, sequestration, exile, and everlasting infamy. And hark ye, you can enclose a copy of the papers drawn up by Van Brunow, which prove the marriage of my mother, together with the attestations of the witnesses. Have them ready by tomorrow at daybreak, when the messenger may start."

"They shall be ready, your majesty," said Wade.

"In that case, gentlemen," continued King Monmouth, "I may now dismiss ye to your posts. Should anything fresh arise

I shall summon ye again, that I may profit by your wisdom. Here we shall stay, if Sir Stephen Timewell will have us, until the men are refreshed and the recruits enrolled. We shall then make our way Bristolward, and see what luck awaits us in the North. If Beaufort comes over, all will be well. Farewell, my kind friends. I need not tell ye to be diligent and faithful."

The council rose at the king's salutation, and bowing to him, they began to file out of the castle hall. Several of the members clustered round me with hints for my journey or suggestions as to my conduct.

"He is a proud, forward man," said one. "Speak humbly to him, or he will never hearken to your message, but will order you to be scourged out of his presence."

"Nay, nay," cried another. "He is hot, but he loves a man that is a man. Speak boldly and honestly to him, and he is more like to listen to reason."

"Leave him alone," cried Saxon. "The lad hath as much sense as any of ye. He will see which way the cat jumps. Come, friend, let us make our way back to our men."

"I am sorry indeed to lose you," he said, as we threaded our way through the throng of peasants and soldiers upon the Castle Green. "Your company will miss you sorely. Lockarby must see to the two. If all goes well you should be back in three or four days. I need not tell you that there is a real danger. Have you any message to leave?"

"None, save my love to my mother," said I.

"It is well. Should you fall in any unfair way, I shall not forget his grace of Beaufort, and the next of his gentlemen who comes in my way shall hang as high as Haman. And now you had best make for your chamber and have as good a slumber as you may, since to-morrow at cock-crow begins your new mission."

CHAPTER TWENTY-TWO

OF THE NEWS FROM HAVANT

HAVING given my orders that Covenant should be saddled and bridled by daybreak, I had gone to my room and was preparing for a long night's rest, when Sir Gervas, who slept in the same apartment, came dancing in with a bundle of papers waving over his head.

"Three guesses, Clarke!" he cried. "What would you most desire?"

"Letters from Havant," said I, eagerly.

"Right," he answered, throwing them into my lap. "Three of them, and not a woman's hand among them. Sink me, if I can understand what you have been doing all your life.

> " 'How can youthful heart resign
> Lovely woman, sparkling wine?'

But you are so lost in your news that you have not observed my transformation."

"Why, where did you get these?" I asked in astonishment, for he was attired in a delicate plum-colored suit with gold buttons and trimmings, set off by silken hosen and Spanish leather shoes with roses on the instep. "But how came these things?"

"Some horsemen have come in from Petersfield, bearing them with them. As to my little box, it chanced to find its way, however, to the Bruton inn, and the good woman there, whom I had conciliated, found means to send it after me. I have few fixed principles, I fear, but two there are which I can say from my heart that I never transgress: I always carry a corkscrew, and I never forget to kiss the landlady."

"From what I have seen of you," said I, laughing, "I could be warranty that those two duties are ever fulfilled."

"I have letters, too," said he, sitting on the side of the bed and turning over a sheaf of papers. " 'Your broken-hearted Araminta.' Hum! The wench cannot know that I am ruined or her heart would speedily be restored. How now? From Mrs. Butterworth! No money for three weeks! Bailiffs in the house! Now curse me if this is not too bad!"

"What is the matter?" I asked, glancing up from my own letters. The baronet's pale face had taken a tinge of red, and he was striding furiously up and down the bedroom with a letter crumpled up in his hand.

"It is a burning shame, Clarke," he cried. "Hang it, she shall have my watch. It is by Tompion, of the sign of the Three Crowns in Paul's Yard, and cost a hundred when new. It should keep her for a few months. Mortimer shall measure swords with me for this. I shall write villain upon him with my rapier's point."

"I have never seen you ruffled before," said I.

"No," he answered, laughing. "Many have lived with me for years and would give me a certificate for temper. But this is too much. Sir Edward Mortimer is my mother's younger brother, Clarke, but he is not many years older than myself. So when I found that all was up with me I received from Mortimer an advance, which was sufficient to take me, according to my wish, over to Virginia, together with a horse and a personal outfit. This Mistress Butterworth is mine old wet-nurse, and it hath been the custom of the family to provide for her. My only request to Mortimer, therefore, made on the score of old friendship, was that he should continue this pittance, I promising that should I prosper I would return whatever he should disburse. The mean-hearted villain wrung my hand and swore that it should be so. How vile a thing is human nature, Clarke! For the sake of this paltry sum he, a rich man, hath broken his pledge, and left this poor woman to starve. But he shall answer to me for it. He thinks that I am on the Atlantic. If I march back to London with these brave boys I shall disturb the tenor of his sainted existence. Meanwhile I shall trust to sundials, and off goes my watch to Mother Butterworth. But how of your own letters? You have been frowning and smiling like an April day."

"There is one from my father, with a few words attached from my mother," said I. "The second is from an old friend of mine, Zachariah Palmer, the village carpenter. The third is from Solomon Sprent, a retired seaman, for whom I have an affection and respect."

"You have a rare trio of newsmen. I would I knew your father, Clarke. He must, from what you say, be a stout bit of British oak. I spoke even now of your knowing little of the world, but indeed it may be that in your village you can see mankind without the varnish, and so come to learn more of the good of human nature. I would not be wealthy again, Micah! How goes the old lilt?

> " 'Our money shall never indite us
> Or drag us to Goldsmith Hall,
> No pirates or wrecks can affright us.
> We that have no estates
> Fear no plunder or rates,
> Nor care to lock gates.
> He that lies on the ground cannot fall!'

That last would make a good motto for an almshouse."

"You will have Sir Stephen up," said I, warningly, for he was carolling away at the pitch of his lungs.

"Never fear! He and his prentices were all at the broadsword exercise in the hall as I came by. It is worth something to see the old fellow stamp, and swing his sword, and cry 'Ha!' on the down-cut. Mistress Ruth and friend Lockarby are in the tapestried room, she spinning, and he reading aloud one of those entertaining volumes which she would have me read. Methinks she hath taken his conversion in hand, which may end in his converting her from a maid into a wife. And so you go to the Duke of Beaufort! Well, I would that I could travel with you, but Saxon will not hear of it, and my musketeers must be my first care. God send you safe back! Where is my jasmine powder and the patchbox? Read me your letters if there be aught in them of interest. I have been splitting a flask with our gallant colonel at his inn, and he hath told me enough of your home at Havant to make me wish to know more."

"I must to sleep," said I, laying aside my pipe. "I should be on the road by daybreak."

"Nay, I prithee, complete your kindness by letting me have a glimpse of your respected parent, the Roundhead."

" 'Tis but a few lines," I answered. "He was ever short of speech. But if they interest you, you shall hear them.

" 'I am sending this by a godly man, my dear son, to say that I trust that you are bearing yourself as becomes you. In all danger and difficulty trust not to yourself, but ask help from on high. If you are in authority, teach your men to sing psalms when they fall on, as is the good old custom. In action give point rather than edge. A thrust must beat a cut. Your mother and the others send their affection to you. Sir John Lawson hath been down here like a ravening wolf, but could find no proof against me. John Marchbank, of Bedhampton, is cast into prison. Truly Antichrist reigns in the land, but the kingdom of light is at hand. Strike lustily for truth and conscience.

" 'Your loving father,

" 'JOSEPH CLARK.

" 'Postscriptum' (from my mother)—'I trust that you will remember what I have said concerning your hosen and also the broad linen collars, which you will find in the bag. It is little over a week since you left, yet it seems a year. When cold or wet, take ten drops of Daffy's Elixir in a small glass of strong waters. Should your feet chafe, rub tallow on the inside of your boots. Commend me to Master Saxon and to Master Lockarby, if he be with you. His father was mad at his going, for he hath a great brewing going forward, and none to mind the mash-tub. Ruth hath baked a cake, but the oven hath played her false, and it is lumpy in the inside. A thousand kisses, dear heart, from your loving mother,

"'M. C.'"

"A right sensible couple," quoth Sir Gervas, who, having completed his toilet, had betaken him to his couch. "I now begin to understand your manufacture, Clarke. I see the threads that are used in the weaving of you. Your father looks to your spiritual wants. Your mother concerns herself with the material. Well, out with the light, for we should both be stirring at cock-crow. That is our religion at present."

"Early Christians," I suggested, and we both laughed as we settled down to sleep.

CHAPTER TWENTY-THREE

OF THE SNARE ON THE WESTERN ROAD

JUST after sunrise I was waked by one of the mayor's servants, who brought word that the Honorable Master Wade
was awaiting me down-stairs. Having dressed and descended, I
found him seated by the table in the sitting-room with papers
and wafer-box, sealing up the missive which I was to carry. He
was a small, worn, gray-faced man, very erect in his bearing and
sudden in his speech, with more of the soldier than of the lawyer
in his appearance.

"So," said he, pressing his seal above the fastening of the string, "I see that your horse is ready for you outside. You had best make your way round by Nether Stowey and the Bristol Channel, for we have heard that the enemy's horse guard the roads on the far side of Wells. Here is your packet."

I bowed, and placed it in the inside of my tunic.

"It is a written order, as suggested in the council. The duke's reply may be written, or it may be by word of mouth. In either case, guard it well. This packet contains also a copy of the depositions of the clergyman at the Hague, and of the other witnesses who saw Charles of England marry Lucy Walters, the mother of his majesty. Your mission is one of such importance that the whole success of our enterprise may turn upon it. See that you serve the paper upon Beaufort in person, and not through any intermediary, or it might not stand in a court of law."

I promised to do so if possible.

"I should advise you also," he continued, "to carry sword and pistol as a protection against the chance dangers of the road, but to discard your head-piece and steel-front as giving you too warlike an aspect for a peaceful messenger."

"I had already come to that resolve," said I.

"There is nothing more to be said, captain," said the lawyer, giving me his hand. "May all good-fortune go with you. Keep a still tongue and a quick ear. Watch keenly how all things go. Mark whose face is gloomy and whose content. The duke may be at Bristol, but you had best make for his seat at Badminton. Our sign of the day is Tewkesbury."

Thanking my instructor for his advice, I went out and mounted Covenant, who pawed and champed at his bit in his delight at getting started once more. Few of the townsmen were stirring, though here and there a night-bonneted head stared out at me through a casement. At the north gate a guard of half a company was stationed, who let me pass upon hearing the word. Once beyond the old walls, I found myself out on the countryside, with my face to the north and a clear road in front of me.

It was a blithesome morning. The sun was rising over the Brendon Hills, and heaven and earth were ruddy and golden. From the high ground to the north I looked back upon the sleeping town, with the broad edging of tents and wagons, which showed how suddenly its population had outgrown it. Beyond the town, and on either side of it, stretched a glorious view of the Somersetshire downs, rolling away to the distant sea, with town and hamlet, castle turret and church tower, wooded coombe and stretch of grainland—as fair a scene as the eye could wish to rest upon. As I wheeled my horse and sped upon my way I felt that this was a land worth fighting for, and that a man's life was a small thing if he could but aid, in however trifling a degree, in working out its freedom and its happiness. At a little village over the hill I fell in with an outpost of horse, the commander of which rode some distance with me and set me on my road to Nether Stowey.

My course ran along by the foot of the beautiful Quantock Hills, where heavy-wooded coombes are scattered over the broad heathery downs, deep with bracken and whortle-bushes. On either side of the track steep winding glens sloped downward, lined with yellow gorse, which blazed out from the deep-red soil like a flame from embers. Peat-colored streams splashed down these valleys and over the road, through which Covenant ploughed fetlock deep, and shied to see the broad-backed trout darting from between his fore-feet.

All day I rode through this beautiful country, meeting few folk, for I kept away from the main roads. It was not until evening that I at last came out upon the banks of the Bristol Channel, at a place called Shurton Bars, where the muddy Parret makes its way into the sea. At this point the channel is so broad that the Welsh mountains can scarcely be distinguished. The shore is flat and black and oozy, flecked over with white patches of sea-birds, but farther to the east there rises a line of

MY COURSE RAN ALONG THE FOOT OF THE BEAUTIFUL QUANTOCK HILLS,
WHERE HEAVY-WOODED COOMBES ARE SCATTERED OVER THE BROAD
HEATHERY DOWNS

hills, very wild and rugged, rising in places into steep precipices. As the night drew in, the country became bleaker and more deserted. An occasional light twinkling in the distance from some lonely hill-side cottage was the only sign of the presence of man. The rough track still skirted the sea, and, high as it was, the spray from the breakers drifted across it. The salt pringled on my lips, and the air was filled with the hoarse roar of the surge and the thin piping of curlews, who flitted past in the darkness like white, shadowy, sad-voiced creatures from some other world. The wind blew in short, quick, angry puffs from the westward, and far out on the black waters a single glimmer of light rising and falling, tossing up, and then sinking out of sight, showed how fierce a sea had risen in the channel.

Riding through the gloaming in this strange wild scenery, my mind naturally turned towards the past. I had just fallen into a dream in which I saw Reuben Lockarby crowned King of England by Mistress Ruth Timewell, while Decimus Saxon endeavored to shoot him with a bottle of Daffy's Elixir, when in an instant, without warning, I was dashed violently from my horse, and left lying half conscious on the stony track.

So stunned and shaken was I by the sudden fall that though I had a dim knowledge of shadowy figures bending over me, and of hoarse laughter sounding in my ears, I could not tell for a few minutes where I was nor what had befallen me. When at last I did make an attempt to recover my feet, I found that a loop of rope had been slipped round my arms and my legs so as to secure them. With a hard struggle I got one hand free, and dashed it in the face of one of the men who were holding me down; but the whole gang of a dozen or more set upon me at once, and while some thumped and kicked at me, others tied a fresh cord round my elbows, and deftly fastened it in such a way as to pinion me completely. Finding that in my weak and dazed state all efforts were of no avail, I lay sullen and watchful, taking no heed of the random blows which were still showered upon me. So dark was it that I could neither see the

faces of my attackers, nor form any guess as to who they might
be or how they had hurled me from my saddle. The champing
and stamping of a horse hard by showed me that Covenant was
a prisoner as well as his master.

"Dutch Pete's got as much as he can carry," said a rough,
harsh voice. "He lies on the track as limp as a conger."

As he spoke the edge of the moon peeped over a cliff and
threw a flood of cold clear light upon the scene. Looking up,
I saw that a strong rope had been tied across the road from
one tree trunk to another, about eight feet above the ground.
I made no attempt to move, however, but waited in silence to
find out who these men were into whose hands I had fallen. My
one fear was lest my letters should be taken away from me, and
my mission rendered of no avail. That in this, my first trust,
I should be disarmed without a blow, and lose the papers which
had been confided to me, was a chance which made me flush and
tingle with shame at the very thought.

The gang who had seized me were rough-bearded fellows in
fur caps and fustian jackets, with buff belts round their waists,
from which hung short straight whinyards. Their dark, sun-
dried faces, and their great boots, marked them as fishermen or
seamen, as might be guessed from their rude sailor speech. A
pair knelt on either side with their hands upon my arms, a third
stood behind with a cocked pistol pointed at my head, while the
others, seven or eight in number, were helping to his feet the
man whom I had struck, who was bleeding freely from a cut
over the eye.

"Take the horse up to Daddy Mycroft's," said a stout,
black-bearded man, who seemed to be their leader. "It is no
mere dragooner hack, but a comely, full-blooded brute which
will fetch sixty pieces at the least. Your share of that, Peter,
will buy salve and plaster for your cut."

"Ha, houndsfoot!" cried the Dutchman, shaking his fist at
me. "You would strike Peter, would you? You would draw
Peter's blood, would you? We shall see. Take that, you deyvil's

spawn, take that!" He ran at me, and kicked me as hard as he could with his heavy sea-boots.

Some of the gang laughed, but the man who had spoken before gave the Dutchman a shove that sent him whirling. "None of that," he said, sternly. "We'll have British fair play on British soil, and none of your cursed longshore tricks. I won't stand by and see an Englishman kicked, d'ye see, by a tub-bellied, round-starned, schnapps-swilling, chicken-hearted son of an Amsterdam lust-vrouw. Hang him, if the skipper likes. That's all above-board, but, by thunder, if it's a fight that you will have, touch that man again."

"All right, Dicon," said their leader, soothingly. "We all know that Pete's not a fighting man, but he's the best cooper on the coast; eh, Pete? But enough said! Up with the prisoner, and let us get him safely into the bilboes."

I was raised to my feet and half carried, half dragged along in the midst of the gang. My horse had already been led away in the opposite direction. Our course lay off the road, down a very rocky and rugged ravine which sloped away towards the sea. There seemed to be no trace of a path, and I could only stumble along over rocks and bushes as best I might in my fettered and crippled state. The blood, however, had dried over my wounds, and the cool sea-breeze playing upon my forehead refreshed me, and helped me to take a clearer view of my position.

It was plain from their talk that these men were smugglers. As such, they were not likely to have any great love for the government, or desire to uphold King James in any way. But I could not but wonder, as I was dragged along, what had led these men to lie in wait for me as they had done. The smugglers were a lawless and desperate body, but they did not, as a rule, descend to foot-paddery or robbery. Could it possibly be that I had been betrayed? I was still turning over these questions in my mind when we all came to a halt, and the captain blew a shrill note on a whistle which hung round his neck.

The place where we found ourselves was the darkest and most rugged spot in the whole wild gorge. On either side great cliffs shot up, which arched over our heads, with a fringe of ferns and bracken on either lip, so that the dark sky and the few twinkling stars were wellnigh hid. Great black rocks loomed vaguely out in the shadowy light, while in front a high tangle of what seemed to be brushwood barred our road. At a second whistle, however, a glint of light was seen through the branches, and the whole mass was swung to one side as though it moved upon a hinge. Beyond it a dark winding passage opened into the side of the hill, down which we went with our backs bowed, for the rock ceiling was of no great height. On every side of us sounded the throbbing of the sea.

Passing through the entrance, which must have been dug with great labor through the solid rock, we came out into a lofty and roomy cave, lit up by a fire at one end, and by several torches.

In this rock-girt space, which may have been sixty paces long and thirty across, there were gathered great piles of casks, kegs, and cases; muskets, cutlasses, staves, cudgels, and straw were littered about upon the floor. At one end a high wood fire blazed merrily, casting strange shadows along the walls, and sparkling like a thousand diamonds among the crystals on the roof. The smoke was carried away through a great cleft in the rocks. Seated on boxes, or stretched on the sand round the fire, there were seven or eight more of the band, who sprang to their feet and ran eagerly towards us as we entered.

"Have ye got him?" they cried. "Did he indeed come? Had he attendants?"

"He is here and he is alone," the captain answered. "Our hawser fetched him off his horse as neatly as ever a gull was netted by a cragsman. What have ye done in our absence, Silas?"

"We have the packs ready for carriage," said the man addressed, a sturdy, weather-beaten seaman of middle-age. "The silk and lace are down in these squares covered over with sacking. The one I have marked 'yarn' and the other 'jute'—a thousand of Mechlin to a hundred of the shiny. They will sling over a mule's back. Brandy, schnapps, Schiedam, and Hamburg Goldwasser are all set out in due order. The 'baccy is in the flat cases over by the Black Drop there. A plaguy job we had carrying it all out, but here it is ship-shape at last, and the lugger floats like a skimming-dish, with scarce ballast enough to stand up to a five-knot breeze."

"Any signs of the *Fairy Queen?*" asked the smuggler.

"None. Long John is down at the water's edge looking out for her flashlight. This wind should bring her up if she has rounded Combe-Martin Point. There was a sail about ten mile to the east-nor'-east at sundown. She might have been a bristol schooner, or she might have been a king's fly-boat."

"A king's crawl-boat," said Captain Murgatroyd, with a sneer. "We cannot hang the gauger until Venables brings up the *Fairy Queen,* for after all it was one of his hands that was snackled. Let him do his own dirty work."

"Tausend blitzen!" cried the ruffian Dutchman, "would it not be a kindly gruss to Captain Venables to chuck the gauger down the Black Drop ere he come? He may have such another job to do for us some day."

"Zounds, man, are you in command or am I?" said the leader, angrily. "Bring the prisoner forward to the fire! Now, hark ye, dog of a land-shark; you are as surely a dead man as though you were laid out with the tapers burning. See here"— he lifted a torch, and showed by its red light a great crack in the floor across the far end of the cave—"you can judge of the Black Drop's depth!" he said, raising an empty keg and tossing it over into the yawning gulf. For half a minute we stood silent before a dull distant clatter told that it had at last reached the bottom.

"It will carry him half-way to hell before the breath leaves him," said one.

"It's an easier death than the Devizes gallows!" cried a second.

"Nay, he shall have the gallows first!" a third shouted. "It is but his burial that we are arranging."

"He hath not opened his mouth since we took him," said the man who is called Dicon. "Is he a mute, then? Find your tongue, my fine fellow, and let us hear what your name is. It would have been well for you if you had been born dumb, so that you could not have sworn our comrade's life away."

"I have been waiting for a civil question after all this brawling and babbling," said I. "My name is Micah Clarke. Now, pray inform me who ye may be, and by what warrant ye stop peaceful travellers upon the public highway?"

"This is our warrant," Murgatroyd answered, touching the hilt of his cutlass. "As to who we are, ye know that well enough. Your name is not Clarke, but Westhouse, or Waterhouse, and you are the same cursed exciseman who snackled our poor comrade, Cooper Dick, and swore away his life at Ilchester."

"I swear that you are mistaken," I replied. "I have never in my life been in these parts before."

"Fine words! Fine words!" cried another smuggler. "Gauger or no, you must jump for it, since you know the secret of our cave."

"Your secret is safe with me," I answered. "But if you wish to murder me I shall meet my fate as a soldier should. I should have chosen to die on the field of battle, rather than to lie at the mercy of such a pack of water-rats in their burrow."

"My faith!" said Murgatroyd. "This is too tall talk for a gauger. He bears himself like a soldier, too. It is possible that in snaring the owl we have caught the falcon. Yet we had certain token that he would come this way, and on such another horse."

"Call up Long John," suggested the Dutchman. "I vould not give a plug of Trinidado for the Schelm's word. Long John was with Cooper Dick when he was taken."

"Aye," growled the mate Silas. "He got a wipe over the arm from the gauger's whinyard. He'll know his face, if any will."

"Call him, then," said Murgatroyd, and presently a long, loose-limbed seaman came up from the mouth of the cave, where he had been on watch. He wore a red kerchief round his forehead, and a blue jerkin, the sleeve of which he slowly rolled up as he came nigh.

"Where is Gauger Westhouse?" he cried. "He has left his mark on my arm. Rat me if the scar is healed yet. The sun is on our side of the wall now, gauger. But hullo, mates! who be this that ye have clapped into irons? This is not our man!"

"Not our man!" they cried, with a volley of curses.

"Why, this fellow would make two of the gauger, and leave enough over to fashion a magistrate's clerk. Ye may hang him to make sure, but still he's not the man."

"Yes, hang him!" said Dutch Pete. "Sapperment! is our cave to be the talk of all the country? Vere is the pretty *Maria* to go then, vid her silks and her satins, her kegs and her cases? Are we to risk our cave for the sake of this fellow? Besides, has he not schlagged my kopf—schlagged your cooper's kopf— as if he had hit me mit mine own mallet? Is that not vorth a hemp cravat?"

"Worth a jorum of rumbo," cried Dicon. "By your leave, captain, I would say that we are not a gang of padders and michers, but a crew of honest seamen, who harm none but those who harm us. Exciseman Westhouse hath slain Cooper Dick, and it is just that he should die for it; but as to taking this young soldier's life, I'd as soon think of scuttling the saucy *Maria,* or of mounting the Jolly Roger at her peak."

What answer would have been given to this speech I cannot tell, for at that moment a shrill whistle resounded outside the cave, and two smugglers appeared bearing between them the body of a man. It hung so limp that I thought at first that he might be dead, but when they threw him on the sand he moved, and at last sat up like one who is but half awake from a swoon. He was a square, dogged-faced fellow, with a long white scar down his cheek, and a close-fitting blue coat with brass buttons.

"It's Gauger Westhouse!" cried a chorus of voices.

"Yes, it is Gauger Westhouse," said the man, calmly, giving his neck a wriggle as though he were in pain. "I represent the king's law, and in its name I arrest ye all, and declare all the contraband goods which I see around me to be confiscate and forfeited, according to the second section of the first clause of the statute upon illegal dealing. If there are any honest men in this company, they will assist me in the execution of my duty." He staggered to his feet as he spoke, but his spirit was greater than his strength, and he sank back upon the sand amid a roar of laughter from the rough seamen.

"We found him lying on the road when we came from Daddy Mycroft's," said one of the new-comers, who were the same men who had led away my horse. "He must have passed just after you left, and the rope caught him under the chin and threw him a dozen paces. We saw the revenue button on his coat, so we brought him down. Body o' me, but he kicked and plunged for all that he was three-quarters stunned."

"Have ye slacked the hawser?" the captain asked.

"We cast one end loose and let it hang."

"'Tis well. We must keep him for Captain Venables. But now, as to our other prisoner: we must overhaul him and examine his papers, for so many craft are sailing under false colors that we must needs be careful. Hark ye, Mister Soldier! What brings you to these parts, and what king do you serve? for I hear there's a mutiny broke out, and two skippers claim equal rating in the old British ship."

"I am serving under King Monmouth," I answered, seeing that the proposed search must end in the finding of my papers.

"Under King Monmouth!" cried the smuggler. "Nay, friend, that rings somewhat false. The good king hath, I hear, too much need of his friends in the south to let an able soldier go wandering along the sea-coast like a Cornish wrecker in a sou'wester."

"I bear despatches," said I, "from the king's own hand to Henry Duke of Beaufort, at his castle of Badminton. Ye can find them in my inner pocket, but I pray ye not to break the seal, lest it bring discredit upon my mission."

"Sir," cried the gauger, raising himself upon his elbow, "I do hereby arrest you on the charge of being a traitor, a promoter of treason, a vagrant, and a masterless man within the meaning of the fourth statute of the Act. As an officer of the law I call upon you to submit to my warrant."

"Brace up his jaw with your scarf, Jim," said Murgatroyd. "When Venables comes he will soon find a way to check his gab. Yes," he continued, looking at the back of my papers, "it is marked, as you say, 'From James the Second of England, known lately as the Duke of Monmouth, to Henry Duke of Beaufort, President of Wales, by the hand of Captain Micah Clarke, of Saxon's regiment of Wiltshire foot.' Cast off the lashings, Dicon. So, captain, you are a free man once more, and I grieve that we should have unwittingly harmed you. We are good Lutherans to a man, and would rather speed you than hinder you on this mission."

"Could we not indeed help him on his way?" said the mate Silas. "For myself, I don't fear a wet jacket or a tarry hand for the cause, and I doubt not ye are all of my way of thinking. Now, with this breeze we could run up to Bristol and drop the captain by morning, which would save him from being snapped up by any land-sharks on the road."

"Aye, aye," cried Long John. "The king's horse are out beyond Weston, but he could give them the slip if he had the *Maria* under him."

"Well," said Murgatroyd, "we could get back by three long tacks. Venables will need a day or so to get his goods ashore.

If we are to sail back in company we shall have time on our hands. How would the plan suit you, captain?"

"My horse!" I objected.

"It need not stop us. I can rig up a handy horse-stall with my spare spars and the grating. The wind has died down. The lugger could be brought to Dead Man's Edge, and the horse led down to it. Run up to Daddy's, Jim; and you, Silas, see to the boat. Here is some cold junk and biscuit—seaman's fare, captain—and a glass o' the real Jamaica to wash it down, an thy stomach be not too dainty for rough living."

I seated myself on a barrel by the fire, and stretched my limbs, which were cramped and stiffened by their confinement, while one of the seamen bathed the cut on my head with a wet kerchief, and another laid out some food on a case in front of me. The rest of the gang had trooped away to the mouth of the cave to prepare the lugger, save only two or three who stood on guard round the ill-fated gauger. I was turning it over in my own mind whether aught could be done to help him, when Murgatroyd came over, and dipping a tin pannikin into the open rum-tub, drained it to the success of my mission.

"I shall send Silas Bolitho with you," said he, "while I bide here to meet Venables, who commands my consort. If there is aught that I can do to repay you for your ill-usage——"

"There is but one thing, captain," I broke in, eagerly. "It is as much, or more, for your own sake than mine that I ask it. Do not allow this unhappy man to be murdered."

Murgatroyd's face flushed with anger. "You are a plain speaker, Captain Clarke," said he. "This is no murder. It is justice. What harm do we here? There is not an old house-wife over the whole countryside who does not bless us. Where is she to buy her souchong or her strong waters except from us? We charge little, and force our goods on no one. We are peaceful traders. Yet this man and his fellows are ever yelping at our heels, like so many dog-fish on a cod-bank. We have been harried and chevied and shot at until we are driven into such dens as this. A month ago four of our men were bearing a keg up the hill-side to Farmer Black, who hath dealt with us these five years back. Of a sudden down came half a score of horse, led by this gauger, hacked and slashed by their broadswords, cut Long John's arm open, and took Cooper Dick prisoner. Dick was haled to Ilchester Jail, and hung up after the assizes like a stoat on a game-keeper's door. This night we had news that this very gauger was coming this way, little knowing that we should be on the lookout for him. Is it a wonder that we should lay a trap for him, and that, having caught him, we should give him the same justice as he gave our comrades?"

"He is but a servant," I argued. "He hath not made the law. It is his duty to enforce it. It is with the law itself that your quarrel is."

"You are right," said the smuggler, gloomily. "It is with Judge Moorcroft that we have our chief account to square. He may pass this road upon his circuit. Heaven send he does! But we shall hang the gauger too. He knows our cave now, and it would be madness to let him go."

I saw that it was useless to argue longer, so I contented myself with dropping my pocket-knife on the sand within reach of the prisoner, in the hope that it might prove to be of some service to him. His guards were laughing and joking together, and giving little heed to their charge, but the gauger was keen enough, for I saw his hand close over it.

I had walked and smoked for an hour or more when Silas the mate appeared, and said that the lugger was ready and the horse aboard. Bidding Murgatroyd farewell, I ventured a few more words in favor of the gauger, which were received with a frown and an angry shake of the head. A boat was drawn up on the sand, inside the cave, at the water's edge. Into this I stepped, as directed, with my sword and pistols, which had been given back to me, while the crew pushed her off and sprang in as she glided into deep water.

I could see by the dim light of the single torch which Mur-

gatroyd held upon the margin that the roof of the cave sloped
sheer down upon us as we sculled slowly out towards the entrance. So low did it come at last that there was only a space
of a few feet between it and the water, and we had to bend our
heads to avoid the rocks above us. The boatmen gave two
strong strokes, and we shot out from under the overhanging
ledge, and found ourselves in the open, with the stars shining
murkily above us, and the moon showing herself dimly and
cloudily through a gathering haze. Right in front of us was
a dark blur, which, as we pulled towards it, took the outline
of a large lugger rising and falling with the pulse of the sea.
Her tall thin spars and delicate net-work of cordage towered
above us as we glided under the counter, while the creaking
of blocks and rattle of ropes showed that she was all ready to
glide off upon her journey. Lightly and daintily she rode upon
the waters, like some giant sea-fowl, spreading one white pinion
after another in preparation for her flight. The boatmen ran
us alongside, and steadied the dingy while I climbed over the
bulwarks on to the deck.

She was a roomy vessel, very broad in the beam, with a graceful curve in her bows, and masts which were taller than any
that I had seen on such a boat in the Solent. In the midst of
this after-deck the mariners had built a strong stall, in which
my good steed was standing, with a bucketful of oats in front
of him. My old friend shoved his nose against my face as I
came aboard, and neighed his pleasure at finding his master
once more. We were still exchanging caresses when the grizzled
head of Silas Bolitho, the mate, popped out of the cabin hatchway.

"We are fairly on our way now, Captain Clarke," said he.
"The breeze has fallen away to nothing, as you can see, and
we may be some time in running down to our port. Are you
not aweary?"

"I am a little tired," I confessed. "My head is throbbing

from the crack I got when that hawser of yours dashed me from my saddle."

"An hour or two of sleep will make you as fresh as a Mother Carey's chicken," said the smuggler. "Your horse is well cared for, and you can leave him without fear. Yet no harm can come to him—so you had best come down and turn in."

I descended the steep stairs which led down into the low-roofed cabin of the lugger. On either side a recess in the wall had been fitted up as a couch.

"This is your bed," said he, pointing to one of them. "We shall call you if there be aught to report." I needed no second invitation, but flinging myself down, without undressing, I sank in a few minutes into a dreamless sleep, which neither the gentle motion of the boat nor the clank of feet above my head could break off.

CHAPTER TWENTY-FOUR

OF THE WELCOME THAT MET ME AT BADMINTON

WHEN I opened my eyes I had some ado to recall where I was, but on sitting up it was brought home to me by my head striking the low ceiling with a sharp rap. The vessel was rising and falling with a gentle motion, but from the flapping of canvas I judged that there was little wind. Slipping quietly from my couch, so as not to wake the mate, I stole upon deck.

We were, I found, not only becalmed, but hemmed in by a dense fog-bank, which rolled in thick, choking wreaths all round us, and hid the very water beneath us. Covenant was staring right and left with great questioning eyes. The crew were gathered along the bulwarks, and smoking their pipes, while they peered out into the dense fog.

"God den, captain," said Dicon, touching his fur cap. "We have had a rare run while the breeze lasted, and the mate reckoned before he turned in that we were not many miles from Bristol town."

"In that case, my good fellow," I answered, "ye can set me ashore, for I have not far to go."

"We must e'en wait till the fog lifts," said Long John.

"There's only one place along here, d'ye see, where we can land cargoes unquestioned. When it clears we shall turn her head for it, but until we can take our bearings it is anxious work wi' the sands under our lee."

"Keep a lookout there, Tom Baldock!" cried Dixon to a man in the bows. "We are in the track of every Bristol ship, and though there's so little wind, a high-sparred craft might catch a breeze which we miss."

"Sh!" said Long John, suddenly, holding up his hand in warning. "Sh!"

We listened with all our ears, but there was no sound, save the gentle wash of the unseen waves against our sides.

"Call the mate!" whispered the seaman. "There's a craft close by us. I heard the rattle of a rope upon her deck."

Silas Bolitho was up in an instant, and we all stood straining our ears, and peering through the dense fog-bank. We had wellnigh made up our minds that it was a false alarm, and the mate was turning back in no very good humor, when a clear loud bell sounded seven times quite close to us, followed by a shrill whistle and a confused shouting and stamping.

"It's a king's ship," growled the mate. "That's seven bells, and the bo'sun is turning out the watch below."

"It was on our quarter," whispered one.

"Nay, I think it was on our port bow," said another.

The mate held up his hand, and we all listened for some fresh sign of the whereabouts of our scurvy neighbor. The wind had freshened a little, and we were slipping through the water at four or five knots an hour. Of a sudden a hoarse voice was heard roaring at our very side. "'Bout ship!" it shouted. "Bear a hand on the lee braces, there! Stand by the halyards! Bear a hand, ye lazy rogues, or I'll be among ye with my cane, with a wannion to ye!"

"It is a king's ship, sure enough, and she lies just there," said Long John, pointing out over the quarter. "Merchant adventurers have civil tongues. It's your blue-coated, gold-braided, swivel-eyed quarter-deckers that talk of canes. Ha! did I not tell ye?"

As he spoke the white screen of vapor rolled up like the curtain in a playhouse, and uncovered a stately war-ship, lying so close that we could have thrown a biscuit aboard. On the high poop stood an elderly officer with cocked hat and trim white wig, who at once whipped up his glass and gazed at us through it.

"Ahoy, there!" he shouted, leaning over the taffrail. "What lugger is that?"

"The *Lucy*," answered the mate, "bound from Porlock Quay to Bristol with hides and tallow. Stand ready to tack!" he added, in a lower voice, "the fog is coming down again."

"Ye have one of the hides with the horse still in it," cried the officer. "Run down under our counter. We must have a closer look at ye."

"Aye, aye, sir!" said the mate, and putting his helm hard down, the boom swung across, and the *Maria* darted off, like a scared sea-bird, into the fog. Looking back, there was nothing but a dim loom to show where we had left the great vessel. We could hear, however, the hoarse shouting of orders and the bustle of men.

"Look out for squalls, lads!" cried the mate. "He'll let us have it now."

He had scarcely spoken before there were half a dozen throbs of flame in the mist behind, and as many balls sung among our rigging. One cut away the end of the yard, and left it dangling; another grazed the bowsprit, and sent a puff of white splinters into the air.

"Warm work, captain, eh?" said old Silas, rubbing his hands. "Zounds, they shoot better in the dark than ever they did in the light. There have been more shots fired at this lugger than she could carry were she loaded with them. And yet they never so much as knocked the paint off her before. There they go again!"

A fresh discharge burst from the man-of-war, but this time they had lost all trace of us, and were firing by guess.

"That is their last bark, sir," said Dicon.

"No fear. They'll blaze away for the rest of the day," growled another of the smugglers. "Why, Lor' bless ye, it's good exercise for the crew, and the 'munition is the king's, so it don't cost nobody a groat."

"It's well the breeze freshened," said Long John. "I heard the creak o' davits just after the first discharge. She was lowering her boats, or I'm a Dutchman."

"The fog lifts a little towards the land," Silas remarked. "Methinks I see the loom of St. Austin's Point. It rises there upon the starboard bow."

"There it is, sure enough, sir!" cried one of the seamen, pointing to a dark cape which cut into the mist.

"Steer for the three-fathom creek, then," said the mate. "When we are on the other side of the point, Captain Clarke, we shall be able to land your horse and yourself. You will then be within a few hours' ride of your destination."

I led the old seaman aside, and having thanked him for the kindness which he had shown me, I spoke to him of the gauger, and implored him to use his influence to save the man.

"It rests with Captain Venables," said he, gloomily. "If we let him go, what becomes of our cave?"

"Is there no way of insuring his silence?" I asked.

"Well we might ship him to the Plantations," said the mate. "We could take him to the Texel with us, and get Captain Donders or some other to give him a lift across the western ocean."

"Do so," said I, "and I shall take care that King Monmouth shall hear of the help which ye have given his messenger."

"Well, we shall be there in a brace of shakes," he remarked. "Let us go below and load your ground-tier, for there is nothing like starting well trimmed with plenty of ballast in the hold."

Following the sailor's advice, I went down with him and

enjoyed a rude but plentiful meal. By the time that we had finished, the lugger had been run into a narrow creek, with shelving sandy banks on either side. The district was wild and marshy, with few signs of any inhabitants. With much coaxing and pushing, Covenant was induced to take to the water, and swam easily ashore, while I followed in the smuggler's dingy. A few words of rough, kindly leave-taking were shouted after me; I saw the dingy return, and the beautiful craft glided out to sea and faded away once more into the mists which still hung over the face of the waters.

Being now alone, my first care was to bathe my face and hands in a stream which ran down to the sea, and to wipe away any trace of my adventures of the night before. My cut was but a small one, and was concealed by my hair. Having reduced myself to some sort of order, I next rubbed down my horse as best I could, and rearranged his girth and his saddle. I then led him by the bridle to the top of a sand-hill hard by, whence I might gain some idea as to my position.

The fog lay thick upon the channel, but all inland was very clear and bright. The glittering Avon wound its way over the countryside like a silver snake in a flower-bed. Close to its mouth, and not more than two leagues from where I stood, rose the spires and towers of stately Bristol, the Queen of the West, which was and still may be the second city in the kingdom.

As I knew that the duke's seat was miles on the Gloucestershire side of the city, and as I feared lest I might be arrested and examined should I attempt to pass the gates, I struck inland, with intent to ride round the walls and so avoid the peril. The path which I followed led me into a country lane, which in turn opened into a broad highway crowded with travellers, both on horseback and on foot. As the troublous times required that a man should journey with his arms, there was naught in my outfit to excite remark, and I was able to jog on among the other horsemen without question or suspicion.

From their appearance they were, I judged, country farmers or squires, for the most part, who were riding into Bristol to hear the news, and to store away their things of price in a place of safety.

"By your leave, zur!" said a burly, heavy-faced man in a velveteen jacket, riding up upon my bridle-arm. "Can you tell me whether his Grace of Beaufort is in Bristol or at his house o' Badminton?"

I answered that I could not tell, but that I was myself bound for his presence.

"He was in Bristol yestreen, a-drilling o' the trainbands," said the stranger; "but, indeed, his grace be that loyal, and works that hard for his majesty's cause, that he's a' ower the county, and it is but chance-work for to try and to catch him. But if you are about to zeek him, whither shall you go?"

"I will go to Badminton," I answered, "and await him there. Can you tell me the way?"

"What! Not know the way to Badminton!" he cried, with a blank stare of wonder. "Whoy, I thought all the warld knew that. You're not fra Wales or the border counties, zur, that be very clear."

"I am a Hampshire man," said I. "I have come some distance to see the duke."

"Aye, so I should think!" he cried, laughing loudly. "If you doan't know the way to Badminton you doan't know much! But I'll go with you, danged if I doan't, and I'll show you your road, and run my chance o' finding the duke there. What be your name?"

"Micah Clarke is my name."

"And Vairmer Brown is mine—John Brown by the register, but better knowed as the Vairmer. Tak' this turn to the right off the high-road. Now we can trot our beasts, and not be smothered in other folks' dust. And what be you going to Beaufort for?"

"On private matters, which will not brook discussion," I answered.

"Lor', now! Affairs o' state, belike," said he, with a whistle. "Well, a still tongue saves many a neck. I'm a cautious man myself, and these be times when I wouldna' whisper some o' my thoughts—no, not into the ears o' my old brown mare here—for fear I'd see her some day standing over against me in the witness-box."

"They seem very busy over there," I remarked, for we were now in full sight of the walls of Bristol, where gangs of men were working hard with pick and shovel, improving the defences.

"Aye, they be busy, sure enough, makin' ready in case the rebels come this road. Cromwell and his tawnies found it a rasper in my vather's time, and Monmouth is like to do the same."

"It hath a strong garrison, too," said I, bethinking me of Saxon's advice at Salisbury. "I see two or three regiments out yonder on the bare open space."

"They have four thousand foot and a thousand horse," the farmer answered; "but the foot are only trainbands, and there's no trusting them after Axminster. They say up here that the rebels run to nigh twenty thousand, and that they give no quarter. Well, if we must have civil war, I hope it may be hot and sudden, not spun out for a dozen years like the last one. If our throats are to be cut, let it be with a shairp knife, and not with a blunt hedge-shears."

"What say you to a stoup of cider?" I asked, for we were passing an iron-clad inn, with "The Beaufort Arms" printed upon the sign.

"With all my heart, lad," my companion answered. "Ho, there! two pints of the old hard-brewed! That will serve to wash the dust down. The real Beaufort Arms is up yonder at Badminton, for at the buttery-hatch one may call for what one will in reason and never put hand to pocket."

"You speak of the house as though you knew it well," said I.

"And who should know it better?" asked the sturdy farmer, wiping his lips, as we resumed our journey. "Why, it seems but yesterday that I played hide-and-seek wi' my brothers in the old Boteler Castle, that stood where the new house o' Badminton, or Acton Turville, as some calls it, now stands. The duke hath built it but a few years, and, indeed, his dukedom itself is scarce older. There are some who think that he would have done better to stick by the old name that his forebears bore."

"What manner of man is the duke?" I asked.

"Hot and hasty, like all of his blood. Yet when he hath time to think, and hath cooled down, he is just in the main. Your horse hath been in the water this morning, vriend."

"Yes," said I, shortly, "he hath had a bath."

"I am going to his grace on the business of a horse," quoth my companion. "His officers have pressed my piebald four-year-old, and taken it without a 'with your leave,' or 'by your leave,' for the use of the king. I would have them know that there is something higher than the duke, or even than the king. There is the English law, which will preserve a man's goods and his chattels. I would do aught in reason for King James's service, but my piebald four-year-old is too much."

"I fear that the needs of the public service will override your objection," said I.

"Why, it is enough to make a man a Whig," he cried. "Even the Roundheads always paid their vair penny for every pennyworth they had, though they wanted a vair pennyworth for each penny. I have heard my father say that trade was never so brisk as in 'forty-six, when they were down this way. Old Noll had a noose of hemp ready for horse-stealers, were they for king or for Parliament. But here comes his grace's carriage, if I mistake not."

As he spoke a great heavy yellow coach, drawn by six cream-colored Flemish mares, dashed down the road, and came swiftly towards us. Two mounted lackeys galloped in front, and two others, all in light blue and silver liveries, rode on either side.

"His grace is not within, else there had been an escort behind," said the farmer, as we reined our horses aside to let the carriage pass. As they swept by he shouted out a question as to whether the duke was at Badminton, and received a nod from the stately bewigged coachman in reply.

"We are in luck to catch him," said Farmer Brown. "He's as hard to find these days as a crake in a wheat-field. We should be there in an hour or less. I must thank you that I did not take a fruitless journey into Bristol. What did you say your errand was?"

I was again compelled to assure him that the matter was not one of which I could speak with a stranger, on which he appeared to be huffed, and rode for some miles without opening his mouth.

"'Tis the bell from Chipping Sodbury," said my companion, at last, wiping his ruddy face. "That's Sodbury Church yonder over the brow of the hill, and here on the right is the entrance of Badminton Park."

High iron gates, with the leopard and griffin, which are the supporters of the Beaufort arms, fixed on the pillars which flanked them, opened into a beautiful domain of lawn and grassland, with clumps of trees scattered over it, and broad sheets of water, thick with wild-fowl. At every turn as we rode up the winding avenue some new beauty caught our eyes, all of which were pointed out and expounded by Farmer Brown, who seemed to take as much pride in the place as though it belonged to him.

As we drew near the house we came on a large extent of level sward on which a troop of horse were exercising, who were raised, as my companion informed me, entirely from the duke's own personal attendants. Passing them, we rode through a grove of rare trees and came out on a broad space of gravel which lay in front of the house. The main doorway was led up to by lines of columns and a broad flight of marble steps, on which stood a group of footmen and grooms who took our horses when we dismounted. A gray-haired steward or major-domo inquired our business, and, on learning that we wished to see the duke in person, he told us that his grace would give audience to strangers in the afternoon at half after three by the clock. In the meantime he said that the guests' dinner had just been laid in the hall, and it was his master's wish that none who came to Badminton should depart hungry. My companion and I were but too glad to accept the steward's invitation, so, having attended to the needs of the toilet, we followed a foot-man, who ushered us into a great room, where the company had already assembled. The guests may have numbered fifty or sixty, old and young, gentle and simple, of the most varied types and appearance.

After dinner we were all shown into a small ante-chamber, set round with velvet settees, where we were to wait till the duke was ready to see us. In the centre of this room there stood several cases, glass-topped and lined with silk, wherein were little steel and iron rods, with brass tubes and divers other things, very bright and ingenious, though I could not devise for what end they had been put together. A gentleman-in-waiting came round with paper and inkhorn, making notes of our names and of our business. Him I asked whether it might not be possible for me to have an entirely private audience.

"His grace never sees in private," he replied. "He has ever his chosen councillors and officers in attendance."

"But the business is one which is only fit for his own ear," I urged.

"His grace holds that there is no business fit only for his own ear," said the gentleman. "You must arrange matters as best you can when you are shown in to him. I will prom-ise, however, that your request be carried to him, though I warn you that it cannot be granted."

I thanked him for his good offices, and turned away with the farmer to look at the strange little engines within the cases.

"What is it?" I asked. "I have never seen aught that was like it."

"It is the work of the mad Marquis of Worcester," quoth he. "He was the duke's grandfather. He was ever making and devising such toys, but they were never of any service to himself or to others. Now, look ye here! This wi' the wheels were called the water-engine, and it was his crazy thought that, by heating the water in that ere kettle, ye might make the wheels go round, and thereby travel along iron bars quicker nor a horse could run. 'Oons! I'd match my old brown mare against all such contrivances to the end o' time. But to our places, for the duke is coming."

We had scarce taken our seats with the other suitors when the folding doors were flung open, and a stout, thick, short man of fifty, or thereabouts, came bustling into the room, and strode down it between two lines of bowing clients. He had large, projecting, blue eyes, with great pouches of skin beneath them, and a yellow, sallow visage. At his heels walked a dozen officers and men of rank, with flowing wigs and clanking swords. They had hardly passed through the opposite door into the duke's own room when the gentleman with the list called out a name, and the guests began one after the other to file into the great man's presence.

"Methinks his grace is in no very gentle temper," quoth Farmer Brown. "Did you not mark how he gnawed his nether lip as he passed?"

"He seemed a quiet gentleman enough," I answered. "It would try Job himself to see all these folk of an afternoon."

"Hark at that!" he whispered, raising his finger. As he spoke the sound of the duke's voice in a storm of wrath was heard from the inner chamber, and a little, sharp-faced man came out and flew through the ante-chamber as though fright had turned his head.

"He is an armorer of Bristol," whispered one of my neighbors. "It is likely that the duke cannot come to terms with him over a contract."

"Nay," said another. "He supplied Sir Marmaduke Hyson's troop with sabres, and it is said that the blades will bend as though they were lead. Once used they can never be fitted back into the scabbard again."

I had been sitting all this time wondering how in the world I was to conduct my business amid the swarm of suppliants and the crowd of officers who were attending the duke. Had there been any likelihood of my gaining audience with him in any other way I should gladly have adopted it, but all my endeavors to that end had been useless. On the whole, it seemed best that I should make the fittest use I could of my present position, in the hope that the duke's own discretion and self-command might, when he saw the address upon my despatches, lead to a more private interview.

I had just come to this resolution when my name was read out, on which I rose and advanced into the inner chamber. It was a small but lofty room, hung in blue silk with a broad gold cornice. In the centre was a square table, littered over with piles of papers, and behind this sat his grace, with full-bottomed wig rolling down to his shoulders, very stately and imposing. His private scrivener sat beside him, taking notes of his directions, while the others stood behind in a half circle, or took snuff in the deep recess of the window.

"Captain Micah Clarke," said the duke, reading from the list in front of him. "What is your wish, captain?"

"One which it would be better if I could deliver privately to your grace," I answered.

"Ah, you are he who desired private audience? Well, captain, these are my council, and they are as myself. So we may look upon ourselves as alone. What I may hear they may hear. Zounds, man, never stammer and boggle, but out with it!"

My request had roused the interest of the company, and

those who were in the window came over to the table. Nothing could have been worse for the success of my mission, and yet there was no help for it but to deliver my despatches. I can say with a clear conscience, without any vainglory, that I had no fears for myself. The doing of my duty was the one thought in my mind.

My short delay and hesitation had sent a hot flush of anger into the duke's face, so I drew the packet of papers from my inner pocket and handed them to him with a respectful bow. As his eyes fell upon the superscription, he gave a sudden start of surprise and agitation, making a motion as though to hide them in his bosom. If this were his impulse he overcame it, and sat lost in thought for a minute or more with the papers in his hand. Then, with a quick toss of the head, like a man who hath formed his resolution, he broke the seals and cast his eyes over the contents, which he then threw down upon the table with a bitter laugh.

"What think ye, gentlemen?" he cried, looking round with scornful eyes—"what think ye this private message hath proved to be? It is a letter from the traitor Monmouth, calling upon me to resign the allegiance of my natural sovereign and to draw my sword in his behalf! If I do this I am to have his gracious favor and protection. If not, I incur sequestration, banishment, and ruin. He thinks Beaufort's loyalty is to be bought like a packman's ware, or bullied out of him by ruffling words. The descendant of John of Gaunt is to render fealty to the brat of a wandering playwoman!"

Several of the company sprang to their feet, and a general buzz of surprise and anger greeted the duke's words. He sat with bent brows, beating his foot against the ground, and turning over the papers upon the table.

"What hath raised his hopes to such mad heights?" he cried. "How doth he presume to send such a missive to one of my quality? Is it because he hath seen the backs of a parcel of rascally militiamen, and because he hath drawn a few hundred chaw-bacons from the plough's tail to his standard, that he ventures to hold such language to the President of Wales? But ye will be my witnesses as to the spirit in which I received it."

"We can preserve your grace from all danger of slander on that point," said an elderly officer, while a murmur of assent from the others greeted the remark.

"And you!" cried Beaufort, raising his voice and turning his flashing eyes upon me; "who are you that dare to bring such a message to Badminton? You had surely taken leave of your senses ere you did set out upon such an errand!"

"I am in the hands of God here as elsewhere," I answered, with some flash of my father's fatalism. "I have done what I promised to do, and the rest is no concern of mine."

"You shall find it a very close concern of thine," he shouted, springing from his chair and pacing up and down the room; "so close as to put an end to all thy other concerns in this life. Call in the halberdiers from the outer hall! Now, fellow, what have you to say for yourself?"

"There is naught to be said," I answered.

"But something to be done," he retorted, in a fury. "Seize this man and secure his hands!"

Four halberdiers who had answered the summons closed in upon me and laid hands on me. Resistance would have been folly, for I had no wish to harm the men in the doing of their duty. This being so, I stood erect, with my eyes fixed upon the angry nobleman, while his soldiers were putting the gyves about my wrists.

CHAPTER TWENTY-FIVE

OF STRANGE DOINGS IN THE BOTELER DUNGEON

"TAKE down this fellow's statement," said the duke to his scrivener. "Now, sirrah, it may not be known to you that his gracious majesty the king hath conferred plenary powers upon me during these troubled times, and that I have his warrant to deal with all traitors without either jury or judge. You do bear a commission, I understand, in the rebellious body which is here described as Saxon's regiment of Wiltshire foot? Speak the truth for your neck's sake."

"I will speak the truth for the sake of something higher than that, your grace," I answered. "I command a company in that regiment."

"And who is this Saxon?"

"I will answer all that I may concerning myself," said I, "but not a word which may reflect upon others."

"Ha!" he roared, hot with anger. "Our pretty gentleman must needs stand upon the niceties of honor after taking up arms against his king. I tell you, sir, that your honor is in such a parlous state already that you may well throw it over and look to your safety. The sun is sinking in the west. Ere it set your life, too, may have set forever."

"I am the keeper of my own honor, your grace," I answered. "As to my life, I should not be standing here this moment if I had any great dread of losing it. It is right that I should tell you that my colonel hath sworn to exact a return for any evil that may befall me from you or any of your household who may come into his power. This I say, not as a threat, but as a warning, for I know him to be a man who is like to be as good as his word."

"Your colonel, as you call him, may find it hard enough to save himself soon," the duke answered, with a sneer. "How many men hath Monmouth with him?"

I smiled and shook my head.

"How shall we make this traitor find his tongue?" he asked, furiously, turning to his council.

"I should clap on the thumbkins," said one fierce-faced old soldier.

"I have known a lighted match between the fingers work wonders," another suggested.

"Enough, gentlemen, enough!" cried the duke. "We shall discuss this at greater length in privacy. Halberdiers, remove the prisoner, and let a clergyman be sent to look to his spiritual needs!"

"Shall we take him to the strong room, your grace?" asked the captain of the guard.

"No, to the old Boteler dungeon," he replied; and I heard the next name upon the list called out, while I was led through a side door with a guard in front and behind me. We passed through endless passages and corridors, with heavy step and clank of arms, until we reached the ancient wing. Here, in the corner turret, was a small, bare room, mouldy and damp, with a high, arched roof, and a single long slit in the outer wall to admit light. A small wooden couch and a rude chair formed the whole of the furniture. Into this I was shown by the captain, who stationed a guard at the door, and then came in after me and loosened my wrists. He was a sad-faced man, with solemn, sunken eyes and a dreary expression, which matched ill with his bright trappings and gay sword-knot.

"Keep your heart up, friend," said he, in a hollow voice. "It is but a choke and a struggle. A day or two since we had the same job to do, and the man scarcely groaned. Old Spender, the duke's marshal, hath as sure a trick of tying and as good judgment in arranging a drop as hath Dun of Tyburn. Be of

good heart, therefore, for you shall not fall into the hands
of a bungler.''

"I would that I could let Monmouth know that his letters
were delivered," I exclaimed, seating myself on the side of
the bed.

"I' faith, they were delivered. Had you been the penny
postman of Mr. Robert Murray, of whom we heard so much
in London last spring, you could not have handed it in more
directly. Why did you not talk the duke fair? He is a gracious nobleman, and kind of heart, save when he is thwarted
or angered. Some little talk as to the rebels' numbers and
dispositions might have saved you."

"I wonder that you, as a soldier, should speak or think of
such a thing," said I, coldly.

"Well, well! Your neck is your own. If it please you to
take a leap into nothing it were a pity to thwart you. But
his grace commanded that you should have the chaplain. I
must away to him."

"I prithee do not bring him," said I. "I am one of a dis-
senting stock, and I see that there is a Bible in yonder recess.
No man can aid me in making my peace with God."

"No? Well, what I can do for you in reason shall be done,
since you will not be long upon our hands. Above all, keep
a cheery heart."

He left the cell, but presently unlocked the door and pushed
his dismal face round the corner. "I am Captain Sinclair, of
the duke's household," he said, "should you have occasion to
ask for me."

I was seated with my head bowed upon my breast, deeply
buried in a solemn train of thoughts, when I was startled by
hearing a sharp click, such as a man might give who wished
to attract attention. I sprang to my feet and gazed round in
the gathering gloom without being able to tell whence it came.
I had wellnigh persuaded myself that my senses had deceived
me, when the sound was repeated louder than before, and cast-

ing my eyes upward I saw a face peering in at me through the slit, or part of a face rather, for I could but see the eye and corner of the cheek. Standing on my chair I made out that it was none other than the farmer who had been my companion upon the road.

"Hush, lad!" he whispered, with a warning forefinger pushed through the narrow crack. "Speak low, or the guard may chance to hear. What can I do for you?"

"How did you come to know where I was?" I asked, in astonishment.

"Whoy, mun," he answered, "I know as much of this 'ere house as Beaufort does himsel'. Afore Badminton was built, me and my brothers has spent many a day in climbing over the old Boteler tower. It's not the first time that I have spoke through this window. But, quick; what can I do for you?"

"I am much beholden to you, sir," I answered, "but I fear that there is no help which you can give me, unless, indeed, you could convey news to my friends in the army of what hath befallen me."

"I might do that," whispered Farmer Brown. "Hark ye in your ear, lad, what I never breathed to man yet. Mine own conscience pricks me at times over this bolstering up of a Papist to rule over a Protestant nation. Let like rule like, say I. At the 'lections I rode to Sudbury, and I put in my vote for Maister Evans, of Turnford, who was in favor o' the Exclusionists. Sure enough, if that same bill had been carried, the duke would be sitting on his father's throne. Let Monmouth get the law changed, and it will do more for him than all the dukes in England. For all that he's a Protestant, and I would do what I might to serve him."

"There is a Captain Lockarby, who is serving in Colonel Saxon's regiment, in Monmouth's army," said I. "Should things go wrong with me, I would take it as a great kindness if you would bear him my love, and ask him to break it gently, by word or by letter, to those at Havant. If I were sure that this would be done, it would be a great ease to my mind."

"It shall be done, lad," said the good farmer. "I shall send my best man and fleetest horse this very night, that they may know the straits in which you are. I have a file here if it would help you."

"Nay," I answered, "human aid can do little to help me here."

"There used to be a hole in the roof. Look up and see if you can see aught of it."

"It arches high above my head," I answered, looking upward; "but there is no sign of any opening."

"There was one," he repeated. "My brother Roger hath swung himself down wi' a rope. In the old time the prisoners were put in so, like Joseph into the pit. The door is but a new thing."

"Hole or no hole, it cannot help me," I answered. "I have no means of climbing to it. Do not wait longer, kind friend, or you may find yourself in trouble."

"Good-bye, then, my brave heart," he whispered, and the honest gray eye and corner of ruddy cheek disappeared from the casement. Many a time during the course of the long evening I glanced up with some wild hope that he might return, and every creak of the branches outside brought me on to the chair, but it was the last that I saw of Farmer Brown.

This kindly visit, short as it was, relieved my mind greatly, for I had a trusty man's word that, come what might, my friends should at least have some news of my fate. It was now quite dark, and I was pacing up and down the little chamber when the key turned in the door, and the captain entered with a rushlight and a great bowl of bread and milk.

"Here is your supper, friend," said he. "Take it down, appetite or no, for it will give you strength to play the man at the time ye wot of. They say it was beautiful to see my Lord Russell die upon Tower Hill. Be of good cheer! Folk may say as much of you. His grace is in a terrible way. He walketh up and down, and biteth his lip, and clincheth his hands like one who can scarce contain his wrath. It may not be against you, but I know not what else can have angered him."

I made no answer to this Job's comforter, so he presently left me, placing the bowl upon the chair, with the rushlight beside it. I finished the food, and, feeling the better for it, stretched myself upon the couch, and fell into a heavy and dreamless sleep. This may have lasted three or four hours; when I was suddenly awakened by a sound like the creaking of hinges. Sitting up on the pallet, I gazed around me. The rushlight had burned out, and the cell was impenetrably dark. I rose and felt my way slowly round the room, passing my hand over the walls and door. Then I paced backward and forward to test the flooring. Neither around me nor beneath me was there any change. Whence did the sound come from, then? I sat down upon the side of the bed and waited patiently in the hope of hearing it once again.

Presently it was repeated, a low groaning and creaking, as though a door or shutter long disused was being slowly and stealthily opened. At the same time a dull yellow light streamed down from above, issuing from a thin slit in the centre of the arched roof above me. Slowly, as I watched it, this slit widened and extended, as if a sliding panel were being pulled out, until a good-sized hole was left, through which I saw a head, looking down at me, outlined against the misty light behind it. The knotted end of a rope was passed through this aperture, and came dangling down to the dungeon floor. It was a good, stout piece of hemp, strong enough to bear the weight of a heavy man, and I found, upon pulling at it, that it was firmly secured above. Clearly it was the desire of my unknown benefactor that I should ascend by it, so I went up hand over hand, and after some difficulty in squeezing my shoulders through the hole I succeeded in reaching the room above. While I was still rubbing my eyes after the sudden change from darkness into light, the rope was swiftly whisked up and the sliding shutter closed once more. To those who were not in the secret there was nothing to throw light upon my disappearance.

I found myself in the presence of a stout, short man clad in a rude jerkin and leather breeches, which gave him somewhat the appearance of a groom. He wore a broad felt hat drawn down very low over his eyes, while the lower part of his face was swathed round with a broad cravat. In his hand he bore a horn lanthorn, by the light of which I saw that the room in which we were was of the same size as the dungeon beneath, and differed from it only in having a broad casement which looked out upon the park. There was no furniture in the chamber, but a great beam ran across it, to which the rope had been fastened by which I ascended.

"Speak low, friend," said the stranger. "The walls are thick, and the doors are closed, yet I would not have your guardians know by what means you have been spirited away."

"Truly, sir," I answered, "I can scarce credit that it is other than a dream. It is wondrous that my dungeon should be so easily broken into, and more wondrous still that I should find a friend who would be willing to risk so much for my sake."

"Look there!" quoth he, holding down his lanthorn so as to cast its light on the part of the floor where the panel was fitted. "Can you not see how old and crumbled is the stonework which surrounds it? This opening in the roof is as old as the dungeon itself, and older far than the door by which you were led into it. For this was one of those bottle-shaped cells or oubliettes which hard men of old devised for the safe keeping of their captives. Once lowered through this hole into the stone-girt pit a man might eat his heart out, for his fate was sealed. Yet you see that the very device which once hindered escape has now brought freedom within your reach."

"Thanks to your clemency, your grace," I answered, looking keenly at my companion.

"Now out on these disguises!" he cried, peevishly pushing

back the broad-edged hat and disclosing, as I expected, the features of the duke. "Even a blunt soldier lad can see through my attempts at concealment. I fear, captain, that I should make a bad plotter, for my nature is as open—well, as thine is. I cannot better the simile."

"Your grace's voice once heard is not easily forgot," said I.

"Especially when it talks of hemp and dungeons," he answered, with a smile. "But if I clapped you into prison you must confess that I have made you amends by pulling you out again at the end of my line like a minnow out of a bottle. But how came you to deliver such papers in the presence of my council?"

"I did what I could to deliver them in private," said I. "I sent you a message to that effect."

"It is true," he answered; "but such messages come in to me from every soldier who wishes to sell his sword, and every inventor who hath a long tongue and a short purse. How could I tell that the matter was of real import?"

"I feared to let the chance slip, lest it might never return," said I. "I hear that your grace hath little leisure during these times."

"I cannot blame you," he answered, pacing up and down the room. "But it was untoward. I might have hid the despatches, yet it would have roused suspicions. Your errand would have leaked out. There are many who envy my lofty fortunes, and who would seize upon a chance of injuring me with King James. Sunderland or Somers would, either of them, blow the least rumor into a flame which might prove unquenchable. There was naught for it, therefore, but to show the papers and to turn a harsh face on the messenger. The most venomous tongue could not find fault in my conduct. What course would you have advised under such circumstances?"

"The most direct," I answered.

"Aye, aye, Sir Honesty. Public men have, however, to pick their steps as best they may, for the straight path would lead too often to the cliff-edge. The tower would be too scanty for its guests were we all to wear our hearts upon our sleeves. But to you in this privacy I can tell my real thoughts without fear of betrayal or misconstruction. On paper I will not write one word. Your memory must be the sheet which bears my answer to Monmouth. And, first of all, erase from it all that you have heard me say in the council-room. Let it be as though it never were spoken. Is that done?"

"I understand that it did not really represent your grace's thoughts."

"Very far from it, captain. But prithee tell me what expectation of success is there among the rebels themselves? You must have heard your colonel and others discuss the question, or noted by their bearing which way their thoughts lay. Have they good hopes of holding out against the king's troops?"

"They have met with naught but success hitherto," I answered.

"Against the militia. But they will find it another thing when they have trained troops to deal with. And yet—and yet— One thing I know, that any defeat of Feversham's army would cause a general rising throughout the country. On the other hand, the king's party are active. Every post brings news of some fresh levy. Albemarle still holds the militia together in the west. The Earl of Pembroke is in arms in Wiltshire. Lord Lumley is moving from the east with the Sussex forces. The Earl of Abingdon is up in Oxfordshire. At the university the caps and gowns are all turning into head-pieces and steel fronts. James's Dutch regiments have sailed from Amsterdam. Yet Monmouth hath gained two fights, and why not a third? They are troubled waters—troubled waters!" The duke paced backward and forward with brows drawn down, muttering all this to himself rather than to me, and shaking his head like one in the sorest perplexity.

"I would have you tell Monmouth," he said at last, "that I thank him for the papers which he hath sent me, and that I

will duly read and weigh them. Tell him also that I wish
him well in his enterprise, and would help him were it not that
I am hemmed in by those who watch me closely, and who would
denounce me were I to show my true thoughts. Tell him that,
should he move his army into these parts, I may then openly
declare myself; but to do so now would be to ruin the fortunes
of my house without in any way helping him. Can you bear
him that message?"

"I shall do so, your grace."

"Tell me," he asked, "how doth Monmouth bear himself in
this enterprise?"

"Like a wise and gallant leader," I answered.

"Strange," he murmured; "it was ever the jest at court
that he had scarce energy or constancy enough to finish a game
at ball, but would ever throw his racquet down ere the winning-
point was scored. Methinks he resembles that Brutus in Roman
history who feigned weakness of mind as a cover to his ambi-
tions."

The duke was once again conversing with himself rather
than with me, so that I made no remark, save to observe that
Monmouth had won the hearts of the lower people.

"There lies his strength," said Beaufort. "The blood of
his mother runs in his veins. He doth not think it beneath him
to shake the dirty paw of Jerry the tinker or to run a race
against a bumpkin on the village green. Well, events have
shown that he hath been right. These same bumpkins have
stood by him when nobler friends have held aloof. I would
I could see into the future. But you have my message, captain,
and I trust that, if you change it in the delivery, it will be in
the direction of greater warmth and kindliness. It is time now
that you depart, for within three hours the guard is changed,
and your escape will be discovered."

"But how depart?" I asked.

"Through here," he answered, pushing open the casement
and sliding the rope along the beam in that direction. The

rope may be a foot or two short, but you have extra inches
to make matters even. When you have reached the ground,
take the gravel path which turns to the right, and follow it
until it leads you to the high trees which skirt the park. The
seventh of these hath a bough which shoots over the boundary
wall. Climb along the bough, drop over upon the other side,
and you will find my own valet waiting with your horse. Up
with you, and ride, haste, haste, post-haste, for the south. By
morn you should be well out of danger's way."

"My sword?" I asked.

"All your property is there. Tell Monmouth what I have
said, and let him know that I have used you as kindly as was
possible."

"But what will your grace's council say when they find that
I am gone?" I asked.

"Pshaw, man! never fret about that! I will off to Bristol
at daybreak, and give my council enough to think of without
their having time to devote to your fate. But time presses.
Gently through the casement! So! Remember the message."

"Adieu, your grace!" I answered, and seizing the rope,
slipped rapidly and noiselessly to the ground, upon which he
drew it up and closed the casement. As I looked round my
eye fell upon the dark, narrow slit which opened into my cell,
and through which honest Farmer Brown had held converse
with me. Half an hour ago I had been stretched upon the
prison pallet without a hope or a thought of escape. Now I
was out in the open, with no hand to stay me, breathing the
air of freedom.

The path to the right led through groves and past carp
ponds for a mile or more, until I reached the line of trees which
skirted the boundary wall. Not a living thing did I see upon
my way, save a herd of fallow-deer, which scudded away like
swift shadows through the shimmering moonshine. Looking
back, the high turrets and gables of the Boteler wing stood out,
dark and threatening, against the starlit sky. Having reached

the seventh tree, I clambered along the projecting bough which shot over the park wall, and dropped down upon the other side, where I found my good old dapple-gray awaiting me in the charge of a groom. Springing to my saddle, I strapped my sword once more to my side, and galloped off, as fast as the four willing feet could carry me, on my return journey.

All that night I rode hard, without drawing bridle, through sleeping hamlets, by moon-bathed farm-houses, past shining, stealthy rivers, and over birch-clad hills. When the eastern sky deepened from pink into scarlet, and the great sun pushed his rim over the blue North Somerset hills, I was already far upon my journey.

My road lay through Shepton-Mallet, Piper's Inn, Bridgewater, and North Petherton, until in the cool of the evening I pulled up my weary horse at the Cross Hands, and saw the towers of Taunton in the valley beneath me. A flagon of beer for the rider and a sieveful of oats for the steed put fresh mettle into both of us, and we were jogging on our way once more, when there came galloping down the side of the hill about forty cavaliers, as hard as their horses could carry them. So wild was their riding that I pulled up, uncertain whether they were friend or foe, until, as they came whirling towards me, I recognized that the two officers who rode in front of them were none other than Reuben Lockarby and Sir Gervas Jerome. At the sight of me they flung up their hands, and Reuben shot on to his horse's neck, where he sat for a moment astride of the mane, until the brute tossed him back into the saddle.

"It's Micah! It's Micah!" he gasped, with his mouth open and the tears dropping down his honest face.

"Od's pitikins, man! how did you come here?" asked Sir Gervas, poking me with his forefinger as though to see if I were really of flesh and blood. "We were leading a forlorn of horse into Beaufort's country to beat him up, and to burn his fine house about his ears if you had come to harm. There has just come a groom from some farmer in those parts who hath brought us news that you were under sentence of death, on which I came away with my wig half frizzled, and found that friend Lockarby had leave from Lord Grey to go north with these troopers. But how have you fared?"

"Well and ill," I answered, wringing their kindly hands. "I had not thought last night to see another sun rise, and yet ye see that I am here sound in life and limb. But all these things will take some time in the telling."

"Aye, and King Monmouth will be on thorns to see you. Right about, my lads, and back for the camp. Never was errand so rapidly and happily finished as this of ours. It would have fared ill with Badminton had you been hurt."

The troopers turned their horses and trotted slowly back to Taunton, while I rode behind them between my two faithful friends, hearing from them all that had occurred in my absence, and telling my own adventures in return. The night had fallen ere we rode through the gates, where I handed Covenant over to the mayor's groom, and went direct to the castle to deliver an account of my mission.

CHAPTER TWENTY-SIX

OF THE STRIFE IN THE COUNCIL

KING MONMOUTH'S council was assembled at the time
of my coming, and my entrance caused the utmost surprise
and joy, as they had just heard news of my sore danger. Even
the royal presence could not prevent several members, among
whom were the old mayor and two soldiers of fortune, from
springing to their feet and shaking me warmly by the hand.
Monmouth himself said a few gracious words, and requested
that I should be seated at the board with the others.

"You have earned the right to be of our council," said he,
"and, lest there should be a jealousy among other captains that
you should come among us, I do hereby confer upon you the
special title of scout-master, which, though it entail few if any
duties in the present state of our force, will yet give you pre-
cedence over your fellows. We had heard that your greeting
from Beaufort was of the roughest, and that you were in sore
straits in his dungeons. But you have happily come yourself
on the very heels of him who bore the tidings. Tell us, then,
from the beginning, how things have fared with you."

I should have wished to have limited my story to Beaufort
and his message, but as the council seemed to be intent upon
hearing a full account of my journey, I told, in as short and
simple speech as I could, the various passages which had befallen me—the ambuscado of the smugglers, the cave, the capture of the gauger, the journey in the lugger, the acquaintance
with Farmer Brown, my being cast into prison, with the manner
of my release and the message wherewith I had been commis-
sioned. To all of this the council hearkened with the uttermost

attention, while a muttered oath, ever and anon, from a courtier or a groan and prayer from a Puritan showed how keenly they followed the various phases of my fortunes. Above all, they gave the greatest heed to Beaufort's words, and stopped me more than once when I appeared to be passing over any saying or event before they had due time to weigh it. When I at last finished they all sat speechless, looking into one another's faces and waiting for an expression of opinion.

"On my word," said Monmouth, at last, "this is a young Ulysses, though his Odyssey doth but take three days in the acting. Scudéry might not be so dull were she to take a hint from these smugglers' caves and sliding panels. How say you, Grey?"

"He hath indeed had his share of adventure," the nobleman answered, "and hath also performed his mission like a fearless and zealous messenger. You say that Beaufort gave you naught in writing?"

"Not a word, my lord," I replied.

"And his private message was that he wished us well and would join us if we were in his country?"

"That was the effect, my lord."

"Yet in his council, as I understand, he did utter bitter things against us, putting affronts upon the king, and making light of his just claims upon the fealty of his nobility?"

"He did," I answered.

"He would fain stand upon both sides of the hedge at once," said King Monmouth. "Such a man is very like to find himself on neither side, but in the very heart of the briars. It may be as well, however, that we should move his way, so as to give him the chance of declaring himself."

"In any case, as your majesty remembers," said Saxon, "we had determined to march Bristolwards and attempt the town."

"The works are being strengthened," said I, "and there are five thousand of the Gloucestershire trainbands assembled within. I saw the laborers at work upon the ramparts as I passed."

"If we gain Beaufort we shall gain the town," quoth Sir Stephen Timewell. "There are already a strong body of godly and honest folk therein who would rejoice to see a Protestant army within their gates. Should we have to beleaguer it we may count upon some help from within."

"Hegel und blitzen!" exclaimed the German soldier, with an impatience which even the presence of the king could not keep in bounds. "How can we talk of sieges and leaguers when we have not a breaching-piece in the army?"

"The Lard will find us the breaching-pieces," cried Ferguson, in his strange, nasal voice. "What is there he canna do? Hosannah! Hosannah!"

"The doctor is right," said a square-faced, leather-skinned English Independent. "Yes, gentlemen," he continued, raising his voice and glancing across the table at some of the courtiers, "ye may sneer at words of piety, but I say that it is you and those like you who will bring down God's anger upon this army."

"And I say so too," cried another sectary, fiercely.

"And I," "And I," shouted several, with Saxon, I think, among them.

"Is it your wish, your majesty, that we should be insulted at your very council-board?" cried one of the courtiers, springing to his feet with a flushed face. "How long are we to be subject to this insolence because we have the religion of a gentleman, and prefer to practise it in the privacy of our hearts rather than at the street corners with these Pharisees?"

Several had sprung to their feet on either side. Hands were laid upon sword-hilts, and glances as stern and as deadly as rapier thrusts were flashing backward and forward; but the more neutral and reasonable members of the council succeeded in restoring peace, and in persuading the angry disputants to resume their seats.

"How now, gentlemen?" cried the king, his face dark with

anger, when silence was at last restored. "Is this the extent of my authority that ye should babble and brawl as though my council-chamber were a Fleet Street pot-house? Ye may now separate, each to your quarters, and to-morrow morning we shall, with the blessing of God, start for the north to see what luck may await our enterprise in those parts."

The king bowed as a sign that the formal meeting was over, and, taking Lord Grey aside, he conversed with him anxiously in a recess. The courtiers swaggered out of the room in a body, with much clinking of spurs and clanking of swords. The Puritans drew gravely together and followed after them, walking not with demure and downcast looks, as was their common use, but with grim faces and knitted brows.

Indeed, religious dissension and sectarian heat were in the very air. Outside, on the Castle Green, the voices of preachers rose up like the drone of insects. Every wagon or barrel or chance provision case had been converted into a pulpit, each with its own orator and little knot of eager hearkeners. Here was a russet-coated Taunton volunteer, in jack-boots and bandolier, holding forth on the justification by works. Farther on a grenadier of the militia, with blazing red coat and white cross-belt, was deep in the mystery of the Trinity. In one or two places, where the rude pulpits were too near to each other, the sermons had changed into a hot discussion between the two preachers, in which the audience took part by hums or groans, each applauding the champion whose creed was most in accordance with his own. Through this wild scene, made more striking by the ruddy, flickering glare of the camp-fires, I picked my way, with a weight at my heart, for I felt how vain it must be to hope for success where such division reigned. Saxon looked on, however, with glistening eyes, and rubbed his hands with satisfaction.

"The leaven is working," quoth he. "Something will come of all this ferment."

"I see not what can come of it save disorder and weakness," I answered.

"Good soldiers will come of it, lad," said he. "They are all sharpening themselves, each after his own fashion, on the whetstone of religion. I tell you I would rather see them thus employed than at their drill, for all their wrangling and jangling."

"But how of this split in the council?" I asked.

"Ah, that is indeed a graver matter. All creeds may be welded together, but the Puritan and the scoffer are like oil and water. Yet the Puritan is the oil, for he will be ever atop. These courtiers do but stand for themselves, while the others are backed up by the pith and marrow of the army. It is well that we are afoot to-morrow. The king's troops are, I hear, pouring across Salisbury Plain, but their ordnance and stores are delaying them, for they know well that they must bring all they need, since they can expect little from the good-will of the country folk. Ah, friend Buyse, wie geht es?"

"Ganz gut," said the big German, looming up before us through the darkness. "But, sapperment, what a cawing and croaking, like a rookery at sunset! You English are a strange people—yes, donnerwetter, a very strange people! There are no two of you who think alike upon any subject under Himmel! The Cavalier will have his gay coat and his loose word. The Puritan will cut your throat rather than give up his sad-colored dress and his Bible. But, my young Hercules, I am right glad to see you back in safety. I am half in fear to give you my hand now, after your recent treatment of it. I trust that you are none the worse for the danger that you have gone through."

"Mine eyelids are, in truth, a little heavy," I answered. "Save for an hour or two aboard the lugger, and about as long on a prison couch, I have not closed eye since I left the camp."

"We shall fall in at the second bugle call, about eight of the clock," said Saxon. "We shall leave you, therefore, that you may restore yourself after your fatigues." With a parting nod the two old soldiers strode off together down the crowded fore street, while I made the best of my way back to the mayor's hospitable dwelling, where I had to repeat my story all over again to the assembled household before I was at last suffered to seek my room.

CHAPTER TWENTY-SEVEN

OF THE AFFAIR NEAR KEYNSHAM BRIDGE

MONDAY, June 21, 1685, broke very dark and windy, with dull clouds moving heavily across the sky, and a constant sputter of rain. Yet, a little after daybreak, Monmouth's bugles were blowing in every quarter of the town, from Tone Bridge to Shuttern, and by the hour appointed the regiments had mustered, the roll had been called, and the vanguard was marching briskly out through the eastern gate. It went forth in the same order as it entered, our own regiment and the Taunton burghers bringing up the rear. It was remarked on all sides that the army had improved in order and discipline during the three days' halt, owing perchance to the example of our own unceasing drill and soldierly bearing. In numbers it had increased to nigh eight thousand, and the men were well fed and light of heart. With sturdy, close-locked ranks, they splashed their way through mud and puddle, with many a rough country joke and many a lusty stave from song or hymn. So the long line wound its way over the hills.

All day we trudged along roads which were quagmires, over our ankles in mud, until, in the evening, we made our way to Bridgewater, where we gained some recruits, and also some hundred pounds for our military chest, for it was a well-to-do place, with a thriving coast-trade carried on down the river Parret. After a night in snug quarters we set off again in even worse weather than before. All day it was splashing and swashing through mud and mire, the rain-drops shining on the gun-barrels and dripping from the heavy-footed horses. On and on, through the pitiless rain, past the wooded park of Piper's Inn, through Walton, where the floods were threatening the cottages, past the orchards of Street, and so, in the dusk of the evening, into the gray old town of Glastonbury, where the good folk did their best by the warmth of their welcome to atone for the bitterness of the weather.

The next morning was still wet and inclement, so the army made a short march to Wells. On this march we first began to come into touch with the royal horse. More than once, when the rain-mist cleared, we saw the gleam of arms upon the low hills which overlook the road, and our scouts came in with reports of strong bodies of dragoons on either flank. At one time they massed heavily upon our rear, as though planning a descent upon the baggage. Saxon, however, planted a regiment of pikes on either side, so that they broke up again and glinted off over the hills.

From Wells we marched, upon the 24th, to Shepton-Mallet, with the ominous sabres and helmets still twinkling behind and on either side of us.

That evening we were at Keynsham Bridge, less than two leagues from Bristol, as the crow flies, and some of our horse forded the river and pushed on almost to the walls.

By morning the rain-clouds had at last cleared, so Reuben and I rode slowly up one of the sloping green hills which rose behind the camp, in the hope of gaining some sight of the enemy. Our men we left littered about upon the grass, trying to light fires with the damp sticks, or laying out their clothes to dry in the sunshine. A strange-looking band they were, coated and splashed with mud from head to heel, their hats all limp and draggled, their arms rusted, and their boots so worn that many walked barefoot, and others had swathed their kerchiefs round their feet. Yet this short spell of soldiering had changed them from honest-faced yokels into fierce-eyed, half-shaven, gaunt-cheeked fellows, who could carry arms or port pikes as though they had done naught else since childhood.

"There was a time when I was called plump Reuben," quoth my friend, as we rode together up the winding track. "What

with too little that is solid and too much that is liquid, I am
like to be skeleton Reuben ere I see Havant again. I am as
full of rain-water as my father's casks are of October. I would,
Micah, that you would wring me out and hang me to dry upon
one of these bushes."

"If we are wet, King James's men must be wetter," said I,
"for at least we have had such shelter as there was."

"It is poor comfort, when you are starved, to know that
another is in the same plight. I give you my word, Micah, I
took in one hole of my sword-belt on Monday, two on Tuesday,
one yesterday, and one to-day. I tell you I am thawing like
an icicle in the sun."

"If you should chance to dwindle to naught," said I, laughing, "what account are we to give of you in Taunton? Since
you have donned armor and taken to winning the hearts of fair
maidens, you have outstripped us all in importance, and become
a man of weight and substance."

"I had more substance and weight ere I began trailing over
the countryside like a Hambledon packman," quoth he. "But,
in very truth and with all gravity, Micah, it is a strange thing
to feel that the whole world for you, your hopes, your am-
bitions, your all, are gathered into so small a compass that a
hood might cover it and two little pattens support it. I feel as
if she were my own higher self, my loftier part, and that I,
should I be torn from her, would remain forever an incomplete
and half-formed being. With her I ask nothing else. Without
her all else is nothing."

"But have you spoken to the old man?" I asked. "Are
you indeed betrothed?"

"I have spoken to him," my friend answered, "but he was
so busy in filling ammunition-cases that I could not gain his
attention. When I tried once more he was counting the spare
pikes in the castle armory with a tally and an inkhorn. I told
him that I had come to crave his granddaughter's hand, on
which he turned to me and asked, 'Which hand?' with so blank

a stare that it was clear that his mind was elsewhere. On the third trial, though, the day that you did come back from Badminton, I did at last prefer my request, but he flashed out at me that this was no time for such fooleries, and he bade me wait until King Monmouth was on the throne, when I might ask him again. I warrant that he did not call such things fooleries fifty years ago, when he went a-courting himself."

"At least he did not refuse you," said I. "It is as good as a promise that, should the cause be successful, you shall be so too."

"By my faith," cried Reuben, "if a man could, by his own single blade, bring that about, there is none who hath so strong an interest in it as I. No, not Monmouth himself!"

Just beneath us ran the Avon, curving in long bends through the woodlands, with the gleam of the sun striking back from it here and there, as though a row of baby suns had been set upon a silver string. A road ran along the Somersetshire bank of the Avon, and down this two troops of our horse were advancing, with intent to establish outposts upon our eastern flank. As they jangled past in somewhat loose order, their course lay through a pinewood, into which the road takes a sharp bend. We were gazing down at the scene when, like lightning from a cloud, a troop of the Horse Guards wheeled out into the open, and, breaking from trot to canter, and from canter to gallop, dashed down in a whirlwind of blue and steel upon our unprepared squadrons. A crackle of hastily unslung carbines broke from the leading ranks, but in an instant the Guards burst through them and plunged on into the second troop. For a space the gallant rustics held their own, and the dense mass of men and horses swayed backward and forward, with the swirling swordblades playing above them in flashes of angry light. Then blue coats began to break from among the russet, the fight rolled wildly back for a hundred paces, the dense throng was split asunder, and the Royal Guards came pouring through the rent, and swerved off to right and left through hedges and over ditches, stabbing and hacking at the fleeing horsemen. The whole scene, with the stamping horses, tossing manes, shouts of triumph or despair, gasping of hard-drawn breath and musical clink and clatter of steel, was to us upon the hill like some wild vision, so swiftly did it come and so swiftly go. A sharp, stern bugle call summoned the Blues back into the road, where they formed up and trotted slowly away before fresh squadrons could come up from the camp. The sun gleamed and the river rippled as ever, and there was nothing save the long litter of men and horses to mark the course of the hell blast which had broken so suddenly upon us.

As the Blues retired we observed that a single officer brought up the rear, riding very slowly, as though it went much against his mood to turn his back, even to an army. The space betwixt the troop and him was steadily growing greater, yet he made no effort to quicken his pace, but jogged quietly on, looking back from time to time to see if he were followed. The same thought sprang into my comrade's mind and my own at the same instant, and we read it in each other's faces.

"This path," cried he, eagerly. "It brings us out beyond the grove, and is in the hollow all the way."

"Lead the horses until we get on better ground," I answered. "We may just cut him off if we are lucky."

There was no time for another word, for we hurried off down the uneven track, sliding and slipping on the rain-soaked turf. Springing into our saddles, we dashed down the gorge, through the grove, and so out on to the road in time to see the troop disappear in the distance, and to meet the solitary officer face to face.

He was a sunburned, high-featured man, with black mustachios, mounted on a great, raw-boned, chestnut charger. As we broke out on to the road he pulled up to have a good look at us. Then, having fully made up his mind as to our hostile intent, he drew his sword, plucked a pistol out of his holster with his left hand, and, griping the bridle between his teeth, dug his spurs into his horse's flanks, and charged down upon us at the top of his speed. As we dashed at him, Reuben on his bridle arm and I on the other, he cut fiercely at me, and at the same moment fired at my companion. The ball grazed Reuben's cheek, leaving a red weal behind it like a lash from a whip, and blackening his face with the powder. His cut, however, fell short, and, throwing my arm round his waist as

the two horses dashed past each other, I plucked him from the saddle and drew him face upward across my saddle-bow. Brave Covenant lumbered on with his double burden, and before the Guards had learned that they had lost their officer, we had brought him safe, in spite of his struggles and writhings, to within sight of Monmouth's camp.

"A narrow shave, friend," quoth Reuben, with his hand

to his cheek. "He hath tattooed my face with powder until I shall be taken for Solomon Sprent's younger brother."

"Thank God that you are unhurt," said I. "See, our horse are advancing along the upper road. Lord Grey himself rides at their head. We had best take our prisoner into camp, since we can do naught here."

"For Christ's sake, either slay me or set me down!" he cried. "I cannot bear to be carried in this plight, like a half-weaned infant, through your campful of grinning yokels."

"I would not make sport of a brave man," I answered. "If you will give your word to stay with us, you shall walk between us."

"Willingly," said he, scrambling down and arranging his ruffled attire. "By my faith, sirs, ye have taught me a lesson, not to think too meanly of mine enemies. I should have ridden with my troop had I thought that there was a chance of falling in with outposts or videttes."

"We were upon the hill before we cut you off," quoth Reuben. "Had that pistol-ball been a thought straighter, it is I that should have been truly the cut-off one. Zounds, Micah! I was grumbling even now that I had fallen away, but had my cheek been as round as of old the slug had been through it."

"Where have I seen you before?" asked our captive, bending his dark eyes upon me. "Aye, I have it! It was in the inn at Salisbury, where my light-headed comrade Horsford did draw upon an old soldier who was riding with you. Mine own name is Ogilvy—Major Ogilvy, of the Horse Guards Blue. I was right glad that ye did come off safely from the hounds. Some word had come of your errand after your departure, so this same Horsford with the mayor and one or two other Tantivies, whose zeal methinks outran their humanity, slipped the dogs upon your trail."

"I remember you well," I answered. "You will find Colonel Decimus Saxon, my former companion, in the camp. No doubt you will be shortly exchanged for some prisoner of ours."

"Much more likely to have my throat cut," said he, with a smile. "I fear that Feversham in his present temper will scarce pause to make prisoners, and Monmouth may be tempted to pay him back in his own coin. Yet it is the fortune of war, and I should pay for my want of all soldierly caution. Truth to tell, my mind was far from battles and ruses at the moment, for it had wandered away to aqua regia and its action upon the metals, until your appearance brought me back to soldiership."

"The horse are out of sight," said Reuben, looking backward, "ours as well as theirs. Yet I see a clump of men over yonder at the other side of the Avon, and there on the hillside, can you not see the gleam of steel?"

"There are foot there," I answered, puckering my eyes. "It seems to me that I can discern four or five regiments and as many colors of horse. King Monmouth should know of this with all speed."

"He does know of it," said Reuben. "Yonder he stands under the trees, with his council about him. See, one of them rides this way!"

A trooper had indeed detached himself from the group and galloped towards us. "If you are Captain Clarke, sir," he said, with a salute, "the king orders you to join his council."

"Then I leave the major in your keeping, Reuben," I cried. "See that he hath what our means allow." So saying, I spurred my horse, and soon joined the group who were gathered round the king. They were Grey, Wade, Buyse, Ferguson, Saxon, Hollis, and a score more, all looking very grave and peering down the valley with their glasses. Monmouth himself had dismounted and was leaning against the trunk of a tree, with his arms folded upon his breast, and a look of white despair upon his face. Behind the tree a lackey paced up and down, leading his glossy black charger, who pranced and tossed his lordly mane, a very king among horses.

"You see, friends," said Monmouth, turning lack-lustre eyes

from one leader to another, "Providence would seem to be against us. Some new mishap is ever at our heels."

"Not Providence, your majesty, but our own negligence," cried Saxon, boldly. "Had we advanced on Bristol last night we might have been on the right side of the ramparts by now."

"But we had no thought that the enemy's foot was so near!" exclaimed Wade.

"I told ye what would come of it, and so did Oberst Buyse and the worthy Mayor of Taunton," Saxon answered. "However, there is naught to be gained by mourning over a broken pipkin. We must e'en piece it together as best we may."

"Let us advance on Bristol, and put oor trust in the High-est," quoth Ferguson. "If it be his mighty wull that we should tak' it, then shall we enter into it, yea, though drakes and sakers lay as thick as cobble-stanes in the streets."

"Aye, aye! On to Bristol! God with us!" cried several of the Puritans, excitedly.

"But it is madness—dummheit—utter foolishness," Buyse broke in, hotly. "You have the chance, and you will not take it. Now the chance is gone, and you are all eager to go. Here is an army of, as near as I can judge, five thousand men on the right side of the river. We are on the wrong side, and yet you talk of crossing and making a beleaguering of Bristol without breaching-pieces or spades, and with this force in our rear. Will the town make terms when they can see from their ramparts the van of the army which comes to help them? Or does it assist us in fighting the army to have a strong town beside us, from which horse and foot can make an outfall upon our flank? I say again that it is madness."

What the German soldier said was so clearly the truth that even the fanatics were silenced. Away in the east the long, shimmering lines of steel and the patches of scarlet upon the green hill-side were arguments which the most thoughtless could not overlook.

"What would you advise, then?" asked Monmouth, moodily, tapping his jewelled riding-whip against his high boots.

"To cross the river and come to hand-gripes with them ere they can get help from the town," the burly German answered, bluntly. "I cannot understand what we are here for if it be not to fight. If we win, the town must fall. If we lose, we have had a bold stroke for it, and can do no more."

"Is that your opinion, too, Colonel Saxon?" the king asked.

"Assuredly, your majesty, if we can fight to advantage. We can scarce do that, however, by crossing the river on a single narrow bridge in the face of such a force. I should advise that we destroy this Keynsham Bridge, and march down this southern bank in the hope of forcing a fight in a position which we may choose."

"We have not yet summoned Bath," said Wade. "Let us do as Colonel Saxon proposes, and let us in the meantime march in that direction and send a trumpet to the governor."

"There is yet another plan," quoth Sir Stephen Timewell, "which is to hasten to Gloucester, to cross the Severn there, and so march through Worcestershire into Shropshire and Cheshire. Your majesty has many friends in those parts."

Monmouth paced up and down, with his hand to his forehead, like one distrait. "What am I to do," he cried, at last, "in the midst of all this conflicting advice, when I know that not only my own success but the lives of these poor, faithful peasants and craftsmen depend upon my resolution."

"With all humbleness, your majesty," said Lord Grey, who had just returned with the horse, "I should suggest, since there are only a few troops of their cavalry on this side of the Avon, that we blow up the bridge and move onward to Bath, whence we can pass into Wiltshire, which we know to be friendly."

"So be it!" cried the king, with the reckless air of one who accepts a plan, not because it is the best, but because he feels that all are equally hopeless. "What think you, gentlemen?" he added, with a bitter smile. "I have heard news from Lon-

don this morning that my uncle has clapped two hundred mer-
chants and others who are suspected of being true to their creed
into the Tower and the Fleet. He will have one-half of the
nation mounting guard over the other half ere long."

"Or the whole, your majesty, mounting guard over him,"
suggested Wade. "He may himself see the Traitor's Gate
some of these mornings."

"Ha, ha! Think ye so? think ye so?" cried Monmouth,
rubbing his hands and brightening into a smile. "Well, mayhap you have nicked the truth. Who knows? Henry's cause
seemed a losing one until Bosworth Field settled the contention. To your charges, gentlemen. We shall march in half
an hour. Colonel Saxon and you, Sir Stephen, shall cover the
rear and guard the baggage—a service of honor, with this fringe
of horse upon your skirts."

The council broke up forthwith, every man riding off to his
own regiment. The whole camp was in a stir, bugles blowing
and drums rattling, until in a very short time the army was
drawn up in order, and the forlorn of cavalry had already started
along the road which leads to Bath. On our march we could
see the red coats of Feversham keeping pace with us upon the
other side of the Avon. A large body of his horse and dragoons
had forded the stream and hovered upon our skirts, but Saxon
and Sir Stephen covered the baggage so skilfully, and faced
round so fiercely with such a snarl of musketry whenever they
came too nigh, that they never ventured to charge home.

CHAPTER TWENTY-EIGHT

OF THE FIGHT IN WELLS CATHEDRAL

I AM fairly tied to the chariot-wheels of history now and must follow on with name and place and date, whether my tale suffer by it or no. I am very sure that the sacrifices of these brave men were not thrown away, and that their strivings were not as profitless as might at first sight appear. Monmouth's army was but the vanguard of that which marched three years later into London, when James and his cruel ministers were flying as outcasts over the face of the earth.

On the night of June 27th, or rather early in the morning of June 28th, we reached the town of Frome, very wet and miserable, for the rain had come on again, and all the roads were quagmires. From this next day we pushed on once more to Wells, where we spent the night and the whole of the next day, to give the men time to get their clothes dry, and to recover themselves after their privations.

In the forenoon a parade of our Wiltshire regiment was held in the Cathedral Close, when Monmouth praised it, as it well deserved, for the soldierly progress made in so short a time.

As we returned to our quarters after dismissing our men, we came upon a great throng of the rough Bagworthy and Oare miners, who were assembled in the open space in front of the cathedral, listening to one of their own number, who was addressing them from a cart. The wild and frenzied gestures of the man showed us that he was one of those extreme sectaries whose religion runs perilously near to madness. The hums and groans which rose from the crowd proved, however, that his fiery words were well suited to his hearers, so we halted on the verge of the multitude and hearkened to his address. A red-bearded, fierce-faced man he was, with tangled, shaggy hair tumbling over his gleaming eyes, and a hoarse voice which resounded over the whole square.

"What shall we not do for the Lord?" he cried; "what shall we not do for the Holy of Holies? Why is it that His hand is heavy upon us? Truly, brothers, it is because we have slighted the Lord, because we have not been whole-hearted towards Him. Woe unto ye if, after having put your hands to God's plough, ye turn back from the work! See there!" he howled, facing round to the beautiful cathedral, "what means this great heap of stones? Is it not an altar of Baal? Is it not built for man-worship rather than God-worship? Is it not there that the man Ken, tricked out in his foolish rochet and baubles, may preach his soulless and lying doctrines, which are but the old dish of Popery served up under a new cover? And shall we suffer this thing? Shall we, the chosen children of the Great One, allow this plague-spot to remain? Can we expect the Almighty to help us when we will not stretch out a hand to help Him? We have left the other temples of Prelacy behind us. Shall we leave this one too, my brothers?"

"No, no!" yelled the crowd, tossing and swaying.

"Shall we pluck it down, then, until no one stone is left upon another?"

"Yes, yes!" they shouted.

"Now, at once?"

"Yes, yes!"

"Then to work!" he cried, and, springing from the cart, he rushed towards the cathedral, with the whole mob of wild fanatics at his heels. Some crowded in, shouting and yelling, through the open doors, while others swarmed up the pillars and pedestals of the front, hacking at the sculptured ornaments, and tugging at the gray old images which filled every niche.

"This must be stopped," said Saxon, curtly. "We cannot afford to insult and estray the whole Church of England to please a few hot-headed ranters. The pillage of this cathedral would do our cause more harm than a pitched battle lost. Do you bring up your company, Sir Gervas, and we shall do what we can to hold them in check until they come."

"Hi, Masterton!" cried the baronet, spying one of his under-officers among the crowd who were looking on, neither assisting nor opposing the rioters. "Do you hasten to the quarters, and tell Barker to bring up the company with their matches burning. I may be of use here."

"Ha, here is Buyse!" cried Saxon, joyously, as the huge German ploughed his way through the crowd. "And Lord Grey, too! We must save the cathedral, my lord! They would sack and burn it."

"This way, gentlemen," cried an old, gray-haired man, running out towards us with hands outspread, and a bunch of keys clanking at his girdle. "Oh, hasten, gentlemen, if ye can indeed prevail over these lawless men! They have pulled down Saint Peter, and they will have Paul down too unless help comes. There will not be an apostle left. The east window is broken. They have brought a hogshead of beer, and are broaching it upon the high altar. Oh, alas, alas! that such things should be in a Christian land!" He sobbed aloud and stamped about in a very frenzy of grief.

"It is the verger, sirs," said one of the townsfolk. "He hath grown gray in the cathedral."

"This way to the vestry door, my lords and gentlemen," cried the old man, pushing a way strenuously through the crowd. "Now, lack-a-day, the sainted Paul hath gone too!"

As he spoke a splintering crash from inside the cathedral announced some fresh outrage on the part of the zealots. Our guide hastened on with renewed speed, until he came to a low oaken door heavily arched, which he unlocked with much rasping of wards and creaking of hinges. Through this we sidled as best we might, and hurried after the old man down a stone-flagged corridor, which led through a wicket into the cathedral, close by the high altar.

The great building was full of the rioters, who were rushing hither and thither, destroying and breaking everything which they could lay their hands on. In the centre of the side aisle a small group had a rope round the neck of Mark the Evangelist, and were dragging lustily upon it, until, even as we entered, the statue, after tottering for a few moments, came crashing down upon the marble floor. The shouts which greeted every fresh outrage, with the splintering of wood-work, the smashing of windows, and the clatter of falling masonry, made up a most deafening uproar, which was increased by the droning of the organ, until some of the rioters silenced it by slitting up the bellows.

What more immediately concerned ourselves was the scene which was being enacted just in front of us at the high altar. A barrel of beer had been placed upon it, and a dozen ruffians gathered round it. As we entered the brown mead was foaming over, while the mob, with roars of laughter, were passing up their dippers and pannikins. The German soldier rapped out a rough, jagged oath at this spectacle, and shouldering his way through the roisterers he sprang upon the altar. The ring-leader was bending over his cask when the soldier's iron grip fell upon his collar, and in a moment his heels were flapping in the air and his head three feet deep in the cask, while the beer splashed and foamed in every direction. With a mighty heave Buyse picked up the barrel, with the half-drowned miner inside, and hurled it clattering down the broad marble steps which led from the body of the church. At the same time, with the aid of a dozen of our men who had followed us into the cathedral, we drove back the fellow's comrades, and thrust them out beyond the rails which divided the choir from the nave.

Our inroad had the effect of checking the riot, but it simply did so by turning the fury of the zealots from the walls and windows to ourselves. Images, stone-work, and wood-carvings were all abandoned, and the whole swarm came rushing up, with a hoarse buzz of rage, all discipline and order completely lost

in their religious frenzy. "Smite the Prelatists!" they howled.
"Down with the friends of Antichrist! Cut them off, even at
the horns of the altar! Down with them!" On either side they
massed, a wild, half-demented crowd, some with arms and some
without, but filled to a man with the very spirit of murder.

"This is a civil war within a civil war," said Lord Grey, with
a quiet smile. "We had best draw, gentlemen, and defend the
gap in the rails, if we may hold it good until help arrives." He
flashed out his rapier as he spoke and took his stand on the
top of the steps, with Saxon and Sir Gervas upon one side of
him, Buyse, Reuben, and myself upon the other. There was only
room for six to wield their weapons with effect, so our scanty
band of followers scattered themselves along the line of the
rails, which were luckily so high and strong as to make an
escalado difficult in the face of any opposition.

The riot had now changed into open mutiny among these
marshmen and miners. Pikes, scythes, and knives glimmered
through the dim light, while their wild cries re-echoed from the
high, arched roof like the howling of a pack of wolves. From
either side they came on, gathering speed and volume, until at
last, with a wild cry, they surged right down upon our sword-
points.

I can say nothing of what took place to right or left of me
during the ruffle, for, indeed, there were so many pressing upon
us, and the fight was so hot, that it was all that each of us could
do to hold our own. The very number of our assailants was in
our favor, by hampering their sword-arms. One burly miner
cut fiercely at me with his scythe, but missing me he swung half
round with the force of the blow, and I passed my sword through
his body before he could recover himself. A marshman, looking more like a shaggy wild beast than a human being, darted
under my weapon and caught me around the knees, while another
brought a flail down upon my head-piece, from which it glanced
on to my shoulder. A third thrust at me with a pike, and
pricked me on the thigh, but I shore his weapon in two with one

blow, and split his head with the next. The man with the flail
gave back at sight of this, and a kick freed me from the unarmed,
ape-like creature at my feet, so that I found myself clear of my
assailants, and none the worse for my encounter, save for a
touch on the leg and some stiffness of the neck and shoulder.

Looking round I found that my comrades had also beaten
off those who were opposed to them. Saxon was holding his
bloody rapier in his left hand, while the blood was trickling
from a slight wound upon his right. Two miners lay across
each other in front of him, but at the feet of Sir Gervas Jerome
no fewer than four bodies were piled together. He had plucked
out his snuff-box as I glanced at him, and was offering it, with
a bow and a flourish, to Lord Grey, as unconcernedly as though
he were back once more in his London coffee-house. Buyse
leaned upon his long broadsword, and looked gloomily at a head-
less trunk in front of him, which I recognized, from the dress,
as being that of the preacher. As to Reuben, he was unhurt
himself, but in sore distress over my own trifling scar, though
I assured the faithful lad that it was a less thing than many a
tear from branch or thorn which we had had when blackberry-
ing together.

The fanatics, though driven back, were not men to be content with a single repulse. They had lost ten of their number,
including their leader, without being able to break our line, but
the failure only served to increase their fury. For a minute or
so they gathered panting in the aisle. Then, with a mad yell,
they dashed in once more, and made a desperate effort to cut a
way through to the altar. It was a fiercer and more prolonged
struggle than before. One of our followers was stabbed to the
heart over the rails, and fell without a groan. Another was
stunned by a mass of masonry hurled at him by a giant cragsman.
Reuben was felled by a club, and would have been dragged out
and hacked to pieces had I not stood over him and beaten off
his assailants. Sir Gervas was borne off his legs by the rush,
but lay like a wounded wild-cat, striking out furiously at every-

thing which came within his reach. Buyse and Saxon, back to back, stood firm amid the seething, rushing crowd, cutting down every man within sweep of their swords. Yet in such a struggle numbers must in the end prevail, and I confess that I for one had begun to have fears for the upshot of our contest, when the heavy tramp of disciplined feet rang through the cathedral, and the baronet's musketeers came at a quick run up the central aisle. The fanatics did not await their charge, but darted off over benches and pews, followed by our allies, who were furious on seeing their beloved captain upon the ground. There was a wild minute or two, with confused shuffling of feet, stabs, groans, and the clatter of musket butts on the marble floor. Of the rioters some were slain, but the greater part threw down their arms and were arrested at the command of Lord Grey, while a strong guard was placed at the gates to prevent any fresh outburst of sectarian fury.

When at last the cathedral was cleared and order restored, we had time to look around us and to reckon our own injuries. In all my wanderings, and the many wars in which I afterwards fought—wars compared to which this affair of Monmouth's was but the merest skirmish—I have never seen a stranger or more impressive scene. In the dim, solemn light the pile of bodies in front of the rails, with their twisted limbs and white, set faces, had a most sad and ghost-like aspect. The evening light, shining through one of the few unbroken stained-glass windows, cast great splotches of vivid crimson and of sickly green upon the heap of motionless figures. A few wounded men sat about in the front pews or lay upon the steps moaning for water. Of our own small company not one had escaped unscathed. Three of our followers had been slain outright, while a fourth was lying stunned from a blow. Buyse and Sir Gervas were much bruised. Saxon was cut on the right arm. Reuben had been felled by a bludgeon stroke, and would certainly have been slain but for the fine temper of Sir Jacob Clancing's breastplate, which had turned a fierce pike-thrust. As to myself it is scarce worth the mention, but my head sang for some hours like a good-wife's kettle, and my boot was full of blood, which may have been a blessing in disguise, for Sneckson, our Havant barber, was ever dinning into my ears how much the better I should be for a phlebotomy.

In the meantime all the troops had assembled and the mutiny been swiftly stamped out.   There were doubtless many among the Puritans who had no love for the Prelatists, but none save the most crack-brained fanatics could fail to see that the sacking of the cathedral would set the whole Church of England in arms, and ruin the cause for which they were fighting.   As it was, much damage had been done, for while the gang within had been smashing all which they could lay their hands upon, others outside had chipped off cornices and gargoyles, and had even dragged the lead covering from the roof and hurled it down in great sheets to their companions beneath.   This last led to some profit, for the army had no great store of ammunition, so the lead was gathered up by Monmouth's orders and recast into bullets.   The prisoners were held in custody for a time, but it was deemed unwise to punish them, so they were finally pardoned and dismissed from the army.

The enemy's horse hovered about us during these days, but the foot had been delayed through the heavy weather and the swollen streams.   On the last day of June we marched out of Wells, and made our way across flat, sedgy plains and over the low Polden Hills to Bridgewater, where we found some few recruits awaiting us.   Here Monmouth had some thoughts of making a stand, and even set to work raising earthworks; but it was pointed out to him that, even could he hold the town, there was not more than a few days' provisions within it, while the country round had been already swept so bare that little more could be expected from it.   The works were therefore abandoned, and, fairly driven to bay, without a loophole of escape left, we awaited the approach of the enemy.

CHAPTER TWENTY-NINE

OF THE GREAT CRY FROM THE LONELY HOUSE

AND so our weary marching and counter-marching came at last to an end, and we found ourselves with our backs fairly against the wall, and the whole strength of the government turned against us. Not a word came to us of a rising or movement in our favor in any part of England. Everywhere the Dissenters were cast into prison and the Church dominant. From north and east and west the militia of the counties was on its march against us. In London six regiments of Dutch troops had arrived as a loan from the Prince of Orange. Others were said to be on their way. The city had enrolled ten thousand men. Everywhere there was mustering and marching to succor the flower of the English army, which was already in Somersetshire. And all for the purpose of crushing some five or six thousand clodhoppers and fishermen, half-armed and penniless, who were ready to throw their lives away for a man and for an idea.

But if the idea for which these poor men fought was a worthy one, what shall we say of the man who had been chosen as the champion of their cause? Alas, that such men should have had such a leader! Swinging from the heights of confidence to the depths of despair, choosing his future council of state one day and proposing to fly from the army on the next, he appeared from the start to be possessed by the very spirit of fickleness.

I will do Monmouth the justice to say that from the time when it was at last decided to fight—for the very good reason that no other course was open—he showed up in a more soldierly and manlier spirit. For the first few days in July no means were neglected to hearten our troops and to nerve them for the coming battle. As to their courage there was no occasion to quicken that, for they were as fearless as lions, and the only danger was lest their fiery daring should lead them into foolhardiness. Their desire was to hurl themselves upon the enemy like a horde of Moslem fanatics, and it was no easy matter to drill such hot-headed fellows into the steadiness and caution which war demands.

Provisions ran low upon the third day of our stay in Bridge-water, which was due to our having exhausted that part of the country before, and also to the vigilance of the Royal Horse, who scoured the district round and cut off our supplies. Lord Grey determined, therefore, to send out two troops of horse under cover of night, to do what they could to refill the larder. The command of the small expedition was given over to Major Martin Hooker, an old life-guardsman of rough speech and curt manners, who had done good service in drilling the headstrong farmers and yeomen into some sort of order. Sir Gervas Jerome and I asked leave from Lord Grey to join the foray—a favor which was readily granted, since there was little stirring in the town.

It was about eleven o'clock on a moonless night that we sallied out of Bridgewater, intending to explore the country in the direction of Boroughbridge and Athelney. We had word that there was no large body of the enemy in that quarter, and it was a fertile district where good store of supplies might be hoped for. We took with us four empty wagons, to carry whatever we might have the luck to find. Our commander arranged that one troop should ride before these and one behind, while a small advance party, under the charge of Sir Gervas, kept some hundreds of paces in front. In this order we clattered out of the town just as the late bugles were blowing, and swept away down the quiet, shadowy roads, bringing anxious, peering faces to the casements of the wayside cottages as we whirled past in the darkness.

That ride comes very clearly before me as I think of it. The baronet and I rode in front, knee against knee, and his light-hearted chatter of life in town, with his little snatches of verse or song from Cowley or Waller, were a very balm of Gilead to my sombre and somewhat heavy spirit.

"Life is indeed life on such a night as this," quoth he, as we breathed in the fresh country air with the reeks of crops and of kine. "Rabbit me! but you are to be envied, Clarke, for having been born and bred in the country! What pleasures has the town to offer compared to the free gifts of nature, provided always that there be a perruquier's and a snuff merchant's and a scent vendor's and one or two tolerable outfitters within reach? With these, and a good coffee-house and a playhouse, I think I could make shift to lead a simple pastoral life for some months."

"In the country," said I, laughing, "we have ever the feeling that the true life of mankind, with the growth of knowledge and wisdom, are being wrought out in the towns."

"Ventre Saint-Gris! It was little knowledge or wisdom that I acquired there," he answered. "Truth to tell, I have lived more and learned more during these few weeks that we have been sliding about in the rain with our ragged lads than ever I did when I was page of the court, with the ball of fortune at my feet. Ged, it is a new creed for me to be preaching!"

"But," said I, "when you were a wealthy man you must have been of service to some one, for how could one spend so much money and yet none be the better?"

"You dear, bucolic Micah!" he cried, with a gay laugh. "You will ever speak of my poor fortune with bated breath and in an awe-struck voice, as though it were the wealth of the Indies. You cannot think, lad, how easy it is for a money-bag to take unto itself wings and fly. Od's fish, lad! when I think of the swarms of needy beggars, the nose-slitting bullies, the toadies, and the flatterers who were reared by us, I feel that in hatching such a poisonous brood our money hath done what no money can undo. Have I not seen them thirty deep of a morning when I have held my levee, cringing up to my bedside——"

"Your bedside!" I exclaimed.

"Aye; it was the mode to receive in bed, attired in laced cambric shirt and periwig, though afterwards it was permitted to sit up in your chamber, but dressed, *à la négligence,* in gown and slippers. The mode is a terrible tyrant, Clarke, though its arm may not extend as far as Havant. The idle man of the town must have some rule of life, so he becomes a slave to the law of the fashions. Mark you those lights upon the left! Would it not be well to see if there is not something to be had there?"

"Hooker hath orders to proceed to a certain farm," I answered. "This we could take upon our return should we still have space. We shall be back here before morning."

"We must get supplies, if I have to ride back to Surrey for them," said he. "Rat me, if I dare look my musketeers in the face again unless I bring them something to toast upon the ends of their ramrods! They had little more savory than their own bullets to put in their mouths when I left them. But I was speaking of old days in London. Our time was well filled. You see, Clarke, that we were active in our idleness, and that there was no lack of employment. Then as evening came on, there were the playhouses to draw us, Dorset Gardens, Lincoln's Inn, Drury Lane, and the Queen's—among the four there was ever some amusement to be found."

"There, at least, your time was well employed," said I; "you could not hearken to the grand thoughts or lofty words of Shakespeare or of Massinger without feeling some image of them in your own soul."

Sir Gervas chuckled quietly. "You are as fresh to me, Micah, as this sweet country air," said he. "Know, thou dear babe, that it was not to see the play that we frequented the playhouse."

"Then why, in Heaven's name?" I asked.

"To see each other," he answered. "It was the mode, I assure you, for a man of fashion to stand with his back turned to the stage from the rise of the curtain to the fall of it. There were the orange wenches to quiz and there were the vizards of the pit, and there were the beauties of the town and the toasts of the court, all fair mark for our quizzing-glasses. Play, indeed! 'Tis true that if La Jeune were dancing, or if Mrs. Bracegirdle or Mrs. Oldfield came upon the boards, we would hum and clap, but it was the fine woman that we applauded rather than the actress."

"And when the play was over you went doubtless to supper and so to bed?"

"To supper, certainly. Sometimes to the Rhenish House, sometimes to Pontack's in Abchurch Lane. Every one had his own taste in that matter. Then there were dice and cards at the Groom Parter's or under the arches at Covent Garden, piquet, passage, hazard, primero—what you choose. After that you could find all the world at the coffee-houses, where an arrière supper was often served with devilled bones and prunes, to drive the fumes of wine from the head. Zounds, Micah! if the Jews should relax their pressure, or if this war brings us any luck, you shall come to town with me and shall see all these things for yourself."

"Truth to tell, it doth not tempt me much," I answered. "Slow and solemn I am by nature, and in such scenes as you have described I should feel a very death's head at a banquet."

Sir Gervas was about to reply when of a sudden, out of the silence of the night, there rose a long-drawn, piercing scream, which thrilled through every nerve of our bodies. I have never heard such a wail of despair. We pulled up our horses, as did the troopers behind us, and strained our ears for some sign as to whence the sound proceeded, for some were of opinion that it came from our right and some from our left. The main body with the wagons had come up, and we all listened intently for any return of the terrible cry. Presently it broke upon us again, wild, shrill, and agonized, the scream of a woman in mortal distress.

" 'Tis over there, Major Hooker," cried Sir Gervas, standing up in his stirrups and peering through the darkness. "There is a house about two fields off. I can see some glimmer, as from a window with the blind drawn."

"Shall we not make for it at once?" I asked, impatiently, for our commander sat stolidly upon his horse as though by no means sure what course he should pursue.

"I am here, Captain Clarke," said he, "to convey supplies to the army, and I am by no means justified in turning from my course to pursue other adventures."

"Death, man! there is a woman in distress," cried Sir Gervas. "Why, major, you would not ride past and let her call in vain for help? Hark, there she is again!" As he spoke the wild scream rang out once more from the lonely house.

"Nay, I can abide this no longer," I cried, my blood boiling in my veins; "do you go on your errand, Major Hooker, and my friend and I shall leave you here. We shall know how to justify our action to the king. Come, Sir Gervas!"

"Mark ye, this is flat mutiny, Captain Clarke," said Hooker; "you are under my orders, and should you desert me you do so at your peril."

"In such a case I care not a groat for thy orders," I answered, hotly. Turning Covenant, I spurred down a narrow, deeply rutted lane which led towards the house, followed by Sir Gervas and two or three of the troopers. At the same moment I heard a sharp word of command from Hooker and the creaking of wheels, showing that he had indeed abandoned us and proceeded on his mission.

"He is right," quoth the baronet, as we rode down the lane; "Saxon or any other old soldier would commend his discipline."

"There are things which are higher than discipline," I muttered. "I could not pass on and leave this poor soul in her distress. But see—what have we here?"

A dark mass loomed in front of us, which proved, as we approached, to be four horses fastened by their bridles to the hedge.

"Cavalry horses, Captain Clarke!" cried one of the troopers who had sprung down to examine them. "They have the government saddle and holsters. Here is a wooden gate which opens on a pathway leading to the house."

"We had best dismount, then," said Sir Gervas, jumping down and tying his horse beside the others. "Do you lads stay by the horses, and if we call for ye come to our aid. Sergeant Holloway, you can come with us. Bring your pistols with you."

CHAPTER THIRTY

OF THE SWORDSMAN WITH THE BROWN JACKET

THE sergeant, who was a great, rawboned west-countryman, pushed the gate open, and we were advancing up the winding pathway, when a stream of yellow light flooded out from a suddenly opened door, and we saw a dark, squat figure dart through it into the inside of the house. At the same moment there rose up a babel of sounds, followed by two pistol shots, and a roaring, gasping hubbub, with clash of swords and storm of oaths. At this sudden uproar we all three ran at our topmost speed up the pathway and peered in through the open door.

The room was large and lofty, with long rows of hams and salted meats dangling from the smoke-browned rafters, as is usual in Somersetshire farm-houses. Right in front of the door a great fire of wood fagots was blazing, and before this, to our unutterable horror, there hung a man head downward, suspended by a rope which was knotted round his ankles, and which, passing over a hook in a beam, had been made fast to a ring in the floor. The struggles of this unhappy man had caused the rope to whirl round, so that he was spinning in front of the blaze like a joint of meat. Across the threshold lay a woman, the one whose cries had attracted us, but her rigid face and twisted body showed that our aid had come too late to save her from the fate which she had seen impending. Close by her two swarthy dragoons in the glaring red coats of the royal army lay stretched across each other upon the floor, dark and scowling even in death. In the centre of the room two other dragoons were cutting and stabbing with their broadswords at a thick, short, heavy-shouldered man, clad in coarse brown kersey stuff, who sprang about among the chairs and round the table with a long, basket-hilted rapier in his hand, parrying or dodging their blows with wonderful adroitness, and every now and then putting in a thrust in return. Hard pressed as he was, and even as we gazed he sprang back to avoid a fierce rush of the furious soldiers, and by a quick, sharp side stroke he severed the rope by which the victim was hung and the body fell with a heavy thud upon the brick floor.

This strange scene held us spellbound for a few seconds, but there was no time for delay, for a slip or trip would prove fatal to the gallant stranger. Rushing into the chamber, sword in hand, we fell upon the dragoons, who, outnumbered as they were, backed into a corner and struck out fiercely, knowing that they need expect no mercy after the devil's work in which they had been engaged. Holloway, our sergeant of horse, springing furiously in, laid himself open to a thrust which stretched him dead upon the ground. Before the dragoon could disengage his weapon, Sir Gervas cut him down, while at the same moment the stranger got past the guard of his antagonist, and wounded him mortally in the throat. Of the four redcoats not one escaped alive, while the bodies of our sergeant and of the old couple who had been the first victims increased the horror of the scene.

"Poor Holloway is gone," said I, placing my hand over his heart. "Who ever saw such a shambles? I feel sick and ill."

"Here is *eau de vie*, if I mistake not," cried the stranger, clambering up on a chair and reaching a bottle from the shelf. "Good, too, by the smell. Take a sup, for you are as white as a new-bleached sheet."

"Honest warfare I can abide, but scenes like this make my blood run cold," I answered, taking a gulp from the flask.

"The woman is dead," said Sir Gervas, "and the man is also, I fear, past recovery. He is not burned, but suffers, I should judge, poor devil! from the rush of blood to the head."

"If that be all it may well be cured," remarked the stranger; and, taking a small knife from his pocket, he rolled up the old

THE SERGEANT PUSHED THE GATE OPEN

man's sleeve and opened one of his veins. At first only a few sluggish black drops oozed from the wound, but presently the blood began to flow more freely, and the injured man showed signs of returning sense.

"He will live," said the little swordsman, putting his lancet back in his pocket. "And now, who may you be to whom I owe this interference which shortened the affair, though mayhap the result would have been the same had you left us to settle it among ourselves?"

"We are from Monmouth's army," I answered. "He lies at Bridgewater, and we are scouting and seeking supplies."

"And who are you?" asked Sir Gervas. "And how came you into this ruffle? S'bud, you are a game little rooster to fight four such great cockerels!"

"My name is Hector Marot," the man answered, cleaning out his empty pistols and very carefully reloading them. "As to whom I am, it is a matter of small moment. Suffice it that I have helped to lessen Kirke's horse by four of his rogues. The Lord help Monmouth's men should they be beaten! These vermin are more to be feared than hangman's cord or headsman's axe."

"But how did you chance upon the spot at the very nick of time?" I asked.

"Why, marry, I was jogging down the road on my mare when I heard the clatter of hoofs behind me, and, concealing myself in a field, as a prudent man would while the country is in its present state, I saw these four rouges gallop past. They made their way up to the farm-house here, and presently from cries and other tokens I knew what manner of hell-fire business they had on hand. On that I left my mare in the field and ran up, when I saw them through the casement, tricing the good man up in front of his fire to make him confess where his wealth lay hidden. Finding that his mouth remained closed, they ran him up, as you saw, and would assuredly have toasted him like a snipe, had I not stepped in and winged two of them with my barkers. The others set upon me, but I pinked one through the forearm, and should doubtless have given a good account of both of them but for your incoming."

"Right gallantly done!" I exclaimed.

Sir Gervas, who had been staring very hard at the man, suddenly gave a start, and slapped his hand against his leg.

"Of course!" he cried. "Sink me, if I could remember where I had seen your face, but now it comes back to me very clearly."

The man glanced doggedly from under his bent brows at each of us in turn. "It seems that I have fallen among acquaintances," he said, gruffly; "yet I have no memory of ye. Methinks, young sir, that your fancy doth play ye false."

"Not a whit," the baronet answered, quietly, and bending forward, he whispered a few words into the man's ear, which caused him to spring from his seat and take a couple of quick strides forward, as though to escape from the house.

"Nay, nay!" cried Sir Gervas, springing between him and the door, "you shall not run away from us. Pshaw, man! never lay your hand upon your sword. We have had bloody work enough for one night. Besides, we would not harm you."

"What mean ye, then? What would ye have?" he asked, glancing about like some fierce wild beast in a trap.

"I have a most kindly feeling to you, man, after this night's work," cried Sir Gervas. "What is it to me how ye pick up a living, as long as you are a true man at heart? Let me perish if I ever forget a face which I have once seen, and your *bonne mine,* with the trade-mark upon your forehead, is especially hard to overlook."

"Suppose I be the same? What then?" the man asked, sullenly.

"There is no suppose in the matter. I could swear to you. But I would not, lad—not if I caught you red-handed. You must know, Clarke, since there is none to overhear us, that in the old days I was a justice of the peace in Surrey, and that our friend here was brought up before me on a charge of riding somewhat late o' night, and of being plaguy short with travellers. You will understand me. He was referred to assizes, but got away in the meanwhile, and so saved his neck. Right glad I am of it, for you will agree with me that he is too proper a man to give a tight-rope dance at Tyburn."

"Nay, gentlemen," he replied, seating himself on the edge of the table and carelessly swinging his legs, "since ye know so much it would be folly for me to attempt to deceive ye. I am indeed the same Hector Marot who hath made his name a terror on the great western road. With truth, however, I can say that though I have been ten years upon the roads, I have never yet taken a groat from the poor, or injured any man who did not wish to injure me. On the contrary, I have often risked life and limb to save those who were in trouble."

"We can bear you out in that," I answered, "for if these four red-coat devils have paid the price of their crimes, it is your doing rather than ours."

"Nay, I can take little credit for that," our new acquaintance answered. "Indeed, I had other scores to settle with Colonel Kirke's horse, and was but too glad to have this breather with them."

While we were talking the men whom we had left with the horses had come up, together with some of the neighboring farmers and cottagers, who were aghast at the scene of slaughter, and much troubled in their minds over the vengeance which might be exacted by the royal troops next day.

"For Christ's zake, zur," cried one of them, an old, ruddy-faced countryman, "move the bodies o' these soldier rogues into the road, and let it zeem as how they have perished in a chance fight wi' your troopers loike. Should it be known as they have met their end within a varm-house there will not be a thatch left unlighted over t' whole countryside; as it is, us can scarce keep these murthering Tangiers devils from our throats."

"His request is in reason," said the highwayman, bluntly.

"We have no right to have our fun and then go our way, leaving others to pay the score."

"Well, hark ye," said Sir Gervas, turning to the group of frightened rustics, "I'll strike a bargain with ye over the matter. We have come out for supplies, and can scarce go back empty-handed. If ye will among ye provide us with a cart, filling it with such bread-stuffs and greens as ye may, with a dozen bullocks as well, we shall not only screen ye in this matter, but I shall promise payment at fair market rates if ye will come to the Protestant camp for the money."

"I'll spare the bullocks," quoth the old man whom we had rescued, who was now sufficiently recovered to sit up. "Zince my poor dame is foully murthered, it matters little to me what becomes o' the stock."

"You say well, gaffer!" cried Hector Marot; "you show the true spirit."

"Her's been a true mate to me for more'n thirty year," said the old man, the tears coursing down his wrinkled cheeks. "Thirty zeed-toimes and thirty harvests we've worked together. But this is a zeed-toime which shall have a harvest o' blood if my right hand can compass it."

"If you go to t' wars, Gaffer Swain, we'll look to your homestead," said the farmer who had spoken before. "As to t' green stuffs as this gentleman asks for, he shall have not one wain-load, but three, if he will but gi' us half an hour to fill them up."

"Then we had set about our part of the contract," said Hector Marot. With the aid of our troopers he carried out the four dragoons and our dead sergeant, and laid them on the ground some way down the lane, leading the horses all round and between their bodies, so as to trample the earth, and bear out the idea of a cavalry skirmish. While this was doing, some of the laborers had washed down the brick floor of the kitchen and removed all traces of the tragedy. The murdered woman had been carried up to her own chamber, so that nothing was left to recall what had occurred save the unhappy farmer, who sat moodily in the same place, unconscious apparently, of all that was going on around him.

The loading of the wagons had been quickly accomplished, and the little drove of oxen gathered from a neighboring field. We were just starting upon our return journey when a young countryman rode up with the news that a troop of the Royal Horse were between the camp and ourselves. This was grave tidings, for we were but seven all told, and our pace was necessarily slow while we were hampered with the supplies.

"How about Hooker?" I suggested. "Should we not send after him and give him warning?"

"I'll goo at once," said the countryman.

"While we have such volunteer scouts as this," I remarked, "it is easy to see which side the country folk have in their hearts. But how are we to make our way back?"

"Zounds, Clarke! let us extemporize a fortress," suggested Sir Gervas. "We could hold this farm-house against all comers until Hooker returns, and then join our forces to his."

"Nay," I answered, "after leaving Major Hooker in a somewhat cavalier fashion, it would be a bitter thing to have to ask his help now that there is danger."

"Ho, ho!" cried the baronet. "For all your cold-blooded stolidity, you are keen enough where pride or honor is concerned. Shall we then ride onward, and chance it? I'll lay an even crown that we never so much as see a red-coat."

"If you will take my advice, gentlemen," said the highwayman, trotting up upon a beautiful bay mare, "I should say that your best course is to allow me to act as guide to you as far as the camp. It will be strange if I cannot find roads which shall baffle these blundering soldiers."

"A very wise and seasonable proposition," cried Sir Gervas. "Master Marot, a pinch from my snuffbox, which is ever a covenant of friendship with its owner. Adslidikins, man! though our acquaintance at present is limited to my having nearly hanged you on one occasion, yet I have a kindly feeling towards you, though I wish you had some more savory trade."

"So do many who ride o' night," Marot answered, with a chuckle. "But we had best start, for the east is whitening, and it will be daylight ere we come to Bridgewater."

Leaving the ill-omened farm-house behind us, we set off with all military precautions, Marot riding with me some distance in front, while two of the troopers covered the rear. So frequent were our turnings, and so often did we change the direction of our advance, that I feared more than once that our guide was at fault; yet, when at last the first rays of the sun brightened the landscape, we saw the steeple of Bridgewater parish church shooting up right in front of us.

"Zounds, man! you must have something of the cat in you to pick your way so in the dark," cried Sir Gervas, riding up to us. "I am right glad to see the town, for my poor wagons have been creaking and straining until my ears are weary with listening for the snap of the axle-bar. Master Marot, we owe you something for this."

"Is this your own particular district?" I asked, "or have you a like knowledge of every part of the south?"

"My range," said he, lighting his short, black pipe, "is from Kent to Cornwall, though never north of the Thames or Bristol Channel. Through that district there is no road which is not familiar to me, nor as much as a break in the hedge which I could not find in blackest midnight. It is my calling. But the trade is not what it was. If I had a son I should not bring him up to it. It hath been spoiled by the armed guards to the mail-coaches, and by the accursed goldsmiths, who have opened their banks and so taken the hard money into their strong-boxes, giving out instead slips of paper, which are as useless to us as an old news-letter. Truly the country is coming to a pretty pass when such trash as that is allowed to take the place of the king's coinage."

"And here we are within our own outposts," quoth Sir Gervas. "Now, mine honest friend, for honest you have been to us, whatever others may say to you, will you not come with us and strike in for a good cause? Zounds, man! you have many an ill deed to atone for, I'll warrant. Why not add one good one to your account, by risking your life for the reformed faith?"

"Not I," the highwayman answered, reining up his horse. "My own skin is nothing, but why should I risk my mare in such a fool's quarrel? Besides, it matters nothing to her whether Papist or Protestant sits on the throne of England—does it, my beauty?"

"But you might chance to gain preferment," I said. "Our colonel, Decimus Saxon, is one who loves a good swordsman, and his word hath power with King Monmouth and the council."

"Nay, nay!" cried Hector Marot, gruffly. "Let every man stick to his own trade. Kirke's horse I am ever ready to have a brush with, for a party of them hung old blind Jim Houston of Milverton, who was a friend of mine. But I will not fight against King James, nor will I risk the mare, so let me hear no more of it. And now I must leave ye, for I have much to do. Farewell to you!"

"Farewell, farewell!" we cried, pressing his brown, horny hands, "our thanks to you for your guidance." Raising his hat, he shook his bridle and galloped off down the road in a rolling cloud of dust.

"Rat me, if I ever say a word against the thieves again!" said Sir Gervas. "I never saw a man wield sword more deftly in my life, and he must be a rare hand with a pistol to bring those two tall fellows down with two shots. But look over there, Clarke! Can you not see bodies of red-coats?"

"Surely I can," I answered. "I can see them over yonder in the direction of Westonzoyland, as bright as the poppies among corn."

"There are more upon the left, near Chedzoy," quoth Sir

Gervas. "One, two, three, and one yonder, and two others behind—six regiments of foot in all. Faith! Monmouth must fight now, if he ever hopes to feel the gold rim upon his temples. The whole of King James's army hath closed upon him."

"We must get back to our command, then," I answered. "If I mistake not I see the flutter of our standards in the market-place." We spurred our weary steeds forward, and made our way with our little party and the supplies which we had collected, until we found ourselves back in our quarters, where we were hailed by the lusty cheers of our hungry comrades. Major Hooker came in shortly after with a good store of provisions, but in no very good case, for he had had a skirmish with the dragoons, and had lost eight or ten of his men. He bore a complaint straightway to the council concerning the manner in which we had deserted him; but great events were coming fast upon us now, and there was small time to inquire into petty matters of discipline.

CHAPTER THIRTY-ONE

OF THE MAID OF THE MARSH AND THE BUBBLE
WHICH ROSE FROM THE BOG

ALL Bridgewater was in a ferment as we rode in, for King James's forces were within four miles, on the Sedgemoor Plain, and it was likely that they would push on at once and storm the town. Towards afternoon, however, parties of our horse and peasants from the fen country came in with the news that there was no fear of an assault being attempted. The royal troops had quartered themselves snugly in the little villages of the neighborhood, and having levied contributions of cider and of beer from the farmers, they showed no sign of any wish to advance.

The town was full of women, the wives, mothers, and sisters of our peasants, who had come in from far and near to see their loved ones once more. Jack-booted, buff-coated troopers; scarlet militiamen, brown, stern-faced Tauntonians; serge-clad pikemen; wild, ragged miners; smock-frocked yokels; reckless, weather-tanned seamen; gaunt cragsmen from the northern coast, all pushed and jostled each other in a thick, many-colored crowd.

Our regiments had been taken off duty whenever it was clear that Feversham did not mean to advance, and they were now busy upon the victuals which our night-foray had furnished. It was a Sunday, fresh and warm, with a clear, unclouded sky and a gentle breeze, sweet with the smack of the country. At four o'clock Monmouth held a last council of war upon the square tower, whence a good view can be obtained of all the country round. Since my ride to Beaufort I had always been honored with a summons to attend, in spite of my humble rank in the army. There were some thirty councillors in all, as many as the space would hold, soldiers and courtiers, Cavaliers and Puritans, all drawn together now by the bond of a common danger.

King Monmouth stood among his chiefs, pale and haggard, with the dishevelled, unkempt look of a man whose distress of mind has made him forgetful of the care of his person. He held a pair of ivory glasses, and as he raised them to his eyes his thin white hands shook and twitched until it was grievous to watch him. Lord Grey handed his own glasses to Saxon, who leaned his elbows upon the rough stone breastwork and stared long and earnestly at the enemy.

"They are the very men I have myself led," said Monmouth, at last, in a low voice, as though uttering his thoughts aloud. "Over yonder at the right I see Dumbarton's foot. I know these men well. They will fight. Had we them with us, all would be well."

"Nay, your majesty," Lord Grey answered, with spirit, "you do your brave followers an injustice. They too will fight to the last drop of their blood in your quarrel."

"Look down at them!" said Monmouth, sadly, pointing at the swarming streets beneath us. "Braver hearts never beat in English breasts, yet do but mark how they brabble and clamor like clowns on a Saturday night. Compare them with the stern, orderly array of the trained battalions. Alas! that I should have dragged these honest souls from their little homes to fight so hopeless a battle!"

"Hark at that!" cried Wade. "They do not think it hopeless, nor do we." As he spoke a wild shout rose from the dense crowd beneath, who were listening to a preacher who was holding forth from a window.

"It is worthy Dr. Ferguson," said Sir Stephen Timewell, who had just come up. "He is as one inspired, powerfully borne onward in his discourse."

"They do indeed seem to be hot for battle," said Monmouth, with a more sprightly look. "It may be that one who has commanded regular troops, as I have done, is prone to lay too much weight upon the difference which discipline and training make. These brave lads seem high of heart. What think you of the enemy's dispositions, Colonel Saxon?"

"By my faith, I think very little of them, your majesty," Saxon answered, bluntly.

"How call you the hamlet on the left—that with the square, ivy-clad church-tower?" asked Monmouth, turning to the Mayor of Bridgewater, a small, anxious-faced man, who was evidently far from easy at the prominence which his office had brought upon him.

"Westonzoyland, your honor—that is, your grace—I mean, your majesty," he stammered. "The other, two miles farther off, is Middlezoy, and away to the left, just on the far side of the rhine, is Chedzoy."

"The rhine, sir! What do you mean?" asked the king, starting violently and turning so fiercely upon the timid burgher that he lost the little balance of wits which was left to him.

"Why, the rhine, your grace, your majesty," he quavered. "The rhine, which, as your majesty's grace cannot but perceive, is what the country-folk call the rhine."

"It is a name, your majesty, for the deep and broad ditches which drain off the water from the great morass of Sedgemoor," said Sir Stephen Timewell.

Monmouth turned white to his very lips, and several of the council exchanged significant glances, recalling the strange prophetic jingle which I had been the means of bringing to the camp. The silence was broken, however, by an old Cromwellian major named Hollis, who had been drawing the position of the villages where the enemy was quartered.

"If it please your majesty, there is something in their order which recalls to my mind that of the army of the Scots upon the occasion of the battle of Dunbar. Cromwell lay in Dunbar, even as we lie in Bridgewater. The ground around, which was boggy and treacherous, was held by the enemy. Now your majesty will see through your glass that a mile of bogland intervenes between these villages, and that the nearest one, Chedzoy, as I think they call it, might be approached without ourselves entering the morass. Very sure I am that were the lord-general with us now he would counsel us to venture some such attack."

"It is a bold thing, with raw peasants, to attack old soldiers," quoth Sir Stephen Timewell. "Yet, if it is to be done, I know well that there is not a man born within sound of the bells of St. Mary Magdalene who will flinch from it."

"You say well, Sir Stephen," said Monmouth. "At Dunbar Cromwell had veterans at his back, and was opposed to troops who had small experience of war."

"Yet there is much good sense in what Major Hollis has said," remarked Lord Grey. "We must either fall on, or be gradually girt round and starved out. That being so, why not take advantage at once of the chance which Feversham's ignorance or carelessness hath given us? To-morrow, if Churchill can prevail over his chief, I have little doubt that we shall find their camp rearranged, and so have cause to regret our lost opportunity."

"If we could break those, all would be well," cried Monmouth. "What is your advice, Colonel Buyse?"

"My advice is ever the same," the German answered. "We are here to fight, and the sooner we get to work the better."

"And yours, Colonel Saxon? Do you agree with the opinion of your friend?"

"I think, with Major Hollis, your majesty, that Feversham, by his dispositions, hath laid himself open to attack, and that we should take advantage of it forthwith. I should be in favor of a night onfall."

"The same thought was in my mind," said Grey. "Our friends here know every inch of the ground, and could guide us to Chedzoy as surely in the darkness as in the day."

"I have heard," said Saxon, "that much beer and cider, with wine and strong waters, have found their way into their camp. If this be so, we may give them a rouse while their heads are still buzzing with the liquor, when they shall scarce know whether it is ourselves or the blue devils which have come upon them."

A chorus of approval from the whole council showed that the prospect of at last coming to an engagement was welcome.

"Has any Cavalier anything to say against this plan?" asked the king.

We all looked from one to the other, but, though many faces were doubtful or desponding, none had a word to say against the night attack. Yet I dare say the boldest of us felt a sinking at the heart as we looked at our downcast, sad-faced leader, and asked ourselves whether this was a likely man to bring so desperate an enterprise to a success.

"If all are agreed," said he, "let our word be 'Soho,' and let us come upon them as soon after midnight as may be. What remains to be settled as to the order of battle may be left for the meantime. You will now, gentlemen, return to your regiments, and you will remember that be the upshot of this what it may, whether Monmouth be the crowned king of England or a hunted fugitive, his heart, while it can still beat, will ever bear in memory the brave friends who stood at his side in the hour of his trouble."

At this simple and kindly speech a flush of devotion, mingled in my own case at least with a heart-whole pity for the poor, weak gentleman, swept over us. We pressed round him with our hands upon the hilts of our swords, swearing that we would stand by him, though all the world stood between him and his rights.

"May God defend the right!" cried the council, solemnly, and separated, leaving the king with Grey to make the final dispositions for the attack.

"These popinjays of the court are ready enough to wave their rapiers and shout when there are four good miles between them and the foe," said Saxon, as we made our way through the crowd. "I fear that they will scarce be as forward when there is a line of musketeers to be faced, and a brigade of horse, perhaps, charging down upon their flank. But here comes friend Lockarby, with news written upon his face."

"I have a report to make, colonel," said Reuben, hurrying breathlessly up to us. "You may remember that I and my company were placed on guard this day at the eastern gate."

Saxon nodded.

"Being desirous of seeing all that I could of the enemy, I clambered up a lofty tree which stands just without the town. From this post, by the aid of a glass, I was able to make out their lines and camp. While I was gazing I chanced to observe a man slinking along under cover of the birch-trees, half-way between their lines and the town. Presently he came so near that I was able to distinguish who it was. He is a man, however, who, I have reason to believe, has no true love for the cause, and it is my belief that he hath been to the royal camp with news of our doings, and hath now come back for further information."

"Aye!" said Saxon, raising his eyebrows. "And what is the man's name?"

"His name is Derrick, one time chief apprentice to Master Timewell at Taunton, and now an officer of the Taunton foot."

"What, the young springald who had his eye upon pretty Mistress Ruth! Now, out on love, if it is to turn a true man into a traitor! But methought he was one of the elect? I have heard him hold forth to the pikemen. How comes it that one of his kidney should lend help to the Prelatist cause?"

"Love again," quoth I. "This same love is a pretty flower when it grows unchecked, but a sorry weed if thwarted."

"He hath an ill-feeling towards many in the camp," said Reuben, "and he would ruin the army to avenge himself on them, as a rogue might sink a ship in the hope of drowning one enemy. Sir Stephen himself hath incurred his hatred for refusing to force his daughter into accepting his suit. He has now returned into the camp, and I have reported the matter to you, that you may judge whether it would not be well to send a file of pikemen and lay him by the heels."

"Perhaps it would be best so," Saxon answered, full of thought; "and yet no doubt the fellow would have some tale prepared which would outweigh our mere suspicions. Could we not take him in the very act?"

A thought slipped into my head. I had observed from the tower that there was a single lonely cottage about a third of the way to the enemy's camp, standing by the road at a place where there were marshes on either side. Any one journeying that way must pass it. If Derrick tried to carry our plans to Feversham he might be cut off at this point by a party placed to lie in wait for him.

"Most excellent!" Saxon exclaimed, when I had explained the project. "My learned Fleming himself could not have devised a better *rusus belli*. Do you convey as many files as ye may think fit to this point, and I shall see that Master Derrick is primed up with some fresh news."

"Nay, a body of troops marching out would set tongues wagging," said Reuben. "Why should not Micah and I go?"

"That would indeed be better," Saxon answered. "But ye must pledge your words, come what may, to be back at sundown, for your companies must stand to arms an hour before the advance."

We both gladly gave the desired promise, and having learned for certain that Derrick had indeed returned to the camp, Saxon undertook to let drop in his presence some words as to the plans for the night, while we set off at once for our post. Our horses we left behind, and, slipping out through the eastern gate, we made our way over bog and moor, concealing ourselves as best we could, until we came out upon the lonely roadway and found ourselves in front of the house.

It was a plain, whitewashed, thatch-roofed cottage, with a small board above the door, whereon was written a notice that the occupier sold milk and butter. No smoke reeked up from the chimney, and the shutters of the window were closed. We knocked at the weather-blotched door, but receiving, as we expected, no reply, I presently put my shoulder against it and forced the staple from its fastenings. There was but a single chamber within, with a straight ladder in the corner, leading through a square hole in the ceiling to the sleeping-chamber under the roof. To our surprise it had still one inmate within its walls. In the centre of the room, facing the door as we entered, stood a little bright golden-haired maid, five or six years of age. Her tiny head was thrown back, and her large blue eyes were full of mingled wonder and defiance. As we entered the little witch flapped her kerchief at us and shooed as though we were two of the intrusive fowl whom she was wont to chivy out of the house.

"Go 'way!" she cried, still waving her hands and shaking her kerchief. "Go 'way! Granny told me to tell any one that came to go 'way!"

"But if they would not go away, little mistress," asked Reuben, "what were you to do then?"

"I was to drive them 'way," she answered, advancing boldly against us with many flaps. "You bad man!" she continued, flashing out at me, "you have broken granny's bolt."

"Nay, I'll mend it again," I answered, penitently, and catching up a stone I soon fastened the injured staple. "There, mistress, your granddam will never tell the difference."

"Ye must go 'way all the same," she persisted; "this is granny's house, not yours."

What were we to do with this resolute little dame of the marshes? That we should stay in the house was a crying need, for there was no other cover or shelter among the dreary bogs where we could hide ourselves. Yet she was bent upon driving us out, with a decision and fearlessness which might have put Monmouth to shame.

"You sell milk," said Reuben. "We are tired and thirsty, so we have come to have a horn of it."

"Nay," she cried, breaking into smiles, "will ye pay me just as the folk pay granny? Oh, heart alive! but that will be fine!" She skipped up on to a stool and filled a pair of deep mugs from the basins upon the table. "A penny, please!" said she.

It was strange to see the little wife hide the coin away in her smock, with pride and joy in her innocent face at this rare stroke of business which she had done for her absent granny.

We bore our milk away to the window, and having loosed the shutters, we seated ourselves so as to have an outlook down the road.

"For the Lord's sake, drink slow!" whispered Reuben, under his breath. "We must keep on swilling milk, or she will want to turn us out."

"We have paid toll now," I answered; "surely she will let us bide."

"If you have done you must go 'way," said she, firmly.

"Were ever two men-at-arms so tyrannized over by a little dolly like this!" said I, laughing. "Nay, little one, we shall compound with you by paying you this shilling, which will buy all your milk. We can stay here and drink it at our ease."

"Jinny, the cow, is just across the marsh," quoth she. "It is nigh milking-time, and I shall fetch her round if ye wish more."

"Now, God forbid!" cried Reuben. "It will end in our having to buy the cow. Where is your granny, little maid?"

"She hath gone into the town," the child answered. "There are bad men with red coats and guns coming to steal and to fight, but granny will soon make them go 'way. Granny has gone to set it all right."

"We are fighting against the men with the red coats, my chuck," said I; "we shall take care of your house with you, and let no one steal anything."

"Nay, then ye may stay," quoth she, climbing up on my knee as grave as a sparrow upon a bough.

"A day of this child would sicken me forever of soldiering," Reuben answered. "The cavalier and the butcher become too near of kin as I listen to her."

"Perhaps both are equally needful," said I, shrugging my shoulders. "We have put our hands to the plough. But methinks I see the man for whom we wait coming down under the shadow of yonder line of pollard willows."

"It is he, sure enough," cried Reuben, peeping through the diamond-paned window.

"Then, little one, you must sit here," said I, raising her up from my knee and placing her on a chair in a corner. "You must be a brave lass and sit still, whatever may chance. Will you do so?"

She pursed up her rosy lips and nodded her head.

"He comes on apace, Micah," quoth my comrade, who was still standing by the casement. "Is he not like some treacherous fox or other beast of prey?"

As he came abreast of our ambush we both sprang out from the open door and barred his way. The man's dark face whitened into a sickly and mottled pallor, while he drew back with a long sharp intaking of the breath and a venomous flash from his black eyes, glancing swiftly from right to left for some means of escape. For an instant his hand shot towards his sword-hilt, but his reason told him that he could scarce expect to fight his way past us. Then he glanced round, but any retreat would lead him back to the men whom he had betrayed. So he stood sullen and stolid, with heavy downcast face and shifting, restless eye, the very symbol of treachery.

"We have waited some time for you, Master John Derrick," said I. "You must now return with us to the town."

"On what grounds do you arrest me?" he asked, in hoarse, broken tones. "Where is your warranty? Who hath given you a commission to molest travellers upon the king's highway?"

"I have my colonel's commission," I answered, shortly. "You have been once already to Feversham's camp this morning."

"It is a lie," he snarled, fiercely. "I do but take a stroll to enjoy the air."

"It is the truth," said Reuben. "I saw you myself on your return. Let us see that paper which peeps from your doublet."

"We all know why you should set this trap for me," Derrick cried, bitterly. "You have set evil reports afloat against me, lest I stand in your light with the mayor's daughter."

"It is not a matter which I shall discuss save at a more fitting time and place," Reuben answered, quietly. "Do you give over your sword and come back with us. For my part, I promise to do what I can to save your life. Should we win this night, your poor efforts can do little to harm us. Should we lose, there may be few of us left to harm."

"I thank you for your kindly protection," he replied, in the same white, cold, bitter manner, unbuckling his sword as he spoke and walking slowly up to my companion. "You can take this as a gift to Mistress Ruth," he said, presenting the weapon in his left hand, "and this!" he added, plucking a knife from his belt and burying it in my poor friend's side.

The villain set up a shrill cry of triumph, and bounding back in time to avoid the savage sword-thrust which I made at him, he turned and fled down the road at the top of his speed. He was a far lighter man than I, and more scantily clad, yet I had from my long wind and length of limb been the best runner of my district, and he soon learned by the sound of my feet that he had no chance of shaking me off. I never dreamed of giving mercy nor did he of claiming it. At last, hearing my steps close upon him and my breathing at his very shoulder, he sprang wildly through the reeds and dashed into the treacherous morass. Ankle-deep, knee-deep, thigh-deep, waist-deep, we struggled and staggered, I still gaining upon him until I was within arm's reach of him, and had whirled up my sword to strike. It had been ordained, however, that he should not die the death of a man, but that of the reptile which he was, for even as I closed upon him he sank of a sudden with a gurgling sound, and the green marsh scum met above his head. As I stood with upraised sword still gazing upon the spot, one single great bubble rose and burst upon the surface, and then all was still once more, and the dreary fens lay stretched before me, the very home of death and of desolation.

I made my way as best I could through the oozy clinging mud to the margin, and hastened back to where Reuben was lying. Bending over him, I found that the knife had pierced through the side leather which connected his back and front plates, and that the blood was not only pouring out of the wound, but was trickling from the corner of his mouth. With trembling fingers I undid the straps and buckles, loosened the armor, and pressed my kerchief to his side to stanch the flow.

"I trust that you have not slain him, Micah," he said, of a sudden, opening his eyes.

"A higher power than ours has judged him, Reuben," I answered.

"Poor devil! He has had much to imbitter him," he murmured, and straightway fainted again. As I knelt over him, marking the lad's white face and labored breathing, and bethought me of his simple, kindly nature, and of the affection which I had done so little to deserve, I am not ashamed to say that my tears were mingled with his blood.

As it chanced, Decimus Saxon had found time to ascend the church-tower for the purpose of watching us through his glass and seeing how we fared. Noting that there was something amiss, he had hurried down for a skilled chirurgeon, whom he brought out to us under an escort of scythemen. I was still kneeling by my senseless friend, doing what an ignorant man might to assist him, when the party arrived and helped me to bear him into the cottage out of the glare of the sun. The minutes were as hours while the man of physic, with a grave face, examined and probed the wound.

"It will scarce prove fatal," he said at last, and I could have embraced him for the words. "The blade has glanced on a rib, though the lung is slightly torn. We shall bear him back with us to the town."

"You hear what he says," said Saxon, kindly. "He is a man whose opinion is of weight. Cheer up, man! You are as white as though it were your blood and not his which was drained away. Where is Derrick?"

"Drowned in the marshes," I answered, at once.

" 'Tis well. It will save us six feet of good hemp. But

our position here is somewhat exposed, since the Royal Horse might make a dash at us. Who is this little maid who sits so white and still in the corner?"

" 'Tis the guardian of the house. Her granny has left her here."

"You had better come with us. There may be rough work here ere all is over."

"Nay, I must wait for granny," she answered, with the tears running down her cheeks.

"But how if I take you to granny, little one?" said I. "We cannot leave you here." I held out my arms, and the child sprang into them and nestled up against my bosom, sobbing as though her heart would break. "Take me away," she cried; "I'se frightened."

I soothed the little trembling thing as best I might, and bore her off with me upon my shoulder. The scythemen had passed the handles of their long weapons through the sleeves of their jerkins in such a way as to form a couch or litter, upon which poor Reuben was laid. A slight dash of color had come back to his cheeks in answer to some cordial given him by the chirurgeon, and he nodded and smiled at Saxon. Thus, pacing slowly we returned to Bridgewater, where Reuben was carried to our quarters, and I bore the little maid of the marshes to kind townsfolk, who promised to restore her to her home when the troubles were over.

CHAPTER THIRTY-TWO

OF THE ONFALL AT SEDGEMOOR

HOWEVER pressing our own private griefs and needs, we had little time now to dwell upon them, for the moment was at hand which was to decide for the time not only our own fates, but that of the Protestant cause in England.

The whole town was loud with the preaching. Every troop or company had its own chosen orator, and sometimes more than one, who held forth and expounded. Men were drunk with religion as with wine. Their faces were flushed, their speech thick, their gestures wild. Sir Stephen and Saxon smiled at each other as they watched them, for they knew, as old soldiers, that of all causes which make a man valiant in deed and careless of life, this religious fit is the strongest and the most enduring.

In the evening I found time to look in upon my wounded

friend, and found him propped up with cushions upon his couch, breathing with some pain, but as bright and merry as ever. Our prisoner, Major Ogilvy, who had conceived a warm affection for us, sat by his side and read aloud to him.

"This wound hath come at an evil moment," said Reuben, impatiently. "Is it not too much that a little prick like this should send my men captainless into battle, after all our marching and drilling? I have been present at the grace, and am cut off from the dinner."

"Your company hath been joined to mine," I answered, "though, indeed, the honest fellows are cast down at not having their own captain. Has the physician been to see you?"

"He has left even now," said Major Ogilvy. "He pronounces our friend to be doing right well, but hath warned me against allowing him to talk."

"Hark to that, lad!" said I, shaking my finger at him. "If I hear a word from you I go. You will escape a rough waking this night, major. What think you of our chance?"

"I have thought little of your chance from the first," he replied, frankly. "Monmouth is like a ruined gamester, who is now putting his last piece upon the board. He cannot win much, and he may lose all."

"Nay, that is a hard saying," said I. "A success might set the whole of the Midlands in arms."

"England is not ripe for it," the major answered, with a shake of his head. "Besides, the man whom ye support has shown that he is unworthy of confidence. Did he not in his declaration promise to leave the choice of a monarch to the Commons? And yet, in less than a week, he proclaimed himself at Taunton Market Cross! Who could believe one who has so little regard for truth?"

"Treason, major, rank treason," I answered, laughing. "Yet if we could order a leader as one does a coat, we might, perchance, have chosen one of the stronger texture. We are in arms not for him, but for the old liberties and rights of Englishmen. Have you seen Sir Gervas?"

Major Ogilvy, and even Reuben, burst out laughing. "You will find him in the room above," said our prisoner. "Never did a famous toast prepare herself for a court ball as he is preparing for his battle. If the king's troops take him, they will assuredly think that they have the duke. He hath been in here to consult us as to his patches, hosen, and I know not what beside. You had best go up to him."

"Adieu, then, Reuben!" I said, grasping his hand in mine.

"Adieu, Micah! God shield you from harm," said he.

"Can I speak to you aside, major?" I whispered. "I think," I went on, as he followed me into the passage, "that you will not say that your captivity hath been made very harsh for you. May I ask, therefore, that you will keep an eye upon my friend should we be indeed defeated this night? No doubt if Feversham gains the upper hand there will be bloody work. The hale can look after themselves, but he is helpless, and will need a friend."

The major pressed my hand. "I swear to God," he said, "that no harm shall befall him."

"You have taken a load from my heart," I answered; "I know that I leave him in safety. I can now ride to battle with an easy mind." With a friendly smile the soldier returned to the sick-room, while I ascended the stair and entered the quarters of Sir Gervas Jerome.

He was standing before a table which was littered all over with pots, brushes, boxes, and a score of the like trifles, which he had either bought or borrowed for the occasion. A large hand-mirror was balanced against the wall, with rushlights on either side of it. In front of this, with a most solemn and serious expression upon his pale, handsome face, the baronet was arranging and rearranging a white berdash cravat. From his dainty riding-hat to his shining spur there was no speck or stain upon him—a sad set-off to my own state, plastered as

I was with a thick frost of the Sedgemoor mud, and disordered from having ridden and worked for two days without rest or repose.

"Split me, but you have come in good time!" he exclaimed, as I entered. "I have even now sent down for a flask of canary. Ah, and here it comes!" as a maid from the inn tripped upstairs with the bottle and glasses. "Here is a gold-piece, my pretty dear, the very last I have in the whole world. It is the only survivor of a goodly family. Pay mine host for the wine, little one, and keep the change for thyself, to buy ribbons for the next holiday. Now curse me if I can get this cravat to fit unwrinkled!"

"There is naught amiss with it," I answered. "How can such trifles occupy you at such a time?"

"Trifles!" he cried, angrily. "Trifles! Well, there, it boots not to argue with you. Fill up your glass!"

"Your company awaits you by the church," I remarked; "I saw them as I passed."

"How looked they?" he asked. "Were they powdered and clean?"

"Nay, I had little leisure to observe. I saw that they were cutting their matches and arranging their priming."

"I would that they had all snaphances," he answered, sprinkling himself with scented water; "the matchlocks are slow and cumbersome. Have you had wine enough?"

"I will take no more," I answered.

"Then mayhap the major may care to finish it. It is not often I ask help with a bottle, but I would keep my head cool this night. Let us go down and see to our men."

It was ten o'clock when we descended into the street. The hubbub of the preachers and the shouting of the people had died away, for the regiments had fallen into their places, and stood silent and stern, with the faint light from the lamps and windows playing over their dark, serried ranks.

"It is half after ten by St. Mary's clock," said Saxon, as we rode up to the regiment. "Have we nothing to give the men?"

"There is a hogshead of Zoyland cider in the yard of yonder inn," said Sir Gervas. "Here, Dawson, do you take these gold sleeve-links and give them to mine host in exchange. Broach the barrel, and let each man have his horn full. Sink me if they shall fight with naught but cold water in them."

"They will feel the need of it ere morning," said Saxon, as a score of pikemen hastened off to the inn. "The marsh air is chilling to the blood."

"I feel cool already, and Covenant is stamping with it," said I. "Might we not, if we have time upon our hands, canter our horses down the line?"

"Of a surety," Saxon answered, gladly, "we could not do better;" so, shaking our bridles, we rode off, our horses' hoofs striking fire from the flint-paved streets as we passed.

As we rode down the long line a buzz of greeting and welcome rose now and again from the ranks as they recognized through the gloom Saxon's tall, gaunt figure. The clock was on the stroke of eleven as we returned to our own men, and at that very moment King Monmouth rode out from the inn where he was quartered and trotted with his staff down the High Street. All cheering had been forbidden, but waving caps and brandished arms spoke the ardor of his devoted followers. No bugle was to sound the march, but as each company received the word the one in its rear followed its movements. The clatter and shuffle of hundreds of moving feet came nearer and nearer, until the Frome men in front of us began to march, and we found ourselves fairly started.

Our road lay across the Parret, through Eastover, and so along the winding track past the spot where Derrick met his fate, and the lonely cottage of the little maid. At the other side of this the road becomes a mere pathway over the plain. Very slow our march was, and very careful, for the plain was, as Sir Stephen Timewell had told us, cut across by great ditches or rhines, which could not be passed save at some few places. At last, however, the two main ones, the Black Ditch and the Langmoor Rhine, were safely traversed, and a halt was called while the foot was formed in line, for we had reason to believe that no other force lay between the royal camp and ourselves. So far our enterprise had succeeded admirably. We were within half a mile of the camp without mistake or accident, and none of the enemy's scouts had shown sign of their presence. If ever a general deserved a beating it was Feversham that night. As we drew up on the moor the clock of Chedzoy struck one.

"Is it not glorious?" whispered Sir Gervas, as we reined up on the farther side of the Langmoor Rhine. "What is there on earth to compare with the excitement of this?"

"You speak as though it were a cocking-match or a bull-baiting," I answered, with some little coldness. "It is a solemn and a sad occasion. Win who will, English blood must soak the soil of England this night."

"The more room for those who are left," said he, lightly.

"I have told friend Reuben such few things as I should desire to be done in case I should fall," said I. "It has eased my mind much to know that I leave behind some word of farewell and little remembrance to all whom I have known. Is there no service of the sort which I can do for you?"

"Hum!" said he, musing. "If I go under, you can tell Araminta—nay, let the poor wench alone! There is Mother Butterworth, too, whom I might commend to your notice. She was the queen of wet-nurses, but alas! cruel time hath dried up her business, and she hath need of some little nursing herself."

"If I live and you should fall, I shall do what may be done for her," said I. "Have you aught else to say?"

"One other thing!" he answered. "I have a trinket or two left which might serve as a gift for the pretty Puritan maid, should our friend lead her to the altar. Od's my life, but she will make him read some queer books! How now, colonel, why are we stuck out on the moor like a row of herons among the sedges?"

"They are ordering the line for the attack," said Saxon, who had ridden up during our conversation. "Donnerblitz! Who ever saw a camp so exposed to an onfall? Oh, for twelve hundred good horse—for an hour of Wessenburg's Pandours! Would I not trample them down until their camp was like a field of young corn after a hail-storm!"

"May not our horse advance?" I asked.

The old soldier gave a deep snort of disdain. "If this fight is to be won, it must be by our foot," said he; "what can we hope for from such cavalry? Keep your men well in hand, for we may have to bear the brunt of the king's dragoons. A flank attack would fall upon us, for we are in the post of honor."

"There are troops to the right of us," I answered, peering through the darkness.

"Aye! the Taunton burghers and the Frome peasants. Our brigade covers the right flank. Next us are the Mendip miners, nor could I wish for better comrades, if their zeal do not outrun their discretion. They are on their knees in the mud at this moment."

"They will fight none the worse for that," I remarked; "but surely the troops are advancing!"

"Aye, aye!" cried Saxon, joyously, plucking out his sword and tying his handkerchief round the handle to strengthen his gripe. "The hour has come! Forward!"

Very slowly and silently we crept on through the dense fog, our feet splashing and slipping in the sodden soil. With all the care which we could take, the advance of so great a number of men could not be conducted without a deep, sonorous sound from the thousands of marching feet. Of a sudden out of the darkness there came a sharp challenge and a shout, with the discharge of a carbine and the sound of galloping hoofs. Away down the line we heard a ripple of shots. The first line of outposts had been reached. At the alarm our horse charged forward with a huzza, and we followed them as fast as our men could run. We had crossed two or three hundred yards of moor, and could hear the blowing of the royal bugles quite close to us, when our horse came to a sudden halt, and our whole advance was at a stand-still.

"Sancta Maria!" cried Saxon, dashing forward with the rest of us to find out the cause of the delay. "We must on at any cost! A halt now will ruin our camisado."

"Forward, forward!" cried Sir Gervas and I, waving our swords.

"It is no use, gentlemen," cried a cornet of horse, wringing his hands; "we are undone and betrayed. There is a broad ditch without a ford in front of us, full twenty feet across!"

"Give me room for my horse, and I shall show ye the way across!" cried the baronet, backing his steed. "Now, lads, who's for a jump?"

"Nay, sir, for God's sake!" said a trooper, laying his hand upon his bridle. "Sergeant Sexton hath sprung in even now, and horse and man have gone to the bottom!"

"Let us see it, then!" cried Saxon, pushing his way through the crowd of horsemen. We followed close at his heels, until we found ourselves on the borders of the vast trench which impeded our advance.

"There must be a passage somewhere," cried Saxon, furiously. "Every moment is worth a troop of horse to them. Where is my Lord Grey? Hath the guide met with his deserts?"

"Major Hollis hath hurled the guide into the ditch," the young cornet answered. "My Lord Grey hath ridden along the bank seeking for a ford."

I caught a pike out of a footman's hand, and probed into the black, oozy mud, standing myself up to the waist in it, and holding Covenant's bridle in my left hand. Nowhere could I touch bottom or find any hope of solid foothold.

"Here, fellow!" cried Saxon, seizing a trooper by the arm. "Make for the rear! Gallop as though the devil were behind you! Bring up a pair of ammunition wagons, and we shall see whether we cannot bridge this infernal puddle."

"If a few of us could make a lodgement upon the other side we might make it good until help came," said Sir Gervas, as the horseman galloped off upon his mission.

All down the rebel line a fierce, low roar of disappointment and rage showed that the whole army had met the same obstacle which hindered our attack. On the other side of the ditch the drums beat, the bugles screamed, and the shouts and oaths of the officers could be heard as they marshalled their men. Glancing lights in Chedzoy, Westonzoyland, and the other hamlets to left and right showed how fast the alarm was extending. Decimus Saxon rode up and down the edge of the fosse, pattering forth foreign oaths, grinding his teeth in his fury, and rising now and again in his stirrups to shake his gauntleted hands at the enemy.

"For whom are ye?" shouted a hoarse voice of the haze.

"For the king!" roared the peasants in answer.

"For which king?" cried the voice.

"For King Monmouth!"

"Let them have it, lads!" and instantly a storm of musket-bullets whistled and sung about our ears. As the sheet of flame sprang out of the darkness the maddened, half-broken horses dashed wildly away across the plain, resisting the efforts of the riders to pull them up. There are some, indeed, who say that those efforts were not very strong, and that our troopers, disheartened at the check at the ditch, were not sorry to show their heels to the enemy. As to my Lord Grey, I can say truly that I saw him in the dim light among the flying squadrons, doing all that a brave cavalier could do to bring them to a stand. Away they went, however, thundering through the ranks of the foot and out over the moor, leaving their companions to bear the brunt of battle.

MICAH CLARKE

"Onto your faces, men!" shouted Saxon, in a voice which rose high above the crash of the musketry and the cries of the wounded. The pikemen and scythemen threw themselves down at his command, while the musketeers knelt in front of them, loading and firing, with nothing to aim at save the burning matches of the enemy's pieces, which could be seen twinkling through the darkness. All along, both to the right and the left, a rolling fire had broken out, coming in short, quick volleys from the soldiers, and in a continuous, confused rattle from the peasants. On the farther wing our four guns had been brought into play, and we could hear their dull growling in the distance.

"Sing, brothers, sing!" cried our stout-hearted chaplain, Master Joshua Pettigrue, bustling backward and forward among the prostrate ranks. "Let us call upon the Lord in our day of trial!" The men raised a loud hymn of praise, which swelled into a great chorus as it was taken up by the Taunton burghers upon our right and the miners upon our left. At the sound the soldiers on the other side raised a fierce huzza, and the whole air was full of clamor.

Our musketeers had been brought to the very edge of the Bussex Rhine, and the royal troops had also advanced as far as they were able, so that there were not five pike's-lengths between the lines. Yet that short distance was so impassable that, save for the more deadly fire, a quarter of a mile might have divided us. Yet, though the air was alive with bullets, the aim of the soldiers was too high for our kneeling ranks, and very few of the men were struck. For our part, we did what we could to keep the barrels of our muskets from inclining upward. The groans and cries from the other side of the ditch showed that some, at least, of our bullets had not been fired in vain.

"We hold our own in this quarter," said I to Saxon. "It seems to me that their fire slackens."

"It is their horse that I fear," he answered. "They can avoid the ditch, since they come from the hamlets on the flank. They may be upon us at any time."

"Hullo, sir!" shouted Sir Gervas, reining up his steed upon the very brink of the ditch, and raising his cap in salute to a mounted officer upon the other side. "Can you tell me if we have the honor to be opposed to the foot guards?"

"We are Dumbarton's regiment, sir," cried the other. "We shall give ye good cause to remember having met us."

"We shall be across presently to make your further acquaintance," Sir Gervas answered, and at the same moment rolled, horse and all, into the ditch, amid a roar of exultation from the soldiers. Half a dozen of his musketeers sprang instantly, waist-deep, into the mud, and dragged our friend out of danger, but the charger, which had been shot through the heart, sank without a struggle.

"There is no harm!" cried the baronet, springing to his feet, "I would rather fight on foot like my brave musketeers." The men broke out a-cheering at his words, and the fire on both sides became hotter than ever.

The gray light of morning was stealing over the moor, and still the fight was undecided. The fog hung about us in feathery streaks, and the smoke from our guns drifted across in a dun-colored cloud, through which the long lines of red-coats upon the other side of the Rhine loomed up like a battalion of giants. My eyes ached and my lips pringled with the smack of the powder. On every side of me men were falling fast, for the increased light had improved the aim of the soldiers.

Ever and anon as the light waxed I could note through the rifts in the smoke and the fog how the fight was progressing in other parts of the field. On the right the heath was brown with the Taunton and Frome men, who, like ourselves, were lying down to avoid the fire. Along the borders of the Bussex Rhine a deep fringe of their musketeers were exchanging murderous volleys, almost muzzle to muzzle, with the left wing of the same regiment with which we were engaged, which was supported by a second regiment in broad white facings, which I believe to have belonged to the Wiltshire militia. On either bank of the black trench a thick line of dead, brown on the one side and scarlet on the other, served as a screen to their companions, who sheltered themselves behind them and rested their musket-barrels upon their prostrate bodies.

The battle was in this state when there rose a cry of "The king, the king!" and Monmouth rode through our ranks, bareheaded and wild-eyed, with Buyse, Wade, and a dozen more beside him. They pulled up within a spear's-length of me, and Saxon, spurring forward to meet them, raised his sword to the salute. I could not but mark the contrast between the calm, grave face of the veteran, composed yet alert, and the half-frantic bearing of the man whom we were compelled to look upon as our leader.

"How think ye, Colonel Saxon?" he cried, wildly. "How goes the fight? Is all well with ye? What an error, alas! what an error! Shall we draw off, eh? How say you?"

"We hold our own here, your majesty," Saxon answered. "Methinks had we something after the nature of palisados or stockados, after the Swedish fashion, we might even make it good against the horse."

"Ah, the horse!" cried the unhappy Monmouth. "If we get over this, my Lord Grey shall answer for it. They ran like a flock of sheep. What leader could do anything with such troops? Oh, lackaday, lackaday! Shall we not advance?"

"There is no reason to advance, your majesty, now that the surprise has failed," said Saxon. "We can but fight it out as we are."

"To throw troops across would be to sacrifice them," said Wade. "Ye have lost heavily, Colonel Saxon, but I think from the look of yonder bank that ye have given a good account of the red-coats."

"Stand firm! For God's sake, stand firm!" cried Monmouth, distractedly. "The horse have fled, and the cannoneers also. Oh, what can I do with such men? What shall I do? Alas, alas!" He set spurs to his horse and galloped off down the line, still wringing his hands and uttering his dismal wailings.

As his escort trooped after him, the great German man-at-arms separated from them and turned back to us. "I am weary of trotting up and down like a lust-ritter at a fair," said he. "If I bide with ye I am like to have my share of any fighting which is going. So, steady, mein Liebchen. That ball grazed her tail, but she is too old a soldier to wince at trifles. Hullo, friend, where is your horse?"

"At the bottom of the ditch," said Sir Gervas, scraping the mud off his dress with his sword-blade. " 'Tis now half-past two," he continued, "and we have been at this child's play for an hour and more. With a line regiment, too! It is not what I had looked forward to!"

"You shall have something to console you anon," cried the German, with his eyes shining. "Mein Gott! Is it not splendid? Look to it, friend Saxon, look to it!"

It was no light matter which had so roused the soldier's admiration. Out of the haze which still lay thick upon our right there twinkled here and there a bright gleam of silvery light, while a dull thundering noise broke upon our ears like that of the surf upon a rocky shore. More and more frequent came the fitful flashes of steel, louder and yet louder grew the hoarse, gathering tumult, until of a sudden the fog was rent, and the long lines of the royal cavalry broke out from it, wave after wave, rich in scarlet and blue and gold, as grand a sight as ever the eye rested upon. Rank after rank, and line after line, with waving standards, tossing manes, and gleaming steel, they poured onward, an army in themselves, with either flank still shrouded in the mist. As they thundered along, knee to knee and bridle to bridle, there came from them such a gust of deep-chested oaths, with the jangle of harness, the clash of steel, and the measured beat of multitudinous hoofs, that no man who hath not stood up against such a whirlwind, with nothing but a seven-foot pike in his hand, can know how hard it is to face it with a steady lip and a firm grip.

Saxon and the German flung themselves among the pikemen, and did all that men could do to thicken their array. Sir Gervas and I did the same with the scythemen, who had been trained to form a triple front, after the German fashion, one rank kneeling, one stooping, and one standing erect, with weapons advanced. Close to us the Taunton men had hardened into a dark sullen ring, bristling with steel, in the centre of which might be seen and heard their venerable mayor, his long beard fluttering in the breeze, and his strident voice clanging over the field. Louder and louder grew the roar of the horse. "Steady, my brave lads!" cried Saxon, in trumpet tones. "Dig the pike-butt into the earth! Rest it on the right foot! Give not an inch! Steady!" A great shout went up from either side, and then the living wave broke over us.

What hope is there to describe such a scene as that—the crashing of wood, the sharp gasping cries, the snorting of horses, the jar when the push of pike met with the sweep of sword? Thus my memories are confined to a swirl of smoke, with steel caps and fierce, eager faces breaking through it, with the red gaping nostrils of horses, and their pawing fore-feet as they recoiled from the hedge of steel. All round rose a fierce babel of shouts and cries—godly ejaculations from the peasants and oaths from the horsemen—with Saxon's voice above all, imploring his pikemen to stand firm. Then the cloud of horsemen recoiled, circling off over the plain, and the shout of triumph from my comrades, and an open snuffbox thrust out in front of me, proclaimed that we had seen the back of as stout squadrons as ever followed a kettle-drum.

But if we could claim it as a victory, the army in general could scarce say as much. None but the very pick of the troops could stand against the flood of heavy horses and steel-clad men. The Frome peasants were gone—swept utterly from the field. Many of them had been driven by pure weight and pressure into the fatal mud which had checked our advance. Many others, sorely cut and slashed, lay in ghastly heaps all over the ground which they had held. A few, by joining our ranks, had saved themselves from the fate of their companions. Farther off the men of Taunton still stood fast, though in sadly diminished numbers. A long ridge of horses and cavaliers in front of them showed how stern had been the attack, and how fierce the resistance. On our left the wild miners had been broken at the first rush, but had fought so savagely, throwing themselves upon the ground and stabbing upward at the stomachs of the horses, that they had at last beaten off the dragoons. The Devonshire militiamen, however, had been scattered, and shared the fate of the men of Frome. During the whole of the struggle the foot upon the farther bank of the Bussex Rhine were pouring in a hail of bullets, which our musketeers, having to defend themselves against the horse, were unable to reply to.

It needed no great amount of soldierly experience to see that the battle was lost, and that Monmouth's cause was doomed. It was broad daylight now, though the sun had not yet risen. Our cavalry was gone, our ordnance was silent, our line was pierced in many places, and more than one of our regiments had been destroyed.

"Is Captain Clarke there?" cried Decimus Saxon, riding up, with his sword-arm flecked with blood. "Ride over to Sir Stephen Timewell and tell him to join his men to ours. Apart we shall be broken—together we may stand another charge."

Setting spurs to Covenant, I rode to our companions and delivered the message. Sir Stephen, who had been struck by a petronel-bullet, and wore a crimson kerchief bound round his snow-white head, saw the wisdom of the advice, and moved his townsmen as directed. His musketeers, being better provided with powder than ours, did good service by keeping down for a time the deadly fire from across the fosse.

"Who would have thought it of him?" cried Sir Stephen, with flashing eyes, as Buyse and Saxon rode out to meet him.

"What think ye now of our noble monarch, our champion of the Protestant cause?"

"He is no very great Krieger," said Buyse. "Yet perhaps it may be from want of habit as much as from want of courage."

"Courage!" cried the old mayor, in a voice of scorn. "Look over yonder and behold your king." He pointed out over the moor with a finger which shook as much from anger as from age. There, far away, showing up against the dark peat-colored soil, rode a gayly dressed cavalier, followed by a knot of attendants, galloping as fast as his horse would carry him from the field of battle. There was no mistaking the fugitive. It was the recreant Monmouth.

"Hush!" cried Saxon, as we all gave a cry of horror and execration; "do not dishearten our brave lads! Cowardice is catching and will run through any army like the putrid fever."

"Der Feigherzige!" cried Buyse, grinding his teeth. "And the brave country folk! It is too much."

"Stand to your pikes, men!" roared Saxon, in a voice of thunder, and we had scarce time to form our square and throw ourselves inside of it before the whirlwind of horse was upon us once more. When the Taunton men had joined us a weak spot had been left in our ranks, and through this in an instant the Blue Guards smashed their way, pouring through the opening, and cutting fiercely to right and left. The burghers on the one side and our own men on the other replied by savage stabs from their pikes and scythes, which emptied many a saddle; but while the struggle was at its hottest the king's cannon opened for the first time with a deafening roar upon the other side of the rhine, and a storm of balls ploughed their way through our dense ranks, leaving furrows of dead and wounded behind them. At the same moment a great cry of "Powder! For Christ's sake, powder!" arose from the musketeers, whose last charge had been fired. Again the cannon roared, and again our men were mowed down as though Death himself with his scythe were among us. At last our ranks were breaking. Again and again the guards crashed through them from side to side, and yet the shattered ranks closed up behind them and continued the long-drawn struggle. So hopeless was it and so pitiable that I could have found it in my heart to wish that they would break and fly, were it not that on the broad moor there was no refuge which they could make for. And all this time, while they struggled and fought, blackened with powder and parched with thirst, spilling their blood as though it were water, the man who called himself their king was spurring over the countryside with a loose rein and a quaking heart, his thoughts centred upon saving his own neck, come what might to his gallant followers.

Large numbers of the foot fought to the death, neither giving nor receiving quarter, but at last, scattered, broken, and without ammunition, the main body of the peasants dispersed and fled across the moor, closely followed by the horse. Saxon, Buyse, and I had done all that we could to rally them once more, and had cut down some of the foremost of the pursuers, when my eye fell suddenly upon Sir Gervas, standing hatless with a few of his musketeers in the midst of a swarm of dragoons. Spurring our horses, we cut a way to his rescue, and laid our swords about us until we had cleared off his assailants for the moment.

"Jump up behind me!" I cried. "We can make good our escape."

He looked up smiling and shook his head. "I stay with my company," said he.

"Your company!" Saxon cried. "Why, man, you are mad! Your company is cut off to the last man."

"That's what I mean," he answered, flicking some dirt from his cravat. "Don't ye mind! Look out for yourselves. Good-bye, Clarke! Present my compliments to ———" The dragoons charged down upon us again. We were all borne backward, fighting desperately, and when we could look round the baronet was gone forever. We heard afterwards that the king's troops found upon the field a body which they mistook for that of Monmouth, on account of the effeminate grace of the features and the richness of the attire. No doubt it was that of our undaunted friend, Sir Gervas Jerome, a name which shall ever be dear to my heart.

And now it was every man for himself. In no part of the field did the insurgents continue to resist. The first rays of the sun shining slantwise across the great dreary plain lit up the long line of the scarlet battalions, and glittered upon the cruel swords which rose and fell among the struggling drove of resistless fugitives. The German had become separated from us in the tumult, and we knew not whether he lived or was slain, though long afterwards we learned that he made good his escape, only to be captured with the ill-fated Duke of Monmouth. Grey, Wade, Ferguson, and others had contrived to save themselves, while Stephen Timewell lay in the midst of a stern ring of his hard-faced burghers, dying as he had lived, a gallant Puritan Englishman. All this we learned afterwards. At present we rode for our lives across the moor, followed by a few scattered bodies of horse, who soon abandoned their pursuit in order to fasten upon some more easy prey.

Looking back from the summit of the low hills which lie to the westward of the moor, we could see the cloud of horsemen streaming over the bridge of the Parret and into the town of Bridgewater, with the helpless drove of fugitives still flying in front of them. We had pulled up our horses, and were looking sadly and silently back at the fatal plain, when the thud of hoofs fell upon our ears, and, turning round, we found two horsemen in the dress of the Guards riding towards us. They had made a circuit to cut us off, for they were riding straight for us with drawn swords and eager gestures.

"More slaughter," I said, wearily. "Why will they force us to it?"

Saxon glanced keenly from beneath his drooping lids at the approaching horsemen, and a grim smile wreathed his face in a thousand lines and wrinkles.

"It is our friend who set the hounds upon our track at Salisbury," he said. "This is a happy meeting. I have a score to settle with him."

It was, indeed, the hot-headed young cornet whom we had met at the outset of our adventures. Some evil chance had led him to recognize the tall figure of my companion as we rode from the field, and to follow him, in the hope of obtaining revenge for the humiliation which he had met with at his hands. The other was a lance-corporal, a man of square, soldierly build, riding a heavy black horse with a white blaze upon its forehead.

Saxon rode slowly towards the officer, while the trooper and I fixed our eyes upon each other.

"Well, boy," I heard my companion say, "I trust that you have learned to fence since we met last."

The young guardsman gave a snarl of rage at the taunt, and an instant afterwards the clink of their sword-blades showed that they had met. For my own part, I dared not spare a glance upon them, for my opponent attacked me with such fury that it was all that I could do to keep him off. No pistol was drawn upon either side. It was an honest contest of steel against steel. So constant were the corporal's thrusts, now at my face, now at my body, that I had never an opening for one of the heavy cuts which might have ended the matter. He plucked a dagger from his belt and struck it into my left arm, but I dealt him a blow with my gauntleted hand which smote him off his horse and stretched him speechless upon the plain. Almost at the same moment the cornet dropped from his horse, wounded in several places. Saxon sprang from his saddle, and picking the soldier's dagger from the ground, would have finished them both had I not jumped down also and restrained him. He flashed round upon me with so savage a face that I could see that the wild-beast nature within him was fairly roused.

"What hath thou to do?" he snarled. "Let go!"

"Nay, nay! Blood enough hath been shed," said I. "Let them lie."

"What mercy would they have had upon us?" he cried, passionately, struggling to get his wrist free. "They have lost, and must pay forfeit."

"Not in cold blood," I said, firmly. "I shall not abide it."

"Indeed, your lordship," he sneered, with the devil peeping out through his eyes. With a violent wrench he freed himself from my grasp, and springing back, picked up the sword which he had dropped.

"What then?" I asked, standing on my guard astride of the wounded man.

He stood for a minute or more looking at me from under his heavy-hung brows, with his whole face writhing with passion. Every instant I expected that he would fly at me, but at last, with a gulp in his throat, he sheathed his rapier with a sharp clang, and sprang back into the saddle.

"We part here," he said, coldly. "I have twice been on the verge of slaying you, and the third time might be too much for my patience. You are no fit companion for a cavalier of fortune. Join the clergy, lad; it is your vocation."

Gathering up his bridle in his left hand, he shot one last malignant glance at the bleeding officer, and I galloped off along one of the tracks which lead to the southward. I stood gazing after him, but he never sent so much as a hand-wave back, riding on with a rigid neck until he vanished in a dip in the moor.

"There goes one friend," thought I, sadly, "and all forsooth because I will not stand by and see a helpless man's throat cut. Another friend is dead on the field. A third, the oldest and dearest of all, lies wounded at Bridgewater, at the mercy of a brutal soldiery."

A muttered oath followed by a groan roused me from my meditations. The corporal was sitting up rubbing his head, with a look of stupid astonishment upon his face, as though he were not very sure either of where he was or how he came there. The officer, too, had opened his eyes and shown other signs of returning consciousness. His wounds were clearly of no very serious

FROM HEAD TO FOOT I WAS SPLASHED AND CRIMSONED WITH BLOOD

nature. There was no danger of their pursuing me even should they wish to do so, for their horses had trotted off to join the numerous other riderless steeds who were wandering all over the moorlands. I mounted and rode slowly away, saving my good charger as much as possible.

There were many scattered bodies of horse riding hither and thither over the marshes, but I was able to avoid them, and trotted onward, keeping to the waste country until I found myself eight or ten miles from the battle-field. At last, after riding for three hours, I chose out a sheltered spot where a clump of bushes overhung a little brook. There, seated upon a bank of velvet moss, I rested my weary limbs, and tried to wash the stains of battle from my person.

It was only now when I could look quietly at my own attire that it was brought home to me how terrible the encounter must have been in which I had been engaged, and how wonderful it was that I had come off so scatheless. From head to foot I was splashed and crimsoned with blood, partly my own, but mostly that of others. My left arm was stiff and wellnigh powerless from the corporal's stab; but on stripping off my doublet and examining the place, I found that though there had been much bleeding the wound was on the outer side of the bone, and was therefore of no great import. A kerchief dipped in water and bound tightly round it eased the smart and stanched the blood. Beyond this scratch I had no injuries, though from my own efforts I felt as stiff and sore all over as though I had been well cudgelled, and the slight wound got in Wells Cathedral had reopened and was bleeding. With a little patience and cold water, however, I was able to dress it and to tie myself up as well as any chirurgeon in the kingdom.

Having seen to my injuries, I had now to attend to my appearance. A good wash, however, in the brook soon removed those traces of war, and I was able to get the marks off my breastplate and boots. In the case of my clothes, however, it was so hopeless to clean them that I gave it up in despair. My good old horse had been never so much as grazed by steel or bullet, so that with a little watering and tending he was soon as fresh as ever, and we turned our backs on the streamlet a better favored pair than we had approached its banks.

It was now going on to mid-day, and I began to feel very hungry, for I had tasted nothing since the evening before. Two or three houses stood in a cluster upon the moor, but the blackened walls and scorched thatch showed that it was hopeless to expect anything from them. At last, when I was fairly weary of my fruitless search for food, I espied a windmill standing upon a green hill at the other side of some fields. Judging from its appearance that it had escaped the general pillage, I took the pathway which branched away to it from the high-road.

CHAPTER THIRTY-THREE

OF MY PERILOUS ADVENTURE AT THE MILL

AT THE base of the mill there stood a shed which was evidently used to stall the horses which brought the farmers'
grain. Some grass was heaped up inside it, so I loosened
Covenant's girths and left him to have a hearty meal. The
mill itself appeared to be silent and empty. I climbed the steep
wood ladder, and, pushing the door open, walked into a round,
stone-flagged room, from which a second ladder led to the loft
above. On one side of this chamber was a long wooden box,
and all round the walls were ranged rows of sacks full of flour.
In the fireplace stood a pile of fagots ready for lighting, so with
the aid of my tinder-box I soon had a cheerful blaze. Taking

a large handful of flour from the nearest bag, I moistened it with water from a pitcher, and, having rolled it out into a flat cake, proceeded to bake it, smiling the while to think of what my mother would say to such rough cookery.

I was lost in thought, brooding sadly over the blow which the news would be to my father, when I was startled by a loud sneeze, which sounded as though it were delivered in my very ear. Drawing my sword, I walked round, pricking the great flour-sacks, but without being able to find cause for the sound. I was still marvelling over the matter, when a most extraordinary chorus of gasps, snorts, and whistles broke out, with cries of "Oh, holy mother!" "Blessed Redeemer!" and other such exclamations. This time there could be no doubt as to whence the uproar came. Rushing up to the great chest upon which I had been seated, I threw back the heavy lid and gazed in.

It was more than half full of flour, in the midst of which was floundering some creature which was so coated and caked with the white powder that it would have been hard to say that it was human were it not for the pitiable cries which it was uttering. Stooping down, I dragged the man from his hiding-place, when he dropped upon his knees upon the floor and yelled for mercy, raising such a cloud of dust from every wriggle of his body that I began to cough and to sneeze. Thinking that there was something familiar about his voice, I drew my hand across his face, which set him yelling as though I had slain him. There was no mistaking the heavy cheeks and the little greedy eyes. It was none other than Master Tetheridge, the noisy town-clerk of Taunton.

"I am but a poor scrivener man, your serene highness," he bawled. "Indeed, I am a most unhappy clerk, your honor, who has been driven into these courses by the tyranny of those above him."

"Do you renounce the Duke of Monmouth?" I asked, in a stern voice.

"I do, from my heart," said he, fervently.

THE MILL APPEARED TO BE SILENT AND EMPTY

"Then prepare to die," I roared, whipping out my sword, "for I am one of his officers."

At the sight of the steel the wretched clerk gave a perfect bellow of terror, and falling upon his face, he wriggled and twisted, until, looking up, he perceived that I was laughing. On that he crawled up on to his knees once more, and from that to his feet, glancing at me askance, as though by no means assured of my intentions.

"You must remember me, Master Tetheridge," I said. "I am Captain Clarke, of Saxon's regiment of Wiltshire foot. I am surprised, indeed, that you should have fallen away from that allegiance to which you did not only swear yourself, but did administer the oath to so many others."

"Not a whit, captain, not a whit," he answered, resuming his old bantam-cock manner as soon as he saw that there was no danger. "I am upon oath as true and as leal a man as ever I was."

"That I can fully believe," I immediately answered.

"I did but dissimulate," he continued, brushing the flour from his person. "I did but practise that cunning of the serpent which should in every warrior accompany the courage of the lion. Master Ulysses is my type, even as thine, I take it, is Master Ajax."

"Methinks that Master Jack-in-the-box would fit you better," said I. "Wilt have a half of this cake? How came you in the flour-bin?"

"Why, marry, in this wise," he answered, with his mouth full of dough. "When the fight was lost, and I had cut and hacked until my arm was weary and my edge blunted, I found that I was left alone alive of all the Taunton men. Were we on the field you could see where I had stood by the ring of slain which would be found within the sweep of my sword-arm. Finding that all was lost, and that our rogues were fled, I mounted our worthy mayor's charger, seeing that the gallant gentleman had no further need for it, and rode slowly from the field. God of mercy, what is that?"

"'Tis but my horse in the stall below," I answered.

"I thought it was the dragoons," quoth the clerk, wiping away the drops which had started out upon his brow. "You and I would have gone forth and smitten them."

"Or climbed into the flour-bin," said I.

"I have not yet made clear to you how I came there," he continued. "Having ridden, then, some leagues from the field, and noting this windmill, it did occur to me that a stout man might single-handed make it good against a troop of horse. We have no great love of flight, we Tetheridges. I pulled up, there-fore, and had dismounted to take my observations, when my brute of a charger gave the bridle a twitch, jerked itself free, and was off in an instant over hedges and ditches. I had, there-fore, only my good sword left to trust to. I climbed up the ladder, and was engaged in planning how the defence could best be conducted, when I heard the clank of hoofs, and on the top of it you did ascend from below. I retired at once into ambush, from which I should assuredly have made a sudden outfall or sally, had not the flour so choked my breathing that I felt as though I had a two-pound loaf stuck in my gizzard."

"All very clear and explicit, Master Tetheridge," said I, relighting my pipe. "No doubt your demeanor when I did draw you from your hiding-place was also a mere cloak for your valor. But enough of that. It is to the future that we have to look. What are your intentions?"

"To remain with you, captain," said he.

"Nay, that you shall not," I answered; "I have no great fancy for your companionship. Your overflowing valor may bring me into ruffles which I had otherwise avoided."

"Nay, nay! I shall moderate my spirit," he cried. "In such troublous times you will find yourself none the worse for the company of a tried fighting-man."

"Tried and found wanting," said I, weary of the man's braggart talk. "I tell you I will go alone."

"Nay, you need not be so hot about it!" he exclaimed, shrinking away from me. "In any case, we had best stay here until nightfall, when we may make our way to the coast."

"That is the first mark of sense that you have shown," said I. "The king's horse will find enough to do with the Zoyland cider and the Bridgewater ale. If we can pass through, I have friends on the north coast who would give us a lift in their lugger as far as Holland. This help I will not refuse to give you, since you are my fellow in misfortune. I would that Saxon had stayed with me! I fear he will be taken."

"If you mean Colonel Saxon," said the clerk, "I think that he also is one who hath much guile as well as valor. It would have been well for the army had they had more such commanders."

"You say truly," I answered; "but now that we have refreshed ourselves, it is time that we bethought us of taking some rest, since we may have far to travel this night. I would that I could lay my hand upon a flagon of ale."

"I would gladly drink to our further acquaintanceship in the same," said my companion; "but as to the matter of slumber, that may be readily arranged. If you ascend that ladder you will find in the loft a litter of empty sacks, upon which you can repose. For myself, I will stay down here for a while and cook myself another cake."

"Do you remain on watch for two hours, and then arouse me," I replied. "I shall then keep guard while you sleep." He touched the hilt of his sword as a sign that he would be true to his post; so, not without some misgivings, I climbed up into the loft, and throwing myself upon the rude couch, was soon in a deep and dreamless slumber, lulled by the low, mournful groaning and creaking of the sails.

I was awakened by steps beside me, and found that the little clerk had come up the ladder and was bending over me. I asked him if the time had come for me to rouse; on which he answered in a strange, quavering voice that I had yet an hour, and that he had come up to see if there was any service which he could render me.

My next waking was a rougher and a sterner one. There came a sudden rush of heavy feet up the ladder, and a dozen red-coats swarmed into the room. Springing to my feet, I put out my hand for the sword which I had laid all ready by my side, but the trusty weapon was gone. It had been stolen while I slumbered. Unarmed and taken at a vantage, I was struck down and pinioned in a moment.

Having lashed my arms, the soldiers dragged me down the ladder as though I had been a truss of hay, into the room beneath, which was also crowded with troopers. In one corner was the wretched scrivener, a picture of abject terror, with chattering teeth and trembling knees, only prevented from falling upon the floor by the grasp of a stalwart corporal. In front of him stood two officers, one a little, hard, brown man with dark, twinkling eyes and an alert manner, the other tall and slender, with a long golden mustache, which drooped down half-way to his shoulders. The former had my sword in his hand, and they were both examining the blade curiously.

"It is a good bit of steel, Dick," said one, putting the point against the stone floor and pressing down until he touched it with the handle. "See with what a snap it rebounds! No maker's name, but the date, 1638, is stamped upon the pommel. Where did you get it, fellow?" he asked, fixing his keen gaze upon my face.

"It was my father's before me," I answered.

"Then I trust that he drew it in a better quarrel than his son hath done," said the taller officer, with a sneer.

"In as good, though not in a better," I returned. "That sword hath always been drawn for the rights and liberties of Englishmen, and against the tyranny of kings and the bigotry of priests."

"What a tag for a playhouse, Dick!" cried the officer. "How doth it run? 'The bigotry of kings and the tyranny of priests.' Why, if well delivered by Betterton close up to the footlights, with one hand upon his heart and the other pointing to the sky, I warrant the pit would rise at it."

"Very like," said the other, twirling his mustache. "But we have no time for fine speeches now. What are we to do with the little one?"

"Hang him!" the other answered, carelessly.

"No, no, your most gracious honors," howled Master Tetheridge, suddenly writhing out of the corporal's gripe and flinging himself upon the floor at their feet. "Did I not tell ye where ye could find one of the stoutest soldiers of the rebel army? Did I not guide ye to him? Did not I even creep up and remove his sword lest any of the king's subjects be slain in the taking of him? I have given him over to ye. Surely ye will let me go?"

"Very well delivered—plaguily so!" quoth the little officer, clapping the palm of one hand softly against the back of the other.

"What this reptile hath said is true," cried the other. "We must keep faith with him if we wish that others of the country folk should give up the fugitives. There is no help for it."

"For myself, I believe in Jeddart law," his companion answered. "I would hang the man first, and then discuss the question of our promise."

"Nay, it cannot be," the taller said. "Corporal, do you take him down. Henderson will go with you. Take from him that plate and sword, which his mother would wear with as good a grace. And hark ye, corporal, a few touches of thy stirrup-leathers across his fat shoulders might not be amiss, as helping him to remember the king's dragoons."

My treacherous companion was dragged off, struggling and yelping, and presently a series of piercing howls, growing fainter and fainter as he fled before his tormentors, announced that the hint had been taken.

"And now for the other," said the little officer, turning away from the window and wiping the tears of laughter from his face. "That beam over yonder would serve our purpose. Where is Hangman Broderick, the Jack Ketch of the Royals?"

"Here I am, sir," responded a sullen, heavy-faced trooper, shuffling forward; "I have a rope here with a noose."

"Throw it over the beam, then. Do you proceed to do your office."

Three or four troopers caught me by the arms, but I shook them off as best I might, and walked with, as I trust, a steady step and a cheerful face under the beam, which was a great smoke-blackened rafter passing from one side of the chamber to the other. The rope was thrown over this, and the noose placed round my neck. Half a dozen dragoons seized the farther end of the coil, and stood ready to swing me into eternity. Through all my adventurous life I have never been so close upon the threshold of death as at that moment, and yet I was keenly alive to all that was going on around me.

"We must do our work with order," remarked the taller captain, taking a note-book from his pocket. "Colonel Sarsfield may desire some details. Let me see! This is the seventeenth, is it not?"

"Four at the farm and five at the cross-roads," the other answered, counting upon his fingers. "Then there was the one whom we shot in the hedge, and the wounded one who nearly saved himself by dying, and the two in the grove under the hill. I can remember no more, save those who were strung up in Bridgewater immediately after the action."

"It is well to do it in an orderly fashion," quoth the other, scribbling in his book. "It is very well for Kirke and his men, who are half Moors themselves, to hang and to slaughter without discrimination or ceremony, but we should set them a better example. What is your name, sirrah?"

"My name is Captain Micah Clarke," I answered.

The two officers looked at each other, and the smaller one gave a long whistle. "It is the very man!" said he. "This comes of asking questions! Rat me if I had not misgivings that it might prove to be so. They said that he was large of limb."

"Tell me, sirrah, have you ever known one Major Ogilvy of the Horse Guards Blue?" asked the captain.

"Seeing that I had the honor of taking him prisoner," I replied, "and seeing also that he hath shared soldier's fare and quarters with me ever since, I think I may fairly say that I do know him."

"Cast loose the cord!" said the officer, and the hangman reluctantly slipped the cord over my head once more. "Young man, you are surely reserved for something great, for you will never be nearer your grave until you do actually step into it. This Major Ogilvy hath made great interest both for you and for a wounded comrade of yours who lies at Bridgewater. Your name hath been given to the commanders of horse, with orders to bring you in unscathed should you be taken. Yet it is but fair to tell you that though the major's good word may save you from martial law, it will stand you in small stead before a civil judge, before whom you must in the end take your trial."

"I desire to share the same lot and fortune as has befallen my companions in arms," I answered.

"Nay, that is but a sullen way to take your deliverance," cried the officer. "The situation is as flat as sutler's beer. Sergeant Gredder, do you with two troopers conduct the prisoner to Gommatch Church. It is time that we were once more upon our way, for in a few hours the darkness will hinder the pursuit."

At the word of command the troopers descended into the field where their horses were picketed, and were speedily on the march once more, the tall captain leading them, and the stage-struck cornet bringing up the rear. The sergeant to whose care I had been committed—a great, square-shouldered, dark-browed man—ordered my own horse to be brought out, and helped me

to mount it. He removed the pistols from the holsters, however, and hung them with my sword at his own saddle-bow.

"Shall I tie his feet under the horse's belly?" asked one of
the dragoons.

"Nay, the lad hath an honest face," the sergeant answered.
"If he promises to be quiet we shall cast free his arms."

"I have no desire to escape," said I.

"Then untie the rope. A brave man in misfortune hath ever
my good-will, strike me dumb else! Do ye ride on either side,
and I behind! Our carbines are primed, friend, so stand true
to your promise!"

"Nay, you can rely upon it," I answered.

"Your little comrade did play you a scurvy trick," said the
sergeant; "for seeing us ride down the road, he did make across
to us, and bargained with the captain that his life should be
spared, on condition that he should deliver into our hands what
he described as one of the stoutest soldiers in the rebel army.
Truly you have thews and sinews enough, though you are surely
too young to have seen much service."

"This hath been my first campaign," I answered.

"And is like to be your last one," he remarked, with soldierly
frankness. "I hear that the Privy Council intend to make such
an example as will take the heart out of the Whigs for twenty
years to come."

When we at last rode into the little village of Gommatch,
which overlooks the plain of Sedgemoor, it was with regret on
each side that I bade my guardian adieu. As a parting favor
I begged him to take charge of Covenant for me, promising to
pay a certain sum by the month for his keep, and commissioning him to retain the horse for his own use should I fail to
claim him within the year. It was a load off my mind when I
saw my trusty companion led away, staring back at me with
questioning eyes, as though unable to understand the separation.

CHAPTER THIRTY-FOUR

OF THE COMING OF SOLOMON SPRENT

THE church of Gommatch was a small ivy-clad building with a square Norman tower, standing in the centre of the hamlet of that name. Its great oaken doors, studded with iron, and high narrow windows, fitted it well for the use to which it was now turned. Two companies of Dumbarton's foot had been quartered in the village, with a portly major at their head, to whom I was handed over by the sergeant, with some account of my capture, and of the reasons which had prevented my summary execution.

Night was now drawing in, but a few dim lamps, hung here and there upon the walls, cast an uncertain, flickering light over the scene. A hundred or more prisoners were scattered about upon the stone floor, many of them wounded, and some evidently dying. The hale had gathered in silent, subdued groups round their stricken friends, and were doing what they could to lessen their sufferings. Here and there in the shadows dark kneeling figures might be seen, and the measured sound of their prayers ran through the aisles, with a groan now and again, or a choking gasp as some poor sufferer battled for breath.

On Thursday morning, the third day after the battle, we were all conveyed into Bridgewater, where we were confined for the remainder of the week in St. Mary's Church, the very one from the tower of which Monmouth and his commanders had inspected Feversham's position. The more we heard of the fight from the soldiers and others, the more clear it became that, but for the most unfortunate accidents, there was every chance that our night attack might have succeeded. The ferocity of the Privy Council, after the rebellion was quelled, arose from their knowledge of how very close it had been to success.

I do not wish to say too much of the cruelty and barbarity of the victors. The sluggard Feversham and the brutal Kirke have earned themselves a name in the west which is second only to that of the arch villain who came after them. They did all that wicked and callous-hearted men could do, knowing well that such deeds were acceptable to the cold-blooded, bigoted hypocrite who sat upon the throne. They worked to win his favor and they won it. Men were hanged and cut down and hanged again. Every cross-road in the country was ghastly with gibbets.

At the end of a week or two news came of the fugitives. Monmouth, it seems, had been captured by Portman's yellow-coats when trying to make his way to the New Forest, whence he hoped to escape to the Continent. He was dragged, gaunt, unshaven, and trembling, out of a bean-field in which he had taken refuge, and was carried to Ringwood, in Dorsetshire. Strange rumors reached us concerning his behavior—rumors which came to our ears through the coarse jests of our guards. Some said that he had gone on his knees to the yokels who had seized him. Others that he had written to the king offering to do anything, even to throw over the Protestant cause, to save his head from the scaffold. Alas! time showed that the stories were indeed true, and that there was no depth of infamy to which this unhappy man would not descend, in the hope of pro-longing for a few years that existence which had proved a curse to so many who trusted him.

Of Saxon no news had come, good or bad, which encouraged me to hope that he had found a hiding-place for himself. Reuben was still confined to his couch by his wound, and was under the care and protection of Major Ogilvy. The good gentleman came to see me more than once, and endeavored to add to my comfort, until I made him understand that it pained me to find myself upon a different footing to the brave fellows with whom I had shared the perils of the campaign. One great favor he did me in writing to my father, and informing him that I was well and in no pressing danger. In reply to this letter I had a stout Christian answer from the old man, bidding me to be of good courage. My poor mother, he said, was in deep distress at my position, but was held up by her confidence in the decrees of Providence. He enclosed a draft for Major Ogilvy, commissioning him to use it in whatever way I should suggest. This money, together with the small hoard which my mother had sewed into my collar, proved to be invaluable, for when the jail-fever broke out among us I was able to get fitting food for the sick, and also to pay for the services of physicians, so that the disease was stamped out ere it had time to spread.

Early in August we were brought from Bridgewater to Taunton, where we were thrown with hundreds of others into the same wool storehouse where our regiment had been quartered in the early days of the campaign. We gained little by the change, save that we found that our new guards were somewhat more satiated with cruelty than our old ones, and were therefore less exacting upon their prisoners. Not only were friends allowed in occasionally to see us, but books and papers could be obtained by the aid of a small present to the sergeant on duty. We were able, therefore, to spend our time with some degree of comfort during the month or more which passed before our trial.

One evening I was standing listlessly with my back against the wall, looking up at the thin slit of blue sky which showed itself through the narrow window, and fancying myself back in the meadows of Havant once more, when a voice fell upon my ear which did, indeed, recall me to my Hampshire home. Those deep, husky tones, rising at times into an angry roar, could belong to none other than my old friend the seaman. I approached the door from which the uproar came, and all doubt vanished as I listened to the conversation.

"Won't let me pass, won't ye?" he was shouting. "Let me tell you I've held on my course when better men than you have asked me to veil top-sails. I tell you I have the admiral's permit, and I won't clew up for a bit of a red-painted cockboat; so move from athwart my hawse, or I may chance to run you down."

"We don't know nothing about admirals here," said the sergeant of the guard. "The time for seeing prisoners is over for the day, and if you do not take your ill-favored body out of this I may try the weight o' my halberd on your back."

"I have taken blows and given them ere you were ever thought of, you land-swab," roared old Solomon. "I was yard-arm and yard-arm with De Ruyter when you were learning to suck milk. If I tack back to Major Ogilvy and signal him the way that I have been welcomed, he'll make your hide redder than ever your coat was."

"Major Ogilvy!" exclaimed the sergeant in a more respect-ful voice. "If you had said that your permit was from Major Ogilvy it would have been another thing, but you did rave of admirals and commodores, and God knows what other out-landish talk! Whom is it that you would see?"

"If I had you in my watch," returned the seaman, "I would make a man of you yet."

"Pass the old man through!" cried the sergeant, furiously, and the sailor came stumping in, with his bronzed face all screwed up and twisted, partly with amusement at his victory over the sergeant, and partly from a great chunk of tobacco which he was wont to stow within his cheek. Having glanced round without perceiving me, he put his hands to his mouth and bellowed out my name, with a string of "Ahoys!" which rang through the building.

"Here I am, Solomon," said I, touching him on the shoulder.

"God bless you, lad! God bless you!" he cried, wringing my hand. "I could not see you, for my port eye is as foggy as the Newfoundland banks, and has been ever since Long Sue Williams of the Point hove a quart pot at it in the Tiger Inn, nigh thirty year agone. How are you? All sound, alow and aloft?"

"As well as might be," I answered. "I have little to complain of."

"None of your standing rigging shot away?" said he. "No spars crippled? No shots between wind and water, eh? You have not been hulled, nor raked, nor laid aboard of?"

"None of these things," said I, laughing.

"Faith! you are leaner than of old, and have aged ten years in two months. You did go forth as smart and trim a fighting-ship as ever answered helm, and now you are like the same ship when the battle and the storm have taken the gloss from her sides and torn the love-pennants from her peak. Yet am I right glad to see you sound in wind and limb."

"I have looked upon sights," said I, "which might well add ten years to a man's age."

"Aye, aye," he answered, with a hollow groan, shaking his head from side to side. "It is a most accursed affair. Yet, bad as the tempest is, the calm will ever come afterwards if you will but ride it out with your anchor placed deep in Providence. Ah, lad, that is good holding-ground! But if I know you aright, your grief is more for these poor wretches around you than for yourself."

"It is, indeed, a sore sight to see them suffer so patiently and uncomplainingly," I answered; "and for such a man, too!"

"Aye, the chicken-livered swab!" growled the seaman, grinding his teeth.

"How are my mother and my father?" I asked.

"Thy father hath set his face hard, and goes about his work as usual, though much troubled by the justices, who have twice had him up to Winchester for examination, but have found his papers all right and no charge to be brought against him. Your mother, poor soul, hath little time to mope or to pipe her eye. They have taken to prayer as some would to rum, and warm their hearts with it when the wind of misfortune blows chill. They were right glad that I should come down to you, and I gave them the word of a sailor that I would get you out of the bilboes if it might anyhow be done."

"Get me out, Solomon!" said I; "nay, that may be put outside the question. How could you get me out?"

"There are many ways," he answered, sinking his voice to a whisper, and nodding his grizzled head as one who talks upon what has cost him much time and thought. "There is scuttling."

"If this wool-house were galley *Providence*, and Taunton Deane were the Bay of Biscay, it might be attempted," I said.

"I have indeed got out o' the channel," he answered, with a wrinkled brow. "There is, however, another most excellent plan which I have conceived, which is to blow up the building."

"To blow it up!" I cried.

"Aye! a brace of kegs and a slow match would do it any dark night. Then where would be these walls which now shut ye in?"

"Where would be the folk that are now inside them?" I asked. "Would you not blow them up as well?"

"Plague take it, I had forgot that," cried Solomon. "Nay, then, I leave it with you. What have you to propose?"

"Then my advice is, my dear old friend," said I, "that you leave matters to take their course, and hie back to Havant. Do what you can to cheer my mother's heart, and commend me to Zachary Palmer. Your visit hath been a joy to me, and your return will be the same to them. You can serve me better so than by biding here."

"Sink me if I like going back without a blow struck," he growled; "yet, if it is your will, there is an end of the matter. Tell me, lad—has that lank-sparred, slab-sided, herring-gutted friend of yours played you false? I know where he hath laid himself up, moored stem and stern, all snug and ship-shape, waiting for the turn of the tide."

"What, Saxon!" I cried; "do you indeed know where he is? For God's sake speak low, for it would mean a commission and five hundred good pounds to any one of these soldiers could he lay hands upon him."

"They are scarce like to do that," said Solomon. "On my journey hither I chanced to put into port at a place called Bruton, where there is an inn that will compare with most, and the skipper is a wench with a glib tongue and a merry eye. I was drinking a glass of spiced ale, as is my custom about six bells of the middle watch, when I chanced to notice a great lanky carter, who was loading up a wagon in the yard with a cargo o' beer casks. Looking closer, it seemed to me that the man's nose, like the beak of a goshawk, and his glinting eyes, with the lids only half-reefed, were known to me; but when I overheard him swearing to himself in good High Dutch, then his figurehead came back to me in a moment. I put out into the yard, and touched him on the shoulder. Zounds, lad! you should have seen him spring back and spit at me—like a wildcat, with every hair of his head in a bristle. I told him that his secret was safe with me, and I asked him if he had heard that you were laid by the heels. He answered that he knew it, and that he would be answerable that no harm befell you, though in truth it seemed to me that he had his hands full in trimming his own sails without acting as pilot to another. However, there I left him, and there I shall find him again, if so be as he has done you an injury."

"Nay," I answered; "I am right glad that he has found this refuge. We did separate upon a difference of opinion, but I have no cause to complain of him. In many ways he hath shown me both kindness and good-will."

"He is as crafty as a purser's clerk," quoth Solomon. "I have seen Reuben Lockarby, who sends his love to you. He is still kept in his bunk from his wound, but he meets with good treatment. Major Ogilvy tells me that he has made such interest for him that there is every chance that he will gain his discharge, the more particularly since he was not present at the battle.

Your own chance of pardon would, he thinks, be greater if you had fought less stoutly."

The good old seaman stayed with me until late in the night, listening to my adventures, and narrating in return the simple gossip of the village, which is of more interest to the absent wanderer than the rise and fall of empires. Before he left he drew a great handful of silver-pieces from his pouch, and went round among the prisoners, listening to their wants, and doing what he could, with rough sailor talk and dropping coins, to lighten their troubles. I felt as though he had brought a whiff of his own pure ocean breezes into our close and noisome prison, and left us the sweeter and the healthier.

It was late in August when the lord Chief-justice Jeffreys made his entry. From one of the windows of the room in which we were confined I saw him pass. First rode the dragoons with their standards and kettle-drums, then the javelin men with their halberds, and behind them the line of coaches full of the high dignitaries of the law. Last of all, drawn by six long-tailed Flemish mares, came a great open coach, thickly crusted with gold, in which, reclining amid velvet cushions, sat the infamous judge, wrapped in a cloak of crimson plush, with a heavy white periwig upon his head, which was so long that it drooped down over his shoulders. They say that he wore scarlet in order to strike terror into the hearts of the people, and that his courts were, for the same reason, draped in the color of blood.

CHAPTER THIRTY-FIVE

OF THE DEVIL IN WIG AND GOWN

THERE was no delay in the work of slaughter. That very
night the great gallows was erected outside the White Hart
Inn. Among the prisoners the night was passed in prayer and
meditation, the stout-hearted holding forth to their weaker
brethren, and exhorting them to play the man, and to go to their
death in a fashion which should be an example to true Prot-
estants throughout the world. Never have I seen anything so
admirable as the cool and cheerful bravery wherewith these poor

clowns faced their fate. Their courage on the battle-field paled before that which they showed in the shambles of the law. So amid the low murmur of prayer, and appeals for mercy to God from tongues which never yet asked mercy from man, the morning broke, the last morning which many of us were to spend upon earth.

The court should have opened at nine, but my lord chief-justice was indisposed, having set up somewhat late with Colonel Kirke. It was nearly eleven before the trumpeters and criers announced that he had taken his seat. One by one my fellow-prisoners were called out by name, the more prominent being chosen first. They went out from among us amid hand-shakings and blessings, but we saw and heard no more of them, save that a sudden fierce rattle of kettle-drums would rise up now and again, which was, as our guards told us, to drown any dying words which might fall from the sufferers and bear fruit in the breasts of those who heard them. With firm steps and smiling faces the roll of martyrs went forth to their fate during the whole of that long autumn day, until the rough soldiers of the guard stood silent and awed in the presence of a courage which they could not but recognize as higher and nobler than their own. Folk may call it a trial that they received, and a trial it really was, but not in the sense that we Englishmen use it. It was but being haled before a judge, and insulted before being dragged to the gibbet. Nearly a hundred were either executed or condemned to death upon that opening day.

I had expected to be among the first of those called, and no doubt I should have been so but for the exertions of Major Ogilvy. As it was, the second day passed, but I still found myself overlooked. On the third and fourth days the slaughter was slackened, not on account of any awakening grace on the part of the judge, but because the great Tory land-owners and the chief supporters of the government revolted at this butchery of defenceless men. As it was, two hundred and fifty fell victims to this accursed monster's thirst for human blood.

On the eighth day of the assizes there were but fifty of us left in the wool warehouse. For the last few days prisoners had been tried in batches of ten and twenty, but now the whole of us were taken in a drove under escort to the courthouse, where as many as could be squeezed in were ranged in the dock, while the rest were penned, like calves in the market, in the body of the hall. The judge reclined in a high chair, with a scarlet dais above him, while two other judges, in less elevated seats, were stationed on either side of him. On the right hand was a jury-box, containing twelve carefully picked men—Tories of the old school—firm upholders of the doctrines of non-resistance and the divine right of kings. Just under the judge was a broad table, covered with green cloth and strewn with papers. On the right hand of this were a long array of crown lawyers, grim, ferret-faced men, each with a sheaf of papers in his hands, which they sniffed through again and again as though they were so many bloodhounds picking up the trail along which they were to hunt us down. On the other side of the table sat a single, fresh-faced young man, in silk gown and wig, with a nervous, shuffling manner. This was the barrister, Master Helstrop, whom the crown in its clemency had allowed us for our defence, lest any should be bold enough to say that we had not had every fairness in our trial. The remainder of the courtroom was filled with the servants of the justices' retinue and the soldiers of the garrison, who used the place as their common lounge, looking on the whole thing as a mighty cheap form of sport, and roaring with laughter at the rude banter and coarse pleasantries of his lordship.

The clerk having gabbled through the usual form, the lord justice proceeded to take matters into his own hands.

"I trust that we shall come well out of this!" he broke out. "I trust that no judgment will fall upon this building! Was ever so much wickedness fitted into one courthouse before? Who ever saw such an array of villanous faces? Ah, rogues, I see a rope ready for every one of ye! And you, you great hulking rebel, have you not grace enough to cast your eyes down, but must needs look justice in the face as though you were an honest man? Are you not afeard, sirrah? Do you not see death close upon you?"

"I have seen that before now, my lord, and I was not afeard," I answered.

"Generation of vipers!" he cried, throwing up his hands. "Rogues, we shall be merciful to ye—oh, merciful, merciful! How many are here, recorder?"

"Fifty and one, my lord."

"Oh, sink of villany! Fifty and one as arrant knaves as ever lay on a hurdle! Oh, what a mass of corruption have we here! Who defends the villains?"

"I defend the prisoners, your lordship," replied the young lawyer.

"Master Helstrop, Master Helstrop!" cried Jeffreys, shaking his great wig until the powder flew out of it, "you are in all these dirty cases, Master Helstrop. Oh, Master Helstrop, I fear that I shall live to see some evil come upon you!"

"I crave your lordship's pardon!" cried the faint-hearted barrister, with his face the color of his brief.

"Keep a guard upon your words and upon your actions!" Jeffreys answered, in a menacing voice. "See that you are not too zealous in the cause of the scum of the earth. How now, then? What do these one and fifty villains desire to say for themselves?"

"Forty of them desire to plead guilty to the charge of taking up arms against the king," replied our barrister.

"Ah!" roared the judge. "Was ever such unparalleled impudence? Guilty, quotha! Put down those words on the record, clerk!"

"They have refused to express repentance, your lordship!" replied the counsel for the defence.

"Oh, the parricides! Oh, the shameless rogues!" cried the judge. "Put the forty together on this side of the enclosure.

Oh, gentlemen, have ye ever seen such a concentration of vice?
But the other eleven. How can they expect us to believe this
transparent falsehood—this palpable device? How can they
foist it upon the court?"

"My lord, their defence hath not yet been advanced!" stammered Master Helstrop.

"I can sniff a lie before it is uttered," roared the judge, by
no means abashed. "I can read it as quick as ye can think it.
Come, come, the court's time is precious. Put forward a
defence, or seat yourself, and let judgment be passed."

"These men, my lord," said the counsel, who was trembling
until the parchment rattled in his hand—"these eleven men, my
lord ——"

"Eleven devils, my lord," interrupted Jeffreys.

"They are innocent peasants, my lord, who love God and
the king, and have in nowise mingled themselves in this recent
business. They have been dragged from their homes, my lord,
not because there was suspicion against them, but because they
could not satisfy the greed of certain common soldiers who were
balked of plunder in ——"

"Oh, shame, shame!" cried Jeffreys, in a voice of thunder.
"Oh, threefold shame, Master Helstrop! Are you not content
with bolstering up rebels but you must go out of your way to
slander the king's troops? What is the world coming to?
What, in a word, is the defence of these rogues?"

"An *alibi,* your lordship."

"Ha! The common plea of every scoundrel. Have they
witnesses?"

"We have here a list of forty witnesses, your lordship.
They are waiting below, many of them having come great dis-
tances and with much toil and trouble."

"Who are they? What are they?" cried Jeffreys.

"They are country folk, your lordship. Cottagers and
farmers, the neighbors of these poor men, who knew them well,
and can speak as to their doings."

"Cottagers and farmers!" the judge shouted. "Why, then, they are drawn from the very class from which these men come."

"Will you not hear the witnesses, your lordship?" cried our counsel, shamed into some little sense of manhood by this outrage.

"Not a word from them, sirrah," said Jeffreys. "It is a question whether my duty towards my kind master the king— write down 'kind master,' clerk—doth not warrant me in placing all your witnesses in the dock as the aiders and abettors of treason."

"If it please your lordship," cried one of the prisoners, "I have for witnesses Mr. Johnson, of Nether Stowey, who is a good Tory, and also Mr. Shepperton, the clergyman."

"The more shame to them to appear in such a cause," replied Jeffreys. "What are we to say, gentlemen of the jury, when we see county gentry and the clergy of the Established Church supporting treason and rebellion in this fashion?"

"But hear me, my lord!" cried one of the prisoners.

"Hear you, you bellowing calf!" shouted the judge. "We can hear naught else. We shall hear you at the end of a rope ere many days."

"We scarce think, your lordship," said one of the crown lawyers, springing to his feet amid a great rustling of papers— "we scarce think that it is necessary for the crown to state any case. We have already heard the whole tale of this most damnable and execrable attempt many times over. The gentlemen of the long robe are therefore unanimously of opinion that the jury may at once be required to pronounce a single verdict upon the whole of the prisoners."

"Which is?" asked Jeffreys, glancing round at the foreman.

"Guilty, your lordship," said he, with a grin, while his brother jurymen nodded their heads and laughed to one another.

"Of course, of course! guilty as Judas Iscariot!" cried the judge, looking down with exultant eyes at the throng of peasants and burghers before him. "Move them a little forward, ushers,

MICAH CLARKE

349

that I may see them to more advantage." The very devil seemed to be in the man, for as he spoke he writhed with unholy laughter, and drummed his hand upon the red cushion in front of him. I glanced round at my companions, but their faces were all as though they had been chiselled out of marble. If he had hoped to see a moist eye or a quivering lip, the satisfaction was denied him.

"Had I my way," said he, "there is not one of ye but should swing for it. But have ye not heard how your most soft-hearted and compassionate monarch, the best of men—put it down in the record, clerk—on the intercession of that great and charitable statesman, Lord Sunderland—mark it down, clerk—hath had pity on ye? Hath it not melted ye? I declare, when I think of it"—here, with a sudden catching of the breath, he burst out a-sobbing, the tears running down his cheeks—"when I think of it, the Christian forbearance, the ineffable mercy, it doth bring forcibly to my mind that great Judge before whom all of us— even I—shall one day have to render an account. Shall I repeat it, clerk, or have you it down?"

"I have it down, your lordship."

"Then write 'sobs' in the margin. 'Tis well that the king should know our opinion on such matters. At his command we withhold from ye the chastisement which ye have merited. Drop on your knees and offer up thanks when I tell ye that he hath ordained that ye shall all have a free pardon." Here the judge rose from his seat, as though about to descend from the tribunal, and we gazed upon each other in the utmost astonishment at this most unlooked-for end to the trial. The soldiers and lawyers were equally amazed, while a hum of joy and applause rose up from the few country folk who had dared to venture within the accursed precincts.

"This pardon, however," continued Jeffreys, turning round with a malicious smile upon his face, "is coupled with certain conditions and limitations. Ye shall all be removed from here to Poole, in chains, where ye shall find a vessel awaiting ye.

With others ye shall be stowed away in the hold of the said vessel, and conveyed at the king's expense to the Plantations, there to be sold as slaves. God send ye masters who will know by the free use of wood and leather how to soften your stubborn thoughts and incline your mind to better things!" He was again about to withdraw, when one of the crown lawyers whispered something across to him.

"Well thought of, coz," cried the judge. "I had forgot. Bring back the prisoners, ushers! Perhaps ye think that by the Plantations I mean his majesty's American dominions. By the Plantations, therefore, I mean Barbadoes and the Indies, where ye shall live with the other slaves, whose skins may be blacker than yours, but I dare warrant that their souls are more white." With this concluding speech the trial ended, and we were led back through the crowded streets to the prison from which we had been brought. On either side of the street, as we passed, we could see the limbs of former companions dangling in the wind, and their heads grinning at us from the tops of poles and pikes.

We were scarce back in the wool-house once more when a file of guards with a sergeant entered, escorting a long, pale-faced man with protruding teeth, whose bright blue coat and white silk breeches, gold-headed sword, and glancing shoe-buckles proclaimed him to be one of those London exquisites whom interest or curiosity had brought down to the scene of the rebellion. He tripped along upon his tiptoes like a French dancing-master, waving his scented kerchief in front of his thin high nose, and inhaling aromatic salts from a blue vial which he carried in his left hand.

"By the Lard!" he cried, "but the stench of these filthy wretches is enough to stap one's breath. It is, by the Lard! I have a grant of a dozen of them, and Captain Pogram hath offered me twelve pounds a head. But they must be brawny rogues—strong and brawny, for the voyage kills many, sergeant, and the climate doth also tell upon them. Now here is one whom

I must have. Yes, in very truth, he is a young man, and hath much life in him and much strength. Tick him off, sergeant, tick him off!"

"His name is Clarke," said the soldier. "I have marked him down."

"There is yonder man with the brown face, you can mark him down," cried the fop, sniffing at his bottle. "And the young man beside him also. Tick him off. There is yonder lusty fellow with the red head, sergeant! The blacks will think he is afire. Those, and these six stout yokels, will make up my dozen."

"You have indeed the pick of them," said the sergeant.

"Aye, sink me, but I have a quick eye for horse, man, or woman! I'll pick the best of a batch with most. Twelve twelves, close on a hundred and fifty pieces, sergeant, and all for a few words, my friend, all for a few words. I did but send my wife, a demmed handsome woman, mark you, and dresses in the mode, to my good friend the secretary to ask for some rebels. 'How many?' says he. 'A dozen will do,' says she. It was all done in a pen-stroke. What a cursed fool she was not to have asked for a hundred!"

Three days after our trial we were drawn up in North Street in front of the castle, with others from the other prisons who were to share our fate. We were placed four abreast, with a rope connecting each rank, and of these ranks I counted fifty, which would bring our total to two hundred. On each side of us rode dragoons, and in front and behind were companies of musketeers to prevent any attempt at rescue or escape. In this order we set off upon the tenth day of September, amid the weeping and wailing of the townsfolk, many of whom saw their sons or brothers marching off into exile without their being able to exchange a last word or embrace with them. Some of these

poor folk, doddering old men and wrinkled, decrepit women, toiled for miles after us down the high-road until the rear-guard of foot-faced round upon them, and drove them away with curses and blows from their ramrods.

Late in the afternoon of the third day the spars and rigging of the shipping in Poole Harbor rose up before us, and in another hour we had descended the steep and craggy path which leads to the town. Here we were drawn up on the quay opposite the broad-decked, heavy-sparred brig which was destined to carry us into slavery.

We were marched aboard and led below by the mate of the vessel, a tall, red-faced seaman with ear-rings in his ears, while the captain stood on the poop with his legs apart and a pipe in his mouth, checking us off one by one by means of a list which he held in his hand. As he looked at the sturdy build and rustic health of the peasants, which even their long confinement had been unable to break down, his eyes glistened, and he rubbed his big red hands together with delight.

"Show them down, Jem!" he kept shouting to the mate. "Stow them safe, Jem! There's lodgings for a duchess down there; s' help me, there's lodgings for a duchess! Pack 'em away!"

One by one we passed before the delighted captain, and down the steep ladder which led into the hold. Here we were led along a narrow passage, on either side of which opened the stalls which were prepared for us. As each man came opposite to the one set aside for him, he was thrown into it by the brawny mate, and fastened down with anklets of iron by the seaman armorer in attendance. It was dark before we were all secured, but the captain came round with a lantern to satisfy himself that all his property was really safe. I could hear the mate and him reckoning the value of each prisoner, and counting what he would fetch in the Barbadoes market.

"Have you served out their fodder, Jem?" he asked, flash-

ing his light into each stall in turn. "Have you seen that they
had their rations?"

"A rye-bread loaf and a pint o' water," answered the mate.

"Fit for a duchess, s' help me!" cried the captain. "Look
to this one, Jem. He is a lusty rogue. Look to his great hands.
He might work for years in the rice-swamps ere the land-crabs
have the picking of him."

"Aye, we'll have smart bidding amid the settlers for this lot.
'Cod, captain, but you have made a bargain of it! Od's bud!
you have done these London fools to some purpose."

"If it please your honor," said a seaman, coming hurriedly
down from the deck, "there is a stranger upon the poop who
will have speech with your honor."

"What manner of man, sirrah?"

"Surely he is a person of quality, your honor. He is as free
wi' his words as though he were the captain o' the ship. The
boatswain did but jog against him, and he swore so woundily
at him and stared at him so, wi' een like a tiger-cat, that Job
Harrison says we have shipped the devil himsel'. The men
don't like the look of him, your honor."

"Curse his blood, whoever he be!" growled the seaman.
"Every cock on his own dunghill. What doth the rogue mean?
Were he the lord high privy seal, I would have him to know
that I am lord of my own quarter-deck!" So saying, with many
snorts of indignation, the mate and the captain withdrew together up the ladder, banging the heavy hatchways down as they
passed through.

A single oil-lamp swinging from a beam in the centre of the
gangway which led between the rows of cells was the only light
which was vouchsafed us. By its yellow, murky glimmer we
could dimly see the great wooden ribs of the vessel. A grievous
stench from foul bilge-water poisoned the close, heavy air.
Heavy breathing all around me showed that my companions,
wearied out by their journey and their sufferings, had dropped
into a slumber.

I lay long awake full of thought both for myself and for the poor souls around me. At last, however, the measured swash of the water against the side of the vessel and the slight rise and fall had lulled me into a sleep, from which I was suddenly aroused by the flashing of a light in my eyes. Sitting up, I found several sailors gathered about me, and a tall man with a black cloak swathed round him swinging a lantern over me.

"That is the man," he said.

"Come, mate, you are to come on deck!" said the seaman armorer. With a few blows from his hammer he knocked the irons from my feet.

"Follow me!" said the tall stranger, and led the way up the hatchway ladder. It was heavenly to come out into the pure air once more. Close beside us the lights of the town gleamed yellow and cheery. Beyond, the moon was peeping over the Bournemouth hills.

"This way, sir," said the sailor; "right aft into the cabin, sir."

Still following my guide, I found myself in the low cabin of the brig. A square shining table stood in the centre, with a bright swinging lamp above it. At the farther end, in the glare of the light, sat the captain, his face shining with greed and expectation. On the table there stood a small pile of gold-pieces, a rum-flask, glasses, a tobacco-box, and two long pipes.

"My compliments to you, Captain Clarke," said the skipper, bobbing his round, bristling head. "An honest seaman's compliments to you. It seems that we are not to be shipmates this voyage, after all."

"Captain Micah Clarke must do a voyage of his own," said the stranger.

At the sound of his voice I sprang round in amazement. "Good heavens!" I cried, "Saxon!"

"You have nicked it," said he, throwing down his mantle and showing the well-known face and figure of the soldier of fortune. "Zounds, man! if you can pick me out of the Solent,

I suppose that I may pick you out of this accursed rat-trap in which I find you. In truth, I was huffed with you when last we parted, but I have had you in my mind for all that."

"A seat and a glass, Captain Clarke," cried the skipper. "Od's bud! I should think that you would be glad to raise your little finger and wet your whistle after what you have gone through."

I seated myself by the table with my brain in a whirl. "This is more than I can fathom," said I. "What is the meaning of it, and how comes it about?"

"For my own part, the meaning is as clear as the glass of my binnacle," quoth the seaman. "Your good friend Colonel Saxon, as I understand his name to be, has offered me as much as I could hope to gain by selling you in the Indies. Sink it, I may be rough and ready, but my heart is in the right place!"

"Then I am free," said I.

"You are free," he answered. "There is your purchase-money upon the table. You can go where you will, save only upon the land of England, where you are still an outlaw under sentence."

"How have you done this, Saxon?" I asked. "Are you not afraid for yourself?"

"Ho, ho!" laughed the old soldier. "I am a free man, my lad! I hold my pardon, and care not a maravedi for spy or informer. Who should I meet but Colonel Kirke a day or so back. Yes, lad! I met him in the street and I cocked my hat in his face. I can snap this finger and thumb at them, so! They would rather see Decimus Saxon's back than his face, I promise ye!"

"But how comes all this about?" I asked.

"Why, marry, it is no mystery. Cunning old birds are not to be caught with chaff. When I left you I made for a certain inn where I could count upon finding a friend. There I lay by for a while, en cachette, as the messieurs call it, while I could work out the plan that was in my head. Donnerwetter! but I got a fright from that old seaman friend of yours, who should be sold as a picture, for he is of little use as a man. Well, I bethought me early in the affair of your visit to Badminton, and of the Duke of B. We shall mention no names, but you can follow my meaning. To him I sent a messenger, to the effect that I purposed to purchase my own pardon by letting out all that I knew concerning his double dealing with the rebels. He asked my conditions. I replied, a free pardon and a command for myself. For you, money enough to land you safely in some foreign country where you can pursue the noble profession of arms. I got them both, though it was like drawing teeth from his head. His name hath much power at court just now, and the king can refuse him nothing. I have my pardon and a command of troops in New England. For you I have two hundred pieces, of which thirty have been paid in ransom to the captain, while twenty are due to me for my disbursements over the matter. In this bag you will find the odd hundred and fifty, of which you will pay fifteen to the fishermen who have promised to see you safe to Flushing."

I was bewildered by this sudden and most unlooked-for turn which events had taken. When Saxon had ceased to speak I sat as one stunned, trying to realize what he had said to me. There came a thought into my head, however, which chilled the glow of hope and of happiness which had sprung up in me at the thought of recovering my freedom. My presence had been a support and a comfort to my unhappy companions. How could I desert them now?

"I am much beholden to you, Saxon," I said at last, speaking slowly and with some difficulty, for the words were hard to utter. "But I fear that your pains have been thrown away. These poor country folk have none to look after or assist them. They are as simple as babes, and as little fitted to be landed in a strange country. I cannot find it in my heart to leave them!"

Saxon burst out laughing, and leaned back in his seat with

his long legs stretched straight out and his hands in his breeches pockets.

"This is too much!" he said at last. "I saw many difficulties in my way, yet I did not foresee this one. You are in very truth the most contrary man that ever stood in neat's leather. Yet I think that I can overcome these strange scruples of yours by a little persuasion."

"As to the prisoners, Captain Clarke," said the seaman, "I'll be as good as a father to them. S' help me, I will, on the word of an honest sailor! If you should choose to lay out a trifle of twenty pieces upon their comfort, I shall see that their food is such as mayhap many of them never got at their own tables. They shall come on deck, too, in watches, and have an hour or two o' fresh air in the day. I can't say fairer!"

"A word or two with you on deck," said Saxon. He walked out of the cabin, and I followed him to the far end of the poop, where we stood leaning against the bulwarks. One by one the lights had gone out in the town, until the black ocean beat against a blacker shore.

"You need not have any fear of the future of the prisoners," he said, in a low whisper. "They are not bound for the Barbadoes, nor will this skinflint of a captain have the selling of them, for all that he is so cocksure. If he can bring his own skin out of the business it will be more than I expect. He hath a man aboard his ship who would think no more of giving him a tilt over the side than I should."

"What mean you, Saxon?" I cried.

"Hast ever heard of a man named Marot?"

"Hector Marot! Yes, surely I knew him well. A highwayman he was, but a mighty stout man with a kind heart beneath a thief's jacket."

"The same. He is aboard," said Saxon. "It appears that he was much disturbed in his mind over the cruelties which were inflicted on the country folk after the battle at Bridgewater. Being a man of a somewhat stern and fierce turn of mind, his disapproval did vent itself in actions rather than words. Soldiers were found here and there over the countryside pistolled or stabbed, and no trace left of their assailant. A dozen or more were cut off in this way, and soon it came to be whispered about that Marot the highwayman was the man that did it, and the chase became hot at his heels."

"Well, and what then?" I asked, for Saxon had stopped to light his pipe at the same old metal tinder-box which he had used when first I met him.

"I had heard," quoth he, puffing slowly at his pipe, "that Marot was a man of this kidney, and also that he was so compassed round that he was in peril of capture. I sought him out, therefore, and held council with him. His mare, it seems, had been slain by some chance shot, and as he was much attached to the brute, the accident made him more savage and more dangerous than ever. He had no heart, he said, to continue in his old trade. Indeed, he was ripe for anything—the very stuff out of which useful tools are made. I found that in his youth he had had a training for the sea. When I heard that, I saw my way in the snap of a petronel."

"What then?" I asked. "I am still in the dark."

"Nay, it is surely plain enough to you now. Marot's end was to baffle his pursuers and to benefit the exiles. How could he do this better than by engaging as a seaman aboard this brig, the *Dorothy Fox,* and sailing away from England in her? There are but thirty of a crew. Below hatches are close on two hundred men, who, simple as they may be, are, as you and I know, second to none in the cut-and-thrust work, without order or discipline, which will be needed in such an affair. Marot has but to go down among them some dark night, knock off their anklets, and fit them up with a few stanchions or cudgels. Ho, ho, Micah! what think you? The planters may dig their plantations themselves for all the help they are like to get from West-countrymen this bout."

"It is, indeed, a well-conceived plan," said I. "It is a pity,

Saxon, that your ready wit and quick invention hath not had a
fair field. You are, as I know well, as fit to command armies
and to order campaigns as any man that ever bore a truncheon."

"Mark ye there!" whispered Saxon, grasping me by the arm.
"See where the moonlight falls beside the hatchway? Do you
not see that short, squat seaman who stands alone, lost in
thought, with his head sunk upon his breast? It is Marot! I
tell you that if I were Captain Pogram I would rather have the
devil himself, horns, hoofs, and tail, for my first mate and bunk
companion than have that man aboard my ship. You need not
concern yourself about the prisoners, Micah. Their future is
decided."

"Then, Saxon," I answered, "it only remains for me to thank
you and to accept the means of safety which you have placed
within my reach."

"Spoken like a man," said he; "is there aught which I may
do for thee in England? though, by the mass, I may not be here
very long myself, for, as I understand, I am to be intrusted with
the command of an expedition that is fitting out against the
Indians, who have ravaged the plantations of our settlers."

"There is a friend whom Sir Gervas Jerome did commend
to my care," I remarked. "I have, however, already taken
measures to have his wishes carried out. There is naught else
save to assure all in Havant that a king who hath battened upon
his subjects, as this one of ours hath done, is not one who is like
to keep his seat very long upon the throne of England. When
he falls I shall return, and perhaps it may be sooner than folk
think."

"These doings in the west have indeed stirred up much ill-
feeling all over the country," said my companion. "On all hands
I hear that there is more hatred of the king and of his ministers
than before the outbreak. What ho, Captain Pogram, this way!
We have settled the matter, and my friend is willing to go."

"I thought he would tack round," the captain said, staggering
towards us with a gait which showed that he had made the rum-

bottle his companion since we had left him. "S' help me, I was sure of it! Though, by the mass, I don't wonder that he thought twice before leaving the *Dorothy Fox,* for she is fitted up fit for a duchess, s' help me! Where is your boat?"

"Alongside," replied Saxon; "my friend joins with me in hoping that you, Captain Pogram, will have a pleasant and profitable voyage."

"I am cursedly beholden to him," said the captain, with a flourish of his three-cornered hat.

"Also that you will reach Barbadoes in safety."

"Little doubt of that," said the captain.

"And that you will dispose of your ware in a manner which will repay you for your charity and humanity."

"Nay, these are handsome words," cried the captain. "Sir, I am your debtor."

A fishing-boat was lying alongside the brig. By the murky light of the poop lanterns I could see the figures upon her deck, and the great brown sail all ready for hoisting. I climbed the bulwark, and set my foot upon the rope ladder which led down to her.

"Good-bye, Decimus!" said I.

"Good-bye, my lad! You have your pieces all safe?"

"I have them."

"Then I have one other present to make you. It was brought to me by a sergeant of the royal horse. It is that, Micah, on which you must now depend for food, lodging, raiment, and all which you would have. It is that to which a brave man can always look for his living. It is the knife wherewith you can open the world's oyster. See, lad, it is your sword!"

"The old sword! My father's sword!" I cried in delight, as Saxon drew from under his mantle and handed to me the discolored old-fashioned leathern sheath with the heavy brass hilt which I knew so well.

"You are now," said he, "one of the old and honorable guild of soldiers of fortune. I would that I could come with you, but I am promised pay and position which it would be ill to set aside. Farewell, lad, and may fortune go with you!"

I pressed the rough soldier's horny hand, and descended into the fishing-boat. The rope that held us was cast off, the sail mounted up, and the boat shot out across the bay. On the land, scattered twinkling lights at long stretches marked the line of the coast. As I gazed backward a cloud trailed off from the moon, and I saw the hard lines of the brig's rigging stand out against the white cold disk. By the shrouds stood the veteran, holding to a rope with one hand, and waving the other in farewell and encouragement. That lean, sinewy figure, with its long extended arm, was the last which I saw for a weary time of the dear country where I was born and bred.

CHAPTER THIRTY-SIX

OF THE END OF IT ALL

AND so I come to the end of the history of a failure—a brave failure and a noble one, but a failure none the less. In three more years England was to come to herself, to tear the fetters from her free limbs, and to send James and his poisonous brood flying from her shores even as I was flying then.

Of the others I can only tell ye what I know. Some slipped out of my ken entirely. Of others I have heard vague and incomplete accounts. The leaders of the insurrection got off much more lightly than their followers, for they found that the passion of greed was even stronger than the passion of cruelty. Grey, Buyse, Wade, and others bought themselves free at the price of all their possessions. Ferguson escaped. Monmouth was executed on Tower Hill, and showed in his last moments some faint traces of that spirit which spurted up now and again from his feeble nature, like the momentary flash of an expiring fire.

My father and my mother lived to see the Protestant religion regain its place once more, and to see England become the champion of the reformed faith upon the Continent. Three years later I found them in Havant much as I had left them, save that there were more silver hairs among the brown braided tresses of my mother, and that my father's great shoulders were a trifle bowed and his brow furrowed with the lines of care.

Reuben Lockarby was ill for many months, but when he at last recovered he found a pardon awaiting him through the interest of Major Ogilvy. After a time, when the troubles were all blown over, he married the daughter of Mayor Timewell, and he still lives in Taunton, a well-to-do and prosperous citizen.

Thirty years ago there was a little Micah Lockarby, and now I am told that there is another, the son of the first, who promises to be as arrant a little Roundhead as ever marched to the tuck of drum.

Of Saxon I have heard more than once. So skilfully did he use his hold over the Duke of Beaufort that he was appointed through his interest to the command of an expedition which had been sent to chastise the savages of Virginia, who had wrought great cruelties upon the settlers. Having at last driven the tribes far into the wilderness, he was presented with a tract of

country for his services, where he settled down. There he married, and spent the rest of his days in rearing tobacco and in teaching the principles of war to a long line of gaunt and slab-sided children. They tell me that a great nation of exceeding strength and of wondrous size promises some day to rise up on the other side of the water.

What became of Hector Marot and of the strange ship-load which had set sail from Poole Harbor? There was never a word heard of them again, unless indeed a story which was spread some months afterwards, by Captain Elias Hopkins, of the Bristol ship *Caroline*, may be taken as bearing upon their fate.

For Captain Hopkins relates that, being on his homeward voyage from our settlements, he chanced to meet with thick fogs and a head-wind in the neighborhood of the great cod-banks. One night as he was beating about, with the weather so thick that he could scarce see the truck of his own mast, a most strange passage befell him. For as he and others stood upon the deck, they heard to their astonishment the sound of many voices joined in a great chorus, which was at first faint and distant, but which presently waxed and increased until it appeared to pass within a stone's-throw of his vessel, when it slowly died away once more and was lost in the distance. There were some among the crew who set the matter down as the doing of the Evil One, but, as Captain Elias Hopkins was wont to remark, it was a strange thing that the foul fiend should choose West-country hymns for his nightly exercise, and stranger still that the dwellers in the pit should sing with a strong Somersetshire burr. For myself, I have little doubt that it was indeed the *Dorothy Fox* which had swept past in the fog, and that the prisoners, having won their freedom, were celebrating their delivery in true Puritan style. Whether they were driven on to the rocky coast of Labrador, or whether they found a home in some desolate land whence no kingly cruelty could harry them, is what must remain forever unknown.

One word of another friend—the last mentioned, but not the least valued. When Dutch William had been ten years upon the English throne there was still to be seen in the field by my father's house a tall strong-boned horse, whose gray skin was flecked with dashes of white. And it was ever observed that, should the soldiers be passing from Portsmouth, or should the clank of trumpet or the rattle of drum break upon his ear, he would arch his old neck, throw out his gray streaked tail, and raise his stiff knees in a pompous and pedantic canter. The country folk would stop to watch these antics of the old horse, and then the chances are that one of them would tell the rest how that once fine charger had borne one of their own village lads

to the wars, and how, when the rider had to fly the country, a
kindly sergeant in the king's troops had brought the steed as a
remembrance of him to his father at home. So Covenant passed
the last years of his life, a veteran among steeds, well fed and
cared for, and much given mayhap to telling in equine language
to all the poor, silly country steeds, the wonderful passages which
had befallen him in the west.

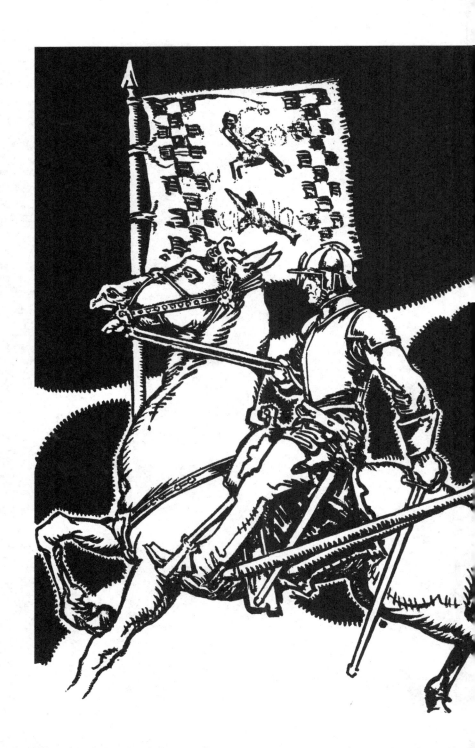